Teferi is running out. Out of friends, out of hope . . .

Teferi pounced. *I'm not asking you to go to war. I'm merely asking you to talk to me, to educate me by sharing your success with Skyshroud.*

Oh, no, Freyalise's tone became sharper, colder, and more cutting. *Teferi would never ask me to fight as Urza did. Teferi does not fight, not when he can run away and hide for three centuries. Not when he can see his own nation and his own tribes to safety. Not when he can skulk away and leave the rest of the world to defend itself.*

Teferi started as if struck. He was not wounded by Freyalise's slanted view of his actions but from one simple detail nigh-lost among her cruel invective.

Three centuries? Teferi said.

. . . out of time.

Scott McGough returns to Magic: The Gathering's home plane of Dominaria to tell a compelling story of passion, insight, and sacrifice.

EXPERIENCE THE MAGIC

ARTIFACTS CYCLE

The Brothers' War
Jeff Grubb

Planeswalker
Lynn Abby

Time Streams
J. Robert King

Bloodlines
Loren Coleman

INVASION CYCLE

The Thran (A Prequel)
J. Robert King

Invasion
J. Robert King

Planeshift
J. Robert King

Apocalypse
J. Robert King

MIRRODIN CYCLE

The Moons of Mirrodin
Will McDermott

The Darksteel Eye
Jess Lebow

The Fifth Dawn
Cory J. Herndon

KAMIGAWA CYCLE

Outlaw:
Champions of Kamigawa
Scott McGough

Heretic:
Betrayers of Kamigawa
Scott McGough

Guardian:
Saviors of Kamigawa
Scott McGough

RAVNICA CYCLE

Ravnica
Cory J. Herndon

Guildpact
Cory J. Herndon

Dissension
Cory J. Herndon

ONSLAUGHT CYCLE

Onslaught
J. Robert King

Legions
J. Robert King

Scourge
J. Robert King

Time Spiral Cycle · Book I

Scott McGough

Time Spiral Cycle, Book I
TIME SPIRAL

Cover art by Scott M. Fischer
First Printing: September 2006

9 8 7 6 5 4 3 2 1

ISBN-10: 0-7869-3988-5
ISBN-13: 978-0-7869-3988-6
620-95470740-001-EN

U.S., CANADA,
ASIA, PACIFIC, & LATIN AMERICA
Wizards of the Coast, Inc.
P.O. Box 707
Renton, WA 98057-0707
+1-800-324-6496

EUROPEAN HEADQUARTERS
Hasbro UK Ltd
Caswell Way
Newport, Gwent NP9 0YH
GREAT BRITAIN
Save this address for your records.

Visit our web site at www.wizards.com

Dedication
This book is dedicated to everyone who thinks
I should have dedicated a book to them by now.
This one's for you . . . now let it go, y'all.

Acknowledgments
This book would not have been possible without contributions
from the following exceptional individuals:

- Elena K., for the daily inspiration
- Susan Morris, for making an editorial/organizational ordeal
  seem so effortless and making the book itself fun to write
- John and Tim, for the lively email brainstorming sessions
  and their encyclopedic knowledge of Magic history
- Daneen McDermott and Jess Lebow, who both helped forge
  so much of the backstory that led to this novel and these
  characters
- Jesper Myrfors, Mark Tedin, Daniel Gelon, and Anthony
  Waters, for their invaluable input way back during a crucial
  Urza's Destiny brainstorm meeting
- Kath, Kim, Sharon, Brett, Kel, and Cujo, for knowing when
  it's time to crack open the Tia Maria and put on the footy
  franks

Her name was Jhoira and she was over one thousand years old. This fact tended to impress people, though Jhoira herself never let it go to her head. She had seen too much of the world, of many worlds, to pride herself on a simple longer-than-usual lifespan. She had witnessed first-hand the creation and destruction of worlds, vicious planet-wide warfare, and the cataclysmic sundering of time itself. Where there is magic and madness literally anything is possible, and a thousand-year-old woman simply doesn't stand out.

Jhoira's humility was also rooted in the hard fact that she was not a true immortal and did not consider herself so. She had known several of the real variety throughout the centuries and had met, dined, and made war with beings who had either embraced infinity or been consumed by it: vampiric lich-lords, elemental avatars, and otherworldly spellcasters with godlike power. Jhoira shared some of the same long-lived perspectives with these supremely powerful beings, but ultimately she was not like them.

If she needed proof or a reminder of that truth, all she had to do was look around. The elegant polished stone of her workshop walls hadn't been quarried or chiseled by mason's tools. They had been conjured out of the aether, created as walls from the first moment of their existence. The entity that shaped these walls into an efficient and aesthetically pleasing structure had done so by taking its design directly from Jhoira's mind.

She was an artificer, a designer, and a builder of machines. She was not an architect and had no actual plan for or notion toward building her perfect workshop. What she did have was the raw idea of it, and that was all it took for a truly infinite immortal to make it real. This was the very real difference between her and a genuinely remarkable being—turning her thoughts into reality required significant research, a fair amount of trial and error, and a great deal of hard work.

She was perhaps their peer by sheer virtue of her longevity—an uninterrupted millennium of existence commands a certain amount of respect in any company—but there was always something grudging and unfriendly about some of the titans she met. To the true gods and demigods of the universe, she was simply an ordinary person with an extraordinary amount of time. Long life was not something Jhoira had achieved or sought after but something that happened to her, no more an achievement than being hit by a falling rock or bitten by a rare snake. Her presence among the mighty sometimes struck Jhoira as decidedly unwelcome, that of a solitary and precocious child in a room full of adults who wished her to be seen and not heard.

Jhoira did not resent this subtle exclusion but prided herself on it. She was *not* one of them—the undying, infinitely powerful, or impervious to harm. She could be injured or killed the same as any shorter-lived person, as the arcane forces that extended her span did nothing to protect her from violence, disease, or deprivation.

Jhoira also aged, albeit very slowly. She seemed to have only gained a few years in the past thousand, but she had definitely grown older. Even at this glacial rate her body would eventually progress through maturity and on into decline and eventually death. It seemed a cheerless thought when she considered it objectively, but the harsh reality was definitely softened by its extreme distance. Like every other finite, mortal being, Jhoira would live until she died or something killed her.

The outwardly young woman pushed her three-legged stool back from the workbench. The table top was a massive block of granite polished as smooth as glass, and it lay half-covered in hand tools, a tall oil lamp in its top corner. The lamp's bone-white flame cast a soft glow across the room.

Jhoira's coarse, chestnut brown hair was gathered into a thick braid at the base of her neck. Her face was wide and open, almost heart-shaped, and her sharp, proud features marked her as a Ghitu, the nomadic, desert-dwelling tribe that thrived where most humans never dared go. She had left the desert young enough to escape the long-term effects of wind-driven sand and searing daytime heat, so her skin was still as soft and unlined as a nineteen-year-old girl's. Her complexion was light brown, almost golden like strong, milky tea, but she knew her tone grew far darker and richer under just a few hours of sunlight. Jhoira privately thought this browning made her seem even younger, as if the face in the mirror belonged to a carefree child with time to lounge and play in the sunshine.

The only parts of Jhoira that hinted at her true age were her eyes. Dark brown and endlessly deep, Jhoira's eyes brimmed both with curiosity and the wisdom that comes from pursuing curious things. For her, time had slowed to a crawl and the years barely touched her body as they washed over it, but Jhoira's eyes displayed a full thousand years of experience.

She whistled, a short, sharp note, and a clicking answered. A large metallic insect whirred to life on the far end of the table top. It stood on six sharp legs as small yellow gems in its eyes glowed ever brighter. The beetlelike creature was the size of a large house cat and it moved stiffly, though it made steady progress across the workbench. As it approached the line of gleaming implements, the green metal shell on its back split and opened to reveal gold-trimmed glass wings. The wings also retracted, exposing a velvet-lined cavity within.

Clicking softly, the beetle balanced on his hindmost legs and its folded-back shell. The mechanical bug took the nearest tool into its mandibles, a polished jeweler's pick. The front pair of legs seized the pick and handed it back to the second pair. These legs tucked the pick neatly into its velvet-lined body, positioning it into a form-fitting niche. The bug continued to select and pack each tool as Jhoira stood and turned away.

"Thank you," she said absently.

She had tried different designs for her ambulatory toolbox over the centuries, but its final form always came back to her original model. Its function was to bring her the items she needed, collect them when she was done, and store them until she needed it again. The metallic beetle's efficiency and familiarity were a comfortable part of her routine. No matter how often she was obliged to move her workshop or how suddenly she had to go, she could always rely on having her tool kit handy.

Jhoira, my dear. Are you already packing up? It's true, then, we can't put it off any longer. It's time to have that talk we keep starting and never finishing.

The voice in Jhoira's head was smooth and thoughtful, mostly because the speaker so loved the sound of his own voice that he strived to capture all of its subtle nuances and timbres even when he communicated mind to mind. The evident pleasure in Teferi's voiceless words told her he had gotten everything just right. Furthermore, since he sounded perfect he was probably already viewing this conversation as a compete success.

She could fairly hear the playful smirk on his face . . . assuming he was currently embodied and had a face. Can one smirk without actual lips? If not, Teferi would have surely invented a way by now.

The succulent, rolling voice came again. *It's not like you to hesitate, milady. Are you waiting for a sign or stalling for time? Perhaps I should come back later? Though in truth it would be far better if—*

"You're nattering, Teferi," Jhoira sighed, "and I'm not stalling, you are. You've got something to say and I'm standing here waiting for you to say it."

Teferi laughed lightly. He materialized before her, fading into view in a cascade of twinkling blue light. "I never get tired of this room," Teferi said. He scanned the workshop with an appreciative arch to his eyebrows.

He appeared as always, clad in his own body at the age of twenty-five. Tall, dark-skinned, and handsome, he wore the colors of his native Zhalfir, blue-white robes trimmed in green and yellow. Teferi's head and face were clean shaven under his elaborate tribal headgear, as they had been since he was a small boy. He was smiling, as usual, with a twinkle of mischievous glee in his eyes.

Jhoira noted that her friend had come outfitted as the court mage complete with an official guild insignia. He even carried the gracefully curved staff that looked impressive but always struck her as the former spine of some hapless creature. Court mages were traditionally minor wizards with big mouths, political ambitions, and a flair for flashy theatrics. They were usually tolerated at court as amusements and distractions, but they were not widely respected.

Seeing Teferi now forced Jhoira to pause and mentally correct what she had said to him earlier: if he were coming to her as a court mage, she was not ready for what he had to say and might never be. For Teferi was no mere mage, no mere wizard, but a planeswalker. He was functionally omnipotent, a being of incalculable power with the ability to go almost anywhere, do almost anything, and appear however he liked. Jhoira had never cared for the relish Teferi took from playing this role, that of the loquacious-yet-mysterious advisor. The manners and wit that delighted kings were tiresome to her, and she was starting to believe lately that they concealed something troubling, even ominous.

Jhoira dismissed her concerns for now, at least until they could be justified by something more dire than Teferi's choice of robes. He was perfectly entitled to the court mage's regalia, as long ago he had held the position for many years. During what Zhalfirin history still called the Golden Age, Teferi famously provided the king with the best magical advice and the most spectacular sorcerous entertainments, and all without ever revealing the true extent of his vast magical power.

History did not record that Teferi's tenure as court mage ended unhappily. He did not like to discuss the circumstances that led to his falling-out with the king and the end of his career as a court mage. Instead, Teferi would brush the matter aside with a laugh, content to repeat the version he had planted in Zhalfir's libraries and history texts: that the king's miracle-worker grew tired of public life and quietly retreated to his own private island to live out his declining years. Jhoira had visited Teferi shortly after this retirement began, and he had already stopped wearing the court mage's regalia. She was almost certain he had not worn it at all since then . . . not until recently.

Jhoira fought back another wave of unease. In Zhalfir, Teferi employed the court mage's hallmarks of distraction and slight-of-hand on a national scale. The humble entertainer and folksy sage inspired wonder in the king at first then awe. With the monarch's complete attention and undiluted admiration, Teferi's witty, quietly offered counsel was always welcome. When it was followed to the letter, it somehow always resulted in stronger peace and deeper prosperity for the king and his nation alike. The more the monarch trusted Teferi, the grander and more successful his reign became.

Teferi the court mage helped shape Zhalfir into a country that achieved unrivaled levels of military dominance and social enlightenment, but he did so secretly and largely through deceit. He concealed his true nature and his true aims from those he was pledged to serve and charmed or manipulated them into adopting his plans as their own. In this way he set the agenda for an entire nation, an entire region, directing that region's initiative and resources toward his own goals and ends. It was all for the best, of course, and on almost every level it worked, perfectly, to the mutual gain of all.

This was Teferi at his most beneficent and productive, but it was also him at his most devious and patronizing. Jhoira knew too well the danger of a planeswalker with hidden agendas, the damage such a powerful being could do inadvertently as they manipulated people and nations on a global scale. She would never blame Teferi for the disasters that plagued Zhalfir after he retired, but the peace and prosperity he so carefully crafted was quickly destroyed by a war fought primarily to claim his secrets. Jhoira had seen the consequences of a planeswalker's folly firsthand, repeatedly throughout her life, and she was not about to sit by and let it happen again.

With that immediate goal firmly in mind, Jhoira tried to relax. Long ago she had stared down perhaps the most powerful planeswalker ever born and shamed him into protecting those who relied on him, but Teferi was not the sort who responded to direct confrontation. He'd been too much of a class clown in his youth and too fond of baiting stern authority figures, so to scold him was to invite greater mischief.

Besides, Teferi's garb may well be the planeswalker equivalent of a false grin, but he was still her friend and still a profoundly logical thinker. He would listen to reason. A strong argument would compel him to examine closely the course he had settled on before he set out upon it.

Teferi cocked his bald head, jovial but puzzled. "If I didn't know you so well," he said, "I'd say you don't look wholly happy to see me."

Jhoira smiled thinly. "It's not that. I just think I know what you're about to say."

"Do you, now?" The planeswalker raised one eyebrow. "Tell me then, and save me the trouble."

Jhoira hesitated. She probed Teferi's face for a familiar flicker of his unguarded personality, but the greater part of his transcendent mind was clearly engaged elsewhere. This breezy aspect of her friend was little more than jovial manners and energetic charm.

"You're ready to go back home," she said. "You've been distracted ever since I said that careless thing I said."

Teferi's face was wide-eyed study in innocent calm. "What careless thing?"

"You know what I mean. When I said that it might have been better if we hadn't done what we did, that I might be happier if we had left things alone."

"Oh," Teferi said. "That."

"Yes, that. I freely admit I could have phrased it more tactfully."

"As I recall, you said it wasn't too far gone from what Urza might have done, and to make the point you called me 'Teferi Planeswalker,' which you know I hate."

"Yes, well. Anyway, I think you took that to heart, and I believe you think I was right. We shouldn't have waited this long to set it right. Maybe we shouldn't have done it in the first place, so you want to fix it, and you want me to help."

Teferi's eyes twinkled. "Very, very good," he said, "but you missed one crucial detail."

Jhoira patiently held Teferi's gaze. "What would that be?"

"That this is all your fault. You brought it up, your idea to fix things. You can't blame any of what happened next on me." Teferi twirled his arm until his sleeve wound tight around his wrist, his long, elegant fingers extended. "Take my hand, old friend, and I will forgive you. Then we can get on with the important business before us."

Jhoira stared coldly at Teferi's hand.

"My fault?" she said.

"Entirely."

"I alone am responsible. I magically took two continents off the map. All by myself."

"Indeed. Well, it's fair to say I helped, but only in the same way that we collaborated on this room." He craned his head around appreciatively. "I did the leg work and the heavy lifting, but the impetus and the main thrust of—"

"Teferi," Jhoira said, "if I agree to take the blame, will you stop babbling? Will you tell me what you want to do? I'm not saying I will agree to do it, but I do want to hear what it is."

Teferi nodded. For a moment Jhoira saw a glimpse of him as she knew him for so long: patient, informed, and concerned. This glimpse of her friend was a welcome sight to Jhoira, even with the weariness and worry on his features.

With a flourish Teferi conjured a large ball of crystal-clear ice. The sphere was solid with a series of irregular shapes across its surface. Jhoira recognized the sphere as a globe and the globe as Dominaria, home world to herself and Teferi both. Each of Dominaria's large continental masses was in its proper place, separated by vast stretches of accurately rendered ocean. The ice model included the surface of the globe and a thin shell of frosty air to represent the planet's breathable atmosphere.

"Recognize the place?"

"Of course." Jhoira let the planeswalker's patronizing tone pass for now, as she was engrossed in studying Teferi's display. There were strange, crackling shapes on the surface of Teferi's model that she did not recognize, that did not correspond to any land or sea she knew. These objects pulsed with a sickly greenish glow, and Jhoira noted that the space directly above or below each glowing mass had a jagged network of thin cracks and fissures radiating from it.

She gestured to the nearest glowing shape and the single

Scott McGough

lightning bolt shaped crack that pierced it. "What does this represent?"

"It's hard to articulate," Teferi said slowly, "but let's call it a disruption . . . a rip in the fabric of things. Time, space, energy, magic—the stresses they exert are all centering on this spot. The stress is starting to show." He shrugged. "I don't know exactly, but it's definitely connected to Shiv's return." Jhoira's eyes narrowed at the mention of her homeland, which they had uprooted and removed from its spot on the map.

At the time, their purpose had been to preserve part of the world before it was completely overrun by the toxic armies of an evil god. At the time, they sought to secure those places and people that could rebuild the social, physical, and magical foundations of society. At the time, she hadn't felt like a person who saves her most prized possession from a burning house instead of trying to fight the fire.

"How is it connected to Shiv?" she said at last.

Teferi paused. "It's better if I just show you."

"Show me, then."

Teferi gestured and the globe spun smoothly around. It stopped with one of the troubling glowing shapes positioned directly in front of Jhoira.

"When we took Shiv out," Teferi said, "we didn't get it all, but we took enough to leave a major hole—a very large, very irregular hole." On the globe, a jagged gap in the ice flared then continued to pulse as Teferi talked about it.

"Now Shiv is coming back, right to the place we took it from, to the hole it left behind. I can't stop it. I can only minimize the impact. If it were a perfectly round hole or perfectly square, we might be able to finesse it back into place—a nudge here, a twist there—but it's not a perfect shape. It's not even the same shape as the hole anymore." Teferi paused for dramatic effect.

"So it's not going to fit," Jhoira said.

Teferi's shoulders slumped. "Yes, yes. You really know how to spoil—"

"What will happen when it doesn't fit?"

Teferi shrugged sadly. He closed his eyes and gave a dismissive wave as he turned away from the globe.

Behind him, a sharp-edged chunk of ice materialized just above the surface of the model. The chunk sank toward the glowing gap they had been inspecting, the one that represented the absent part of Shiv. Jhoira recognized the rough shapes representing the continent on which she was born, and she saw that the two would never match up again.

Ponderously, inexorably, the chunk plowed into the surface of the globe, sending thick cracks deep into its center and showering the floor with shards of brittle ice.

"I see, Teferi," Jhoira said, "so how—"

The globe continued to splinter and crack, loud enough to drown out Jhoira's voice. Huge wedges broke out from the sphere's interior and tumbled to the stone floor. The entire globe shuddered and split into pieces but held its component parts in a roughly spherical shape.

"Teferi, you've made your point. Stop this."

The gaps between pieces of the globe glowed an eerie yellow and Jhoira heard a high-pitched whine. The air around the disintegrating sphere suddenly folded and cracked in on itself, bubbling like boiling oil yet brittle as glass. Jhoira took an involuntary step back as these ripples undulated up across the walls and ceiling, breaking the polished stone open and sending showers of dust and grit across the room.

The floor fell out from below Jhoira's feet as her workshop disintegrated. Outside the walls was a vast, yawning void of blackness and indistinct motion. The cracks in reality crawled across the surface of the void, folding and mashing the emptiness against itself. Jhoira's vision went dark, and she opened her mouth to scream as everything around her heaved and crumbled to a noisy end.

Teferi stepped forward and took her by the shoulders. With his face pressed alongside hers, his lips almost touching her ear, the planeswalker whispered, "It gets much worse from here on."

Then they were both standing once more in Jhoira's shop. The ice globe was still intact before them, the ceiling and walls were intact, and the beetlelike toolbox was still busily at its work.

Jhoira pushed back from Teferi as she cleared her throat and tried to control her breathing. She was determined not to let his awesome display have its intended effect. Instead of looking at him, Jhoira leaned in close to the surface of the globe.

"Show me Zhalfir," she said.

"Zhalfir can wait. Shiv comes first, and if we don't sort it out there won't be anything for Zhalfir to return to."

Jhoira clenched her teeth. Without rising or turning away from the globe, she said, "Show me Zhalfir."

Teferi sighed and gestured. The globe spun. It stopped with the northeast coast of the supercontinent Jamuraa facing Jhoira. There was a glowing space where Teferi's home had been and the ice above it was riven by another large, deep crack.

Jhoira's breath had almost settled to normal and her heartbeat had stopped racing. Slowly, she stood up straight and faced Teferi. "We'd better go see for ourselves," she said. "We can't really do anything for Dominaria from here."

Visibly relieved, Teferi let his eyes close for an extended blink. "I agree," he said as his eyes fluttered open, "and I apologize for the bombast of the presentation, but that's how I see it . . . late at night, when I'm trying to relax."

Jhoira's lip curled. "We can talk later about how necessary that was. Right now I'd like us to start preparing for Shiv."

Teferi's wide, false smile returned. "Well," he said smoothly, "there's going to be a stop or two we have to make elsewhere first."

"Where? What for?" Jhoira crossed her arms. "Why are you being so cagey about this?"

"Because I know you won't like it. I don't like it either, but there are too many good reasons not to do it. It makes too much sense, perfect sense when you think about it."

"Then let me think about it." Jhoira went up on her toes to force Teferi into eye contact. "I'm tired of this, Teferi. Shiv is my home. Dominaria is my home. Tell me where you want to go first so we can get started saving them."

The bald man turned sheepishly. He gestured once more and the globe rotated a half-turn. Jhoira stared until a small, glowing shape in the northern hemisphere caught her attention. A rich emerald dot glowed steadily at the center of the shape's otherwise sickly green pulse. A single thick fissure stabbed down into the center of the dot.

Jhoira stared a few seconds more. Then she closed her eyes. "You can't be serious."

"I am. It has to start here."

Jhoira opened her eyes. "Why?"

"Because it is one of the only places I know where someone has done what we want to do. In fact, it was even harder than what we face because there wasn't even a hole for it to fit into. She made it fit anyway, without disturbing so much as a single snowflake, and," he added, "it's the only such place with the planeswalker who pulled it off still living there."

Jhoira shook her head "That is the best reason I can think of not to go." She paused. "Actually, I can think of ten better reasons right now, off the top of my head. Shall I list them?"

Teferi stepped forward. His eyes were soft and human and he looked more tired than Jhoira had seen him in decades. "Please," he said.

"You were right when you said that careless thing. We should do something. I don't know exactly what it is yet, but I know it starts here." He pointed to the globe. "I promise not to decide without you, but I need to do this. No, I want to. I want to do the right thing and to do it carefully, with no bad consequences. For that I absolutely need you."

Jhoira paused, her keen mind racing. She didn't like the options. Teferi was up to something, obviously, and he was determined to keep her from learning what. Could she bear the responsibility of helping him without fully knowing his mind more easily than she could by letting him act alone?

"All right," she said, "I'm with you, but if we're going into barbarian country I want some protection."

"You'll be traveling with me," Teferi said winningly. "What better protection is there?"

"Warriors," Jhoira said evenly. "Ghitu and viashino both."

Teferi shook his head. "Problem. It's not so easy to take people out of phase, and once we do we still have to prepare them for the rigors of—"

"Nonsense, Teferi Planeswalker. Everything's easy for you, and if I'm taking the entire blame for this mess, I should at least get to bring a few friendly faces along as we fix it."

Teferi sighed. "Viashino, then?"

Jhoira nodded. "And Ghitu. Warriors all."

"Agreed."

Jhoira exhaled. It wasn't much, but adding more people to the equation would force Teferi to interact with other mortals besides her. Also, as they were about to place themselves among the most notoriously bloodthirsty and violent people ever known, it was always a good idea to have strong, loyal bodyguards who knew how to fight. Even when traveling with a planeswalker, it was wise to be prepared for anything.

Teferi's eyes suddenly twinkled anew. "So it's agreed. Warriors all," he said. "Now . . . can we please get to it? I don't know what's going on . . . not fully, anyway . . . and the longer it takes us to find out, the more anxious I become."

"You lead," Jhoira said, "I'll follow." She nodded again, but her eyes were back on the ice globe. "For now."

"For now," Teferi echoed, smiling radiantly, "that's all I need."

CHAPTER 2

An icy mist wallowed over the beach, crowning brackish green waves and charcoal-dark sand with cold, clinging gray. The occasional stinging gust raised mournful sounds from the driftwood and from the skeleton of a fisherman's shack half-standing on the dunes above.

A drop of cobalt blue liquid appeared in the fog halfway between the edge of the bay and the dunes. The speck grew to a line then contracted back down to a marble-sized ball. The ball flattened, spread, then inflated back into a larger sphere. It repeated this process, each time driving the dense fog back.

The glowing blue sphere began to spin and crackle, its substance swirling back into its own center. This vortex gathered momentum but the sphere did not shrink. Instead it expanded, stretching its mouth wider and its tail farther as it shaped itself into a sparkling horizontal cyclone.

Pure white light flashed from inside the funnel. When it faded Teferi was there, majestically floating several feet above the sand. The planeswalker quickly scanned the area. He scowled. He settled down onto the beach rather harder than he'd intended, his fine Zhalfirin sandals disappearing into the wet sand. This would not do.

Teferi shook off the displeasure that was twisting his face and turned back to the open mouth of his funnel-nexus. He didn't want to give Jhoira any more misgivings about this endeavor. She was sure to notice and comment on his ostentatious entrance, sure to remind him that he'd never created such a lightshow for a simple planeswalk before. She might even accuse him of trying to dazzle her and the warriors in their party, to impress them and keep them distracted.

Teferi straightened his robes and extracted his feet from the sand. He planted the end of his ceremonial staff in the beach and reached out toward the vortex. He didn't need to, but he did because simply concentrating and thinking the others through would not sufficiently distract him from the dullness of the scenery. Showing off for Jhoira was a pleasant diversion, and it also provided an obvious explanation for why he was making such a spectacle of their arrival. At the very least, he hoped it would keep Jhoira from delving into the real reasons this planeswalk was so much more difficult than it ought to be.

Teferi gestured dramatically and the vortex spun faster. The sparks circling the cyclone's outer edges crackled and glowed, growing more intense as their velocity increased. The lights became more numerous and more frenzied as Teferi clenched his fist and pale cyan smoke rose from the wind-funnel's edges. The sparks all flared as one and the smoke hissed as the mouth of the nexus flashed blinding white once more.

Jhoira emerged from the cyclone. She stepped down onto the sand and glanced at Teferi, who bowed and presented the beach to her with a lowered head and a wave of his arm. As he bowed, Teferi scanned their surroundings again from the corners of his half-closed eyes.

He was very disappointed. He had expected much more when he set foot on the world of his birth for the first time in over a century. Where was the renewing rush of familiarity? The warm, welcoming sense of being home at last? He didn't expect parades and throngs of well-wishers scattering flower petals before him, but he had hoped for at least a twinge of nostalgia or a dash of regret for the time he'd spent away from this endlessly fascinating place.

Jhoira looked down the beach. She looked up at the murky gray sky and out to the dreary green sea. She carefully pivoted in place, her feet plowing up tiny mounds of sand as she turned, her eyes always on the sky. She was counting or calculating to herself, her lips moving slightly and silently until she faced the mountainous horizon to the north.

Jhoira turned to Teferi, her face wrinkling in annoyance. "This isn't Keld," she said.

"Of course it is," he said. But was it? Was Jhoira right? Was the 'walk even more difficult than he realized, to the point he had missed their destination?

Teferi blinked through a disquieting moment of doubt. That wasn't what he'd expected her to say. He was expert at mind to mind communication and had even mastered a form of telepathy, but he had long ago stopped trying to read Jhoira's mind. It was rude, for one thing, and for another, Jhoira's thoughts were so tightly organized that he never had access to anything she wouldn't tell him herself.

"It can't be Keld." Jhoira glanced up. "See for yourself."

Teferi carefully mimicked her survey of the sky, scanning overhead from the southern sea horizon to the northern mountains. Then he reversed the process and scouted from the mountains back out to the sea, his lips moving all the while.

Then, still peering upward, Teferi said, "What am I looking for again?"

Jhoira paused. Teferi suspected it was only because she was choking back exasperation.

"The weather is wrong," she said at last, her voice calm but stern. "The landscape is wrong. The air, the sea, the mountains . . . everything is wrong. If we could see the stars I could prove it to you, because I bet they're wrong, too."

"I can see the stars." Teferi said. He had not moved or changed his stance, but his eyes darkened to a deep indigo black and their surfaces glistened like metal. "This is definitely Keld." Teferi turned to Jhoira. He blinked and his eyes were back to their usual friendly brown. "This is where I meant for us to be. Where we need to be."

Jhoira tossed her head, unconvinced. "I trust your abilities," she said, "but Keld is one of the strongest sources of red mana in the world. The local culture is founded on fire magic, and there's no fire here. Look, I can hardly raise a decent spark." She concentrated, staring at her own upturned hand. Seconds passed before the faintest red fleck appeared, flickering weakly as it hovered over her palm.

The pale red spark faded quickly. When it was gone Jhoira shook her hand vigorously and flexed her fingers. "If this is Keld, something has gone terribly wrong here."

"This is Keld," Teferi said again, "and something has gone terribly wrong, but not just here." He held her concerned eyes for a moment then motioned to the vortex. "Shall I bring in the rest of the group?"

"Please." She glanced up at the ruins of the half-collapsed shack. "I think we should provide them with an alternative source of mana. If they're counting on the supply here, none of their spells will work. Then again . . . " Jhoira scanned the nearly empty beach. "There don't appear to be as many bloodthirsty barbarians as I expected." She looked back at Teferi. "Or anyone else, for that matter."

Teferi didn't answer, occupying himself with gesturing. Since he could actually bring the rest of the group through with barely a thought, he used the extra time gesturing afforded him to closely examine the world around him.

He was immediately sorry. It was so much worse than he'd feared.

Keld's broad, squat mountains were broken and worn, weathered shadows of their former selves. Instead of the proud, sharp summits Teferi expected, nearly every mountain was topped by a broken bowl of cracked stone. Keld's mountaintops looked to have exploded and collapsed in on themselves. It was similar to a series of large-scale volcanic eruptions, but Keld had not seen a naturally active volcano in all its recorded history. Moreover, there was absolutely no heat or seismic force present, not in any of the calderalike structures. If lava flows had shattered these peaks it had done so eons ago and the aftermath had long since cooled to stone, but if that were true, where were the records of such an event?

Teferi turned this new evidence over in his mind as he brought the Shivan warriors through. The state of these mountains was dire news for all of Dominaria. Jhoira was correct in that Keld was one of the most potent sources of mountain magic in the world, yet there was almost no mana now, almost no magical energy at all.

More sparks spun, flared, and danced around the vortex. Jhoira stepped back, shielding her face against the brilliance. Once more harsh white light flashed from inside the cyclone, this time fading to leave four bipedal shapes.

All were natives of Shiv, taken and preserved long ago with their homeland. Teferi hadn't been exaggerating earlier—even for a planeswalker it was difficult to bring these warriors out of their phased state and transport them here. Luckily, Jhoira knew exactly which of her fellow Shivans were qualified and interested in joining this humble outing. From that small pool of candidates, only these four had been willing and able to answer her call. "Four is enough," Jhoira had said, "if I get the right four."

This group more than satisfied her requirements. Two were human Ghitu tribe members like Jhoira herself, one male and one female. They were both lean and small in stature and each was dressed in the bright red garb of elite Ghitu warriors. Between them they carried a wide array of hand-tooled weapons.

The remaining two were viashino, the tenacious lizard people who thrived in parts of Shiv where human beings could not, where the heat and caustic air roasted and dissolved frailer-skinned species in a matter of seconds. These viashino loomed tall behind the Ghitu, larger and far more massive than their human counterparts, though they both carried cudgels and gleaming silver blades that had been smithed in Ghitu forges.

Teferi could see the comfort Jhoira took from the warriors' presence. Her own tribemates were well versed in the magics of combat and fire and were also experienced hand-to-hand fighters. The viashino were terribly fast despite their size and bulk and wickedly clever despite their bestial appearance. The lizard warriors were rightly feared for their lightning ambush tactics and the ferocity of their charges. Nothing short of an army would get past these defenders, and if an army showed up, well . . . Teferi himself would handle that problem when and if it arose.

"Welcome to Keld," Teferi said, but his tone was stern. "There's something interfering with the mana here. It is inadequate for your needs." He waved his staff horizontally. "Here," he said. "These mana stars will more than make up for the shortfall."

Simple silver chains appeared around each Shivan neck. Jhoira and the others now sported necklaces with vivid, five-pointed star gems that hung down to their collarbones. The multifaceted stones shone with an opalescent glow.

"Be ready to move in the next ninety seconds."

Teferi was relying on the Shivans to conduct themselves with tight military discipline. They were experienced campaigners and had come to do serious work, perhaps even bloody work. They did not need to be flattered or put at ease, so he didn't bother to smooth-talk them as he would a fellow academic or visiting head of state.

The thoughts in their minds were less guarded and more available than Jhoira's, but they were also less comprehensible. Teferi's brand of telepathy worked best when both the reader and the read cooperated. If not, the experience was painful for the subject and taxing for the telepath. He gathered random flashes of anxiety, hubris, and anticipation from these warriors, but he could have easily gleaned such information from their facial expressions and body language. Teferi both liked and disliked the warrior mindset for precisely this reason: they were reliable, predictable, and not given to imaginative thinking.

"Cold," said one of the viashino. He was smaller and leaner than his partner and his scales were a far darker green. The keen edges of his diamond-shaped scales glistened in the mist. He sniffed the air. "Ice storm soon. Or snow. It'll start after sundown."

The viashino language itself was little more than a stream of clicks and hisses, but thankfully all the lizard folk Jhoira knew had mastered human speech. Teferi was once more secretly pleased that these viashino voices were not as breathy or sibilant as those of some other reptilian races. He thought of himself as a tolerant person, open to all cultures and customs, but it did get tiresome when a simple "Yes" took a full five seconds to say.

"Of course you're cold," the planeswalker said. "You're accustomed to the deserts of Shiv. Try to relax and remember to draw mana from the gem, not the land."

The viashino's tail lashed from side to side. It was longer than the warrior was tall, supple and strong. It was ridged with sharp, toothlike scales and its end was a wide, flat crescent with razor sharp edges. The crescent listed back and forth behind the viashino's head as he turned his rounded snout towards Teferi.

"Not me," the viashino said sharply. "This place is cold. The weather. It's too cold here."

"We're in Keld," Teferi said patiently. "It's always cold here."

"I know where we are," the viashino sneered. "I've been in Keld before, and it's not supposed to be this cold." He rose to his full height and glared down at Teferi, his sharp tongue darting between far sharper teeth. "And friend wizard? Stop talking to me like I'm an idiot child."

"Skive is right," Jhoira called. "This is the end of Keld's summer. It shouldn't be this miserable." She glanced back to the north. "The mountains don't look right either."

"Your pardon," Teferi spoke to the viashino called Skive. He didn't want Jhoira to take a closer look at the mountains and come to the same disturbing conclusion he had—not yet, anyway. She could not help but notice them sooner or later, especially since some of the mountain bases were so eroded that Teferi feared they might simply overbalance and fall like a top-heavy toy.

To Skive, Teferi added, "You are right to be concerned. Things are not exactly as I expected, but that won't affect our mission here. If you like, I can raise the temperature around us or whistle up some warmer gear for you." His brown eyes sparkled with blue energy. Teferi smiled. "But we are still moving out in the next sixty seconds."

"I need no help." Skive looked away. "I'm ready to work. Let's just get this done while my blood is still liquid."

Corus, the larger viashino, huffed a ragged laugh. "Cheer up, Skive," he said. "We're working with two Ghitu firestarters. We need never be cold again."

The female Ghitu smiled, happy to take up the challenge. "My fire will do more than warm you, newt."

"Now, Dassene," the male Ghitu chided. "Don't be so rude to our comrades. It's insulting to call such a noble reptile 'newt.' "

"Your pardon, Aprem," Dassene said, mimicking Teferi's tone and head bob. "What should I call him?"

"Skink," Aprem said. He grinned maliciously. "Maybe eft."

Corus interlaced his fingers and stretched his long scaly arms out before him. "I'll 'eft' you, little Ghitu," he said, smiling through a mouth of gleaming white fangs. "Where do you get off calling us names? I understand the Ghitu word for you match-strikers translates directly as 'disposable.' In your own language! It must be inspiring to have your worth as a warrior spelled out in your very rank."

The planeswalker watched them for a moment, wondering if this was the sort of tight military discipline that earned Shivans their fierce reputation. Then Jhoira cleared her throat and said, "When you're through blustering, brothers and sisters, I'd like to move away from this exposed position."

The tension broke at the sound of her voice. The soldiers' bravado cooled and the Shivans shared a guarded chuckle as they moved away from Teferi and Jhoira, readying themselves to move out.

Jhoira came up next to Teferi, her voice low and calm. "They'll be fine," she said. "A little friendly competition among neighbors." She leaned in close to Teferi and added, "What do you think is happening here? I accept that this is Keld, but it doesn't feel like Keld. It certainly doesn't look like Keld."

"I agree," Teferi said.

Jhoira peered out into the bay. "Isn't this the main port of the entire country? Where are the boats? Where are the ships?" She threw her hands out wide. "Where are the Keldons?"

Teferi nodded but did not reply. It was true: this had been Keld's busiest population center and one of the few places outsiders could land and do business without being attacked on sight. He'd expected not only a large number of natives, but also a healthy contingent of commerce-bearing ships and foreign traders. Instead, there was nothing. No warships, no merchant vessels. No marina, no docks, no harbormaster . . . no harbor. Other than the wrecked shack, this Keldon beach had no distinguishing features beyond grim flotsam, an unpleasant breeze, and wet sand.

"I've made a mistake." Teferi spoke quietly so only Jhoira would hear. "Something's wrong here, and I don't know what it is."

Jhoira put a hand on his arm. "That's why we came," she said, "to find things out. And, that being the case, let me bring us back to it: we're not here to fix Keld. This a problem and a mystery for another day. We're here to consult with Freyalise, to study the forest she installed, and then move on."

"True," Teferi said.

He felt his doubts and anxiety fade as he fixed on something concrete and constructive. His plan was far from detailed or complete, but it began at a very logical point. Before he tried to redraw the map by forcing a significant chunk of territory back into it, he intended to talk to another planeswalker who had already done precisely that.

Teferi flashed a smile at Jhoira and said, "To Skyshroud then. Freyalise certainly knows we're here, but I'm sure she won't leave the forest. She's going to make us come to her." His smile tightened. "There's some sort of interference that's making it difficult to planeswalk. I think Freyalise the xenophobe has finally figured out a way to keep people like me away."

"Which puts you on equal footing with the rest of us," Jhoira said. "All right, then. If we can't planeswalk, we simply walk."

Teferi's jovial retort froze in his throat. "Actually," he said. "We're probably going to fight first."

"Fight? But—" Jhoira stopped as the sensation hit her, too. She searched Teferi's eyes for an answer that he did not have, then the two of them simultaneously turned inland.

The fog between the dunes was flowing away from a tall pillar of . . . something. Distorted waves of force churned along its exterior, causing the pillar to scintillate and throb like a living thing. The rectangular mass was translucent, but the view through it was distorted, bent as if seen through a carelessly ground lens. Instead of the dreary and dead Keldon beach around them, looking through the phenomenon showed a Keldon shoreline that was bright, burning, and hot. In fact, it showed a bustling port complete with many buildings and plenty of ships. Teferi's eyes narrowed in the harsh light illuminating the scene inside the pillar, where everything that was visible was also on fire.

"What is that?" Jhoira asked.

"No idea," Teferi said, "but we should call our friends away from it."

The Shivan warriors were all staring at the phenomenon, but none of them had bothered to retreat. As the pillar and the images it contained began to expand toward them, they tensed for battle.

"Fall back," Teferi said urgently.

Thunder rumbled from the growing shape and violent waves of visual distortion rolled out, warping the beach as they passed. Searing pain blasted through Teferi's body, shooting up his spine and slamming into his brain like an ice-cold hammer. An awful grating sound tore through his ears as the pillar split in half lengthwise, fouling the air with a dizzying smell and a shower of white-hot sparks.

A single burly figure fell from the sundered pillar, a broadsword in one hand and a battle-axe in the other. He was almost seven feet tall with thick muscles rippling across every inch of him. His eyes glittered from deep inside their hollow sockets, wide, bulging, and flashing red like the sunset on the edge of a blade. His hair was long and matted, and his jutting brow cast a sinister shadow across his face. The wild man wore leather breeches and wrist gauntlets but no armor. In fact, he was naked to the waist and the damp fog hissed wherever it touched his bare skin.

As his lips curled into a snarl, the barbarian opened his jaws and hungrily snapped his huge, square teeth.

There's going to be a fight, Teferi thought dreamily, but where had this enemy come from? Why was the portal he used causing Teferi pain?

Nearby, the barbarian pulled himself free of the sand. He threw his head back and let out a throaty battle roar. More of the wild-eyed fiends fell from the fissure behind him as he howled, and every one joined in the war cry as soon as they found their footing and drew their own vicious weapons. Soon there were almost a dozen of them, each roaring through a nightmarish expression of feral bloodlust.

Teferi felt his grasp of the situation slipping away. So little of this made sense and what did was crowded out of his mind by the angry, jagged, red-hot thoughts of the incoming Keldons. Teferi tried not to read their minds, to shutter them out, but their thoughts still peppered him like grapeshot from a catapult. The Keldons' thoughts were raw, violent, incoherent things, and Teferi felt himself grow nauseated as they burned and stabbed into his mind.

Were they truly even Keldons? These berserkers were a good deal paler than expected. Oh, they were big enough, but instead of the imposing slate gray color that typified fighting Keldons, this lot was a sallow, sickly shade of gray . . . more ashes and smoke than stone. Like the drab landscape around them, these barbarians seemed drained, leeched of something vital—perhaps even desperate to reclaim it.

Of course, this subtle cosmetic difference didn't make the raiders any less intimidating or dangerous, and he saw that the Shivan warriors shared this conclusion. Corus had extended his claws and Skive's tail curled up over his own head like a scorpion's. Aprem had already produced a six-balled bolas and began whirling it while Dassene drew two polished batons of hard wood from her belt. She held each stick firmly in the center as the ends burst into flame.

"So," Aprem called back to Jhoira, his tone bright, "we start the day in battle against a real Keldon war party." As he spoke, the ends of each weighted bolas ignited, wreathing the air above him in a halo of fire. The mana stars flared crimson each time the Ghitu cast their spells.

"No," Jhoira said. She fixed her eyes on Teferi. "These aren't Keldons, are they? At least, not Keldons that anyone has seen for over five hundred years."

Teferi did not meet Jhoira's eyes. She was right, and what's more, she had just voiced the conclusion he could not bring himself to reach. These were not the Keldons of his era, or any era since.

They were throwbacks, echoes from a dark era long since passed, when the warlike tribe used a dire mix of magic and science to enhance their strength and ferocity.

"They should not exist," he admitted. The planeswalker did not move, doing nothing to address the mounting danger in front of them. He felt dazed with his attention split between the physical threat of the Keldons and the metaphysical threat of the rift that brought them.

There were now almost two dozen berserkers on the beach. The first to emerge stepped forward, eyeing the small party of visitors, and spat contemptuously. The brute turned and called out in the guttural common language of Keld, "Kill them all."

"They do act like Keldons," Teferi said.

"But they're not. They're not supposed to exist anymore." Jhoira's voice was rising to a yell. "How did they get here?"

"Who cares?" Skive said. His sharp-edged tail whipped through the fog around him. "They're here and they're coming fast."

Jhoira turned to Teferi and said, "Stop this." He barely heard her as he stared fixedly at the source of their attackers. The rift in time and space lingered over the dismal patch of shoreline, but no more berserkers fell from it.

Jhoira continued to shout. "Teferi, do not let this continue, not until we know more, until we understand more."

Skive and Corus were not waiting for the barbarians to come to them or for Teferi's paralysis to break. Lighter and faster, Skive led the way, but both viashino were little more than twin blurs as they met the barbarians head-on. Only a few paces behind, Aprem and Dassene joined in the counterattack, gems aglow, leaving ropes of fire in the wake of their weapons.

Jhoira stepped up to Teferi and grabbed him by the shoulders. "Do not let this happen," she said, shoving her face close to his. His eyes felt far away, and his expression was blank. "Make it stop."

"Stop." Teferi blinked. "Yes. Forgive me, Jhoira, I was lost in thought. And thank you." He glanced up at the rift, the sight of the strange phenomenon reviving the pain in Teferi's head and spine. He brushed this sensation aside, defiantly staring deep into the heart of the disruption.

"Stop," he said. His eyes flashed and the entire Keldon beach disappeared under a surge of blue-white light. When the wave faded, only Teferi and the Shivans remained on the shore, the Keldon raiders having disappeared in mid-charge. Robbed of his target, Skive overextended his tail strike and fell clumsily to his knees.

The rift still rippled and wavered overhead. Teferi stared at it, savoring the rare and powerful emotion it inspired in him. He hated it. It confounded him, pained him, and worst of all, it was delaying him. He had come to do other things, important things, but now he had to include this in his larger list of urgent problems to be addressed.

"What's going on?" Dassene shouted. The others echoed her confusion.

"It is a fair question," Jhoira said.

Teferi looked at his friend, and beyond, over her shoulder to the regrouping Ghitu and viashino and the rift that still hung in the air.

"A fair question deserves a swift answer," Teferi said, his voice mellifluous and warm, "which I don't currently have, but just wait. I'll be back in a second." He winked. "At least, I'll be back long before the barbarians will."

Before Jhoira could object, Teferi planeswalked away from the Keldon beach.

* * * * *

The tranquility in the wake of Teferi's' sudden departure only lasted a few moments. After that, the first ghostly images of the Keldon raiders began to reappear. They flickered into view all together, each in precisely the same posture as when they had vanished, and though they were as pale and insubstantial as phantoms, they were growing more solid all the time.

Corus stepped up to one of the ghostly Keldons, tasting the air around it with his long tongue. The viashino grinned unpleasantly. "Think the super-wizard will make it back in time?"

"Absolutely." Jhoira glanced at each of her fellow Shivans in turn then added, "But let's prepare to defend ourselves as well. Just in case."

The Ghitu and viashino formed a quick skirmish line between Jhoira and the returning Keldon raiders. The Shivans were calm and confident, their gems sparkling, and their muscles loose and ready for action.

Jhoira's gaze traveled back and forth between the rift and the spot where Teferi had left them to fend for themselves. For the world's sake, as well as her own, she wondered what he'd do if the berserkers returned in force before he did.

CHAPTER 3

Teferi returned once more to the Blind Eternities. This was the all-encompassing void that separated planar realms, a place between places that was simultaneously everywhere and nowhere. The Blind Eternities had been named by ancient planeswalkers, and since they were still the only beings who could breach such a barrier unaided, the name stuck. Like other planeswalkers before him, Teferi used the Blind Eternities not only as a conduit for his travels but also as a waystation and vantage point from which to consider his grandest cosmic designs.

Teferi paused, gathering strength after another unexpectedly strenuous journey. Before him lay the entire multiverse like a great, chaotic hive, its countless planes all stacked into a seemingly infinite array with no discernable pattern. He skimmed along the surface of this great, untidy mass like a drop of water on polished glass, looking down at the galaxies and arcane nether realms hurtling by below him.

All around, the horizon was filled by countless glittering stars and an army of planets that marched in tight orbital formation. There was vast empty space here as well, unbroken stretches of black vacuum that connected swirling nebulae of colorful ice and dust. The physical and magical stresses here would kill almost instantly anything less than a planeswalker, but to Teferi it was a quiet place that afforded him the solitude he craved.

Alone now, he allowed his thoughts to flow freely. The Keldons he had just seen were creatures out of time. Everything about them was off—their look and feel, their sights and sounds—and Teferi believed it all stemmed from being out of synch with the world around them. Somehow they had been plucked from an earlier era and deposited in modern Keld. Worse, the plucking had happened right in front of him and yet he, the great and patient observer, learned nothing about it. Whatever moved the warriors through time was somehow connected to the strange rift, and the rift's mere presence was harmful to Teferi even without the killers that came through it.

Most troubling of all, Teferi now knew that he had been unable to tell how badly out of temporal tune the barbarians were because his own frame of reference was askew. In other words, while he was sure where he was, he was not so certain about when.

Safe from the Blind Eternities' churning, caustic void, still clothed in the body and robes of a Zhalfirin court mage, Teferi forced himself to relax. This was ultimately a question of time, and time was his special area of expertise. He simply needed to focus his full attention on the matter at hand, and so he now allowed his mind return to his favorite subject, the one that had called him and absorbed him for most of his life.

He had been fascinated by the concept of time for as long as he could remember. As a nine-year-old at the Tolarian Academy, he was celebrated for being more advanced than the other prodigies, and it delighted him to be given special treatment simply for being as he was. At the age of nine he became truly enamored of the concept "wise beyond his years" and strove to live up to it. His first duties as one of Tolaria's advanced students involved the construction and maintenance of a working time machine. Later, as both wizard and planeswalker, Teferi repeatedly focused his energies on the study of time, on its nature and effects.

It was a truly elemental force, perhaps the only unstoppable one.

Time guarded its secrets jealously, and unlocking those secrets in full had always been Teferi's idea of the ultimate reward. It was not greed or ambition that drove him, as he was not interested in personal glory, rewriting history, or channeling this primal force for his own ends. He simply wanted to understand it better. And, if he were being completely honest, he also loved the pure academic pursuit of its secrets.

The time rift on Keld had challenged him, perhaps even bested him, but time had defeated Teferi before, and he still admired it, even loved it. He savored each new priceless bit knowledge that his studies mined from it. Time had defied all of history's greatest thinkers alike, including Teferi, but he was also one of the rare few to whom time had confessed at least some of its secrets.

Teferi paid a heavy price for his fascination over the centuries. The Tolarian time machine he worked on exploded almost as soon as it was switched on, exposing the entire island and its population to the violent effects of unrestrained temporal energy. Many died in the first minutes after the disaster, aged to dust or victims of the heat and toxic fumes from Tolaria's primordial past.

The time disaster left only a handful the students and faculty unharmed. One was the school's headmaster, Urza, the obsessed planeswalker who had disguised himself as a mortal wizard and scholar in order to personally lead his team of hand-picked time-travel researchers. Urza drove the design and construction of the time apparatus, meticulously oversaw the construction and testing of the device, then promptly pushed both the machine and his students past their respective limits.

Another unscathed survivor was Jhoira, whose quick wits and survival skills kept her safe from nearly all of the disaster's negative time effects. Teferi himself was not so lucky. The Tolarian Academy's youngest prodigy was caught in the initial mechanical explosion, which set his heavy robes on fire. Panicking, enveloped in flame, Teferi then stumbled into a pocket of slow time where each grain in the hourglass took months or even years to fall. He spent four decades burning in that bubble of altered time before Jhoira devised a way to get him out. He spent an additional three decades enduring vivid, paralyzing nightmares about burning alive.

This ordeal had an incalculably huge effect on Teferi, of course, but not even this horrific trauma could sever him from his interest in time. As he saw it, the fault lay not with the elemental force or the study of it but with the careless methodology of headmaster Urza. Time was like fire, most dangerous when it was misunderstood or misused. In Urza's hands, time could destroy, as it had the academy, but in Jhoira's it could also heal and protect. She proved that with a device that used the stricken island's slow time against its fast time to cancel each other out and safely extract him from the flames. She was also living proof of the miraculous age-retarding secrets of the island's water supply in the wake of the disaster.

Now, even as they tried to understand its potential impact on their homeland, time was toying with him and Jhoira once more. The continents he had taken and preserved were outside the normal flow of events—virtually no years had passed for Shiv and Zhalfir while they'd been gone. When he compared one hundred years of stasis to the devastation left by the Phyrexian Invasion there was a dangerous discrepancy between the taken part of Shiv and the part that remained. He had plans to adjust for this discrepancy, as he expected Shiv's return to be the most difficult part of his endeavor, but now the Keldon time rift added a new hurdle. If a similar phenomenon existed or appeared while Shiv was rematerializing, the additional stress would be catastrophic for the entire multiverse. At the very least it would accelerate the reality-collapsing disaster he had so vividly demonstrated for Jhoira.

Just as troubling, though less pressing, was the dismal state of Dominaria's mana. Teferi had saved Shiv and Zhalfir from the degradations of a war that destroyed huge sections of the planet, but that war had ended over a hundred years ago. Dominaria's magical resources should have recovered by now, or at least they should have recovered more. Barring a second devastating, planet-wide event, there was still nothing to explain what had so drained an entire world of its vital energy.

Teferi fought to organize his thoughts. He had playfully described his planeswalker status as being "just shy of omnipotent, well short of omniscient," but he was always half-bound by his humbler origins as a normal man. As an immortal, he understood how mortal minds simply aren't well-suited to process the infinite. He had been a planeswalker far longer than he had been a man, but it was still very difficult for him to get anything done if he also had to contemplate the entirety of the universe while he was doing it. Pondering reality often made his eyes glaze over and sometimes his mind would drift for weeks, unfocused but seeing all. For his own sanity and for the sake of a world that needed him to act, Teferi now chose to focus on just the myriad things that affected him and his plans for the immediate future rather than every thing there was.

So the planeswalker marshaled his thoughts. He arranged them and guided them not as a drill instructor, shouting crisp commands to a company that responded without hesitation, but as a lion tamer, urging, cajoling, even whipping the snarling, truculent things through hoops and onto pedestals until they had achieved the formation he sought.

He reviewed his situation and his options, finally acknowledging that his original plans hadn't actually changed very much. He still sought to confer with Freyalise to learn how she had integrated an entire landmass into the existing fabric of Dominaria. Time rifts, mana droughts, and anachronistic Keldons were important but secondary. He needed to find out more before Shiv returned, as everything still hinged on that return. If he learned Freyalise's method, Teferi could adapt it to his own ends.

You overlook an important element, Teferi of Tolaria. What if Freyalise chooses not to receive you?

The woman's voice was confident, measured, and stern. Though Teferi reached out to her now, Freyalise remained a hidden, disembodied voice. Teferi had not spoken to her before, through voice or thought, but he recognized his fellow planeswalker instantly.

Freyalise, he sent back. *Well met, Mistress of Skyshroud.*

Already we disagree. You are not welcome here. Your presence is disruptive here. I do not want you here.

Teferi pressed on, unconcerned. *I will not stay long. If you can grant me just a little of your time in order to save a world, that is all the time I will need.*

I have already saved a world, Freyalise said. *Several, in fact, and several times over.*

Then you shouldn't mind helping me do it once more.

On the contrary. I am openly hostile to anything you might wish to accomplish and will resist you however I can. I have saved worlds before without your help—this world, in fact. You need me, Teferi. I do not need you.

Teferi paused, weighing his next words carefully. Freyalise had always been extremely territorial and hostile to intruders. Now he was in her territory and she was far too powerful to be compelled. She needed to be convinced.

I seek to do what you have done, he said, *but elsewhere. I had hoped that you would be willing to share with me, for no other reason than it's the quickest way to be rid of me, for I am determined, Freyalise. I have just returned to this world and I see that it is in jeopardy. Surely you, who stayed behind, are aware of the current dangers?*

My world and my interests begin and end with the Skyshroud Forest, Freyalise flared. *I will protect both from any danger that arises, be it unnatural phenomena or a planeswalker's interference.*

The danger I've seen threatens everything, inside Skyshroud and out.

Skyshroud has me. Let everything else find its own protector.

Teferi fought back a wave of anger at her selfish short-sightedness. *I seek to be that protector, Freyalise. I want to do for the world what you do for this small part of it. Will you help me?*

I will not.

Why? How can you maintain your isolation when circumstances will not allow it?

You're not listening to me, little man, Freyalise said. *I control the circumstances that affect Skyshroud, and my isolation ends when I choose, not because you desire it. I listened to you Tolarians once before, during the Invasion. It did not suit me, nor the world.*

I'm not Urza, Teferi said earnestly. *I'm not asking to you follow me into battle as he did. I only—*

Very wise. For Urza's planeswalker strike force was as ill-conceived as it was ill-fated. The nine of us hardly lasted a day before we began betraying and murdering each other. Urza himself accounted for at least two of the deaths, sacrificing us like pawns. Of the original number, I mark only two who carried out our mission and returned alive and intact.

Since then, Freyalise sniffed her disdain, *I have been far more selective in my choice of allies.*

Teferi pounced. *I'm not asking you to go to war. I'm merely asking you to talk to me, to educate me by sharing your success with Skyshroud.*

Oh, no, Freyalise's tone became sharper, colder, and more cutting. *Teferi would never ask me to fight as Urza did. Teferi does not fight, not when he can run away and hide for three centuries. Not when he can see his own nation and his own tribes to safety. Not when he can skulk away and leave the rest of the world to defend itself.*

Teferi started as if struck. He was not wounded by Freyalise's slanted view of his actions but from one simple detail nigh-lost among her cruel invective.

Three centuries? Teferi said.

Freyalise paused. When she finally spoke, her glee was savage. *You didn't know? You lose track of how long you've been gone, and you have the gall to ask me to educate you? Leave here at once, meddler, and take your Shivan minions with you. I will protect Skyshroud from the dangers here. Your battle and your burden are where you left them in Shiv.*

Teferi turned his thoughts back to Jhoira and the others. *What else don't I know?*

Freyalise laughed coldly. *That is a subject one could expound on at length.*

Have a care, Freyalise. I have had too many rude shocks today. I will not gladly endure much more of your abuse.

No? Freyalise mirth was obvious. *Let me assure you, there's more to come.* Her voice became dark and menacing. *If you truly object, Teferi, if you wish to challenge me to a formal duel . . . do something.*

"I shall," Teferi said, "and you will help me, Freyalise."

The planeswalker's harsh, mocking laughter echoed across the Blind Eternities. Teferi made a show of ignoring it, but he busily memorized every sound and syllable.

Without another word, Teferi concentrated. There was a moment of disorientation and a flash of stabbing pain, then he took himself back to Keld.

* * * * *

Jhoira scanned the beach in the wake of the abortive battle. It had been a short, savage exchange, and now five berserkers lay motionless on the ground. There were no casualties on the Shivan side.

Two of the prone raiders were definitely dead and the other three were preparing to follow, burned and bleeding in the sand. The rest of the barbarian raiders had retreated in the face of the Shivans' ferocity.

Aprem slowly brought his whirling, flaming bolas under control and holstered them. Grinning, he called out, "That was too easy. Do Keldons usually turn and run away?"

"No," Jhoira said emphatically. "They do not."

"Far too easy," Skive agreed. The end of his tail was streaked with crimson, as three of the berserker casualties were his. "These were just cannon fodder, the lowest of the low. They don't even have a leader—without a warlord, Keldons are just another gang of thugs who pillage and make a lot of noise. No discipline, no danger."

The Shivan warriors were disappointed when their foes pulled back as quickly as they'd attacked. The raiders had retreated back over the dunes, glaring and growling all the way. Though Skive and Corus followed, they only pursued the enemy long enough to make sure they were not regrouping for a second attack. The raiders had been bloodied, but they were by no means beaten. Not yet.

Jhoira had no idea how Teferi wanted to proceed from here, but she was certain the safest and smartest thing they could all do was wait for him. At least the Shivan warriors were savvy enough not to pepper Jhoira with questions about their mission or the planeswalker who commissioned it. She stared up at the mysterious rift that still hovered over them, readying questions of her own for Teferi.

As she waited, the rest of the party quickly grew restless. Skive idly split a piece of driftwood into uniform lengths with his tail while Corus impressed Aprem and Dassene with the quality of his Ghitu-forged blades.

Jhoira heard a grating, low-pitched groan in the air beside her. She turned just as a conical portal opened, Teferi at its wide end.

He looked determined, clear-eyed, and focused, and Jhoira said a silent prayer of thanks.

Grinning and raising his eyebrows, the planeswalker said, "Ready to begin?" He stopped then, eying the dead barbarians. "What happened here?"

"The barbarians came back," Jhoira said. "They phased in far sooner than you anticipated, but they didn't stay long after that."

Dassene twirled her wooden baton in one hand. "We discouraged them from lingering. I hope that was part of your plan."

"If not," Aprem put in, "maybe you should stick around to keep us up to date."

Teferi's eyes narrowed. Jhoira had not often seen the planeswalker angry, but he was clearly approaching the end of his even temper.

"You disappoint me, sir," he said softly. "I am no warrior and never claimed to be. That's why we brought you. I would never have imagined the noble Ghitu and the mighty viashino needed an academic to tell them how to fight, but if I must, shall I also spoonfeed you your meals and tell you where babies come from?"

Corus laughed, but Teferi held Aprem in a withering stare.

The Ghitu mage looked down. "No, sir," he said.

Teferi turned to the other warriors. "We have a job to do and it's time we got started."

"Teferi's right." Jhoira stepped between the warriors and the planeswalker. Softly, to Teferi, she said, "For now, but you really must tell me exactly what is going on here and tell me soon."

"What do you mean?"

"I mean you've been surprised by just about everything we've seen so far. When you left us you were off-balance and confused. Now you've come back all focused and full of purpose. What happened? Did you see Skyshroud or talk with Freyalise?"

"Forget Freyalise. She's more insular than ever. Cattier, too. She won't help us."

Jhoira's stomach sank. "I see."

"I also discovered we have . . . less time than I thought," Teferi added, "Things have deteriorated more than I ever imagined, but we don't need much time, and we certainly don't need Freyalise. One good, hard look at Skyshroud will be enough. It took a colossal effort to do what she did, and an astounding amount of force. The act had to leave some readable signs that we can interpret and put to good use."

"That sounds reasonable. Not as reasonable as heading straight for Shiv, mind you, but since we're here. . . . "

Teferi looked back up at the time rift and winced slightly. "We should go right away. We can march there in a few hours if we leave now and move quickly."

"March?"

Teferi shrugged guiltily. "Until I know more about what we're dealing with, I'm trying to use as little magic as possible. If we march, I'll have time to get a feel for the mana situation straight through my own two feet. Each step will give me a slightly clearer picture of what happened to Keld."

Jhoira nodded. "We march," she said, "but double-time."

"That suits me," called Skive. "Frankly, you warmbloods have been slowing us down." He grinned and his tail sliced the air behind him. Corus tossed the last segment of driftwood into the air and Skive sliced it lengthwise with his tail.

"Excellent," Teferi said. "Then there's nothing left to discuss and no more reason to wait."

Jhoira immediately thought of several good reasons—the fact that they were not prepared for this strangely altered Keld, for example, or the growing list of things Teferi was keeping from her. She decided to keep these issues to herself for just a little while longer.

Whatever had just shocked Teferi into alacrity also made him more determined than ever to visit the forest. Once they had done that and learned all they could, perhaps then he would feel confident enough to share the smaller details of his plans for Shiv. If not, Jhoira would simply have to figure it out for herself.

Teferi winked at her. "So, then. To Skyshroud?"

She nodded. "To Skyshroud, and eventually, Shiv."

Teferi neither agreed nor disagreed, but cocked his head. His only answer to her sober, probing expression was a playfully crooked smile.

CHAPTER 4

The Skyshroud Forest sat in a sheltered valley near the center of Keld. It had always been somewhat absurd when seen from above, a perfectly round garden of leafy green set against a solid sheet of bare rock and snow. The valley was otherwise barren, a cold north wind and shadows from the nearby mountains keeping it in a permanent hard freeze all year. The trees of Skyshroud were thick and strong, and unseen birds filled the frozen air between them with their eerie, hollow songs.

Teferi stood at the crest of a broken ridge overlooking the forest below. Jhoira and the Shivans had already begun climbing down into the valley, carefully picking their way across the jagged cliffs. They moved cautiously but easily down the rocks, comfortable on the rocky terrain. The light and nimble Ghitu were making steady progress, but the heavier viashino moved down the mountainside so quickly it seemed they were falling. They stayed in complete control of their momentum as they descended, and Teferi could hear tiny clicks as their claws found purchase.

Teferi fixed his gaze on the forest beyond as his party descended. His expanded senses told him a great deal about the place even at this distance. He felt the first tingling rush of new discovery, of obtaining information without yet knowing all its implications. He had to get closer, to see more.

Unconsciously, Teferi rose a foot off the ground and floated down the mountain. He continued to stare at Skyshroud as he drifted several yards behind Jhoira and the Ghitu.

He had no firsthand experience with Skyshroud and there was precious little information recorded about it. He knew that the grounds were originally excavated from Dominaria eons ago and cultivated elsewhere, like a rare flower nurtured inside a hothouse.

Skyshroud was then exposed to a viciously hostile environment as part of a mad Phyrexian god's vast and terrible experiment. After millennia of growth and forced evolution, the experiment ended and the forest was to be returned to its original home, but Freyalise intervened. The planeswalker always held herself a goddess among Dominaria's great elf tribes, and she recognized Skyshroud's elves as descendents of her own loyal worshippers. Freyalise took the forest and its elves under her protection and diverted it here, to this inhospitable Keldon valley. She then dedicated a portion of her limitless might to protecting and sustaining the forest against the cold and created this impossible island of growth and abundance in an otherwise unbroken field of frozen rock.

Teferi shifted his perceptions, taking in the view of Skyshroud as patterns of energy that drifted and whorled like oil on water. The forest appeared not as a thick wall of timber and creeping vines, but as a complicated patchwork of pale green lights. Freyalise's magic still enveloped the place, nourishing and warming Skyshroud with the verdant power of nature to make survival possible.

Teferi drifted closer to the forest, easing away from the mountainside and out into empty air. Freyalise's blessing had sustained and helped protect the mana supply from the drought that was crippling the rest of Keld, but the forest was far from robust. He suspected without a direct and continuous infusion of Freyalise's power, Skyshroud would be as desiccated and fallow as Keld proper. As it was Skyshroud was slightly better off, but only because its mana was slower to waste away.

"Teferi." Jhoira's voice was far away, far below. Teferi glanced down and saw that the Shivans had reached the valley floor while he himself was still hovering in place halfway down the mountain.

I'm surveying. Teferi sent his thoughts directly to Jhoira. He was more comfortable keeping their discussions between themselves, and it also spared them the trouble of waiting for their words to stop echoing off the valley walls.

Jhoira's thoughts came back after a short pause. *Seen anything helpful?*

I have, and I'm seeing more all the time.

That's good. We're ready to approach the forest as soon as you catch up.

I'm on my way. Teferi looked once more to Skyshroud as he floated down, this time through the eyes of a planeswalker choosing his next course.

The structure of the multiverse was one of the most difficult things to impart to a non-planeswalker, as so many of its facets were self-contradictory. The infinite array of planes was held together by the Blind Eternities, but it was also separated by them; planes had definite boundaries but indefinite shapes; travel between planes was frequently more difficult when one's origin and destination were adjacent in the multiverse's grand array. There weren't many hard and fast rules that could be applied to every plane, but there were norms that could be codified and discussed. Teferi had used a thousand different metaphors over the years, and a million different examples, but in the end he always felt any explanation was too facile and glib. A student who submitted similar answers for an exam would have found himself in the bottom half of the curve, among the other essayists who had written well but not answered the question.

Teferi looked carefully at Skyshroud, the alien landscape that had been integrated to the existing structure of Keld. It was not an easy fit. Skyshroud's soil was largely clay and loam; Keld was all bedrock. Skyshroud's climate was cool and damp where Keld was dry and lethally cold. Skyshroud's trees had massive exposed roots and grew over and around each other like weeds; Keld's native pines and redwoods were tall, straight, and sharp, and they grew in uniform lines of spiked evergreen. Skyshroud was suffused with nature magic, the magic of growth, abundance, and instinct; Keld seethed with the magic of fire, destruction, and wild, chaotic joy.

No, Skyshroud into Keld had not been an easy fit by any measure, and if all Teferi's observations so far hadn't already proven the forest did not belong in the valley, there was another, supremely obvious proof. Rising from the center of Skyshroud's leafy canopy (and almost certainly descending down through the forest into the Keldon bedrock below) was a massive rent in the fabric of the multiverse. It was superficially similar to the one that had unleashed barbarians on the beach, but only to the extent that a zephyr and a sirocco are both streams of air.

The Skyshroud rift was enormous, stretching high up into the sky and disappearing there among the dense clouds. As Teferi adjusted his vision once more he saw that it did indeed stab deep into the ground below. He looked back up and imagined he could follow the great rift all the way back to Skyshroud's second home, through the Blind Eternities to the far edge of the multiverse, then all the way back to its original location on the other side of Dominaria.

His first presumptions were now confirmed: Freyalise didn't just guide Skyshroud into place; she made a place for it. She had elegantly integrated the forest landscape with that of the mountains, but her elegance was backed by a brute magical power. The ground she prepared for Skyshroud was not fully ready to receive the forest, so she had been obliged to use force. This last inelegant push is almost certainly what cracked the planar structure here, but Teferi was less concerned with fixing this damage than he was with avoiding a similar result when he delivered Shiv. He was already starting to see just how Freyalise had made this happen . . . and how he could improve on her methods.

Teferi picked up speed as he descended, dropping faster even than the viashino could climb. How could he tell Jhoira and tell her quickly? This huge reality fissure was the source of Keld's mana troubles—Teferi could actually see the flow of red and green energy streaming into the rift from all sides like water draining from a cracked basin. Freyalise's work was otherwise so careful, so seamless, but even she had to hammer this particular nail home.

Teferi allowed himself a confident smirk. He was not Freyalise. He had considerably more experience in working with continent-sized landmasses, and he had spent several lifetimes observing, researching, and sometimes causing disruptive space-time events. Having a test case like Skyshroud was all he needed to all but insure Shiv's safe return. All that remained was to crack the mystery of the rift's mana depletion of its surroundings.

Jhoira was waiting for him on the valley floor, her eyes anxious. "New information?"

"Plenty," Teferi said. "Still sorting through it. I was right, by the way: we won't need to stay long. In fact, I expect we'll be in Shiv by lunch time tomorrow."

Jhoira seemed satisfied by that. "What's our next step here?"

Teferi's eyes sparkled. "Stand still," he said, "and enjoy the ride." He stretched out his staff and inscribed a circle in the air over their heads. "Come closer, please." The viashino and Ghitu quickly huddled in so that they were inside the arc of his staff, which Teferi continued to wave.

The group silently floated several inches into the air. There was no magical glow, no dramatic smoke, as he was too keen on this new line of inquiry to bother with theatrics. As one, the group surged forward, one foot above the frozen ground, moving faster than ever.

The warriors seemed comfortable enough, though both Ghitu tended to keep their arms extended so as not to lose their balance.

Jhoira kept her hands folded behind her as she stood alongside Teferi until he noticed she was staring at him. Again.

"What have I done now?" Teferi said.

Jhoira shrugged. "Just wondering what changed. Why you didn't use this trick earlier but can use it now."

"I can't share every thought I have," Teferi said. "We're here to reconnoiter and learn. I'm quickly learning the limits of what this place will let me do."

"Fair enough." Jhoira brought her hands around and held them up in surrender. "But you brought us to help, not to stand by and wait for you to return. We're in this together. If you do need us, put us to work. If not, take us to Shiv and we'll get started there while you run down your leads here."

"I absolutely need you," Teferi said quietly. "All of you. Weren't you listening when I said we'd be in Shiv tomorrow?"

"I was, and you did. I still think that's the best course, but I didn't want to gloat."

"Gloat away," Teferi said. "When we're done here and I have what I need, the smart bet is I'll spend the next fifty years rubbing it in."

"Wouldn't be the first time," Jhoira muttered.

Teferi saw the state of Skyshroud more clearly as they drew closer. The forest was remarkably healthy compared to the rest of Keld, but it was still tired and twisted. The trees were alive, but the wood was soft, weak, and wan. The thickest and tallest trunks were all broken just above thirty or forty feet, with the remaining parts pitted by disease and parasites. The characteristic exposed roots of Skyshroud trees formed a confused tangle of dead, gray tendrils.

The roots and the lower half of each tree were covered in a thick vine that appeared to be equal parts plant and fungus. Ghastly yellow tumors hung from the vines like grotesque fruit, reminding Teferi of diseased muscle tissue and abscessed internal organs. He did not look too closely at the vines, nor did he allow himself to wonder who fertilized them or with what. Sharp, chattering sounds clicked and whistled from the shadows just beyond this heavy vine thicket, the sound of chitinous claws and mandibles snapping and scraping against each other.

Teferi slowed and set the group down twenty yards from the edge of the trees. "From here," he said, "we walk."

Proximity to the massive Skyshroud rift was uncomfortable for Teferi, but it was not as acute as the beach rift had been. Perhaps this one was older, its painful aspect diminished over time? Perhaps Freyalise's blessing had blunted this rift's impact, as it had Keld's frigid weather?

The viashino went ahead, slithering down from the platform onto the cold valley floor. They had barely gone a few paces before a host of tall, lean figures materialized out of the fungus-bearing vines.

"Wait," Teferi said, but the viashino needed no such order.

They each held their position, confident but not hostile, ready to attack or withdraw as needed. Aprem and Dassene fell in behind the two lizards, weapons drawn but unignited.

It was Teferi's first view of a modern Skyshroud elf and he quickly counted ten or more as they silently emerged from the woods. He had been told to expect long, sinewy warriors who favored snakeskin armor—fierce and proud, they would bear a peculiar bluish-green skin tone that made them seem damp and stern in any weather.

What he saw were cadaverous, almost skeletal creatures with hollow eyes, sunken chests, and only the most rudimentary clothing. They were horribly emaciated, each rib and joint clearly visible under their drab gray cloaks. Jaundiced yellow eyes stared dully out from each leathery face, their ragged lips drawn back over stained, broken teeth.

"Gyah," Skive spat. He hissed from the side of his mouth to Corus. "Are these elves or zombies?"

"Maybe both," Corus said.

Teferi wondered if the viashino were correct. They were definitely Skyshroud elves; they definitely had the right demeanor and blue-green tone. They did not seem especially aggressive, but they were all armed with simple square blades of flexible metal or bows and arrows made from bones and fangs of a carnivorous predator. Given the elves' desperate appearance and the clearly stated hostility from Freyalise, Teferi chose not to relax his guard.

"Greetings, you children of Skyshroud." Teferi's voice rolled out from his chest, booming, confident, calling all who heard it to bask in its comforting tones. "I am Teferi of Zhalfir. I have been called many things, planeswalker, wizard, wanderer, loreweaver, and solver of riddles, but the elves of this forest may call me friend or at least respectful visitor, for I mean you no harm. I only wish to view the wonders of your home."

A tall elf in the center of the platoon came forward. He carried himself with the grace and elegance of a chief, though his joints creaked and popped as he walked. When he spoke, his voice was thin and hollow.

"I offer you no greetings, Teferi of Tolaria, nor will any here call you friend." The chieftain did not bow but stared boldly at the planeswalker. "I am Llanach, Captain of the Skyshroud Rangers. Through me Freyalise, our patron and protector, hereby renews her objections to your presence. I have no malice toward you, but in her name I bid you and your cohorts begone."

"Zhalfir," Teferi said gently. "I am Teferi of Zhalfir."

The elf captain's expression did not change. More emaciated bodies shuffled in the brush behind him. "Upon being corrected by a visiting dignitary," Teferi sniffed, "an experienced envoy would apologize."

Llanach face remained fixed and skull-like. Then he spoke, loudly, though his lips barely parted. "Whence you came is not my concern. Only where you are now." Llanach drew his crude sword and crossed it over his chest. "Freyalise herself has decreed it. Praise to her name."

The other elves voices' formed a ragged, monotonous chorus as they responded in unison. "Praise to the goddess Freyalise, protector of Skyshroud." The elf captain called out to his fellow rangers and all six archers nocked arrows onto their strings. They did not take aim or bend the bows, but stood with arrowheads pointed at the hard-packed ground. Though frail, each archer seemed capable, even eager to demonstrate his skills.

The viashino and Ghitu had seen enough. Corus' long claws slid out and Skive's tail curled up over his head. Dassene drew her batons but did not light them. Aprem simply stood with his right hand on his hip, next to the bolas on his belt.

Teferi signed. He opened his eyes wider, taking in all he could about Skyshroud and the valley that supported it before circumstances became too distracting.

He could sweep the elves aside, of course, or shield himself and the Shivans indefinitely as he completed his inspection of the site. That direct action would almost certainly prompt Freyalise into an equally strong response. Things would then escalate, as they invariably did, until a full-fledged planeswalker duel was happening dangerously close to the Skyshroud rift.

Teferi could allow the Shivans and elves to skirmish while he alone observed the forest, but he instantly disliked this option more than he had instantly disliked the previous. Not only did it require significant risk on the part of his allies for no reward—since the Shivans winning the day would just bring Freyalise down to keep her unwanted visitors out—but it also led to the same bad end, two planeswalkers dueling on the rift.

He decided to freeze them all, to stop everyone in their tracks except for himself, Jhoira, and Llanach. It would prevent anyone from getting hurt, but it would also give him a starting argument to head off Freyalise's anger—he wasn't simply paralyzing Skyshroud's defenders, he was pacifying both sides of the conflict as part of a larger, nobler effort.

A sudden blast on a battle horn startled Teferi. It was a strong, clear, sustained note from high on the ridge overhead, roughly where Teferi had paused for his first long look at the forest.

The Shivan warriors all responded to the strong, baleful sound, reacting as a lone wolf does to another wolf's howl. There were other predators in this valley—potential danger and potential competition. The Shivans kept their weapons ready as they split their attention between the elves and the ridge overhead.

The horn's peal drew a more violent reaction from the elves. The archers all drew their bows and oriented on the sound, twitching for the order to fire. Every other elf drew and closed ranks around Llanach. The rangers' captain had not taken his eyes off Teferi, but it looked as if not looking up required considerable effort.

Teferi did not wish to simply turn his back on Freyalise's emissary, so he closed his eyes and bowed to Llanach. Proper protocol observed, he quickly turned as he straightened and scanned the ridge. There, a thousand feet up the mountainside, Teferi saw a single sallow-skinned barbarian. He was shirtless in the cold and steam rose from the twisted mass of tattoos and scar tissue on his chest and shoulders. The squat, burly warrior raised to his lips a hollow ram or steer's horn and blew a second loud, clear note. The horn was bone white, twisted like a nautilus, and as large as the barbarian's forearm.

"That's a colos horn," Skive said. He shielded his eyes against the sun glaring off the ice and snow. "Only warlords use those, and it's blowing an attack call."

"What's a colos?" Aprem asked.

"Think of those yak-goat things you Ghitu shepherd only bigger, much bigger. Five times as tall, twenty times more massive. Bad tempered and aggressive. Sharp hooves"—he angled his head toward the barbarian on the ridge—"and big horns."

Aprem grinned. "How do they taste?"

"The meat's gamey, but it's good for sausage." Skive's tongue flicked out. "Better than field rations, anyway."

Dassene called out, "Is this the same cannon fodder we drove off the beach?"

"Yes," Teferi said.

"No," Skive countered. "If they've got a warlord, they'll be a lot more dangerous."

Aprem drew his weapon. "The horn means they've got a warlord?"

"Someone's giving orders," Jhoira said. "Waiting for a signal is already more organized than they were on the beach."

"Teferi." Llanach's voice was soft but forceful. "You must leave here. Leave the Gathans to us. We have dealt with them before."

Teferi's ears caught on the unfamiliar word, but he had no time to press Llanach for his meaning. "I cannot leave yet, Captain, as I still have work to do. Let me and my associates help you beat back these raiders. That will give me time and us the common cause—"

Llanach's ravaged face twisted in anger. "You are not welcome here! This is not your battle, planeswalker. Leave us to defend our home, as we have always done and will always do: on our own."

"I know you are capable of doing just that, Captain, but I'm not going anywhere until I've got what I came for. Fighting the Keldons with our help has to be preferable to fighting us and the Keldons simultaneously."

The colos horn pealed again. A collection of large, fast-moving figures streamed past the bugler and half-skidded, half-charged down toward the valley.

"They're coming," Skive said.

"How many?" Aprem did not have the viashino's keen vision.

"Thirty," Teferi said. He did not take his eyes from the elf captain. "With twice that held in reserve. Are you equipped and prepared to handle a Keldon warhost of ninety, Llanach? With a colos horn driving it and a warlord close by?"

Llanach hesitated, weighing the options. To his credit, it did not take him long to reach the only possible conclusion.

He turned to his warriors and said, "Target the barbarians and only the barbarians until I say otherwise." He turned back and drew a second sword. "We'll sort out the rest later." To Teferi he said, "Planeswalker. Stay out of our way."

"Count on it," Teferi said. He looked over to Jhoira, who nodded.

"Go," she said. "Learn what you can. We'll help the elves . . . if they allow it."

"And stay out of harm's way," Teferi said.

"Of course."

Behind them, an archer let fly his bone-tipped arrow. The bolt arced high over the valley then plunged down into the front of the charging raiders. Teferi watched a berserker near the front take the elf's arrow squarely in the chest and winced sympathetically as the warrior fell.

His sympathy flickered out like a candle as the stricken raider rolled, recovered, and resumed both his place in the formation and the overall charge. Though the arrow now protruded from both sides of his torso, the brute never lost a step, never acknowledged the wound or the tumble in any way.

Keldons kill quicker than they die. The quotation came to Teferi unbidden from an old Tolarian history scroll, a truism coined by the author to explain the barbarians' long history of prevailing against numerically superior forces. This particular text was one of many that featured sensational, perhaps even slightly exaggerated, firsthand accounts of Keldon campaigns. It told wild, frightening tales of the berserkers' violent excess, terrifying accounts of blood-maddened beasts who ignored fatigue, hunger, the elements, and mortal wounds alike in their mad rush to destroy the enemy.

Dozens of arrows arced up from the valley floor. As Teferi watched, the berserkers come straight through this surge of elven arrows, he saw how this particular battlefield aphorism got its start. Almost all of the raiders took crippling wounds, but not a single one abandoned his headlong plunge into the valley. The sight of their own blood actually seemed to spur them on and drive them into an even deeper frenzy.

"Swords ready," Llanach said. The elves moved into formation and waited for the barbarians to draw closer.

Nearby, Teferi spared one last look at Jhoira. She nodded again and mouthed, "Go." Teferi nodded back. He positioned his elbows on his hips, opened his hands to the sky, and rose into the air on a blue nimbus of light.

As he soared up from the valley floor, Teferi glanced back down. Llanach had thirty elves at his back, and together with the Shivans they would certainly be able to repel the raider's first wave. That would give Teferi the chance to finish here at Skyshroud, and then he could send the entire Keldon population to the far edge of the country. He might even earn Freyalise's help in the process.

Not likely, Freyalise's voice said, *nor even possible.*

Freyalise materialized before Teferi in a foggy bloom of green energy. She appeared, facing him five hundred feet above the forest, and as her body became fully solid and real, the great rift phenomenon behind her let out a deafening blast of thunder.

Teferi screamed in agony. The crack in reality widened, and the Skyshroud rift released a blast of primal energy that engulfed both planeswalkers as well as a huge section of Keldon sky.

CHAPTER 5

Radha watched the barbarians descend. Her eyes were sharp and her view was clear from the highest surviving branches of Skyshroud's tallest surviving trees. She perched among the boughs as solidly and surely as if she'd grown there among them. She was tall and broad shouldered, her long arms and legs wrapped and folded around the trunk and branches of the tree. Her eyes were dark and fierce, and her hair was thick, coarse, and wild. Her dusky skin was the color of some exotic alloy of copper and steel, a rich stony gray tinged with reddish gold. Between her natural coloring and the dark tanned tunic and breeches she wore, Radha was almost perfectly camouflaged against the drawn and wasted timber.

As the false Keldons came roaring down into the valley, they could neither see nor hear Radha, and they would not until she was ready to introduce herself. She absently tightened her grip around the wrist-thick branch in her hand, imagining it was the lead raider's neck. The sturdy Keldon hardwood cracked in Radha's fist, sending a comforting jolt up her forearm.

This brief moment of grim joy faded as Radha turned back to the valley floor and saw that enfeebled stick insect, Llanach, leading Freyalise's rangers. The old ranger had performed his ceremonial duties adequately, meeting the party of strangers and giving them Freyalise's standard greeting. Now he was actually presuming to lead Freyalise's rangers into combat.

Radha's lips twisted into a sneer. Better to say he was leading the worn out, consumptive remnants of Freyalise's rangers, those few who could still walk. Skyshroud's elves had grown too drawn and thin to hold off the false Keldons for long. Radha knew it, Llanach knew it, and deep down, Freyalise knew it too.

Radha smiled, clenching her jaws. They would need her again, and they would need her soon.

She stepped onto a thick branch and gracefully ran out along its length, heading away from the trunk. When her weight began to bend the bough, she hopped down to a lower one and darted along its length until it also began to give. She continued to cascade downward and forward in this manner until she was a prodigious leap away from the tree line and a bare ten feet above the endless tangle of roots and ivy below, where each tough vine was dotted with bulbous, pulsating shapes.

The saproling thicket covered most of the forest floor and made absolutely all land travel in Skyshroud tedious, if not treacherous. The vines could latch on to careless hikers and pull them down, or huge wads of the stuff could separate from the main mass and act independently—saprolings, as these mobile and aggressive drones were called. Half-formed and directed by some foul combination of primal instinct and collective consciousness, saprolings came in all sizes as they limped and shuffled out, engulfing unwary travelers and dragging them back into the main thicket. Once inside a large enough mass of vines, the victims were then torn apart and digested in a matter of hours.

The elves had carved a few relatively safe paths through the center of the forest where the children of Freyalise needed them most, but almost elsewhere else was choked by thick hedges of the revolting, predatory plant-fungus such as the one below her now. Radha watched the thicket surge and undulate like some rank stew coming to a boil. It was an overwhelming sight, but she had not survived in Skyshroud by letting every exotic danger bewitch her to the dangers of every other one.

Beyond the greedy rustling of the vines and the loathsome gurgling of the fungus-bodies came a new sound. Hard, chattering sounds and whiplike slithering echoed in from the distance. Radha peered intently into the dark recesses of the woods. Slivers, the forest's other nuisance, always sounded close, but Radha had never caught more than a quick glimpse of one.

Vaguely insectoid and voracious, slivers were concentrated along the edges of the saproling thicket, mindlessly swarming where the fungus vines were strongest. There were supposedly a dozen different breeds of the voracious little fiends in the forest, each with its own unique adaptations. Some had developed the ability to fly, others delivered toxic stings, and others grew larger and stronger when attacked.

Furthermore, if Llanach's rangers were to be believed, slivers magically shared these specialized abilities with every other sliver nearby. If one of their number could fly and another spit poison, the entire swarm became flying poison-spitters. In the long term, Radha felt this made the sliver swarms more dangerous to Skyshroud than the saproling thicket. Where the thicket encroached slowly and consumed the forest in increments, the slivers would be sudden and devastating.

Freyalise disagreed with Radha, which meant that so did every other elf in the forest. They claimed to have experience with slivers, and they insisted they knew how to handle them.

In the short term, Freyalise and her followers were proven correct. The competition between saprolings and slivers was the only thing keeping both mindless colonies in check. Whenever the thicket rolled in like a viscous green tide, the slivers responded as any voracious hive would to a sudden and large concentration of its primary food source: they rushed in and devoured as much as they could. So the saprolings flowed, the slivers swarmed, and they all killed and consumed each other rather than Skyshroud.

Radha grumbled to herself. Thus the patron of Skyshroud trusted the forest's safety not to action but inaction. She had staked the elves' home on the convenient interaction of two aggressive armies waiting outside their door. One day the slivers or the saprolings would gain the upper hand, and two seconds after that happened the victor would be stronger and battle-hardened when it came for the rest of Skyshroud.

Radha fought the impulse to leap down among the vines and begin slashing them to pieces, to cut down enough vines so that the slivers massing nearby would lose interest or chose a more robust target. She also considered slashing a path through the thicket and on to the swarm to accelerate the inevitable, to start an all-out three-way war between fungus, bug, and Skyshroud.

These were both tempting thoughts, but they paled next to what she already had before her in the valley. She could take her exercise any time she liked by wading into a sea of shambling, twisted fungus creatures or an endless stream of chattering, sharp-taloned slivers. It had delighted her to do precisely that, often in fact. Not today, though. Today, right now, she had more important things to kill.

Radha curled up and dropped into a low squat, gathering her strength as the heavy branch shuddered and sagged beneath her. Arms extended, she rolled forward along the branch until it started to swing back into place. Her heels touched the surface of the branch and Radha sprang upward, using the bough's momentum to launch herself high into the air, past the saproling thicket and on toward the edge of the forest.

Radha turned one last somersault in the air then landed silently among the outermost tendrils of the saproling thicket. Here the vines were no thicker than her bootlaces and the fungus bodies were only the size of chicken eggs.

Radha ducked down among the ivy, staring intently at Llanach and the strangers. There had been six newcomers in all, though now there were five. The dark one had flown off and left three little ones and two big green ones to meet the oncoming raiders. They all wore mana stones and the armed ones seemed capable enough, but they were taking orders from the studious-looking young girl standing safely behind them. Following the girl's lead seemed to leave the warriors standing idle, unable to commit to a fight with either the elves or the barbarians.

Radha resolved to keep an eye on this girl—she was smarter than she looked. Staying neutral was the smart move, as all of the locals had either proven or declared themselves hostile. There was no way for the visitors to guess which native tribe was the more pressing danger, not before the battle started. Once the blood started flowing, however, Radha knew the newcomers would have to side with the defenders of Skyshroud. The raiders were so indiscriminate in combat that there was simply no way stand by without being engaged. If the strangers were the kind to hit back when hit, they would be trading blows with the false Keldons before long.

The first howling barbarians reached the valley floor. Radha shifted her face back and forth, trying to keep track of elves and raiders as they rushed toward each other. A few more seconds and they'd all be close enough to see at once. She wet her lips and crouched lower.

A fist-sized fungus rose up directly beside her face on a six-inch tower of vines. The fungus rippled as the vines below wove themselves together, making a thicker and stronger column. The appendage began to sweep around the area, probing for Radha like a long switch with a meaty bulb on its end.

Utterly fixed on the approaching fight, Radha caught the bulbous end of the saproling stalk and crushed it, splattering yellow goo across the forest floor. She wiped the effluent slime on the still-swaying column of vines, her hand stripping away the small, sharp leaves as it went.

The ragged green stump continued to flail. Radha's hand stole down to her hip. There was a flash of metal and a sharp, whispering sound. The length of vine collapsed, shorn off cleanly at the base. It continued to wriggle and unravel as the thin tendrils crawled back into the main thicket to be reabsorbed.

Radha pushed aside another stray vine with her empty hand. She watched the battle begin, elves, the strangers, and the raiding berserkers all coming together like storm clouds. She could feel the gathering carnage's rhythm, knowing its entire shape, its ebb and flow even as the first blows landed. She was eager to see what the newcomers could do, especially the two big scaly ones. She was eager to see if her battlefield predictions were as accurate as ever.

She was also eager to see the Skyshroud elves defeated—not killed necessarily, but routed. Once Llanach and his dried-up rangers had fallen, the protector of Skyshroud would be forced to turn Radha loose, and this time she would not stop until she had pursued the false Keldons all the way back to their camp. There, she would challenge their leader to single combat, during which she would break off all his arms and his legs and slit him open from groin to gullet before pulling off his head and using it as a commode.

This time, Radha told herself, she would succeed. Not even Freyalise herself would stop her. She smiled again, remembering the feel of the branch as it cracked in her fist.

The raiders and the elves finally met out in the open valley and their swords rang like bells in the frigid air. Away from the battle, the strangers stood ready but did not join in. The little ones, the dark ones in red, had their weapons drawn, and as Radha watched the ends of those weapons burst into bright yellow flame.

Radha's dark eyes widened, glittering in the flames. She stared transfixed, her mouth stretching into a large, hungry grin. She licked her lips. Perhaps she would have to join this battle sooner than she thought.

* * * * *

Teferi's scream lost all its force as soon as he found himself alone and upright in a quiet glade.

It had all happened so fast. Freyalise had appeared and the world had gone away, but the heat and shock from the rift had flared and died like a match struck in a high wind. He had been blind, deaf, and helpless in the skies above Skyshroud, but now he was just as suddenly restored and standing in the heart of the forest.

He sensed a profoundly strong magical aura close by and turned. After a moment Freyalise stepped out from behind a thick tree, glaring at Teferi as she strode into the glade, coming directly at him.

Like Teferi, Freyalise chose to appear in the body of the mortal she had been. She had always been connected to and worshipped by elves, though Freyalise herself was not precisely like any of the elves that lived on Dominaria. Lean and compact, she stood no more than five and a half feet tall. Her skin was fair and her stiff blonde hair hovered around her head like a cloud, spiked up straight and swept back from her face. Only one piercing hazel eye was visible; the other was hidden beneath a gogglelike accessory strapped across her face like a pirate's patch.

Freyalise wore an elegant sleeveless dress that stretched from just below her collarbone to just above her knee. The garment had been woven from two or three wide strips of leathery material that alternated green and white. She also wore a long ranger's cloak that flared out behind her as she moved, pinned to her shoulder by a fanglike splinter of bone. Her arms were encased in a pair of green gloves that covered her from the tips of her fingers up past her elbows.

Everything about the protector of Skyshroud's appearance was piercing, almost threatening, and with good reason. Over the centuries Freyalise had nurtured an especially violent form of isolationism in all of the elf tribes that worshipped her. They would sooner kill an innocent who accidentally ventured into their woods than risk the potential damage an uninvited human could cause. Humans carried axes, built cooking fires, and left the ground strewn with poisons. Humans cleared large sections of timber to clear space and build cages for their livestock, and then they used whatever wood was left to fence themselves in.

Teferi had sat with at least a half-dozen forest avatars, maro-sorcerers, and nature spirits during his lifetime, so he had reliable witnesses to some of the heinous deeds Freyalise's children performed in her name. These were terrible stories of elf warriors maiming farmers who cleared trees and brush to plant crops, hunting poachers for sport and making trophies of their heads, and burning alive families who cut down live trees for wood. The goddess's edict was that humans were inferior to elves, inferior even to trees. When humans transgressed against the forest, human blood would flow until the scales were balanced.

Apart from this anecdotal evidence and what he'd read in the archives, Teferi knew very little about Freyalise. With all his resources, not even he could say where she originally came from, how she became a planeswalker, or how long she had been one. If Freyalise had spoken truly and Teferi had been gone for three centuries, then she herself had been actively traveling the multiverse for at least four thousand years.

Teferi smiled pleasantly as the daunting woman came near. Freyalise would be a true challenge. She was ancient, vastly powerful, a seasoned combatant, and fiendishly smart. She was well-versed in both forest and mountain magic. She was experienced at casting massive, world-altering spells. She was phenomenally self-assured and monumentally stubborn. Most important of all at this juncture, Freyalise hated Teferi and all he stood for and stood openly opposed to his goals.

Teferi's smile was perfect and he kept it that way. Freyalise's discouraging aspects did not outweigh or cancel out his need to speak with her. She had done what Teferi now needed to do. She had also lived here, on the site of that event and this new perplexing rift phenomenon for three hundred years. Formidable as she was, dangerous as she was, Freyalise had information and experience Teferi needed. He might never force it out of her, but that didn't mean he would never get it.

"Before we fight," he said brightly. "Can you at least tell me what just happened?"

Freyalise kept walking until she was within a handsbreadth of Teferi. She stopped and folded her arms as her cloak caught up. After it had re-draped itself across her shoulders, Freyalise tilted her head back and said, "For the last time, none of this concerns you."

"But it does, and it will concern everyone everywhere if I don't act now."

Freyalise's face colored, flushing an angry pink. "What would you know about 'everyone everywhere'? You haven't been here. Nothing you know is still valid." Her face continued to change color, beyond the first flush of rising passion and on toward the brilliant scarlet of a salamander's belly.

Calmly, Teferi noted Freyalise was unaware of her change in appearance as he sank to one knee. "Please," he said. "That is why I'm here. I don't know enough, but you can educate me, Freyalise. Tell me what happened so I can prepare for what is coming."

Eyes averted, Teferi heard the elves' goddess hiss derisively. "Get up, you sycophantic fool."

Teferi craned his head. "I don't want to fight, Freyalise. I have work to do, people to protect, as do you."

Freyalise color slowly returned to normal. She gestured impatiently. "You already know anything I could tell you," she said. "With your resources, you probably know more."

Teferi rose to his feet. "The rift," he said. He pointed up over their heads, to the sky above the forest canopy. "When was that formed?"

Freyalise turned away. She clenched and unclenched her gloved hands. "This one," she said, "existed from the moment I brought Skyshroud here. I thought it was a wound that would heal over time. I thought it was a natural stress fracture in the fabric of the multiverse, the kind you and I see all the time." She paused to glance darkly at Teferi.

"It seems we have something in common after all, Freyalise," Teferi said gently. "We have both cracked a part of the world we were trying to help."

"The rift has always been a problem for planeswalkers," Freyalise said sharply, her tone a stinging rebuke of Teferi. "I felt it fighting me, resisting Skyshroud as I guided the forest here. It has been the forest's shadow since the very beginning, and it has always made planeswalking unpredictable and dangerous. The closer to it you are when you 'walk, the more dramatic the results." Freyalise paused, considering.

"Did it always draw mana to it?"

The goddess glared. "Not always." She clenched her jaw. "Not until Karona came."

"I see. When was that?"

"A century after you left, maybe more. Time has always been hard to quantify when you Tolarians are involved."

Teferi shrugged. "Perhaps. Who is Karona?"

She gaped at him in naked contempt. "How can you pretend not to know?"

"Because I don't."

"She spoke to you. Her followers in Otaria never stopped telling the story of Karona summoning to her the world's mightiest magical beings then dismissing them as if she were interviewing footmen. You were reputedly among the dismissed."

"I've never heard of her, never met her, and never spoken to her. If she says she met me, it was in a dream she had."

Freyalise searched Teferi's face for any sign of deceit. She clenched her jaw once more for a moment and then said, "Karona

was the embodiment of magic, all magic throughout the world."
The planeswalker spoke in bored, practiced tones, an impatient
master lecturing an inattentive student. "She didn't last long,
but while she lived, there was no mana for anyone else. She
commanded it all, controlled it all. After she died, it all came
flooding back." Freyalise shrugged. "But it no longer flowed as it
had before she came. Things changed after she died. They began
to . . . deteriorate."

The bristle-haired planeswalker's voice grew sharp once
more. "It's hard to imagine how you missed Karona's War and
the impact of it." Freyalise gestured to the blasted, stunted trees
around them. "What did occupy your attentions during the last
three centuries?"

"Something went wrong," Teferi admitted. Though he was only
starting to understand exactly what, he did not choose to burden
Freyalise with his theories. "Suffice to say I lost track of time."

"A tragically common failing among scholars from Tolaria."

The hate in Freyalise's tone chilled Teferi's blood once more.
Somewhat shaken, he said, "Why do you keep throwing that at
me, Freyalise? Even the captain of your rangers did it on your
behalf."

Freyalise smiled coldly. "Those barbarians who attacked you,"
she said. "You noticed something different about them."

"I did. They are Keldons from another time."

"Not Keldons," Freyalise interrupted. "Gathans. They named
themselves after the intrepid Tolarian scholar who made them.
Gatha was his name, and he used Tolarian Academy magic, Tolarian Academy artifacts, and Tolarian Academy secrets to make
the most dangerous and bloodthirsty warriors in the world more
dangerous and more bloodthirsty. And he did it on purpose, with
the full support of Urza and the rest of you Tolarian manipulators."
She mock-bowed, lowering her eyes. "In the grand tradition of all
Tolarian success stories, Gatha succeeded, succeeded beyond his

wildest dreams and his test subject's darkest nightmares."

Teferi waited for Freyalise to finish. "So," he said, "the brutes who came through that rift on the beach are not Keldons."

Freyalise shook her head. "True Keldons wiped out the Gathans even before you starting playing the fool in Zhalfir."

Teferi grimaced. "And now they're back."

"Gatha's work did not die easily. The bloodlines he infected took generations to weed out. It took Keld half a millennium to cull the Tolarian interference from their bloodlines."

"What of the true Keldons? Where did they go when the Gathans returned?"

Freyalise shrugged. "We had an arrangement. The Council spoke for Keld and I spoke for Skyshroud. We left each other alone for more than a century. I suspect most of the nation had already ventured out into the world to raid and plunder when the first Gathans appeared, so there weren't enough warlords or warriors at home to stand against them. The Gathans were mighty and numerous, and their warlords did strange things with the mana here. I believe Keld could not support both the Gathans and its own children at once, that its mana was a prize to be claimed only by the strongest.

"The Gathans were stronger. They changed the way Keldon magic worked, turning it to their purposes." She shrugged. "They did to Keld what Keld has done to a hundred other nations: overwhelmed it and took control of its most valuable resources. I didn't truly realize how profound the effects of this change were until the Gathans had already established total dominance."

Teferi spoke softly. "Even then you saw no reason to interfere."

"No," Freyalise said bitterly. "At the time, I did not."

"With all the changes around here, I can understand how you'd overlook something like that. At least until the Gathans came looking for Skyshroud firewood."

The forest's patron simply glared, not deigning to reply.

"When was that, by the way? When did the Gathans first come?"

"Fifty years ago, more or less."

Teferi paced back and forth, puzzling. He looked up at the massive rift over Skyshroud then back at Freyalise. "Too many pieces," he said.

"What?"

"This puzzle has too many pieces. I came to see precisely how you moved Skyshroud in without causing long-term damage, but it seems that you didn't, not completely. Then this Karona threw everything out of balance all over again anyway, which I didn't even know about, despite the fact that everyone seems to think I was there. There's the large rift and the smaller rifts, the Gathans and you, and there's Skyshroud itself, plus a thousand other details that *seem* vital but don't add up." He shook his head, exasperated. "I need time to put all this together for Shiv, but it won't go together. The pieces just won't fit."

The mechanism covering Freyalise's eye flashed and she turned her face west. "I will return to my rangers now. You may accompany me if you wish, but I want us to be absolutely clear: you are not welcome here. Once the Gathans are dealt with, you and your attendants will leave Keld at once."

"Agreed," Teferi said. "Although I hope you and I will speak again soon. If what I've seen is accurate, even this won't be a safe place for your elves much longer."

"Then I will take them somewhere else," Freyalise said. She extended her gloved hand. "Take hold," she said. "Planeswalking this close to the rift requires experience."

Teferi nodded, amused. "Unless you're trying to knock a fellow planeswalker completely off his guard."

Freyalise did not smile. "Come." She took Teferi's hand. "It takes practice, but you can ride the disturbance like a wave and not be battered by it."

Verdant light shone from where Teferi's hand touched hers. He felt a swooping sensation then found himself high above the forest once more.

"Damn her."

Freyalise dropped Teferi's hand but he was quite capable of keeping himself aloft. The forest patron tossed open her cloak, planted her hands on her hips, and glared angrily down at the valley below.

Teferi quickly tallied up the losses, relieved that the Shivan contingent was still unharmed. The elves and Gathans had a worse time of it, with over a dozen on each side cut down during the first violent exchange.

Something pulled Teferi's attention to a small patch of emerald-green fire at the edge of the battle. The planeswalker's eyes went wide and a broad, lazy smile split his features.

"Damn her," Freyalise said again. She saw Teferi and clicked her tongue. "What are you smiling at?"

"That woman," Teferi pointed to the cluster of green-hued flames.

Freyalise waited. Her face registered a moment of something— interest? Concern?

Then she said, "Yes? What about her? She may not survive this day even if she does survive this fight. Why does the mere sight of her delight you?"

Teferi closed his eyes and let relief wash over him. The puzzle had too many pieces and none of them fit—the rift, the Gathans, the centuries-long gap in time. None of it fit.

Teferi opened his eyes and turned to Freyalise, who was still waiting for an answer. He pointed down at the green-fire woman and said dreamily, "She fits."

CHAPTER 6

In the name of Skyshroud's goddess and protector, Radha restrained herself as best she could. True, it was easier to honor the goddess when Radha's chosen target was not among the raiders yet, but Freyalise insisted on patience and forbearance . . . and that is what Radha now offered. It didn't matter why she waited, only that she did.

She began counting to herself, ticking off the seconds in her head as if enough of them would prove her obedience and forestall Freyalise's inevitable ire. Four seconds, five, six . . .

Given the Skyshroud Rangers' current state of decrepitude, Radha did not expect to wait long. The elves so far had provided more resistance than Radha or the Gathan raiders expected, but Llanach and his rangers were but a delay, and not a very taxing one. Each individual berserker in the first charge engaged two or three elves apiece, giving those that came after free access to the rest of the valley, the forest, and the party of strangers. Though elven arrows continued to rain down on the false Keldons, the brutes simply ignored all but the most serious injuries.

Nine seconds, ten, eleven . . .

Radha was mildly impressed by the strangers' choice to go out and meet the barbarians head-on. The smaller of the two scaly ones used his blade-tail to take off a raider's arm at the elbow then ripped another Gathan's throat out with a savage bite. The larger scaly waded straight into the Gathans' formation, trading blows with the raiders and leaving them facedown in his wake.

Radha especially appreciated the humans' fire magic. The unarmed girl was keeping safely out of the way, but the little male in red threw his bolas so that it wrapped tightly around a raider's neck from fifty feet away. When the flaming weights all simultaneously slammed together on the target's head, the entire apparatus exploded. Radha fought to restrain a lusty cheer and almost applauded.

The red-garbed woman was also putting on a spectacular show. Orange fire flared whenever she used her batons to block or deflect an incoming blow. She rolled clear of the enemy, crossed her batons in front of her, and generated a killing blast of flames that cooked two of the lead Gathans where they stood.

Despite their prowess, Radha knew the visitors were destined to lose. They were holding their own, but even now the colos horn sounded again, and a second wave of Gathans started thundering down into the valley. Man for man, the newcomers were up to the challenge, so it was too bad for them they were so badly outnumbered.

Fifteen seconds, sixteen, seventeen . . .

Radha eagerly searched the second wave for the warlord, the leader of the Gathan 'host, but he was not among them. Be patient, she reminded herself. She could forego a dozen bloody battles for the chance to meet the enemy chieftain in single combat.

The horn sounded again, though the Gathan reinforcements weren't even halfway down. Radha glanced up to the bugler and saw that a new barbarian warrior was holding the horn. Her eyes glazed over as she recognized Greht, her enemy, the Gathan's greatest warlord. He had come to personally oversee this raid on the forest.

Radha stopped counting and whispered aloud, "At last."

Greht lowered the colos horn. The Gathan warlord was gigantic, well over seven feet tall and absurdly overmuscled. His chest and arms were so swollen that Radha couldn't imagine how he lifted a sword, much less fought with it. His waist was almost as wide as his shoulders and his legs were, like two barrels stacked on top of each other.

The muscle-bound form was topped by a squat, square head and a flowing mane of black hair. Greht's face was hidden under an angular metal mask that had been riveted directly into his forehead and cheeks. Red coals glowed deep within the mask's iron eye sockets, and its jagged triangular teeth were clogged and coated with a flaky mixture of rust and dried blood.

Patient, Radha repeated to herself. She would be patient, at least until Greht was closer. He would come down to celebrate if the battle went well for his warhost or to salvage the day for them if it went poorly. Either way, Radha would get her chance.

Greht raised the colos horn to his metal mouth. The loudest peal yet floated down the mountain, overtaking the Gathan second wave before reaching those raiders already on the valley floor.

The effect on all of the raiders was immediate. The sound energized them, engorged them, and renewed their vigor and their spirit in the face of a determined enemy. They moved faster, howled louder, and appeared bigger.

A raider who had been caught flat-footed by the little scaly's tail somehow managed to twist away from the killing stroke. Another Gathan swatted flaming bolas out of the air before they could snare him. Captain Llanach of the Skyshroud Rangers was borne to the ground under a lurching barbarian who was himself covered with fighting-mad elves.

The tone of the skirmish quickly changed as the Gathans switched tactics. Instead of simply getting past the forest guardians, they now focused on crippling or killing as many as possible. They were the thin edge of the wedge, and all they had to do now was keep the battle going until the wide end followed them in, until the second wave reached the valley floor . . . which it was on the verge of doing.

A severed elf's head bounced clear of the confused tangle of bodies around Llanach, and the Gathan who chopped it took a dagger in the ribs for his trouble. Seemingly unaware of this injury, the decapitator lunged forward with the elf blade still in him and drove his forehead into that of the ranger who had stabbed him. Radha heard a fearsome crunch and watched as the lean elf warrior fell lifeless to the ground, his face caved in from the bridge of his nose to the top of his skull.

Llanach struck back at the Gathan and missed, but the blow bought enough time for the elf captain to get back to his feet. The remaining rangers regrouped around him.

At the other end of the valley, the barbarian who had dodged the scaly tail now grabbed hold of it and hauled backward with all his might, pulling the reptile warrior down onto one leg. Two other barbarians quickly closed on the vulnerable stranger, but the lizard's larger tribe mate was lightning-fast. The bigger green scaly plowed in and swept aside the Gathans before they could butcher his comrade, taking only one serious axe blow to the chest as he sent all three raiders flying.

A thick stream of flame blasted one of the hurled Gathans out of the air. Radha followed the fire back to the baton woman who'd cast it. She noticed another Gathan silently charging the woman before he pounced on her, but the foreign firecaster did not. The woman was quick enough to cross her weapons defensively in front of herself, but the Gathan's broadsword broke through her guard with a single overhand blow.

The sword cleaved through one of the woman's batons and on through two of the fingers on her left hand. The red-garbed warrior drew a sharp breath, but she did not scream or cry out. Instead, she shoved the rounded tip of her remaining baton into the Gathan's chest. He caught it easily, his huge hand swallowing the baton, the woman's hand, and part of her forearm.

Before he could crush bones and enchanted wood alike into splinters, the woman spat a loud curse in a strange tongue and the raider's entire hand disappeared at the center of a bright yellow fireball. Then the woman planted her foot on the off-balance Gathan's chest and shoved him away. She turned and cradled her wounded hand against her stomach as she withdrew, her feet digging into the hard, cold ground.

She took only a single step before a huge, rough-knuckled hand clamped down on her head from behind. Its fingers were charred black and smoke drifted from cracked knuckles.

"You call that fire?" The wounded Gathan laughed as he tightened his grip. With very little visible effort, he lifted the woman's head until her feet came off the ground. She grabbed his wrist with both hands to keep her spine from separating. Blood from her hand steamed as it flowed across the barbarian's blackened, smoking skin.

"Here," the brute snarled. "Choke on the true fires of Keld." He brought his free hand around and clenched his fist. Smoke started to rise and a small, searing nugget of red light formed, still visible through his thick, callused fingers.

Radha leaped to her feet. There was a flash of metal and a whisper of steel. The Gathan's black hand opened and he dropped the baton woman. Half-blind and bleeding, the eight-fingered stranger rolled away. She looked back as she struggled to her feet, anticipating a death blow that never came.

A large, sharp piece of metal stood imbedded in the Gathan's face. It was about the size of an adult's hand and shaped like an elongated teardrop. The blade's thin, pointed end was buried deep in the bridge of the raider's nose. Its larger, rounded side hung down in front of his chin. Dark blood trickled down both sides of the Gathan's nose and his eyes bulged. He blinked. He teetered backward and fell with his burned hand extended, tightly clenched around the memory of his opponent.

"The fires of Keld," Radha said loudly, "burn only for Keldons." Her voice cut through the other sounds in the valley, and though the melee did not stop, every combatant in the field began factoring this new arrival into the proceedings.

"There's only one Keldon in this valley," Radha snarled, "and you're all looking at her."

Driven by an unseen wind, Radha's hair spread out behind her like a cobra's hood. Her eyes flashed. The air around her head and shoulders hissed and popped as it filled with tiny green flames, each one distinctly shaped like a small oak leaf. Soon there were more than a dozen of the magnificent emerald blooms flickering around her.

Radha relished the looks of surprise and confusion. From her belt she drew another tear-shaped blade, identical to the one she'd stuck in the Gathan's face. The finger-grips along the tear's inner edge allowed it to fit perfectly in her hand, the sharp point emerging from the top of her fist like a small dagger.

Radha turned from the wounded baton woman and the other strangers to face the Gathans. She drew a second tear-shaped blade, holding it with the tip extending from the bottom of her fist. Arms flexed, Radha raised both weapons toward the raiders

"Welcome to Skyshroud, you filthy mongrel bastards." She turned to the remaining elf rangers and waved impatiently.

"Withdraw, Llanach! Return to your camp and prepare for a feast. There'll be fresh meat tonight."

With a raucous howl and without a single thought to Freyalise, Radha sprang toward the nearest Gathan, her blades raised high and a cloud of leafy flames trailing behind her.

* * * * *

Teferi spoke clearly, emphasizing each word to show his interest. "Who is she?"

Freyalise did not seem inclined to answer, but Teferi didn't mind. It was a largely rhetorical question anyway, as he had already learned a great deal about the new arrival simply from observing her.

Her name was Radha, but that was the only bit of information he could easily skim from her mind. The rest of her thoughts were guarded and violent and would require significant effort to pry out. From the few seconds he'd been watching her and reading her, he knew several things for certain. She was a warrior. She was proud. She was physically formidable.

She was also beautiful, the most welcome sight Teferi had seen in quite a long time. Mana flowed to and from her so freely that she glowed and sparkled to his ascended eyes. She was like a fresh, bright flower among dry weeds, a clear mountain spring rising from an otherwise flat and featureless desert.

He examined the battleground below him, his own near-infinite capacity for mana guiding him as a bat's sonar guides it through the densest forest. There was significant combat and fire magic being tossed around down there, though neither Keld nor Skyshroud could provide the mana to fuel it. In this dying environment, all of the factions had turned to alternative sources of magical power: the Shivans had their mana stars, the elves had Freyalise's blessings, and the Gathans had their warlord. The barbarian leader's enhancing magic didn't require much mana, but instead it collected each individual warrior's strength and ferocity, mixed it all together, improved it, and returned it to them fivefold.

Radha, on the other hand, employed no such alternative. She was drawing mana directly to her, the way mages had done on Dominaria for thousands of years. There was still the question of how she was using mana when there was no mana to use . . . or at least, nowhere near enough in the local environment. Somehow Radha had access to magical energy that no one else had, that no one else could even perceive. Teferi himself could not see Radha's magic until it touched her and appeared as part of her flaming mantle.

So many questions he was eager to answer. Where was the mana coming from? How was she drawing it to her? Should he be pleased to at last encounter the kind of robust magic he expected, or should he be concerned that it was so much more powerful than anything else in Keld? What was it about the fierce, unique, and exotic woman that was so distressingly familiar?

He turned to face Freyalise, who was still glaring angrily down at the valley. The forest patron might likewise not be able to see the secret of Radha's abundance, and so she might be interested in letting an experienced scholar investigate. Teferi continued to smile blandly. With this bargaining chip, he might yet convince Freyalise to help.

"I will ask again, Protector of Skyshroud." Teferi spoke solemnly. "But I will be more precise: *what* is she?"

Freyalise glanced up at Teferi. "She is a child of my forest. A disobedient child. A reckless child."

"Does she have the spark?"

The protector of Skyshroud's face was inscrutable. "You tell me. We planeswalkers tend to recognize each other, even before we ascend. What do you see in her?"

Teferi closed his eyes and tilted his head toward the woman. "She has something," he said, "but it's not the spark. She does not have the potential to become like us."

Freyalise's expression softened. "You are correct, or at least, I concur. She will never be like us."

"She claims to be a true Keldon, and she clearly isn't."

"No. Though she denies it daily, Radha is as much an elf of Skyshroud as she is a warrior of Keld."

"She is very important," Teferi said musingly. "To me. And she will be more so."

"Radha is important to me," Freyalise turned and squarely faced Teferi, "and she is mine. I have my own plans for her."

"Of course," Teferi bowed slightly, "but we are reasonable beings. We can reach an understanding."

"We already have. Radha stays here to help me preserve her home. You will leave Skyshroud the instant this battle is complete, without ever meeting her." Freyalise began to shine as her skin became tinged with crimson once more. Her features grew indistinct and alien in the unnatural glow, her eyes gleaming like twin suns. "That is the only understanding I care to come to this day."

"It will do," Teferi nodded, his face unconcerned, "for today. But Radha is the key to my understanding this changed world, Freyalise. I mean to get Shiv back without catastrophe, and to do that I need as perfect an understanding as I can get. I need her."

"Skyshroud needs her more."

"Oh? What will Skyshroud gain by keeping her from me? How long have you been studying her, Freyalise? Skyshroud is still dying.

"Keld can no longer support itself, much less your transplanted kingdom. How much of your power is devoted daily to keeping this place and its inhabitants alive? Is this subsistence-level half-life the abundant future you envisioned for your children when you brought them here?

"Let me have Radha, Protector of Skyshroud. I am as devoted to learning and study as you are to your privacy. I will discover the Keldon elf's secrets, mapping out her place in this strange world. What's more, I will share what I discover with you, for knowing it may well be the answer to both our problems."

Freyalise's angry aura subsided slightly. "You have no idea what you are asking, Tolarian."

"I think I do."

"But you do not." Freyalise quickly returned to her fair-skinned elf guise. "Radha is far more trouble than she's worth, and not only because she continues to defy my understanding."

Teferi smiled. "I have a long history of handling volatile personalities."

Freyalise smiled back, sadly. "Radha's heart is a stone," she said. "A sharp stone. Some who have tried to 'handle' her wound up bleeding and scarred but no closer to their goals."

"If one is careful," Teferi said, "stones can be taken up safely. Stones can be aimed and thrown with precision."

"Stones can also be crushed," Freyalise said, "and when one becomes an obstacle or a hindrance, they often are." She turned back toward the battle. "Yet. . . ."

Teferi watched her think, her face expressionless and inscrutable.

"She seeks to master the battle magic of Keld, to become a leader of armies," Freyalise mused. "That is not so far removed from what I want for her."

"I only want to understand how she accesses mana. She is like the rift in that way, drawing energy to her. I will surely encourage her to increase her command and control over that energy, and that will make her a better warrior, a stronger leader. If she cannot learn to do this on her own, I will learn it myself and show her how." He smiled confidently. "It won't take long. A few days at the most."

Freyalise's cold expression told him his confidence was misplaced, but she said, "You may take her when you go," Freyalise said, "so long as you go quickly. While she is with you, I will be watching and listening."

Teferi nodded. "Of course."

"Then hear the final terms of our agreement, Tolarian. If you and the Shivans are not gone from Keld by sunrise, I will destroy you all. If Radha wishes to return to Skyshroud at any time, I will take her from you." She turned a condescending eye toward Teferi and gestured to the valley below. "I will now withdraw my rangers and leave convincing Radha to you. Can you end this battle quickly and cleanly, or shall I?"

Teferi bowed deeply. "You have done enough, Protector of Skyshroud."

Freyalise shook her head. "Madness," she said. As she started to fade from sight, Freyalise called, "Farewell, Tolarian. Do not return, and remember to 'walk carefully near the rifts."

Teferi waited until he was sure Freyalise was gone then turned back to watch his exciting new prospect run rampant.

CHAPTER 7

Radha left a raider with a foot-long slash across his belly, spinning around behind him to avoid the splatter. She had never felt so alive.

Greht's influence made each of the Gathans her physical equal, but she was tearing through them as if they were children. She was as tall as all but the biggest of the raiders but so much leaner and quicker that she hadn't yet sustained a single injury. She had been equal parts fast and lucky to remain intact for this long, and part of her was disappointed that the enemy wasn't giving a better account of themselves. She had taken a serious toll on them, leaving five dead on the valley floor with spreading crimson stains beneath them.

Llanach's tired rangers had withdrawn mysteriously, but Radha was not concerned. The defenders of Skyshroud could always melt into or appear out of the forest like ghosts. Good riddance in any case. Less of Freyalise's cannon fodder meant more room for Radha to enjoy herself.

The strangers continued to fight as well, though they had pulled back to form a defensive formation around the wounded fire mage and the unarmed girl. The male fire mage and the scalies were able to keep the raiders at bay, but there were plenty of Gathans left to maintain a constant threat.

Radha occupied the rest of the raiding party. She herself was still uninjured, even though the tear-shaped, talonlike blades she used were not designed to defend against a Gathan broadsword. Her rage mounted as she fought, for they were only coming at her one at a time, not afraid of her skills but amused, taking turns like children. They stood and watched, eerily patient as if fighting her were some sort of novelty to be shared.

She had surprised the first few by being faster and stronger than they expected, but they now had the measure of her. What's more, the single combatants were becoming inexplicably more dangerous and more skilled as Radha thinned their numbers. Warlord magic was undeniably tied to the number of combatants on the field, so how was Greht making his warhost stronger as it shrank in size?

She paused for a moment, breathing evenly as the next opponent approached. Her arms and legs were streaked with blood that all but covered her long metal gauntlets and her swooping tribal tattoos. Blood had also matted her hair on one side and stained her cured-hide tunic and leggings. Radha clenched her weapons tightly, green leaves of flame flaring around her. She stared fixedly into the approaching Gathan's eyes and smiled, showing him her teeth.

The colos horn sounded again from the top of the ridge and the berserker approaching her stopped. Though Radha expected a surge of strength from the raider, the klaxon had a very different effect on him. The brute slowed as he heard it, then he stopped.

His bulging muscles relaxed and his eyes narrowed. He nodded at Radha, returning her ruthless smile. Then the brute turned away and lumbered back toward the mountainside.

The other Gathans also stopped fighting at the sound of the horn. Thrown, Radha and the strangers could only stare suspiciously as the raiders withdrew, each uncannily quiet and careful in their movements. The brutes separated into two single-file lines and stood facing each other in perfect, symmetrical ranks.

The colos horn blew again. Radha looked up in time to see the masked figure of Greht cast aside the instrument. He oriented on her in the center of the valley then ran to the edge of the mountain and hurled himself off.

The prodigious leap carried Greht almost halfway down the mountain in one fell swoop. He landed in an explosion of snow and gravel then shot back up into the frigid air before the scattered cloud of debris reached its apex.

Radha's eyes gleamed. Her shroud of flames danced as Greht descended. She had done it. She had goaded him into personal combat. The Gathan warlord would not be an easy opponent, not with so many of his fell raiders backing him, but Radha relished the challenge.

She fortified herself, drawing the innate power of her home to her. As her strength grew, Radha's urge to kill became a burning, driving need. She had two tear-shaped blades in hand and three more on her belt. She was ready. She would kill Greht here and now. She would break the Gathans' dominance in this region and then drive all of them into the sea, preferably in pieces.

Greht landed on the valley floor directly between the two lines of raiders. He glanced neither left nor right as he strode toward Radha, his crackling red eyes boring into hers from behind the mask.

Radha held his gaze. Her heartbeat boomed at her temples so hard the whole world seemed to throb. She gorged herself on the raw power of the land until it filled her, stretching her mind to bursting. The flames around her tripled in number and intensity, burning so brightly that she appeared to be aflame from the waist up. When Radha opened her mouth to give voice to her bloodlust, the sound was distorted by echoes and accompanied by a cloud of verdant fire.

Like a comet wreathed in flames, Radha shot forward. She slammed into Greht's broad chest, engulfing them both in a fiery cloud of green lightning and black, billowing smoke. The impact stunned Radha, crushing the breath from her lungs and sending a jolt of jagged agony through her entire body. Her vision went white and she felt her own body as someone else's, the pain diffuse and distant. Her ears rang, registering only the aftermath of the collision.

Greht had hardly flinched under Radha's attack, immovable as a mountain. He cocked his head, an apelike gesture of confusion without real interest as Radha struggled to regain control of her numbed body. Behind the Gathan warlord, the entirety of his warhost erupted into harsh, mocking laughter.

Greht's massive hand shot out and clamped around Radha's neck. The Gathan lifted her to his masked face. Radha took hold of his wrist and drew another sharp metal tear from her belt. She struggled to breathe, to keep her own weight from choking her to death as she rammed the sharp tip of her weapon deep into the underside of Greht's forearm. Then again. And again and again and again.

Unconcerned by the wounds on his arm or the flecks of his own blood that spattered his face, Greht locked eyes with Radha through his mask.

"Your fire has no heat, elf-girl. And you call yourself a Keldon?" Greht twisted his wrist slightly, closing Radha's windpipe and forcing the blade from her hand. He waited for her eyes to flutter, then he straightened his arm and allowed her to breathe again.

"I am more than a mere Keldon," he said, his face almost touching hers. "I am greater than any 'true' Keldon who ever lived."

Radha coughed, foam and blood spraying from her swollen lips. Her voice was a feral growl, choked and grating. "Prove it."

Sparks popped in Greht's eyes and smoke rose from the sockets in his mask. He snorted. "You speak like a Keldon, but there are no true Keldons left . . . are there, elf-girl?" He shook her slightly. "Certainly not among the old women of Skyshroud."

Radha's nostrils flared. Her eyes sprang open and she extended her neck, stretching her chin up as far as it would go. Then Radha's jaws snapped open and she slammed her face down, biting into the tough wad of flesh between Greht's forefinger and thumb. Radha's teeth clenched tight and the Gathan's blood spilled from her lips.

A jolt of greenish eldritch force surged up Greht's arm from where Radha held him, and when it reached his torso the impact broke his grip and sent him staggering back a step. Radha twisted as she fell so that she could hurl the tear-shaped blade she held into Greht's throat before she hit the ground. She drew back and cast it, straight and true, as her shoulder blades thumped into the stony ground.

But Greht simply tilted his head and Radha's razor-tear bounced harmlessly off the mask's metal chin. The warlord casually followed the deflected blade with his eyes then looked back over his shoulder at his soldiers.

He shrugged, flexing the hand that had held Radha and making a show of noticing his own blood as it dripped from his punctured forearm. To their full-throated approval, he pressed his thick tongue through his mask and licked the wound clean.

Radha forced herself to her feet as Greht turned back to face her. The warlord drew a wide broadsword from a sheath on his back, effortlessly hefting the massive weapon in one hand.

"Elf-girl," he said, his stentorian voice clear and composed, "I've killed a hundred of you walking mana-bladders with this sword. Sometimes they go up in a flash of green before they bleed to death." Greht pointed the tip of the blade at Radha. "What will pour from your body when I split it in two, Skyshroud sow? Liquid or light?"

Radha smiled, her teeth still dripping crimson. "Hate," she said. "I will die spurting great gouts of it upon you, false warlord, and it'll burn clear through wherever it touches."

Greht's eyes popped again as two huge sparks spat from the mask's slit visor. He let out a roar, and then the Gathan warlord lunged.

He was fast, faster than ever, but Radha just managed to

deflect the tip of his broadsword with the flat of her blade. Greht's momentum carried him and the broadsword forward, and Radha slid along its razor edge, her tear striking a stream of yellow sparks. As she neared the hilt of Greht's weapon, he shifted his weight and brought the handle up, twisting it so Radha saw her own reflection in the sword's wide, polished face.

She skidded to avoid slamming face-first into the broadsword. Radha ducked and slashed under Greht's defense, trying to open up the meaty tangle of muscles and veins in the warlord's thigh. Greht twisted and kicked his leg up over Radha's strike so that her blade slashed empty air.

To her open-mouthed amazement, Greht continued to roll, jamming the tip of his sword into the hard, frozen ground and using it to cartwheel a full vertical flip until he came solidly back onto his feet. The Gathan warlord instantly jerked the tip of his sword free and clapped the flat into his waiting hand, turning the polished face once more to Radha as he planted his feet.

Greht grunted and thrust the horizontal blade forward. A semi-visible surge of magical force exploded from the huge weapon, and though Radha was at least twenty yards away it still caught her flat-footed.

She hastily crossed her own blades in front of her face and prepared to weather the storm. It didn't help; she felt the long bones in her forearms bend as they were pressed back awkwardly against her own face. The ground turned to liquid under her as the metal sheathes covering her forearms heated up, searing the skin below.

But Radha held her ground. She wasn't aware of her arms or legs any more, but she saw through bleary eyes that she was still upright. The world pitched like a capsizing ship and Radha stumbled forward. A huge, dark shadow fell across her.

Radha looked up. Greht was there, blocking out the sky, his voice a murky sludge of primal sounds and distorted echoes from behind his mask. Instinctively, Radha slashed at his throat, but her movements were slow and gummy. Her arm slammed against something immovable and the blade sprang from her grip.

Greht held her arm, lifting her up to the tips of her toes. He delivered a savage, tooth-rattling backhand that sent Radha sprawling to the valley floor. The Gathan warhost cheered again, their voices vague and even more incoherent than usual.

Radha felt herself fading. If she blacked out now she would die here, humbled by her most hated foe. She tried to take solace in the fact that at least she had died in combat. At least she had tasted the enemy's blood.

Greht stood over her once more. With a fistful of her long, coarse hair, the warlord hauled Radha up onto her knees, pausing only to swat her head aside when she tried to bite his hand again. Through it all she teetered and swooned, but she also kept her balance and stared fiercely up at her enemy.

The Gathan slowly extended his huge sword out to his right, preparing to take Radha's head with a long, swooping side strike. She struggled to muster a mouthful of spit for one final farewell.

"Excuse me?" The new voice was rich and friendly, a polite inquiry from a cosmopolitan traveler.

Radha forced both eyes open. The dark-skinned wizard who had come with the strangers stood nearby, composed, elegant, and well-mannered.

"Warlord Greht?" he said merrily. "I am Teferi of Zhalfir. I have business with that interesting woman you've got there."

Greht grunted but said nothing. He barely acknowledged the interruption as his arm reached full extension, turning his shoulders slightly to allow himself a stronger, swifter cut.

Radha cursed the stranger. Did he know nothing about barbarians? Did he think a smile and a classy turn of phrase would keep a Gathan warlord from making a kill?

"Oh, dear. Stop that, please," the wizard said. "I really must insist."

Greht half-snorted as he began his swing. The stranger extended his staff.

The air around Radha changed. Her vision fogged. Her skin tingled, even on her numb and smoking arms. She remembered Greht's raised sword and then the sensation of falling freely. She hurled herself back, scrambling clumsily to her feet as she listened for the incoming blow.

Radha circled left of the last place she'd seen Greht, a razor-tear in each hand. Her ability to focus was quickly returning, and her eyes darted left and right as she searched for her enemy.

But Greht was nowhere nearby. In fact, the Gathan warlord was currently fifty yards away and hurtling backward toward the mountainside, right through the center of the carefully assembled ranks of his raiders. Each member of the Gathan warhost followed his flight, craning their heads as he slammed into the deep snow at the base of the mountain.

The wizard's own face appeared, gigantic and glowing, blocking the space between Radha and the Gathans. The wizard manifested this vision of himself without his frivolous hat but with a confident smile. The huge bald phantom filled almost the entire valley from end to end, and its sudden appearance surprised Radha but did not comfort her. She lost her balance and fell back to one knee, two blades pointed at the enormous face.

The wizard's smiling visage remained calm, even friendly. His eyes twinkled as Greht burst out of the snow. The Gathans silently regrouped behind their leader as he assessed this new enemy.

"Begone, Warlord," said the wizard's giant bald head, "and come no more to Skyshroud."

Azure light flared around Greht and his raiders. They each vanished simultaneously, without fanfare. Even those that had fallen and died burst into puffs of powdery blue smoke and were seen no more.

Silence fell across the valley. The wizard reappeared, normal-sized, his head and body attached and his impractical headgear in place. The smiling man dusted his hands together.

"There," he said. He turned to Radha and spoke brightly. "Told her I could handle it. Now then, to business." He bowed deeply, and when he straightened up his eyes were flecked with vivid blue light.

"My name is Teferi," he said, "and you fascinate me."

* * * * *

To Teferi, Radha was even more intoxicating up close. Even now she collected a constant stream of mana, though she seemed to only employ it on that purely cosmetic display of green fire. She was physically and personally imposing, towering over Jhoira and the Ghitu and standing eye-to-eye with Corus and Skive. Though the viashino tended to crane their long necks downward when talking to humans, it was a far shorter trip when they were speaking to Radha.

Radha appeared to be a perfect Keldon/elf hybrid with strong visible traits from both species. Her skin was a striking brownish-gray, like brine-cured hardwood or burnished steel. Physically she favored her barbarian side, evidenced by her size and strength. Keldon blood also bestowed upon her the long arms and legs that characterized the berserkers, as well as the traditional Keldon widow's peak. Radha's long, thick hair flowed wild and free behind her, but it came to a severe point on her face that plunged down almost to her eyebrows.

Radha's elf ancestry was evident in her physical grace and her bone structure. She was not as broad shouldered as her barbarian ancestors, and her arms and legs were less heavily muscled. Her head was smaller and more rounded than a typical Keldon's but broader and more massive than a typical elf's. Unlike the boxy Keldon faces Teferi had researched or the elongated features of the Skyshroud elves, Radha's cheeks and eyebrows were an inviting series of graceful curves and bold, sharp angles. Her lips were thin and elegant, and her teeth were small but square as a row of tombstones.

Those teeth were currently clenched in frustration. Radha was struggling for breath but her mind was clear, as was her voice. "Where is Greht?"

"Gone for now," Teferi said cheerfully. "I wanted very much to meet you, you see, so I sent them away. I have—"

"Where did you send them?" Radha's hand quivered with pent-up energy, almost trembling above the tear-shaped blades on her belt.

Teferi glanced down at her nervous tic and chose his next words very carefully. Radha seemed to be recovering very quickly from her encounter with Greht and her temper was obviously not good. What's more, the language of Keldon politics was far from an exact science and Teferi knew he had to speak with just the right tone of confidence, one that commanded respect without spilling over into actual arrogance. What he had seen and gleaned so far led him to conclude Radha saw herself as a Keldon and would therefore respond to a dominant authority figure.

"I sent them back to their camp," he said. He folded his arms confidently, catching his staff in the crook of his elbow. "But we have business, you and I, important business. You can go and kill Greht another day."

Radha sneered. "What's wrong with today?" She took an unsteady step forward but soon regained her strength and her stride as she swept past Teferi.

"Wait, please," he said. When Radha ignored him, Teferi thumped the bottom of his staff into the ground and said, "Warrior."

His voice boomed impressively and the valley shuddered beneath Radha's feet.

She turned to face him and he took on the terrible aspect of a storm wizard, cloaked in glittering blue metallic fabric, attended by lightning. "Your patron and protector Freyalise has assigned you to my service. I have a great deal of work to do, work worth doing. I need your help. It will be dangerous, but you will be well-rewarded for it."

Radha shrugged, craning her neck sideways until it briefly touched her shoulder. "I have work of my own." She straightened and huffed dismissively. "Let Freyalise keep her own promises."

She turned away once more and Teferi stopped himself on the verge of a planeswalk. It would have been effective to appear suddenly in front of her, dramatic even, but he didn't dare risk it so close to the Skyshroud rift. Instead, he turned to Corus and Skive behind him and sent "Stop her" directly into their minds.

The viashino blinked, caught off-guard by the planeswalker's sudden presence in their heads, but they recovered quickly. They could not move as smoothly across Keldon rock as they could through Shivan sand, but they were still fast enough to catch the deliberate, defiant pace of the Keldon elf before she reached the mountainside.

"Teferi." Jhoira's voice rang out over the valley. "What are you doing?"

The planeswalker kept his eyes on the viashino, who were now standing in front of Radha.

"These two are part of my warhost," Teferi called, "and now so are you. Fall in, warrior, and prepare to fight and die as a true Keldon should."

"No, wait," Jhoira called. She was moving toward Teferi, seemingly with something urgent to add, but things were already in motion. He'd just have to make do on his own.

Radha looked back and forth between the viashino, her back

still turned to Teferi. "I like you scalies," she said to the pair. "I really do. What are you, anyway?"

Before they could answer, Radha struck out with one of her long legs, catching Skive alongside the jaw. She scissored her other foot up and planted it in the blade-tailed viashino's chest, and pushed off of Skive to hurtle face-first at Corus.

Radha hit and bit. An awful crunch sounded as her teeth cracked through the viashino's hide. Corus bellowed and pulled away, hauling Radha along with him. She brought her knees up under her and pushed hard against the viashino's broad chest. A long, ragged piece of pink flesh pulled free as Radha separated from her target and landed lightly on her feet. Corus cursed her in his native viashino and staggered back, his hand pressed to his bleeding collar bone.

Radha turned aside and spit the grisly mouthful out. "Pah!" she said, licking her lips. "The rind is thick and bitter, but the fruit below is sweet."

Enraged, Skive lunged at her with his mouth open wide, looking to return the bite. Radha caught his upper and lower jaws as he came, sank to her knees, and pulled his head down to the ground. The two rolled together, Skive's feet and tail flailing for a moment before the long muscles in Radha's arms and legs bulged. Her strength and their combined momentum made it a simple matter for her to hurl him clear to the edge of the forest, where he landed in the saproling thicket with a thud.

Corus slashed at her with his claws, but Radha easily dodged. He no longer had full reach on the wounded side, as fully extending his arm widened the wound. She rolled past the viashino and dived toward the forest.

Teferi. Jhoira's thoughts were bright and sharp. *What in the name of sanity are you doing?*

Not now. If she reaches the deeper woods—

Talk to her. Let me *talk to her before you—*

It'll take days to pry her out if she goes to ground.
She's not going to ground, is she?

Jhoira was absolutely right—Radha was not trying to reach Skyshroud. The fierce Keldon elf had put some space between herself and the others, but then she stopped well short of the tree line. She wasn't trying to escape.

Corus was wary as he stalked in. He and Skive were far from beaten, but the larger viashino stayed clear, satisfied to maintain a safe distance after facing Radha at close-quarters. Behind Radha, Skive thrashed and cursed among the ivy.

Radha clenched her fists. Dire green light flared behind her pupils and a fresh flurry of fire leaves flickered to life around her. She closed her eyes and crossed her fists before her chest. Opening her eyes, she cast her hands up.

Guided by her motion, the green flames shot upward, then bent and streamed toward the saproling thicket where Skive had landed. The fire sank into the ghastly tangle of vines, and they swelled in response.

Hundreds of thick tendrils erupted around Skive, engulfing him in a many-fingered fist and burying him under an avalanche of leafy green. Teferi could still hear Skive's voice over the sound of the burgeoning thicket, a single, sustained, high-pitched hiss of surprise and annoyance.

Then the viashino shouted, "For slag's sake, someone burn this stuff off me."

She did it again, Teferi thought. Radha carelessly wasted mana when no one else could even find it. What's worse, she used it to feed saprolings, which were little more than cancerous tumors with roots. Freyalise must be beset indeed to have saprolings at all, much less enough to cover the forest floor.

Teferi froze when he heard the cacophony rising behind the noise of the saproling surge. It was a chattering, clicking sound, the advance notice of a thousand hard, sharp-tipped legs charging toward them. Radha's green fire hadn't just invigorated the saprolings; it had also stirred up the slivers.

Slivers were another arcane species he had studied but not encountered. Now Teferi could sense their alien presence nearby as distinctly as that of the time-lost Gathans on the beach, though where the berserkers were creatures out of time, these slivers were out of synch physically and magically.

He saw them for the first time then, a hundred at once as the leading edge of the wide swarm ripped through the underbrush. There were hundreds of them, each as big as a seagull, wedge-shaped, sharp-nosed creatures with tough outer shells and rigid, spiked limbs. Two winglike crests stabbed out from each sliver's back, their barbed double-tails lashing behind like two striking snakes.

Things just got more complicated, he sent to Jhoira.

You just noticed this? His friend's thoughts were as biting as he'd ever heard them.

The second wave of buzzing slivers erupted from the dense woods, swirling through the air like wasps returning to their nest.

They can fly now, Jhoira's voice observed, *and I just saw one punch straight through a tree trunk.*

Which means they all can, Teferi said. *Remind me to congratulate Radha on an excellent diversion.*

She couldn't have heard Teferi's thoughts, but Radha screeched triumphantly as if she had. The mana-gorged slivers and saprolings continued to pour out of the forest. They formed two increasingly large heaps of squirming, scratching chaos that heaved and strained against each other. Away from the center of the mass, stray slivers and a fresh crop of saprolings skittered and crept out into the valley.

The thicket continued to churn behind Radha as she turned to face Corus and the rest of the strangers.

"Look here," she said, her voice bright and nasty. "More work you can do, without me. Work worth doing." She sneered at Teferi. "I hope it's as *fascinating* for you as I am."

Larger faceless, multi-legged forms emerged from the confused mass of vines, fungus, and scissorlike jaws. Engorged by Radha's donation of mana, the smallest of these latest saproling monstrosities was as large as a pony. They moved at different speeds with different gaits, but they all shambled clear of the forest and into the valley, mewling like horrid, mouthless children. Likewise, the slivers were more frenzied and savage than ever in the face of prey that had suddenly become a real threat.

Teferi reached out with his mind. He found Skive at the center of a ten-foot mound of vines and offal. The Shivan warrior was screaming, not in pain or terror but from sheer disgust. Clearly he hadn't noticed the line of slivers chewing its way toward him . . . if he had, if Skive understood the real danger he faced, his screams sound a bit more urgent. Thankfully, it was a simple matter to magically latch onto Skive and levitate him out of the thicket.

By then Radha was gone, of course, vanished into the trees of Skyshroud. Teferi would not have any real trouble finding her, but it would take time. The more time he spent tracking her, the less time he had to prepare the ground for Shiv's return.

Still, first things first. He plucked up Corus as well as Skive, then levitated Jhoira and the other Ghitu. Teferi set them down a safe distance from the forest edge, facing the oncoming line of ghastly fungus monsters and the odd sliver.

"I'd appreciate your help," he said to the Shivans. "There's a lot on my mind at present. Cut back the saprolings or burn them down as quickly as you can; the slivers seem to be following them."

Jhoira looked as if she had quite a lot to say to Teferi. He was glad she chose to limit herself to, "What will you do, Teferi Planeswalker?"

Teferi bowed. "Of course." When he rose, his eyes flashed and a swirling wind swept up dust and granular snow into a perfect circle. The shape filled in, solidified, and hardened into a giant crystalline snowflake.

"A parting gift," Teferi said, "to show that I haven't forgotten my Shivan allies."

The planeswalker nodded. The great snowflake turned on its side and started to spin. It gained momentum, its exquisite crystalline structure becoming a nearly solid blur. The whirling circle of sharp ice shimmered for a moment then shot across the valley, sundering each in the long line of fresh saproling shamblers messily at the waist. The snowflake stayed pristine as it burst through the saprolings, leaving a gleaming silver-blue metallic trail behind it.

Nearly all of the saprolings fell into pieces, covering the valley floor in a grisly stew of gore and fungus chunks. The frenzied slivers quickly descended on the mess, swallowing as much as they could scissor free. Shreds of green and yellow spattered up from the edge of the thicket as it retreated back to the tree line.

"I," Teferi said, his voice full of confidence, "will now begin the figuring out of things once and for all. But first I need to come up with a way to convince our new friend to help us."

Jhoira nodded grimly. "Right," she said. "I'll be doing a little figuring myself while you're gone."

"Stay safe," Teferi smiled. "Though that shouldn't be too hard now."

"Stay in touch," Jhoira said, without smiling.

Without replying or changing his expression, Teferi disappeared.

CHAPTER 8

Radha circled around to the far edge of the forest, emerging at the north end. The saprolings were thinner up here, where it was coldest, and she was soon scaling the steep sides of the mountains that bordered Skyshroud and leaving the whole forest valley behind.

She was forbidden to do this, as all the elves were. Radha had flaunted this restriction several times already, always in the pursuit of her enemies, so she was not concerned. Freyalise's punishment would hardly stack up to the joy and glory she'd get from killing Greht.

She would need a new strategy. Greht had grown too strong, his warhost too large. It pained her to admit it, but he was clearly her physical superior—bigger, stronger, faster, with a higher threshold of pain. She had to find some way of eliminating the gap, of becoming his equal.

Radha moved swiftly through the snow and reached the peak of the mountain in just over an hour. As her long legs and loping stride ate up the ground below her, she turned her thoughts to the upcoming battle.

It was a circular problem, a snake eating its own tail—the stronger Greht was, the more successful his raids; the more successful his raids, the larger his warhost grew, fattened by plunder and press gangs; the larger his 'host, the stronger Greht became; and then the cycle began again.

She had to break that cycle if she were ever going to beat him. She had to separate him from his followers or at least meet him on the battlefield with a warhost of her own.

Only a warlord can lead a 'host, and you are no warlord, Radha.

Radha grinned as she kept moving. She recognized the voice. "Wizard. I see the saprolings and slivers were easily discouraged."

Quite so, and since then I've been following you, Radha. I have heard your thoughts and I would like to talk with you about them.

"Hah!" Radha laughed. "Piss off, baldie."

Do you really think you can break the bond between Greht and his 'host? My understanding is that warlords campaign constantly. The man lives in an armed camp, never far from a huge body of soldiers who are all fervid to kill and die for him. How will you isolate him from that?

"You talk like a tutor. What in nine hells is 'fervid'?"

Until she understood more about the long-winded wizard's voice in her head, Radha would be extremely careful. She tamped down the violent thoughts rising in response to his words and reviewed what she knew. Teferi, he called himself. He had spoken of Freyalise, telling her the patron had placed Radha in his service. Was he Freyalise's ally? Enemy? Unwitting tool? In any case, was he as powerful as the protector of Skyshroud?

How will you stand against that? Teferi continued. He had an irritatingly jovial tone even when he tried to sound solemn and portentous. *How will you raise a warhost of your own to do it? What Keldon would follow a daughter of Skyshroud against Greht?*

Radha stopped, green fire flickering in her eyes. "I am Keldon," she said.

I say you are not. That trick back there with the saproling thicket . . . what kind of Keldon fights a battle by enhancing shrubbery?

"This one," Radha said. "The one that beat you, embarrassed you, and got away clean."

Nonsense. "*Your fire has no heat, elf-girl.*"

Radha drew two tear-shaped blades, holding their sharp tips out as she shouted inarticulate rage into the sky.

Teferi waited until she ran out of breath. *You cannot defeat Greht alone. I can help you.*

"I wipe my feet on your help, clean-head."

Don't be rash. If you want to become a true daughter of Keld—

"I am a true daughter of Keld." She sheathed her weapons and turned back down the mountain. "Now blow away, gas-bag. I've a Gathan to kill." For the next twenty paces the only sounds Radha heard were her own boots whispering through the snow.

Then Teferi's voice said, *Very well, but remember two things, Radha of Skyshroud.*

"Didn't you leave?" Radha snapped. "I'm so bored right now."

Teferi paused. *You are remarkable, Radha, but you are no true Keldon, not until you learn Keld's wisdom for yourself and touch its power with your own hands. You have longed for that all your life but never had it. I can put it in your reach. When you are ready for me to do so, simply call my name. . . .*

"Which one?" Radha slowed to a walk, craning her head around behind her. "Clean-head or gas-bag?"

But the wizard was already gone. Radha waited for a few moments to be sure he had nothing else to add, then she resumed her fast, loping gait.

The bald wizard's riddles could wait, so she pushed the encounter to the back of her mind. She still had a lot of ground to cover before she'd be in Greht's territory. Once in, she next had to find his mobile headquarters.

The Gathans were massing for a major ritual before beginning a large-scale campaign abroad. Greht needed wood to make warships, and he would be traveling among all the campsites he controlled from the southern edge of the forest to the eastern shoreline to make sure they were collecting timber fast enough. It might take Radha several days to pick up his trail, and by then he would have moved on, but eventually she would track him down.

Radha looked up at the endlessly gray sky. As she came down off the mountainside, the landscape grew harder and more barren. There were no trees here, no cover, just miles and miles of blasted, frozen rock. The wind was freezing, but Radha liked the cold. It made her feel restless, like there were too many things to do that she didn't want anyone else to have the pleasure of doing.

She continued to run, now following the long-abandoned footpaths her ancestors had worn into the rock. A large party had recently come this way. Greht and his 'host? Whoever they were, if they stuck to the paths Radha might be able to catch them by daybreak.

* * * * *

Hours later, the trail led Radha to something she hadn't seen in years: a human settlement. It was a drab and awful collection of shacks that sat nestled against a thick, murky stream. The settlers had constructed a crude water wheel to harness the stream's almost nonexistent flow, but Radha could not guess why. There were no crops or lumber to mill.

Something like a sentry hut stood empty by the side of the path. Radha strode past it. The settlement seemed deserted, but as she drew closer to the small cluster of buildings she heard someone weeping.

The sound came from between the first two ramshackle structures, a storage shack and a public house. Radha edged silently up to the mouth of the alley and peered in.

A small, huddled form crouched between two lifeless bodies. Radha could not make out any clear details, but all three figures were dressed in peasant rags. The two on the ground were soaked with crimson, and as the weeping child rocked and sniffled, the wet ground sloshed beneath his threadbare shoes.

Radha turned sideways and forced herself through the narrow alley opening. The buildings on either side were not square to one another, so the space opened up toward the back of the alley. Radha walked to the far end, hands open and in full view of the child, but the small head never looked up from the bodies on the ground.

They were scrawny, wasted creatures like all Keldon humans who hadn't yet been killed or forcibly taken by a Gathan warhost. The child was fair-skinned but sickly, his neck and hands a jaundiced yellow. Liquid dripped from between the fingers pressed over his face.

The boy must have heard Radha's boots because he suddenly stopped sobbing. He pressed his hands harder against his face and held his breath, listening intently.

"I mean you no harm," Radha said. Her voice echoed coldly off of the wet wooden walls.

The child lowered his hands and Radha saw why the Gathans had left this otherwise healthy young recruit behind. Fresh wounds covered his face, a connected series of jagged slashes that had opened his flesh and cruelly destroyed both eyes.

Radha's jaw clenched as she recognized the symbol these wounds formed. It was a Keldon corpse marker, a rough way of honoring the fallen. If they had been valiant foes, the sigil on the body was grudgingly respectful: "Died well" or "Showed No Fear." Far more popular were the marks used to desecrate the bodies of worthless enemies to dishonor a hated foe: "Coward," "Backstabber," and "Leave Me to Rot."

To anyone who could read Keldon runes, this boy was forever marked, "Target."

Only the Gathans used corpse markers on living people. Only Greht would order such a mark carved into a child.

"Boy," she said sharply. "Who did this?"

The shredded, slack-jawed face did not change at the sound of Radha's voice.

"The big men with swords," she prompted. "Did one of them wear a metal mask?"

The boy stared sightlessly at her for a while longer. Then he slowly nodded his head.

"Keldons." The child's voice was thick and hoarse.

"Gathans," Radha said automatically, but the boy scarcely heard.

"They lined us all up." His chest heaved and his slack expression began to waver as fresh sobs came. "They said, 'don't look.' "

"But you looked."

The boy nodded, tears washing through the sticky sheets of red on his cheeks. "I looked."

Radha glanced down at the other two bodies. She wondered if they died before or after the boy was blinded. "Here." Radha crouched down and pressed one of her tear-shaped blades into the child's hand. "Put your fingers here. And here. See how they fit? Now squeeze. Good." She gently took his free hand and pricked his thumb with the tip of the blade. "Watch out for the sharp end. Hold it like this, inside your sleeve."

She pulled a chunk of hard tack from her belt and pressed into the boy's other soft, pliable hand. "That's food. It will keep you strong until they come back."

The boy made a panicked sound but Radha held both his hands tight. "Oh yes, they're coming back. And when they do, wait until they're as close as I am, until their voices are as loud as mine is now. And they will be, because they'll want to look at you and laugh in your face."

She stood, releasing the boy's hands, leaving him with the

blade and the rations. "When you hear that, ram the sharp end up toward the sound as hard as you can. Keep your legs beneath you, lean forward, and push."

Radha turned and walked to the mouth of the alley without a backward glance. She smoothly turned sideways and slipped through the gap. The last thing she saw behind her was the razor-tear in the boy's hand, glittering in the dim light as he tested its weight and feel.

She stepped onto the thoroughfare and something hard slammed into her forehead. Radha's vision blurred and she fell back against the wall of the storage shack. The butt of a club or a farmer's tool cracked across her jaw, this time sending her clumsily to the ground.

Three heavy bodies immediately piled on, pinning her arms and legs. She heard a man's voice call from the alley, "Two more dead in the alley! Bright lady, there's a little boy here, too!"

"What did you do to those people?" The woman's voice was shrill in Radha's ear. She pulled back on Radha's hair and screamed again. "What did you do that child?"

Radha heaved with all her might, driving the back of her head into the raving woman's face. She continued to arch her spine, snarling as she pulled the men holding her arms with her.

"Hold her down, you idiots!"

But Radha had already loosened one captor's grip. She snatched her hand free of his and clamped onto his windpipe. He was a fat man and his neck was wide and rubbery. Radha's fingers sank in as if she were digging into a loaf of uncooked bread.

They held this preposterous position for several seconds, Radha's legs and one arm pinned to the ground, half her torso almost vertical. The settlers had her three-quarters pinned, but she was quickly choking the fat one to death with her free hand.

Radha suddenly turned and spat at the man holding her arm. Green fire flared from her lips, and though it did not burn it startled the settler into easing his grip. Radha pulled her other hand loose, twisted at the waist, and dug it into the fat man's neck.

Using the big man as an anchor, Radha hauled herself forward, out from under the men holding her legs. Some of the people in the street shouted as she kicked free and planted her feet under her, her fingers still buried in the settler's throat. She strained, muscles in her neck and shoulders bunching, and then Radha straight-arm lifted the fat settler over her head.

When her arms and legs were fully extended and his feet were a clear foot off the ground, Radha arched her back again toppled over backward. She flung the big man as she fell, hurling him onto the remaining settlers behind her and taking fully half of them out of the brawl in one loud, clumsy fell swoop.

A nervous-looking man with a saber jumped clear of the muddle and stepped forward. Even with a sword and a half-dozen settlers at his back he was on the verge of panic.

"What do you want?" he yelled. "Haven't you taken enough?"

Radha sneered contemptuously at the man's blade, not even bothering to draw her own. "I am no raider," she said, "no Gathan thug."

"Then why are you attacking us?"

"I didn't. Your friends hit me with a stick and jumped on me. If I weren't in such a hurry you'd all be dead now and we wouldn't even be having this conversation."

The man swallowed hard. "But why are you here?"

"I'm hunting them. The Gathans who just came through here are prey to me."

"What?" The swordsman looked pained. "Bright lady, why would you go looking . . ."

"For sport." In the silence, Radha grinned while the settler with the sword tried to digest her point of view.

"You don't look like one of them," he allowed.

"She's from the forest," another said. "Look at her clothes."

"I thought elves never came out of the forest."

Radha's face darkened. She glared into the shadows, toward the sound of that last comment. "I am a Keldon warrior," she said.

The man with the saber relaxed. "This is some sort of joke, isn't it? You're a Skyshroud elf. Anyone can see that."

A woman with a broken nose stepped forward, speaking through the bloody wad of rags she held pressed to her face. "Id dud madda wud she is. Shees dain-juss."

By now, all of the settlers had disentangled themselves from the pile and were lined up behind the man with the sword, all together a score of them or more. The Gathans must have taken all the conscripts they wanted and left this rabble behind.

Emboldened by superior numbers, or perhaps by the fact that Radha had not harmed anyone since they started talking to her, the crowd's mood began to change.

"She's big for an elf."

"Does this mean we can go into Skyshroud now?"

"I don't trust elves."

"I say she's working for the raiders. She's a scout or something."

"Then why is she so far behind?"

"Maybe she got lost."

"Maybe she tried to join them and they didn't want her. She's just a dog sniffing after the wolf pack."

"Quiet!" The man with the saber was closest to Radha, so it was he who shouted. His warning had come too late, though, as green fire was already licking up past Radha's eyebrows.

"Elf warrior," he began.

"Keldon," Radha growled. "I am Keldon."

Before the swordsman could stop them, two voices rang out over the thoroughfare.

"Sure you are," said the one.

"Prove it," laughed the other.

Radha roared and threw herself at the last settler to speak, the tear-blade in her fist arcing down toward the bridge of his nose.

She had also drawn a second blade and held it out to one side to cut the sword-wielding settler's throat as she passed, but she never reached either target.

Instead, she found herself floating motionless over the thoroughfare. The entire scene had frozen, its players arranged like statues outside the narrow alley. Though she took a split second to appreciate the looks of fear and surprise on the settlers, Radha soon began to chafe at her own immobility.

I thought it was time for me to step in, Teferi's voice said, *before someone got hurt. You seemed to be having trouble assembling an effective and loyal fighting force.*

Radha's jaw would not move and her tongue was like stone. She tried to thrash her entire body from side to side, but none of her muscles would respond. Furious, she screamed at the front of her brain.

Let me go, wizard.

Planeswalker. I am a planeswalker, Radha, not a mere wizard.

Who cares? What's a planeswalker?

His voice sparkled. *I can show you. I can show you a lot of things, take you to a lot of places.*

Radha continued to struggle against her paralysis. *I don't want to go anywhere else. I have work to do here.*

Stupid girl. I'm not talking about anywhere else. I want to show you Keld.

We're in Keld, you ass. I've lived here all my life.

But you've never been to the Necropolis nor to the mountain. You've never known the real fires of Keld.

Radha stopped thrashing. She spoke very slowly.

What do you know about the mountain? Or the Necropolis? Or the fires of Keld?

I know the mountain is where Keld begins, and the Necropolis is where Keldons end. That's the Keldon way in a nutshell, isn't it? Beginnings and endings, followed by new beginnings. Every twilight is followed by a new dawn, and so long as the fire keeps burning through the darkness and the cold, Keld will endure. Do you know the tinder spell?

Radha kept silent, once more suppressing her thoughts to keep them from the wizard. He would not take the information from her mind, but Teferi went on without her help, perfectly reciting the words of the first and oldest Keldon incantation.

Coal and tinder, hearth and spark, Keldons are fire, and Keld commands—

"Burn," Radha cried, and a sheet of emerald flames suddenly covered her from head to toe. Her restraints vanished and she fell to the ground, her body flush with rich, raw mana.

Radha quickly bounced back to a standing position with her blades ready. The settlers had all remained frozen, shock still etched into their pale faces.

Oh, Teferi said. *You do know it.*

"I know it works," Radha said, "and so do you."

Indeed. I have studied Keld's history, but has that spell ever worked so well for you before?

She glanced down at the stone below her. An electric thrill raced through her, as she was standing in the middle of a perfect circle of charred, smoking soot. All of the ice and snow dust had boiled away, leaving the sheer, gray rock.

It seems you are a true Keldon after all, or rather, you could be. As I knew you could.

Radha holstered her weapons. "What else do you know?"

Teferi materialized overhead, floating above the frozen settler's heads. He was smiling warmly as he extended his hand.

"Let me show you," he said.

Radha glared at him. She crossed her arms defiantly, but then she glanced down again at the smoking circle. Radha considered this then slowly extended her arm.

Teferi reached down and took her hand in his. The soft blue glow surrounding him crawled from his fingers to hers, and soon Radha was also covered in a sheet of liquid light.

She felt her stomach drop as she and the wizard rocketed up into the evening sky, the frozen villagers and their ramshackle dwellings shrinking to a pinpoint before Radha's eyes as she soared into the dusky sky on the wings of a wizard's magic.

CHAPTER 9

Teferi suspected Radha had been outside of Skyshroud valley before, but he was certain she had never seen her homeland like this. They were looking down from a thousand feet over the tallest mountain in Keld. The pale fields of rock and snow-covered ridges all reflected the fading daylight, giving Teferi and Radha a clear view of Keld's southern half.

The badly worn mountains with their shattered caldera tops amazed Radha, but she kept her voice and her thoughts to herself as they soared, connected to each other by an envelope of glittering blue energy.

"Behold the embers of Keld," Teferi said. "The forces that fueled the covenant between Keld and your ancestors have faded. They are spent but not gone. Not forever. They may yet slumber deep below the roots of the mountain."

Radha continued to look but did not reply. She maintained the same intense, slightly displeased expression.

"Are those people down there?"

Far below, Radha had singled out one of the larger caldera bowls. From their vantage point Teferi could see small stone structures carved into the walls of the caldera and the natural shelves of rock that had been built up and shaped into dwelling places. Buildings dotted the upper third of the caldera's interior, with one larger longhouse overlooking the rim. The Keldon elf had spotted a dozen or more tiny figures moving among the buildings.

"Yes," Teferi said. "Would you like to see them up close?"

"Not particularly," Radha said. "I'd rather see the Necropolis."

Teferi was tempted to probe Radha's thoughts, which were clearly buzzing inside her head like a swarm of bees. He decided against it and simply said, "Of course."

The climbed higher, frigid air splaying harmlessly off the blue barrier around them. Onward they flew, north towards the center of Keld, until the broad, imposing base of the Necropolis swung into view on the western horizon.

The Keldon Necropolis was a massive mausoleum-fortress that had been carved into the heart of a mountain. It was both a war memorial and soldier's cemetery, but at the height of Keldon prominence it had also been a meeting hall for the ruling council. Far below the great hall and the meeting chambers was a complicated network of tunnels and tombs that once held the remains of every great Keldon warlord.

It had also once held the fabled *Golden Argosy*, a massive, magical warship that only sailed to take the bravest Keldons to the most glorious battles . . . or so the legend said. The tale also said the *Argosy* would return after the battle was over, but the center of the Necropolis stood now cracked and hollow as an empty walnut shell, dominated by a void precisely the size and shape of a massive warship.

Whatever mythical power the *Golden Argosy* held, Teferi knew it had actually sailed during the Phyrexian Invasion, and it had taken Keld's greatest warriors into the heart of that struggle. The ship's last voyage departed shortly after Freyalise installed Skyshroud, and as far as Teferi knew it had never returned.

Now the mountain sat broken, empty, and silent, the glorious ship and the bodies of Keld's heroes both long gone. There had been conflicting accounts of what happened before the *Golden Argosy's* last voyage, but most agreed that Keld's honored dead rose from the Necropolis to take their place in the battle as prophesied, but then attacked their own descendents instead of the Phyrexian invaders. Teferi decided to omit that bit of information if Radha ever asked, if only to spare himself another bad-tempered outburst of her name-calling.

He needn't have worried: Radha was awestruck, wide-eyed and mute from the mere sight of the place. Teferi again resisted the temptation to skim her mind—the satisfaction of knowing what she was thinking was not worth the risk of enraging her if she objected to his snooping.

"There's something important I want to show you."

"Good." Radha's face remained fixed on the Necropolis. "There's something important I want to see. Take me to the upper ridge, down there." She pointed.

Teferi smiled patiently. "We must start at the bottom. That is where Keld's oldest secrets are interred."

"I don't care about that. I want to see the more recent tombs."

"And you shall, but we will start at the bottom." Teferi spread his arms and they began to spiral down into the Necropolis's cavernous interior.

As they passed the rim of the caldera, Teferi saw more of the embedded stone dwellings carved into the rock. Radha saw them too, and she snarled angrily.

"Problem?" Teferi asked.

Radha glared at him then back to the makeshift homes. "This is a place for the honored dead," she spat, "not living worms."

"There is very little left of Keld," Teferi said, "and her children have to survive somehow."

They were now on the same level as most of the buildings. Gaunt, desperate faces peered out from many of the windows and doorways, their frightened eyes wide.

"These are your contemporaries," Teferi said. "Modern Keldons."

Scott McGough

"No." Radha shook her head. "These are just citizens of Keld, those who were not worthy to be warriors."

"They could have been. With the right opportunity and the right leadership. . . ."

"What warlord would want them?" Radha flared.

"A prescient question. I imagine . . . a warlord without a 'host might find them useful? After all, a leader with no followers is hardly a leader at all."

Radha fell quiet. Her eyes darted from one desperate cliff-dweller to another. "Take us away from here," she said quietly. Her voice dropped even lower and she muttered "Even Llanach wouldn't field soldiers like this."

Teferi accelerated their descent and they dropped down in the darker recesses of the cavern. There was no natural light, but Teferi could see clearly. He expected Radha could also see their surroundings, as both sides of her ancestry had excellent night vision.

"Stop here," Radha said. Teferi continued on without replying, and she drew one of her blades.

"If you cut me," he said, "who will keep you aloft?"

"I'd rather fall," Radha said, but the tip of her tear-blade wavered in her hand. After a moment she returned the weapon to its sheath.

The floor of the Necropolis appeared below them. It was dotted with a series of featureless stone vaults, each as large as a small house. They had been constructed and assembled so closely together that there was less than a foot's width between them. Teferi brought them down in the center of this field of stone boxes, touching down as lightly as a bee on a flower.

"These are the ancient treasure troves of Keld," Teferi intoned. He spread his arms out wide to encompass the entire area, his staff glowing softly in his hand. "The rarest spoils ever plundered by her armies, the greatest trophies ever seized by her generals, and somewhere among these vaults lies Keld's history. This is what

I've brought to see, for you must know Keld's history if you intend to be its future."

Teferi turned and saw that he was alone. "Radha?" he called.

He concentrated, opening up all his senses. She couldn't have gone far, he thought . . . but then again, she kept finding ways to surprise him.

There she was. Radha had already climbed a quarter of the way back up the side of the cavern, using the hollowed-out graves of her ancestors as hand- and footholds.

Teferi sighed. He folded his arms and rose back into the air, arrow-straight to the spot where Radha was climbing. He floated alongside her, watching her ascend and listening to her breathy curses as she fought her way up.

"I wasn't through talking," Teferi said.

"You never are." Radha continued to climb.

"If you keep this up I'm going to assume you're not interested in what I have to say."

"Good."

"This is important. Keld's magic is inextricable from Keld's history."

Radha caught hold of a wide, flat ledge with both hands. She hauled herself up until her waist was clear of the edge, then leaned forward and rolled into a sitting position. She turned and read the inscriptions carved into the wall beside her.

"This is my history," she said. She followed the inscription with her eyes, pacing slowly along as she read. Radha nodded to herself, checked the words carved into the opposite wall, then sprinted along the row of empty tombs.

Teferi floated behind her, easily keeping pace. Radha continued to read the characters carved into the walls as she ran. They were an ornate and archaic runeform that he had rarely seen, an ancient language called High Keld. It was the language of Keld's most powerful spells, the language of command on the battlefield.

These inscriptions seemed to be a simple list of names, dates, and titles; Radha was most likely looking for someone in particular. From the way her speed kept increasing and her eyes grew wider and more intense, Teferi guessed they were getting close. Best to just let her find what she was looking for.

At last she stopped before one of the tombs. It was an unremarkable niche, no larger or more ornate than any other on this row, yet Radha wore a look of wonder and awe even more profound than when she had first seen the entire Necropolis. Teferi glanced up at the name on the tomb.

"Astor," he read. "Doyen. Upstart. Bearer of Three Blades. Steward of the Northern Wastes. The Butcher of Bogardan."

"Shh," Radha hissed angrily.

Teferi was impressed. "This is your ancestor? Astor the Upstart?"

"My grandfather," Radha said. She turned sharply to Teferi. "His body was never interred here. My grandmother said that was because he never actually died."

Teferi bowed respectfully. "History says he sailed away in the *Golden Argosy* during the Phyrexian Invasion. There is no record of him after that, but he truly was a great warrior. He helped stop the Phyrexians here and in Urborg." Teferi's face brightened. "My grandfather's name was Mabutho. He was the first in my family to own his own land."

"Don't care," Radha said.

Teferi nodded. Should have seen that coming, he thought. "Now, your grandfather," he said, warming to his subject like the academic he was. "He was blood brothers with Eladamri. You've heard of him, haven't you? The messiah of Skyshroud?"

"Not messiah," Radha muttered. "Korvecdal. He was only a savior in the sense of being a vigorous protector."

"Indeed. Excuse my imprecision, but as I say, Skyshroud's greatest warrior and Astor traded scars before they went into battle together."

Radha laughed harshly. "Astor is said to have done a lot in the short time between Skyshroud's arrival and the *Argosy's* departure. He bonded with Eladamri, saw the Necropolis opened, flooded out the machine invaders, sired my mother. . . ."

Teferi winced a little. "He would have had little reason to stay, what with the war and all. Besides, Keldons in that era put no stock at all in family bonds."

"My own mother never saw him," Radha said, "but he gave us everything we needed." She struck her chest with a closed fist. A dark, emerald flame licked up and surrounded her hand, burning brightly. "Almost."

Using her hand as a torch, Radha strode into the tomb of her grandfather. It was empty but for a small brass brazier and a simple wooden box. She reached down with her free hand and flicked the latch on the box. She paused to glance back at Teferi, who remained respectfully outside the niche, then flipped open the lid.

Inside were two identical long, heavy daggers. The blades were angled near the tip so that their points jutted forward. They were thicker and heavier along their flat edges and the extra weight added chopping power to each blow.

"What are those?" Teferi said.

Radha was consumed by the contents of the box, her eyes fixed and her voice distant. "Icons," she said. "Totems."

"I thought he was the 'Bearer of Three Blades.' Where's the third?"

Radha traced the outer edge of the open box with her finger. "Shut up."

Teferi shrugged. Fascinated, he watched as Radha extinguished her fist and drew one of her own blades. She hefted it in her left hand as she lifted one of the bent daggers in her right. She tested the weight and grip of each, comparing her ancestor's weapon to her own.

Radha nodded to herself, pleased. She sheathed her blade and reached back into the box. With one of Astor's daggers in each hand, Radha turned to face Teferi and held her arms aloft.

"Burn," she said, and a yellow-orange bolt of flame jumped from one dagger to the next. The rope of fire continued to burn brightly over Radha's upturned face, connecting the two daggers. The broad-stroke tattoos on her arms began to glow orange-red, like iron left too long in the blacksmith's forge.

Radha then lowered her arms, bringing the horizontal line of flames down to her face.

"Wait," Teferi said.

Radha's nose touched the fire. Her entire body seemed to ignite in an instant, fire covering her from head to toe in a flickering yellow curtain. Radha stood unharmed inside this burning shroud, her voice ecstatic.

The flames suddenly burned out. Radha was left standing flushed, triumphant, and panting. She still held her grandfather's blades up, and they gleamed in the fading light from her tattoos.

"His blood is in my veins," she said huskily, "and now his *kukri* blades are in my hands."

Radha's strange intensity vanished and she dropped her arms to her sides. "I'm done here," she said. "What else did you want me to see?"

Teferi smiled to himself as the Keldon elf slipped Astor's *kukri* blades into her belt. Freyalise had said Radha would be difficult, and she was, but he was getting more useful information from simply standing near her than he'd get from six months of studying Skyshroud itself. Radha was still drawing mana from nowhere, but she was also channeling it through the ancient daggers. She had no personal connection to Keld, but she was moving closer to one. The tinder spell had been a small step forward; using Astor's daggers was another.

Teferi bowed politely and said, "One thing more to see, but first . . . now that you have your grandfather's blades, do you still seek his fire?"

Radha's eyes narrowed. "His fire and more. Much more."

"Then come." Teferi extended his hand and enveloped Radha once more in blue light. She endured the flight to the cavern floor as she would a brief, unpleasant downpour—arms crossed, defiant, and slightly annoyed.

Teferi decided to dispense with the full introduction this time. He took them directly to the vault he was looking for and bid Radha stand near the edge. Teferi traced a large circle in the center of the roof, inscribing a blue-white shape into the stone with his staff. The light seeped inward, toward the center of the circle until the shape became a solid disc of glittering light. Teferi thumped the end of his staff into the center and the entire section of roof faded away, leaving a clean-cut hole that was wide enough for two.

The planeswalker gestured dramatically. A large box made of tough red wood rose out of the hole on a cloud of fog. Teferi guided it onto the adjacent roof and gently set it down. He pressed both palms together as if praying, then flung his arms apart. The box popped open in response, the hinged door on its front face creaking as it moved.

"Behold," Teferi said, "the *Book of Keld.*"

The volume inside the box was gigantic, half as tall as Teferi himself and as thick as a bale of hay. It was bound in the tough black hide of some unidentified animal and its pages were gilt in reddish gold. Oddly, there was a heavy iron chain attached to the binding that led to a cufflike manacle. The book's cover was dominated by ornate characters written in High Keld. The runes had been carved into the cover, revealing a layer of dusty red underneath the hardened black hide.

Radha looked at the book. "I've heard of it," she said. "It looks heavy."

"It should. It contains the history of Keld from the very beginning, as told and recorded by Keldons. Being Keeper of the Book was one of the most respected offices a Keldon could hold. The first covenant between Kradak and the land is recorded there, taken from firsthand accounts. Each of the apocalyptic Twilights your nation has survived." Teferi gestured again, and the *Book of Keld* floated out of its box, the iron chain clinking on the stone floor.

Teferi steered the book to Radha and said, "Are you ready to take on this awesome responsibility?"

"No."

"No?" Teferi's smile faltered.

"No." Radha cocked her head. "Why would I?"

The Book of Keld fluttered a bit but Teferi managed to keep it aloft. "Beg your pardon?"

"I said, why would I want to lug a table-sized book around with me? Granted, it's big enough to act like a shield, and I bet I could crush a Gathan or two if they got caught under it. Beyond that I really don't see any practical use for it."

"It's full of history," Teferi said, "information you can put to use. Your past is in there, the foundations of Keld itself."

Radha whipped out one of Astor's daggers and twirled it dexterously in her hand. "This is my past," she said, "my foundation. I need no book." She slid the dagger back into her belt. "Now. To the mountain."

Teferi hesitated. "Do you mind if I read it?"

"Maybe." Radha shrugged. "How long will it take you?"

A blue film rolled across Teferi's eyes like a second pair of eyelids. When the film receded, Teferi said, "About that long."

Radha huffed. "You just read the whole *Book of Keld*."

"Read it, memorized it, ready to recite it." His eyes flashed. "For example, I can tick off the names of every warlord, every doyen, every Keeper of the Book. I know by heart all twelve stanzas of the Argivian epic 'The Beasts of Keld.' Want to hear it?"

"No."

"Not even the censored bits?"

"No."

"Come on! There are three stanzas that were deemed too crude and upsetting for the general populace. Never published in New Argive, and then lost until right now, this very second. Don't you want to hear them?" He winked. "You'll like the rhyme the author made for "esophagus," I guarantee it."

Radha rolled her eyes, visibly indifferent. "Take me to the mountain."

"Of course. Just let me put things back in order." He waved his staff again and the *Book of Keld* rose once more into the air. The fierce woman's disinterest in the book was troubling, but Teferi counted the Necropolis visit as a success. He had obtained access to the entire history of Keld, as told by the Keldons. Beyond its sheer value as a historical record, the book's information actually made it possible for him to give Radha what she wanted. She wanted to be a Keldon and to wield true Keldon fire. If that was the reward for assisting Teferi, even she might willingly join his cause.

The fact that he had no special understanding of Keldon fire magic or of fire magic in general was not a real concern. He could acquire that expertise later. All he had to do now was get her attention and hold her interest. Once Shiv had been saved, Teferi had intended to rely on his knack for field research and his power as a planeswalker to provide the whole of Radha's reward.

So far, it seemed to be working, too: the *Book of Keld* had already filled in a number of crucial details that illuminated more of Radha's strange relationship to the local mana supply. It had also helped Teferi better understand the ground where Skyshroud had been planted, information he could apply to Shiv's return.

Nearby, Radha seemed on the verge of climbing out on her own again, so Teferi quickly finished lowering the *Book of Keld* back into its vault. Once it was safely in place, he touched his staff to the hole he'd made. The clean-cut circle filled in with blue smoke, which then hardened back into seamless gray stone.

When Teferi lifted his staff, there was no sign the vault roof had ever been opened.

Radha glanced impatiently at him. Teferi spread his arms, surrounding them once more in the blue nimbus, and they rose quickly up through the Necropolis, past the threadbare settlement, and up into the clouds.

CHAPTER 10

Radha soared high over her homeland. Though its peaks were cracked and broken they still had some of the strange, stark beauty she remembered. Her grandmother had once taken her to the top of Skyshroud's tallest tree, back when Skyshroud still had tall trees. From that perch, Radha had her first glimpse of the craggy peaks that defined Keld.

That had also been her first view of the mountain. Then, as now, there were hundreds of towering peaks in Keld, but only one that never needed a name. It sat near the center of the nation's southern half, separated from the rest of the ranges by a circle of rugged foothills. Even now, when every other Keldon peak was diminished and worn away, this mountain stood whole and proud with its fat, round acme visible from nearly any high ground in the entire country.

The first ancient settlers came here after they fled the frigid northern wastelands and ice giants of Parma. The travelers were fierce warriors all, but winter cannot be killed with a sword. When they arrived at this spot they were more than half-dead, but the mountain sheltered them for the night. As the warriors huddled for warmth, the mountain spoke to their leader, Kradak, and he spoke back. When dawn broke, Kradak had bonded to the land and the settlers had bonded to him. Together they could draw on Keld's primal energy and give it form and purpose. They were no longer wandering refugees: they had become Keldons.

Since then every potential warlord went up the mountain as a grueling rite of passage. If he could survive the cold, the wolves, and the lack of food, he was fit to command troops and lead warriors into battle. More importantly, the candidate established his own personal connection to the mountain, as Kradak and the ancients did, and became a true Keldon warlord. Warlords were the living symbol of the great covenant between the land and its denizens, with the power to mix mana with the ferocity of his troops and combine it on the battlefield into something far more potent.

Radha had not been to the mountain before; she had not even wandered this far from Skyshroud, but she knew the stories. Most came straight from her grandmother's lips, but those same tales that inspired Radha also discouraged her from visiting the mountain herself. Even if Radha survived traveling to the mountain, and the mountain itself, and returned successful, Freyalise would still punish her for breaking the patron's isolationist edicts.

Also, and most frustrating to Radha, the warlord-making ritual was traditionally the sole province of men. No woman had ever been permitted to attempt it, and those who had tried anyway never returned. There was no way to be sure the ritual would work for Radha even if she completed it.

Neither ancient Keldon bias nor Freyalise's edicts had kept Radha from exploring other mountains closer to the forest, of course, but none of them was even a shadow of this one. She was furious with herself for not taking the risk and coming here sooner. Maybe the mountain's power was only for men, but Radha could feel it too.

She was not one for poetry, but some of the older elves sang (much to her annoyance). Inexplicably, Radha's mind now turned over the words to an old elf song, a mournful tune about a young woman who impetuously casts a precious keepsake into a deep, still pond. She returns to the pond every year throughout the rest of her life, through adulthood, old age, and beyond death, and no matter how many years pass, no matter how icy or still the water's surface, she always feels the submerged pull of her personal treasure.

Radha snorted, scornful of her own thoughts. Poems were for elves and minstrels, not warriors. She didn't identify with the woman in the song and didn't understand why she thought of her now. Radha hadn't thrown away the power she felt from the mountain; she hadn't even tasted it yet, so why should her brain conjure up that song with its images of ponds and longing? Poetry only seemed to make sense, but it really just encouraged self-indulgent flights of fancy. Plus, she hated the melody and the cloying way it was performed. She resolved to punch a poet when she returned to the forest.

They began to descend and Teferi wisely took them toward the base of the mountain. He had probably guessed Radha would insist on scaling the sacred site herself. They came to light on the crest of a small ridge, the mountain looming large above them.

Radha paced past Teferi, her eyes fixed and vacant. It felt different here; she felt different. It was invigorating, dangerous, and as exhilarating as balancing on one foot at the edge of a ravine. She began to walk faster, heedless of the planeswalker's voice calling after her.

"Behold, the mountain," he said, but his words sounded tired and thin. Then, with energy, he said, "Radha! Please wait."

She kept on, increasing her pace. The crunch of her boots in the snow kept time with her heartbeat, both growing ever more rapid. Radha reached the edge of the mountain itself and jerked to a sudden stop. Her eyes glittered and her hair began to swirl as if moved by a strong wind. The snow around her feet turned to water, then the water turned to steam.

"Hah!" she cried. Waving her arms, she turned back to Teferi and shouted, "Hoy, clean-head! This way! You follow me for awhile!" Without waiting for an answer, Radha bounded up the mountainside.

She vaulted over a sharp rise into a vicious cross-wind that brought tears to her eyes. Radha pressed on, shielding her face with her hand. The power she felt here did nothing to protect her from the cold but rather spurred her on in spite of it, calling to her from the highest and most frigid parts of the mountain. The mountain's strength, its fire, wasn't hers yet, but she knew it existed and now she knew where it was.

The planeswalker floated up next to her, his sheath of blue energy acting as a windbreak. The howling in Radha's ears died off and she could hear Teferi's voice clearly.

"Do you feel it?" he asked. His eyes were bright and probing. "Does your barbarian heart fill to bursting with the fires of Keld?"

Radha smiled at him wolfishly, pleased by his company for the first time. "I do," she said.

"Excellent. This is your first taste of Keld's true strength, and if you come with me now and do as I ask, I swear to return you here. In less than a week, that mere taste can become a gluttonous meal." He extended his hand. "Join me, Radha of Keld, and fulfill your true destiny."

Radha blinked in confusion. "But I'm here now."

Teferi's confident expression cracked a little. "There is no more time," he said. "I brought you here to experience the mountain's power, not to complete the warlord's walkabout. We have much to do and many other places to go."

" 'We,' 'walker? There is no 'we' leaving this mountain, not unless you have a tapeworm." She turned away from the hand he offered. When she spoke again, she tossed the words carelessly over her shoulder. "You have much to do and many places to go. I have a mountain to climb." The wind kicked up again as she stepped out from behind his blue aura.

Radha. The planeswalker's voice roared through her head like a falling tree, drowning out the wind entirely. The mountainside became eerily still and quiet. Radha found it hard to keep moving, her legs growing heavy and unresponsive.

She turned. Teferi still floated in his curtain of blue, but his eyes had gone bright white. Tiny jags of azure lightning radiated out from the tip of his staff. "I have been more than patient," he said, "but this expedition is over. Come with me now, that we might begin another, far more important journey."

"Stuff you." Radha concentrated and lifted her right boot off the ground. She pushed the foot forward, scraping up tiny ridges of snow, then let it thump back down.

A blue streak crossed her vision from the left and the planeswalker was suddenly blocking her path. "Enough of this, child," Teferi said. "Come with me now. You have no choice."

Gone was the odd-shaped hat and the colorful robes. Teferi was now clad in gleaming metallic robes of electric blue that gave off sizzling sparks. His face seemed leaner and less boyish, and his expression was stern. He stood confident, balanced and ready, his staff clenched firmly in his outstretched hand. The tip of the spinelike walking stick glowed silver-white.

"I have escaped the bonds of time," he said. "I have moved continents as if they were puzzle pieces in a child's playroom. The ceaseless motion of the sea and the boundless sky are mine to command, as is a thousand years of history and exploration.

"You are a warrior, Radha, but I am a planeswalker. Come with me freely or you will be bottled and toted like a store of fine wine, to be opened and poured out at my leisure. Either way, you will help me. There is no alternative."

Radha glared into Teferi's milk white eyes. "Stuff you," she said again.

Teferi blinked. When he opened his eyes, they had lost their white glow. His gaze was no longer soft and friendly, but sharp, hard, and full of dire consequences. "Do not underestimate me," he said, "or overestimate yourself. You are mortal. I am infinite. You cannot hope to stand against me."

"I can and do, you pompous ass. Did you really think you could bring me here and then whisk me away? That a taste of the mountain would be enough? You're right about my true destiny; it's is right here and I mean to claim it, right now. Nothing you can do to can keep me from it."

Teferi held her eyes. "Prove—" he said, but he never finished the two-word phrase that was an instant incitement to violence for every true Keldon.

Instead, Radha sprang forward with one of Astor's kukri daggers in her fist. She rammed the point of the heavy blade up through the bottom of Teferi's chin and drove it in until the blade's tip emerged from the top of his head. The planeswalker's eyes vibrated in their sockets as his lips opened and shut soundlessly. Radha's own eyes flashed and spat out twin plumes of orange flame.

She yanked the blade free and watched Teferi fall. More fire flared around the edge of the weapon and Radha stared at it, half-hypnotized by its gentle flicker. When the flames died out she glanced down at Teferi's body. Oddly, there was no blood, not from the wound or on the blade. She shrugged. Perhaps almighty planeswalkers didn't bleed.

Teferi's blue barrier faded and the wind rose once more. Radha shielded her eyes with the hand that held Astor's blade, scanning the bald man's prone form for any signs of life.

"Are you dead?" she shouted. She reached out and nudged Teferi's leg with the toe of her boot. "Are you that easy to kill?" She stared for a moment longer, drew back, then kicked Teferi solidly in the thigh.

There was no reaction. "You are dead, aren't you?" she said. "You said you were infinite." She spat on him. "Ass."

She was thoroughly annoyed. Teferi dressed like a drunken

harlequin, but he had shown her strong magic in the valley and the Necropolis. She had half-believed he was some sort of demigod, but now she saw he was just another wizard who was best at shoveling words.

Radha allowed herself a cruel grin. Maybe Teferi Planeswalker could only stop time, move continents, and control the oceans if his head *wasn't* skewered clean through by Keldon steel.

She squinted in the glare from Astor's dagger, which was still tinged with a faint red gleam. She brought the kukri blade down, its inner light illuminating her face. On a hunch, Radha pulled out the second kukri and held it up to the first.

As they had in the Necropolis, the blades spat fire toward each other and created a line of flame between their tips. Radha felt the mountain's energy pouring into her, surging up through the soles of her feet. It flowed through her legs and spine, across her shoulders and arms, on into the twin daggers. Wild excitement rose in her once more and she clenched her grandfather's weapons tightly in her fists.

"Burn," she said.

The air around her burst into a cloud of fiery leaf-shapes. Instead of the cold green flames that she had been able to summon all her life, these were red and yellow-orange and they radiated intense heat.

Radha's full-throated laugh echoed up the mountainside. She wept, joyous, and the tears sizzled to steam as they ran down her cheeks. She threw her head back and howled, kukri-flame singeing the ends of her hair.

She brought the daggers together with an icy clang. The fire flew from her, exploding outward and burning a wide circle into the snow. Teferi's body remained as it was, unchanged and unmoving.

Radha slipped both daggers back into her belt and faced down the mountainside. She no longer needed to reach the peak to claim her birthright, just as she no longer needed the long-winded planeswalker's help. Astor's daggers and the sacred ground had given her access to Keld's true might. She had it—she could feel it burning inside her.

The sharp wind still cut across Radha's face, but she did not squint. She lit off down the mountain, her long, loping stride even more efficient downhill. The Gathans were nearby.

Greht would be very surprised to see her again, and more so by what she had to show him. If she did not find Greht this night, she would still find plenty of false Keldon throats to cut until the warlord noticed and came to make her stop.

Burning brighter and hotter than she ever had before, Radha went looking for the fight of her life.

* * * * *

Clumsy, Teferi thought to himself as the kukri punched through the top of his skull. Clumsy, careless, and stupid.

Of course he could not be killed by a blade, not even a well-made blade like Astor's. His physical presence was little more than a full-body mask. There was no real heart to pierce, bones to break, or blood to spill. Stabbing a planeswalker was as lethal as stabbing a sack of flour shaped like a planeswalker—the damage was mostly cosmetic and easily repaired.

His mistake here had been thinking like a barbarian instead of an infinite. In his defense, he was still somewhat giddy from the rush of information in the *Book of Keld*. The berserkers seemed so easy to understand when he had their entire history at his fingertips. Flushed with his newfound understanding of Keld, Teferi had erred by approaching Radha as a fellow warrior, by focusing his energies on physical intimidation.

Planeswalkers were beings of mind and mystical power, but if they grew too fixed or comfortable in the body they chose, they could fall victim to that body's inherent weaknesses. He had been in his familiar human guise so long that his consciousness had naturally settled in his head. When Radha spiked his brain, the wound was temporarily as debilitating as if Teferi had been mortal. Once the initial shock passed, his transcendent mind worked quickly to reform his body around the blade in his head, but until then he was by all measures beaten and bereft of life.

Radha did him a favor by yanking the kukri dagger out. Teferi was aware of falling lifeless to the ground, but rather than struggle back to his feet without his full capacities, he chose to stay facedown and ponder as his nerve endings reestablished contact with his body. It was hard to think with his head as it was, and harder still with Radha taunting and kicking him where he lay.

She had been much faster than he'd expected. She had a longer reach and a quicker hand, too. That was how she had managed to put him in this embarrassing position.

But as Radha stretched her arms out and ignited Astor's daggers, Teferi grudgingly admitted the real reason she had bested him: in their face to face, eye to eye confrontation, he blinked first.

The Keldon ways of dominance and command were their own kind of language, one Teferi didn't yet speak fluently. The *Book of Keld* gave him the form but he was lacking the substance. Intimidating berserkers wasn't a matter of locking eyes and waiting for the weaker or less confident party to back down. It was more active, more aggressive than simply holding one's ground . . . more like an actual attack than the prelude to one.

Radha had been in the moment, ready to fight, kill, and die over their disagreement. Teferi had been thinking ahead, mapping out what he would do once Radha had been brought to heel. When she struck, he was surprised by her speed, but he had also been rooted in place like a mouse before the cobra, lost in the dazzling fury of the predator's eye.

The Keldon elf cried out, "Burn," and the air around her went up in flames. Facedown in the dirt, Teferi still saw Radha clearly, still perceived the changes in her and Keld's mana flow that allowed her to produce real fire.

Now this is interesting, he told himself. Perhaps even worth a dagger in the head. Radha was drawing fire mana to her now as well as nature mana, but she still wasn't drawing it directly from the mountain. Even here, at the source of Keld's mana, she needed her grandfather's daggers and her own mysterious energy supply in order to cast spells. Her connection to the land had not changed. From the savage look of triumph on her face, Radha herself had not realized this.

As she turned and thundered down the mountainside, Teferi worked harder to recover. She would go straight to the nearest Gathan warhost to test her newfound abilities. Once there, she'd find what the *Book of Keld* made clear in a hundred different accounts of a hundred different wars: that a single warrior can win a battle, but you need an army to win a sustained campaign. Even the most terrible warlord with the most devastating spells could not expect to defeat a full Keldon warhost by brute force alone. If Radha had read the book, had even glanced at a page or two, she would not be so hasty to challenge the Gathans.

Teferi continued to lie still on the cold, hard ground. Alas, he thought, some people insist on learning life's hardest lessons for themselves.

CHAPTER 11

Radha found her quarry a short run from the mountain, a hastily assembled Gathan camp between two large ridges. It was clear they would not stay long. Five huge wooden carts were lined up and ready to move out at first light, each full of freshly cut Skyshroud timber. It would take less than two days to march to the sea from here, and Greht clearly intended to assemble his new fleet right there on the beach.

There were a score of drivers and laborers huddled fearfully at the far edge of the camp. A huge Gathan overseer watched them with a long spiked scourge in his hand. Fire shot out of the lash's tip when he cracked it, and he cracked it frequently and without warning.

The overseer grinned maliciously. He had been driving them all night, judging from the way they flinched every time his whip arm flexed.

Radha counted Gathans as they patrolled the camp perimeter and bullied the hapless draught slaves. There were perhaps a dozen of them, towering, swollen-chested, and heavily armed. They were a company of warrior brutes on a degrading, non-combat detail, and Radha could feel their foul temper and frustration hanging in the air like greasy smoke.

There was no sign of Greht. Radha planned to change that by slaughtering his raiders, driving off his slaves, and burning his lumber while it was still on the carts. If missing two ships' worth of wood didn't bring the warlord himself to investigate, Radha would simply hunt down and destroy the next caravan that came through. And the next. Sooner or later, the Gathan warlord would have to personally investigate this significant break in his supply lines.

Radha wrapped her hand around the hilt of Astor's dagger, comforted by the sizzling jolt of heat it produced. The blades were so steeped in fire that they seemed to have retained some of it, yet they always cried out for more.

She smiled thinly. Her grandfather must have channeled thousands of spells through them to make them this fierce, this hungry after his long absence. She narrowed her eyes and drew the second kukri. Astor's power was hers to employ now, and the Gathans would suffer.

She opened her mouth, clenched both kukri blades between her teeth, and bit down hard. Silent as a falling leaf, Radha crept along the ground in the shadow of the outer ridge. Her initial plan of murder, liberation, and destruction still appealed to her, but she decided to reverse the order. She would ignite the wood, scatter the slaves, then destroy the Gathans in the resulting confusion.

She froze as a sentry walked past her, but the Gathan went on without raising an alarm. Radha worked her way along the ridge until she was near the center of the makeshift camp, only a short sprint from the carts.

The sentry returned. Radha froze again as he walked past the edge of the command tent, waiting until he was totally out of sight.

Then Radha rose up behind him like smoke. A heavy kukri dagger in each hand, she pointed their tips at each other and let out a soft, musical whistle. The Gathan whirled at the sound, his fist already closing around his sword, but Radha drove both daggers deep into his rib cage before his blade ever left the scabbard. Their faces stood level, barely inches apart as killer and victim stared into each other's eyes.

Radha twisted the blades up and heard two muffled cracks inside the Gathan's chest. Sparks danced in her eyes.

"Burn," she whispered.

The Gathan's head fell back and he wheezed out a soft, hissing moan. Smoke rose from the wounds in his chest, clinging briefly to Radha's clenched fists before they vanished in the breeze. A strong stench of burning hair and charred meat wafted from the raider's gaping mouth.

The Gathan sentry's breath ran out and he slumped forward. It took a great deal of Radha's strength to keep him from thudding to the ground, but she was able to guide him onto his side and still stay hidden. She knelt on the body for a moment to make sure no other sentries were coming then pulled her weapons free and quietly rolled the dead Gathan into the shadows.

She crouched and circled around the back of the tent, keeping as close to the fabric walls as she could without touching them. The only Gathan who might see her now was the lash-wielding overseer. Once he was down, there was nothing between her and the wood on the carts. She would set the convoy alight in one or two key places and dash back to the slave pen. Before the fire grew large enough to attract attention, she would cut loose the draught slaves then finish off the Gathans. They would be leaderless and confused as they were beset by fire, escaping prisoners, and Radha herself.

She nodded. The first step was the overseer. He kept moving back and forth across the mouth of the pen, almost always facing the slaves. Coming up behind him was still risky since the cowering drivers and bearers would see her approach. Radha didn't know how they would react, so she had to strike before something they said or did gave her away.

Radha waited for the overseer to reach the far end of the holding area, then she darted toward the carts. She reached the first in line and crouched down behind its back wheel, shielded from the overseer and the command tent. Her breathing was even and her heartbeat was calm. She waited for a few moments to make sure no one had seen her.

As she waited, Radha breathed in the rich smell of freshly cut timber. There was a great deal of wood here and she couldn't help but wonder how Freyalise had allowed it to be taken. Greht's hunger for ships was all-consuming, but it had only started recently. How was he able to harvest so much of Skyshroud so quickly, when the wood was so precious and the forest's patron stood against him?

Radha set aside that mystery for now. She crept along the line of carts, intending to set the last on fire, then the first, so that the caravan could not advance or retreat once the fight began.

The last cart was very close the overseer's stalking ground, but the Gathan himself was once more at the opposite end of the pen. The slaves would see her as soon as she stood up . . . if any of them retained the will to turn their heads. A few wore expressions animated by fear or nervous energy, but for the most part they were as docile as kennel full of old, incontinent dogs.

Radha touched the tip of a kukri blade to the bottommost log in the pile. She concentrated, gathering hot fiery mana and pushing it through the blade on into the timber. The wood beneath her knife point began to smolder. A few seconds more and she'd have infused the log with enough magical energy to explode whenever she wanted. Until then, it was just waiting to burn.

The first tiny flames sprang up and danced along the log's bottom side. One of the slaves turned—perhaps the man smelled smoke or heard the sizzle of mana sparks. Radha held the grizzled man's eyes for a moment, but he quickly looked away. She kept her dagger stuck in the log and bared her teeth. She waved curtly until he raised his eyes again, then she broadly pantomimed covering her own mouth with her hand. She tilted her head toward the overseer. With her free hand, she drew her index finger across her throat.

The slave didn't understand. He barely seemed to register the fact that she was there. She saw no recognition in his face, only confusion, exhaustion, and fear.

"Commander," the tired, sallow man said, "there's someone at the carts."

The overseer turned and let out a loud warning shout. Without waiting for his comrades or glancing at his inert charges, the burly warrior drew a short stabbing sword and advanced, blade in one hand and scourge in the other.

Radha snarled at the slave, and though her hand leaped to her hip, she left the blade in its sheath. Letting it fly to kill this tattletale would do no good now—the damage was done, and she would need all the weapons she had against the Gathans. She did pause a moment to memorize the man's face. Someday, she would hunt the coward for sport and cut him to death by inches, but for now she would let him live with being what he was: a cur who kisses the hand that beats him.

She stepped back from the cart and drew the second kukri. Now that the overseer had spotted her, he seemed amused by the sight. Why wouldn't he be? The whip had a far longer range than her daggers, and its tip was already glowing with magical fire. As far as the overseer knew, he could lash Radha to death from a safe distance with just a single stroke of the whip.

She raised one of her grandfather's blades high and let out a shriek that stopped the overseer's advance short and caused each of the slaves to cover their ears. She lifted the other dagger, struck sparks from their sharp edges, then drove one of the blades deep into the smoking log beside her.

The overseer's arm was a blur as he raised his whip and brought it down. Radha made no move to defend herself or avoid the flaming lash. She simply watched the red-hot tip as it sliced through the air bound for her face. She concentrated.

The Gathan's scourge was long and fast, but not longer than the logs in the cart . . . and not faster than Radha's magic. It was trickier to detonate only the far end of the mana-stuffed log, but the extra effort was worth it for priceless look on the overseer's face.

The felled tree burst right beside the tip of the overseer's whip. Still ten feet from its intended target, the tough strip of hide was shredded by the concussion of Radha's explosion before the heat set each shred on fire. Radha was blasted by a cloud of ashy grit, which she bore with a wide, wolfish grin.

As an unexpected bonus, flaming splinters of wood also peppered the overseer and the first two rows of slaves. The man who had betrayed Radha to the overseer fell screaming with a slashed forehead and a sharp wooden splint sticking out of his bicep.

Not enough, Radha thought. Not nearly enough. I'm still going to hunt him.

Her ears were ringing but the explosion had left her otherwise untouched. The rest of the logs in the cart were burning as they rolled into the space cleared by the explosion. The slaves all stayed as they were, curled up like frightened children during a late-night thunderstorm. The rest of the Gathans converged on her position as the overseer tried to shake life back into his truncated scourge, the sword in his other hand forgotten. He seemed far less amused.

The Keldon elf raised her kukri blades once more. The air around her became full of fiery leaves that burned in a colorful patchwork of red, yellow, and green. Backed by his 'host-mates, the overseer threw aside the remains of his whip and extended his sword. As one, the Gathans came forward, their metal boots stomping in unison.

Radha sprang out to meet them on her long, loping legs. She hit the ground hard ten feet from her enemy, bending deep as her feet drove into the frozen dirt. Her long legs rippled and Radha shot straight up in the air, soaring high enough to hurdle the entire band of raiders. Her flight was a feint, however, as Radha tucked and spun so that she came down in front of the charging Gathans instead of among them.

Too late, the overseer realized that Radha had not passed him over as a target. He tried to dodge, but their formation was too tight. Instead of hurling himself aside, he merely jostled the Gathans to his left without changing position.

Howling, Radha came down on the overseer's face with both daggers. The blades stuck fast in the Gathan's forehead, and she savored his expression as most of his face vanished below her clenched fists.

The overseer struck back immediately. Before the blades could sink in, he buried his calloused fist in Radha's stomach. Her body folded around the Gathan's arm and she grunted explosively. The blow was so strong that it actually carried Radha up and cast her back several yards before dropping her seat-first on the ground. Her spine twisted painfully as she bounced and half-rolled into a clumsy heap. Straining, she hauled her face out of the dirt and tried to fix on her enemy.

The overseer smiled as blood from the gashes in his forehead collected in his bushy eyebrows. He rolled his eyes up as if trying to see the wound, then locked onto Radha. Searing orange pinpricks of light sat in the center of his pupils.

"Strike harder, elf-girl," he said. The overseer slammed his bleeding forehead with his own clenched fist and the sound echoed off the rocks on the ridge. "Gathan skulls don't crack so easy."

Radha spat bloody foam to the side and rose. Breathing was exquisite agony, and she had to keep her left arm pressed tight against her side. Each backward step she took sent crippling shivers through her legs and lower torso. She kept her head tilted at an angle because holding it upright made her entire left side go numb.

Worst of all, she had lost one of the kukri she'd stuck in the overseer's forehead. That was less pressing than it would be otherwise, as she only had one free hand anyway (the left being necessary to hold her ribs in place so she could breathe).

Astor's blades should not have balked on the overseer's skull. She had driven them in with all her might and all the momentum of her fall behind it. More, she was physically flush with fire from the mountain, which she still felt like fever in her blood. She was stronger and sharper than she'd ever been and it hadn't mattered at all.

The Gathans advanced on her, an organized, a coherent unit acting in perfect concert. Radha's anger began to blot out her pain. There was no warlord among them, yet their natural strength and durability was somehow being enhanced. She could almost see the flow of vital energy moving back and forth among the raiders with the overseer at its hub.

Had Greht's false Keldons become so strong that his trench-level commanders were now capable of warlord-level magic?

The overseer's shoulder twitched. In response, the two leanest Gathans came out ahead of the others. They split up in a perfectly symmetrical pattern as they approached Radha with their long swords drawn. One circled left and the other right, but Radha stood rock-still, her head positioned precisely to see all the Gathans at once. Only her eyes moved as they shifted between the raiders coming at her.

They attacked simultaneously. Without so much as a glance at each other or a nod from the overseer, the two lanky Gathans both sprang at Radha. Through her haze it seemed she had hours to respond. The one from the left held his sword by his hip, low and angled upward, looking to run Radha through. The one from the right swung his blade in a high, sweeping, overhand chop.

Her left side was useless, indefensible with the arm covering her ribs, so she concentrated on the threat from her right. Dodging the Gathan's chop would be simple but would leave her wide open to the point of the other raider's sword. She could try to twist around the chopper and pull him into his partner's thrust, but such a maneuver required exquisite timing and perfect muscle control, neither of which Radha currently had.

Her options limited, Radha decided to do the least likely thing she could imagine. She dropped Astor's dagger and jerked her other arm off her ribs. Radha grunted in pain as her hands shot to her belt, each ripping free a gleaming silver tear. With the Gathans only a few steps away, Radha threw her arms out and sent a blade spinning end over end toward each of her enemies.

The chopping Gathan on her right stutter-stepped and slid past Radha's blade without losing momentum. The other simply charged through the tumbling blade so that it slashed a deep but nonlethal furrow along his jaw bone.

As she toppled, Radha threw herself to her left. This made her an easy target for the thruster, but the chopper's dodge had taken him totally out of position. His blow missed entirely.

That left Radha free to deal with the raider on her left. If he was surprised or amused by her strange, suicidal move, he gave no sign. He delivered the blow he'd committed to, just as the other had, but this thrust could not help but strike home.

Radha's broken ribs grated painfully against each other as the saber plunged in a few inches above her left hip. She pulled back from the thrust, but the Gathan stepped forward so that the blade continued to penetrate. Radha slapped her hands around the sword, sacrificing the flesh on her palms to slow the saber's progress. She partially succeeded, as only an inch or two of the Gathan's blade emerged on the opposite side.

The raider's muscles tensed as he prepared to shove the sword in to its hilt, but Radha threw herself back. Her tormentor stepped forward again, this time angling his saber so that it would do serious damage even if she succeeded in pulling free. Radha twisted her body and guided the blade with her clasped hands as she hit the ground, so that the protruding tip behind her bit sharply into the rocks. The point skidded slightly as the Gathan thrust down as hard as he could.

Radha gasped as the tip finally caught against the rocks. The blade snapped in two places, an inch from the point and halfway between her hands and the Gathan's. Radha put an arm beneath her and rolled herself away from the enemy.

The raider paused to angrily inspect his sword, part of which was still lodged in Radha. He snorted and cursed at her, raising his broken blade. Radha snarled back, blood dripping from her clenched teeth. He stepped toward her, and Radha plucked the segment of sword from her body, cocked her arm, and hurled it into the center of its former owner's forehead.

No time to celebrate, no time to think. Still halfway between standing and sprawled, Radha now tumbled forward to avoid the whistling sound of the other Gathan's second chop. His sword also bit deep into the rocks in the ground, but this blade remained intact.

Radha rolled up onto her feet, but the pain in her ribs was too much for her to stand. She teetered, lost her balance, then slumped onto her side with her legs folded under her.

With five inches of steel protruding from his face, the first Gathan finally collapsed, falling between Radha and the wild-eyed chopper. The surviving raider changed his grip, ignoring his fallen comrade in favor of glaring at Radha, but the overseer's deep, booming voice called, "Hold."

The chopper lost interest in Radha as if she'd disappeared. He sheathed his sword and stood rock-still.

"Back in line." The overseer was behind her now, standing casually across ten feet of open space. He had had marched the rest of the raiders in close to watch, and now he spread his arms out on each side. The Gathan near Radha sprinted past her and fell in among the rest of the raiders, each of them waiting for their next order.

The overseer glared at Radha. Dark gray vapor steamed from his nose and mouth. She sneered back.

"Well?" she rasped.

She drew another tear-shaped blade with her right hand as she repositioned her left across her abdomen. The left arm was doing double duty now, staunching the deep stab wound as well as holding her broken ribs in place.

The overseer lowered his arms. He lazily lifted his palm so that his bicep bulged. "Fresh whip," he said.

"Understood." One of the Gathans climbed up the lead cart, rummaged around near the driver's seat, and tossed a stout, short-handled scourge to the overseer.

Radha, Teferi's voice came to her, calm and clear-headed. *Your journey can end here, if you like, but I have grander things in mind.*

Radha paused for a moment. It was the planeswalker's voice, as cultured and as self-important as ever. The overseer was still glowering and showing off his new whip. The rest were chuckling at the sad figure she presented or muttering dark threats in their guttural voices.

I liked you better dead, she thought. *You talked less.*

I was never dead, Teferi said, *merely in a state of deep meditation.*

You should try dead. I think it would suit you.

I have been pondering what I learned in the Book of Keld. Teferi went on smoothly. *I have been trying to see how to best make myself understood.*

Radha ignored him and focused on reclaiming the kukri dagger she'd dropped when the two Gathans attacked. She might never find the one she'd stuck in the overseer's head . . . assuming it was still intact . . . but she'd be thrice-damned before she'd abandon this one.

She leaned toward the dagger, stretching her long arm as she tried to keep from overbalancing. She quickly hooked the handle of Astor's weapon with the tip of her metal tear-blade and dragged the kukri to her.

Nearby, the overseer's eyes sparkled with dark joy. His posturing was over; he was ready for her.

Radha, here is what I have learned from my meditation. I won't waste our time by offering a bargain, but I do think it's time I made myself clear.

Radha didn't even have the energy to insult the planeswalker properly. She sheathed her blade and dug the tip of Astor's kukri dagger into the rocks, using it to push herself into an upright sitting position.

The overseer stretched a length of the whip between his hands and said, "Give me some room."

The other raiders backed up, unconsciously clearing a perfect semicircle rimmed with their feral, hungry leers. Carefully, the overseer drew back his arm and sent a lazy, rolling hump along the length of his whip as it stretched out behind him.

Radha got to her knees, still clutching Astor's dagger, her chest rattling and wheezing like an old kettle. The pain in her back and legs was blinding, and though she had to tilt her head like a quizzical bird, Radha stared unwavering into the overseer's eyes.

The Gathan stared right back, but his gaze was diffuse and glassy. Radha squinted, looking closer. Instead of orange flame, there were now tiny pinpricks of blue light in the overseer's pupils. The whip-wielding brute's large, dark eyes vanished behind two growing circles of sapphire. Everything else about the overseer's face remained savage and cruel, but his eyes were now solid blue coins of liquid light. He seemed to Radha some kind of clockwork doll, mindless, lit from within by some arcane engine.

I need to make a point, the overseer said, but it was Teferi's voice and Radha heard it directly in her head. *An example, if you will.* The Gathans must have heard him the same way, because the whole platoon quickly lost the arrogant air of blood-sport spectators and started whispering as they looked nervously at each other.

The overseer turned. His newly acquired scourge glowed red along its entire length. The assembled Gathans grumbled and cursed, openly staring at the strange state of his eyes. Radha saw confusion and disarray in her enemies for the first time, perhaps even fear.

With a gargantuan effort, Radha forced herself up on to one foot, her left knee still folded beneath her. Blood still ran from her lips and she was half-mad with pain, but there was no way she was going to miss this.

But Teferi was not waiting for her. *Any three will do*, he said, speaking through the overseer's lips. The Gathan commander's face was still fixed in a cruel smirk, frozen and immobile, but his arm licked out three times in rapid succession.

From the semicircle of raiders, every third one shrieked or gasped before staggering back with his hands clapped to his face. The overseer's mouth opened wide and stayed that way as Teferi's voice rang out over the campsite.

Hark ye, children of this cold, hard place, he said. *Be you Keldon, Gathan, Skyshroud, or anything in between, take heed: I am Teferi, planeswalker, and I am trying to save your world.*

It does not matter that you do not care. I care, and I am weary of treating you bad-mannered adolescents as adults and getting only violence and abuse for my patience.

I have tried to speak to you in your own language, your own idiom, but I fear I have not made myself plain, so I will try again, using terms even you cannot misinterpret.

The three freshly lashed raiders had all stepped back into formation during Teferi's address. Their whip-torn faces were ragged and bleeding, but the wounds were also glowing pale orange in the gloom.

The overseer's sightless eyes scanned the line of raiders. His mouth remained wide open. Through him, Teferi said, *Now.*

The overseer raised his whip just high enough for the handle to clear his own head. Casually, he brought it down with a small crack, sending up a dry plume of dust and rocks near his feet.

In direct response, each of the lashed Gathan raiders exploded into a steaming shower of meat, mist, and red-hot embers. The others scurried to get clear of the triple-part blast. Though their faces were pale and awe-struck, they did not cry out.

Teferi's voice rose again, freezing the Gathans in place. *Return to your master, the Warlord Greht. Tell him Teferi Planeswalker says, "Greht will not have his armada this year. Nor the next. Nor ever, unless Teferi allows it."*

His voice grew louder, more dire, and the ground shook from the sound. *There will be no more trees felled in Skyshroud, no more villagers press-ganged into combat. Teferi Planeswalker is the new King of Keld, and any warlord who wants to run a 'host here will do so only with Teferi's blessing, or he will face Teferi's wrath.*

Now get out of my sight.

The Gathans stood motionless, unblinking. The overseer's whip flicked out again and burst another raider into smoking fragments where he stood. This time those who stood beside the victim did roar, though Radha could not say if it was shock or rage that moved their tongues.

I said "now."

To hammer the point home, the overseer now twirled his whip overhead, creating a huge loop of glowing red in the air above him. When the sound of the lash cutting the air was loud enough to sting Radha's ears, the overseer's arm shot straight up. The end of his whip rocketed skyward and cracked, its sharp end aglow and sparkling. The whip's own weight carried it gently back down, falling through the icy air to land on the overseer's head. The Gathan commander went up in a loud clap of thunder, a huge cloud of fire, and a ghastly shower of blood.

The remaining Gathans broke and ran. They abandoned the carts and the slaves, knowing Greht valued those potential ships far more than the lives of the convoy escorts. They would all most likely have their throats cut as soon as they delivered their strange report, but right now their fear of Teferi was more immediate.

Moments later, Radha was alone in the Gathan camp. No one else was alive, as she didn't count the draught slaves still huddled in their pen. That state of splendid isolation ended suddenly as Teferi materialized in front of her.

He was no longer dressed in his yellow and white robes of state and he had abandoned the gaudy hat. He was wearing a smart, well-tailored set of robes that were blue and white with a metallic diagonal checkerboard motif. He didn't look angry, but neither did he look as jovial and benevolent as he had before. When he spoke, his voice had none of the smug, playful tone Radha had come to expect.

Teferi extended his hand. "Join me," he said.

Radha grunted. She struggled once more to get to her feet but her muscles wouldn't hold.

"Dagger," she said. Her words were clipped and painful and the less she said the less often the world went gray.

"You have it in your hand."

"Other one."

Teferi's eyes flashed as he scanned the area. "It's not here. One of the Gathans must have pocketed it before he ran off."

Radha stared at Teferi through one half-open eye. "Lying?"

"No."

"Bastard." Radha sagged back onto her seat. Her head rolled to the side, but she jerked it back upright before she overbalanced.

"Did good," she said quietly. "With the whip. Thanks."

"Radha," Teferi spoke coolly, sharply. "Join me. Accompany me on my travels, assist me in my endeavors, answer my questions, and obey my commands."

Radha rose back up to one knee. "Or?" she said.

"Or nothing. Literally nothing, Radha of Skyshroud. If I cannot undo what I have done, if I cannot replace what I removed. . . ." Teferi spread his arms out, and as he spoke the things he described appeared as pale blue visions above him. "All of this will spread. The withered mountains, the dying forest, the saprolings, the slivers, the Gathans. All of this slow, lingering death will expand and deepen. Everything will continue to degrade and decline, then it will all collapse in on itself and everything will die.

"I have seen this, as surely as you see me." He pushed his hand closer. "I will waste no more time here. What is your answer?"

Radha inhaled as deeply as she could. She ground her teeth together and slowly, painfully, rose to her feet. When the jagged tingling sensation in her chest and the back of her head receded, she took another breath and said, "Does . . . does the *Book of Keld* . . . tell you why the Gathans are always stronger than I am?"

Teferi nodded.

"And you'll tell me . . . if I help you."

"No bargains, Radha. You either help me or you don't. Either way you must live with the consequences."

"Ahh," she growled impatiently. "Stuff it. It'll do for now."

Excellent. If you prefer, you may address me this way until we can get your wounds treated.

Not interested. Radha sheathed her grandfather's dagger. *I am with you for now, but as soon as I learn the secret, I'm bringing it back here to burn Greht's bones black.*

Teferi nodded. He extended his hand again. Radha stared at it for a moment, then into Teferi's eyes. He held her gaze without wavering.

Radha took his hand. She felt the sensation of slipping sideways through the world, and then she was gone.

CHAPTER 12

Teferi took Radha back to the Skyshroud valley. Freyalise's advice about 'walking carefully near the rift was well-taken, but he was slowly coming to grips with it. It was akin to steering a ship through dangerous reefs while fighting a high wind and a strong current—dangerous and unpredictable but manageable if you paid careful attention to every detail.

Jhoira and the Shivan warriors were waiting. It was clear from the look on Jhoira's face that she would be asking things soon, and she wouldn't be satisfied with flip half-answers.

"We have returned," Teferi called, though it was completely unnecessary.

Jhoira and the others were already crossing the valley to meet them. The Shivans seemed suspicious of Radha, especially the viashino, but the Keldon elf was so calm and tranquil that Teferi stole a glance to make sure she was still conscious.

She was, but she was also still very badly injured, bleeding from her side and cradling her injured ribs. Radha watched the Shivans approach with a smile so placid that Teferi found it somewhat disturbing.

"Is she friendly now?" Aprem asked.

He and Dassene came within ten feet of Radha and stopped, but the viashino came much closer. They stepped out and stood on either side of the recently arrived pair, their vertical pupils opened wide and fixed on Radha. Corus bore a rough bandage on his scaly throat. He hissed at Radha. She smiled.

"She is," Teferi said. "And she has agreed to join my service, the same as you four. If anyone bears grudges, now is the time to air them or put them aside. Either way, they are not to interfere with work from this point on. I want no more blood shed among ourselves."

"I have a grudge," Corus said. "And it won't be settled until I take a chunk out of her as big as the one she took out of me."

"You're alone there," Dassene said. She held up her bandaged hand that had lost two fingers to a Gathan blade. "She saved my behind back there. I'm her friend for life."

Radha flashed her teeth at Dassene. Then she turned to Corus and tilted her chin back. As she exposed her throat, Radha also put her hand on the remaining kukri dagger in her belt.

"Come on then, scaly," she said. "Take a bite."

Skive laughed. "Run through, half bled-out, and she still wants to fight." His needle-sharp teeth glistened as his lips pulled back into a smile. "She looks like an elf but acts like a Keldon."

Radha lowered her chin. "A Keldon like no other." She continued to hold her square-toothed grin at Corus.

The big viashino crossed his arms, his sharp tongue flickering in and out. "Never mind. Just stop calling me 'scaly' and we'll call it even."

Radha nodded. "Done. What shall I call you?" She looked around at the Shivans. "Who are you people, anyway?"

Aprem bowed and introduced himself, but Dassene pushed past him and loudly swore a Ghitu oath of battlefield gratitude. The viashino still held back. Teferi was looking forward to seeing how the warriors sorted all this out. Jhoira stepped in front of him.

"Hello, my friend," he said. "Believe it or not, we're making progress."

"You said we should air all grudges here and now. I have one."

"I thought you might."

Jhoira shook her head to cut short his frivolous banter before it built up any momentum. "Who is she?"

"She is Radha. By blood she is both Keldon and Skyshroud elf. She believes her grandfather was the great warlord Astor, a hero of the Phyrexian Invasion."

Jhoira looked skeptical. "True?"

"Who can say? I never met the man personally. Radha definitely has Keldon blood, so it might as well be Astor's."

"Hmm. And you recruited her why?"

"Because she is necessary. She is the only being we've seen so far who has a strong and reliable supply of mana. Not even Freyalise can draw much from the land here, nor I, and that's largely because it simply doesn't exist. Keld is as dead and dry as a fallow field, and Skyshroud barely survives because of its patron, but Radha has all the mana she needs, and more, whenever she wants it."

"That makes her unique," Jhoira said, "not necessary."

Teferi hesitated. He didn't want to speculate until he had more time to observe Radha, but something about Jhoira's quiet intensity told him an educated guess was better than a witty rejoinder.

"Radha was born on the Skyshroud rift," he said.

He gestured behind him and the jagged tear in reality over the forest became visible to mortal eyes, soaring high into the sunless afternoon sky. The phenomenon straddled the transplanted forest so that Skyshroud appeared ready to fall into a vast canyon of solid smoke.

Nearby, Radha had moved back to the edge of the forest. The spell that protected Freyalise's children was already beginning to heal her injuries, but it was an accelerated natural process rather than instant-results magic. She was slowly regaining her strength as her wounds closed and her bones knit. Dassene and

Skive accompanied her, but all of the warriors fell silent as the rift appeared overhead . . . even Radha stared at the display in open-mouthed wonder.

Teferi shifted from words to thoughts in order to keep his conversation with Jhoira private. *Freyalise says the rift draws all of the local mana into itself, leeching it from the surrounding environment. I believe Radha gets her mana from that rift, drawing from it the way it draws from Keld. She wasn't even born when the rift formed, but she is bound to it the way Keldons are bound to Keld, or Shivans to Shiv. The rift is her true home. It is her anchor to this world and the source of her magic.*

Jhoira turned this over in her head for a moment then said, "How does this tie back to Shiv's return?"

Teferi winced a little at the sound of her voice. *There is almost certainly a similar rift over Shiv and Zhalfir, as well as several other places around the world where global-scale magic was employed or transplanar events took place. This time rift problem may be even more extensive than we thought. It's entirely possible that every planeswalk to and from Dominaria since the dawn of time has created a miniature version of the phenomenon we see here. There could be millions of these time rifts throughout the multiverse. I plan to start with the larger ones and work my way down.*

"You make it sound like the entire universe has become structurally unsound."

I'm glad to hear it. That's what I truly think has happened.

"Shiv's return will be the nudge that pushes everything past the breaking point."

At this point, that's one of the only things I am completely sure of.

Jhoira nodded. She replied with her thoughts this time. *So you're finally ready to take us home?*

Not quite. Not just yet. Jhoira opened her mouth to speak, but

Teferi quickly added, *We must first make one more stop along the way at the Burning Isles. The Phyrexians sent their mountain Stronghold there just as they sent the Skyshroud forest. There was no planeswalker to divert the Stronghold, however, so it landed on target.*

Jhoira did not look pleased. *In Urborg, you mean.*

Yes. In Urborg.

Hardly "on the way" to Shiv.

Everywhere is "on the way" when you travel with a planeswalker. Unable to help himself, Teferi winked. *Besides, it's also on the way if you go by boat . . . and you go the long way around.*

Jhoira's face remained impassive. *What do you expect to find in Urborg when we reach the Stronghold?*

I expect to find a phenomenon like this one. I also expect to find the Urborg equivalent of her, he turned and pointed to Radha, *a native who is connected to the Stronghold rift and can draw mana from it.*

Realization dawned on Jhoira's face, but it was accompanied by a lingering shadow of doubt. *There could be a Shivan equivalent as well, someone who was born on the section we left behind with an innate connection to the Shivan rift.* She paused. *Assuming it exists and that any of these rifts have any degree of commonality.*

Exactly. Teferi smiled, grateful for Jhoira's quick grasp of the situation.

But then . . . why not go directly to Shiv and examine the rift there? And the people, for that matter?

Because the Phyrexians moved Skyshroud and the Stronghold. They helped make the rift that fuels Radha. We should look at the other rifts they made to find commonalities.

Jhoira's face darkened. *The Phyrexians made rifts all over Dominaria. Will Shiv have to wait until you've searched every one?*

Absolutely not. Urborg is our final detour. I promise you: whatever we find at the Stronghold, we will continue directly to Shiv.

Jhoira nodded, somewhat mollified. *How long do we have?*

Teferi's smile tightened. *A matter of days.*

Days? I thought weeks.

You were *right, but there were variables that I had no way of knowing about. . . .* He thought of Karona and the sudden absence and abrupt return of Dominaria's magic.

Teferi suddenly spoke aloud. "Time flowed differently in your workshop," he said. "While we were there, a magical catastrophe happened in a place called Otaria."

Jhoira stood and stared. Teferi knew she was waiting for him to continue, but the words were flattening his tongue.

"We've been gone three hundred years," he said at last. "There was a second world-wide magical war barely a century or so after the Phyrexian Invasion. Ultimately, that war and the extra time we missed are the reasons Dominaria is so haggard and Shiv is coming back on its own."

His friend said nothing for a while. She looked off, away from Teferi and the forest behind him. Her lips twitched, a sure sign that she was running figures in her head.

"I see," she said, "so we go quickly to Urborg and then on to Shiv. Are you certain you can 'walk us there safely?"

"I am."

"Then we should go." Jhoira turned and strode toward the warriors at the treeline.

"Jhoira," Teferi called. He floated to her side and landed just in front of her. "I'm trying to keep you informed, I truly am, but there's so much happening that I can't tell what's important. Please," he said, "I don't mean to keep secrets. I'll tell you all I know if you'll tell me what's important."

Jhoira appraised his earnest expression and heartfelt words with a cold, clinical eye. She glanced over Teferi's shoulder at the Shivans and said quietly, "Why are you wearing Tolarian robes?"

Teferi shrugged as if nothing could be less important. "I was dealing with berserkers," he said. "Playing the glib diplomat was getting me nowhere. I opted for the more practical, goal-oriented look." He smiled guiltily. "Plus, Radha embarrassed me. I felt I was being made a fool of, so I reverted back to my academy days, when I was the one who did the fool-making."

Jhoira frowned. "You opted for a look that echoed Gatha's. You dressed yourself as a Tolarian scholar in the hope it would impress or intimidate the raiders he helped create."

"That did cross my mind," he said, "but it didn't work. They didn't even see me."

"But I can, and I don't like it. Teferi the court mage is devious and secretive, but Teferi the academic is just plain reckless."

"Is that all?"

The air around Teferi shimmered. When it cleared, he was not dressed as a goal-oriented academic or a glad-handing court mage, but as a simple Zhalfirin wizard in fine white linen with blue accents. He wore a square headdress that covered his bald pate and his shoulders and once more he carried the curved, spinelike staff.

Jhoira did not comment on the change. Instead she looked once more past Teferi to the edge of the forest. Radha was there, standing tall once more, her arms both hanging freely at her sides.

"Your necessary addition to the party seems fully healed," Jhoira said.

"Excellent. Then we can go—"

"I want to talk to her," Jhoira said.

"Oh?" Teferi's interest was piqued. "Why?"

"Because she's a Keldon. Because she's already injured one of us."

"Corus very graciously let that pass."

"That's Corus satisfied then. My name is Jhoira."

"Please," Teferi said. He felt his smile growing strained. "I have extracted a vow of loyalty from her. It was a very trying and laborious process. You must trust me to—"

"Must I? Then we have problem, old friend." She stopped and looked at him coldly. "This isn't about the rifts, or Radha, or the missing time. It's about you keeping your hidden agenda hidden from me, because that's the unpredictable element here that's going to get us all killed."

Teferi stopped, his face a perfect study in forlorn regret. Jhoira didn't see it, however, as she had already begun crossing the valley without glancing back.

* * * * *

Jhoira marched up behind Aprem and Dassene, who were facing Radha.

"Warrior," she said to the Keldon elf, "we need to prepare you for the journey."

Radha rolled her neck. "Shoo, child. Adults are talking. Go back to your lessons and your long-winded mentor."

Jhoira's cheeks flushed. She tapped each Ghitu warrior on the shoulder and said, "Step aside, please."

Aprem moved back without a word, but Dassene hesitated. "Ma'am," Dassene started.

"I said step aside." Dassene did, and Jhoira stood almost face to face with Radha. The Keldon elf was far larger than she was, taller, broader, and longer. Jhoira stood staring up at Radha, their eyes locked.

"Corus," Jhoira called. She raised her hand high overhead. "Toss me your blade."

"Ma'am," Dassene said again, urgently.

"I know what I'm doing," Jhoira said, and Radha doesn't, she added to herself. She opened and closed her hand impatiently, urging Corus to comply.

"Incoming," Corus said.

Jhoira heard a whirling sound. Corus's Ghitu dagger dropped point-first into the cold, hard ground beside her. Jhoira continued to stare at Radha as she bent and pulled the blade free.

"That's a good knife," Radha said, somehow making the casual compliment sound like an ominous threat.

Jhoira nodded. Corus's curved weapon was as heavy and long as a short sword, so Jhoira cradled it casually so Radha would not see how hard it was to hold up. Still holding Radha's fierce eyes, Jhoira extended Corus's weapon, half-presenting it to her and half-threatening her with it. Normally, this much eye contact with a Keldon warrior was suicidal. If you looked away, they took you for a weakling and treated you like one. If you didn't look away, they took it as a challenge and killed you for it.

But Radha saw Jhoira as a mere young girl with an oversized knife in her hands. It already confused the Keldon elf, having such a laughable opponent show so little fear, so little hostility . . . so little interest. There wasn't much that could distract a berserker in mid-confrontation, but the incongruity between the Ghitu's eyes and the rest of her made Radha hesitate.

Jhoira's voice rang out before Radha had a chance to regain the initiative. "We are Ghitu from Shiv. We make metal. We seek it out all across the wasteland, we scratch it from the blasted ground, we heat and hammer it in our forges. We work it and hone it into blades like this one." She rotated Corus's knife so that it glinted in Radha's eyes. "I'm glad you appreciate the craftsmanship. Do you forge, Keldon?"

"No," Radha said, a touch defensively.

"Fire and metal," Jhoira continued. "Ghitu lives are built on fire and metal, and we also use them to make war. Do you know battle magic, Keldon? Ghitu fire, hot from the desert?"

"No, little girl, I don't." Radha's face had split into a wide-eyed grin. She didn't understand where this was going, but she was enjoying the ride. "Show me."

"This is Ghitu magic," Jhoira said. "This is Ghitu sacrament." She opened her hands. Wordlessly, Aprem and Dassene each took hold and the gems at their throats shone red.

The cry started with Jhoira, deep in the back of her throat. It quickly spread to her tribe-mates, the sound simultaneously booming and piercing, hard and sharp as Ghitu voices combined and blistered the ears of everyone nearby.

Much like the Gathan's colos horn had enhanced the raiders, the Ghitu war cry flooded Jhoira, Aprem, and Dassene with power. All three shared a dusty red glow and a predatory gleam in their eyes. They smoked and sparked along the tops of their heads and shoulders as if they were about to burst into flame themselves.

Radha stared, half-hypnotized. Jhoira called out to her.

"That's an excellent weapon you carry. Did you make it?"

Radha kept staring, but her eyes were starting to waver. "The dagger belonged to my ancestor. The tears I made myself." She smiled and some of her bluster returned. "Care to see one up close?"

"No. Did you forge them or file down existing blades?"

Radha blinked, now visibly baffled. "I filed them down," she said. "One Gathan broadsword gets me three, maybe four tears."

Jhoira smiled, allowing Radha to see she was impressed. "How many have you made?"

"Dozens," Radha said.

Jhoira spread her arms out, gesturing to Aprem and Dassene. "See," Jhoira she said, through her distant, heat-distorted voice. "We have much in common, Ghitu and Keldon. An appreciation of fine weaponry, a devotion to fire. We are all creatures of flame, metal, and magic, so I expect you to understand what I'm about to say."

"I don't know what you and he agreed to," Jhoira turned and gestured to Teferi, "but remember this while you travel with us. We are warriors, but we are not Keldons. This is not your warhost.

You will not strike us down for looking at you or casually lop off ears and fingers to get our attention. You will not bite our throats out because we bar your path. We are your comrades, Radha. Do not make us your enemies."

With that, Jhoira opened her hands and ended the connection between she, Dassene, and Aprem. Still holding Radha's eyes in her own, Jhoira tossed Corus's dagger back over her head.

"Clear?" she said.

"Thank you," came Corus's voice.

A flicker of amusement ran across Radha's face, but she nodded and said, "Understood."

"We're going to Urborg," Jhoira declared. "One last stop before we reach Shiv. If we're lucky, we'll find nothing and won't stay long. If we aren't lucky . . ." she gestured at Radha,

". . . we might find another one like her."

Radha barked out a short, harsh laugh. "In your dreams, little doyenne. I'm one of a kind."

"Indeed." Jhoira nodded to her and the Shivans, then she turned and stomped back across the valley to Teferi.

"If we only have a few days," she said. "We should leave now."

"Capital," Teferi said. Jhoira was gratified to see that she'd made her point with Teferi as well as Radha. She had so far allowed him to rush her along because the situation was so urgent and their plans so half-formed . . . but she was starting to suspect that he had already planned the endgame, and that he hadn't told her about it yet because she would certainly try to stop it.

"Shivans," Teferi called grandly, "and Radha. We are leaving."

He was careful to keep from looking at Jhoira as his face screwed up in concentration. Working carefully against the interference from the Skyshroud rift, Teferi extended his aura around the others and sealed them up with him in a wide, bright ball of eldritch blue.

CHAPTER 13

The Burning Isles were more than seven thousand nautical miles from Keld. With Teferi's help, Jhoira and the others made it there in a matter of seconds.

Jhoira's vision went blue-white in transit but quickly cleared as they all materialized. She and Teferi were in front with the warriors fanned out behind them. There was no doubt this time about being in the proper place, as the mountainous Stronghold dominated the horizon. It was a huge wedge of dark rock that pierced the uniform ceiling of blood red clouds and black smoke overhead.

"Welcome to Urborg," Teferi said.

"Phaugh," Radha replied. "It reeks of sulfur rot."

The stench was in fact remarkable, a choking mix of rancid oil, rotten meat, and boiling lye. Jhoira covered her mouth and nose with her robe's wide collar. Teferi didn't need to breathe, and the viashino simply closed their nostrils and kept their tongues behind clenched teeth, but soon everyone else had put a hand or a filtering piece of cloth over their face to keep out the choking vapor. Skive and Corus also lowered their thick, translucent inner eyelids, giving them a milky sheen.

Teferi had placed them on a small hillock that rose from the center of a churning lake of tar. The gummy black marsh was choked with the shattered hulls of ships and floating metal debris. Every viscous bubble that rose to the surface and popped let out a waft of greenish-yellow gas, and these fumes blackened and melted any solid thing they touched.

Jhoira looked up at the Stronghold and said to Teferi, "Do you see a rift?"

Teferi nodded. He was also staring up at the jagged black mountain fortress, his eyes glowing white. "It's there," he said, "but it's not the same."

"Is it affecting Radha? Is she attuned to it, or it to her?"

Teferi frowned. "Can't say," he muttered, "but if I had to guess I'd say 'no.' "

"Show us the rift, please." Teferi nodded, still fixed on the Stronghold. Jhoira called out to the others, "Look to the mountain."

The warriors did as she asked. The top of Teferi's staff glowed and he tapped it on the hillock, producing a metallic clang. As it had above Skyshroud, the Stronghold rift appeared, looming over and around the black mountain.

This phenomenon was not a gentle, flowing canyon of smoke. The Stronghold rift was round, for one, and its insides were a violent, swirling mass of dust and electrical discharge. The flickering light was bright purple, like a half-healed bruise, and often two jags of it would spear out from the edges, meet in the middle, and cancel each other out.

All of the others stared up at the strange vortex, but Jhoira watched Teferi, who was watching Radha. The planeswalker was studying her closely, scanning her for something. Whatever telling detail he sought hadn't revealed itself yet, for Radha's reaction to the rift was no different from the rest of the party's: a touch of confusion, but mostly a warrior's determination in the face of an unfamiliar threat.

Jhoira turned back to the Stronghold. If she concentrated she could almost make out the details of a flickering image inside the rift. It appeared similar to the landscape and horizon surrounding the Stronghold, but this other Urborg was covered in a crackling layer of black machinery. Every tree, every hill, every valley, and every bog was coated with wire, rivets, and tiny clockwork motors.

"The mountain," Radha said. Her voice was low and tight. "It shines."

Jhoira looked closer. The twisted mirror image inside the rift had expanded to include the Stronghold itself. Rather than the lifeless rock that was actually there, Jhoira saw a Stronghold aglow from within, spewing a column of silver-white light from its peak. The entire red-black sky seemed to bend itself around this column's edges, the perpetual cloud cover swirling like an over-stirred bowl.

Teferi tapped his staff on the ground again and the Stronghold rift faded from view. "We should investigate it up close," he said, "and I swear we will not linger any longer than is necessary."

"Suits me," Corus muttered.

Jhoira pulled her view away from the swirling charnel clouds above the black mountain. Teferi's glowing staff and Dassene's flaming baton lit up the area around them, so Jhoira had her first clear look at the swamp they now occupied. With it, her stomach went cold.

The debris floating in the tar was not wreckage from the metal ships or random pieces of shrapnel but distinct Phyrexian body parts. There were at least a hundred of the mechanical monstrosities, all broken apart into a charnel mash of skulls, limbs, cutting blades, and crushing pincers.

Most of these metal bones had been picked clean by scavengers or by the caustic bog, but there were enough with visible muscle tissue and gobbets of rotten flesh to make Jhoira extremely uncomfortable. The Phyrexians were regenerative and cannibalistic—if a single living piece found its way to this fetid graveyard, it could conceivably absorb all of the wreckage and reconstitute itself as a gigantic amalgamation of random parts.

Dassene and Aprem seemed to share her concerns. "Are they all dead?" Aprem asked.

"They are," Teferi said. "I brought us here specifically because it was lifeless, but it won't be safe indefinitely. We shouldn't stay."

Radha looked with disgust upon the muck between where they stood and the Stronghold. "Are we supposed to slog through this stuff all the way there?"

"Not at all. This is as close to the rift as I dare planeswalk, but I have other ways of transporting us."

He stretched his staff out and a flat panel of blue formed under their feet. It lifted them into the air, and though Jhoira could see it was no thicker than a scrap of parchment, the blue field felt as solid and as stable as a castle's stone foundation. This strange conveyance gathered speed as it skimmed just inches over the surface of the tar swamp.

Even without having to walk, it promised to be a wearying trip across the smoking bog. Between clusters of toxic fumes dotted with the remains of Phyrexian monstrosities, the unbroken marsh was a fairly monotonous backdrop for the first long leg of their survey. Jhoira saw clusters of trees and other vegetation in the distance, but they were indistinct in the haze.

"What is this place?" Radha asked.

She sat hunched and cross-legged at the forward edge of their platform, moodily resting her elbows on her knees. Jhoira felt an unexpected wave of sympathy for the fierce Keldon elf. Radha was a creature of the forest and a disciple of fire, so for her the pervasive decay and sodden, poisonous ground must be like several hells at once.

Jhoira had been reviewing what she knew about the Burning Isles ever since Teferi mentioned them outside Skyshroud. She had a lot of information to share, but she was quite certain none of it would answer Radha's question.

Teferi, who had all the information Jhoira had and then some, came to a different conclusion. "The Burning Isles," he said, in his most engaging lecture tone, "sit above the most volcanically active area in the entire world. Urborg and Bogarden are the two largest and most important islands in the chain."

"Bogarden." Radha perked up at the name, recognizing it from Astor's tomb.

"Yes, I think you'd like Bogarden. There is something of a fetish for Bogarden spells and artifacts among Keldons, or at least, there was in my time. Your own tattoos," he tapped his own forearm and gestured to the designs snaking up Radha's arms, "are from Bogarden designs."

"We're not going there," Jhoira added gently, "so don't ask."

Radha shrugged, unconcerned.

"Bogarden is rich in potent fire mana, but Urborg is notorious for swamp magic. In the time leading up to the Phyrexian Invasion, the swamps here were home to a ghastly array of zombies, nightgaunts, and other fell creatures. Urborg's magic fueled the schemes of necromancers and lich lords for centuries, earning it a dark and terrible reputation throughout the world.

"Everything changed during the Invasion, of course. Urborg was subject to a series of staggering arcane forces that altered its very nature. Phyrexia transplanted an entire mountain, complete with a conquering army and some of the most powerful magical machinery every built. They tried to establish a stranglehold on Urborg's mana, but one of nature's greatest champions conjured a lush, green forest. He balanced the consumptive energy of the swamp with the restorative force of the forest. Dominaria's defenders eventually destroyed the invaders, but the transplanted mountain Stronghold remained, a baleful monument to one of the darkest trials of the war."

Teferi fell silent. Radha sat for a few moments, the wind blowing her hair back from her face. She turned to Jhoira with a puzzled, impatient look on her face.

"What is this place?" she said again.

"These days," Jhoira said, "it's a war zone. The forest battles the swamp, the swamp battles the forest, and Phyrexian corpses poison it all. It's dangerous no matter what we find. Urborg was full of horrors before the war. I can't even guess what it's full of now."

Radha nodded. She hunched back over her knees and somberly watched the black sludge below them.

Teferi folded his arms around his staff and looked at Jhoira from the corner of his eye. "My answer was a lot more factually accurate," he said.

"But it didn't actually answer her question." Jhoira stepped closer to Teferi. He was watching the Stronghold as it grew closer and Jhoira gestured to it. "Do you see anything we can use?"

Teferi shook his head. "Not yet." He blinked and turned to face his friend. "There is something, a minor ripple, a small fluctuation. Someone is using Phyrexian powerstones between here and our destination."

"Remnant from the Phyrexian Invasion?" Jhoira knew all about powerstones, the durable crystals that could be infused with an almost limitless supply of mana. She used to make them herself, back when she was still attached to the Tolarian Academy. Phyrexians used their version in all of their living war machines, so a functioning powerstone in Urborg could mean that the invaders were not all dead and gone.

"Possibly," Teferi said, "but it's a small stone. Whatever is running on it won't be too hard to shut down."

Jhoira relaxed. "Good. I'd rather not have to re-fight the battle of Urborg."

"I would," Radha said. "I'd like to kill one of those Phyrexians."

"No, you wouldn't." Jhoira shook her head. "Believe me, you really wouldn't."

Radha glowered. "I say I would."

"You don't even know what a Phyrexian is."

Radha cocked her head quizzically. "So?"

This is why I prefer to talk to you this way, Teferi's thoughts said. He was smiling, though, his tone light and his face relaxed, almost amused.

Jhoira allowed herself to return the smile. Teferi's shifting appearance and secretive behavior were still concerns . . . as were the real reasons for Radha's presence and the entire suspect detour to Urborg . . . but at least they were one step closer to Shiv. It was also encouraging that Teferi had planeswalked from one rift to another without incident and that no one had attacked them yet. Jhoira didn't know the size, shape, or character of modern Urborg's denizens, but she knew a group of strange warriors on a blue carpet of light would be a tempting target for all sorts of creatures.

Teferi started as if he's heard a sharp noise. "Trouble," he said.

Jhoira peered out into the darkness. "Phyrexians?"

"Maybe. There was a surge of powerstone energy, but it died out. Now there seem to be a large number of . . . violent-minded things converging on the site of the surge."

"Things." Jhoira frowned. "Can you be more specific?"

"Not yet." Teferi turned and faced the right side of the platform. It slowly corrected its course until it was going where he was looking. "Live things, anyway, not machines." He turned. "Cheer up, Radha. We're leaving Urborg's swamps behind."

Jhoira looked ahead to their new destination. With a growing sense of unease she added, "Headed for Urborg's forests."

The Keldon elf straightened up, opening her eyes wide. As they skimmed toward the largest clump of black, moss-encrusted trees ahead, Radha tilted her head back and sniffed the air.

"Phaugh," she spat.

Jhoira nodded. "I entirely agree."

Teferi glanced from Radha to Jhoira, his eyes crinkled with mirth.

"Hold your noses," he said to the larger group, "and draw your weapons. I think we're about to see something new."

CHAPTER 14

Venser worked furiously, prying at the damaged access panel with a pronged metal tool. He had already retrieved the first stone from the opposite side of the device and now he just had to recover the second. As usual, he had to work as quickly as possible, as it was literally a matter of life and death.

It had been a very successful trail, his most successful yet. The device had not worked precisely the way he expected but it had worked. Part of the engine was fused and the steering mechanism was cracked, but that all happened after the trip was over. In terms of taking him from a starting point to a destination, it was the best he'd ever done.

The panel popped off and splashed into the watery bog. A multifaceted gem about the size of his fist sat inside the square housing, emitting a dim but steady yellow light. Venser checked all around to make sure he was alone then urgently began prying the powerstone loose.

It was the best he'd managed yet, but it still left him stranded outside the safety of his compound. The gladehunters hadn't come yet, but Venser's arrival had been bright and loud enough to attract them. Hells, simply firing up the engine was enough to attract them. Windgrace's raiders hated all magical machinery and were constantly on the prowl for artifacts to destroy and artificers to devour. They would rip Venser to pieces simply for being human and in their territory. He didn't like to think what they'd do if they found him operating his blasphemous (to their way of thinking) device.

The powerstone came free and Venser caught it in his palm. It was cold for such a significant energy source, and he quickly stashed it alongside its twin in a pouch on his tool belt. He took one last look at the strange, thronelike contraption he had assembled, sorry to leave it behind but confident he could return for it later. If not, he would simply rebuild it as he had a dozen times before by scavenging pieces from the swamp. So long as he had an endless supply of spare parts and his powerstones, he could build and test as many artifact machines as he liked.

Something clicked and whistled nearby. Venser quickly ducked around the device, putting it between himself and the sound. Hiding wouldn't help him much against the gladehunters, but it would keep him alive longer than running.

They emerged from the black-leafed trees and red-berried thorn bushes, their huge spiked legs stabbing into the moist ground. The four dire creatures were unlike any he'd seen before, but each bore the distinctive gladehunter mark somewhere on their bodies. There were four in all, each twice as tall as Venser, each capable of biting him in half with a single snap of their serrated jaws.

Two looked like a kind of lobster-mantis hybrid, skittering on four spearlike legs as they cradled their huge, clawed forelimbs in front of them. Their rear legs kept their bodies stable and clear of the muck, while their thoraxes bent vertical at the waist so that their heads and shoulders were almost level with the trees.

The other two were similar multi-legged insects, but they were definitely not mantises. Each was a boulder-sized wedge of sharp-shelled armor that floated forward on flexible, whiplike limbs. They each had two tails lashing from their anterior ends and crested ridges on their shoulders that put Venser in mind of vestigial wings. He counted himself lucky that these two couldn't fly or, he corrected himself, weren't flying yet.

The quartet of gladehunters stopped at the edge of the clearing and sniffed the area. All four quickly oriented on Venser's machine. If they held true to the credo of their master, these fearsome creatures would reduce the device to splinters and scrap. Anyone they found inside or nearby would receive similar treatment and would be added to the mound of wreckage they'd leave behind as a warning to anyone else who brought artifice into their woods.

Lord Windgrace's agents were not evil or bloodthirsty, but they were mindless, cunning, and ruthless, like well-trained but vicious attack dogs. The insect-things wouldn't ask him what he was doing or try to convert him away from his blasphemous ways; they would simply eviscerate him and flatten his abominable machine because that is what they did.

Venser's mind raced. He needed a way out and he needed not to be seen. He couldn't outrun or outfight the gladehunters with what he had on him. Nothing on his belt qualified as a weapon against such creatures. Even the stones, the most dynamic of his tools, were worthless without a machine to drive. Inside a golem or a mechanized spear gun, the stones would absolutely save him from these enemies, but for now they were little more than shiny rocks.

Venser tensed, gathering his nerve for a headlong rush toward his compound. If he waited until they started wrecking the device, they might be distracted long enough for him to reach the dense trees. He knew every inch of this area, and with enough of a head start he might just stay ahead of them all the way home. It wasn't much of a plan, but it was the best he could do under the circumstances.

Stand still, a man's voice told him. *Don't run until I say.*

Venser's heart began beating faster and cold sweat formed on the back of his neck. Magic was often used to subjugate the mind in Urborg, and Venser had lived in Urborg all his life. To him, someone else's voice in one's head was more alarming than waking up with a poisonous snake coiled on your face, its fangs dripping and aimed at your eyes.

Just relax, the man said. *And keep your head down.*

Venser tried to control his breathing. The voice was very friendly and soothing, though Venser did not feel soothed.

A whirling wheel of flame erupted from the left of the gladehunters, spinning toward them like a saw blade. The insects scattered out of its path, the mantises lunging left and the other two lunging right. Venser took a single step away from the machine toward the safety of the trees, but the man's voice stopped him.

Wait for it, the playful voice said.

A bolt of red-orange fire ripped into the mantis gladehunters. Venser heard an awful, ear-splitting shriek as one of the insects rose high on a single pair of legs, covered in flames from its head to its waist. The other mantis shielded itself with its scimitarlike forelimb, which shunted most of the blast aside. That limb burned as the gladehunter lowered it, and the monster thrust it angrily under the surface of the murky water. Its head flicked back and forth as it searched for its tormentor.

The voice said, *All right, now run*, and Venser did, sprinting to the nearest sturdy tree and pressing his back against the opposite side. He closed his eyes and caught his breath before peering around to watch the battle unfold.

The stranger pair of gladehunters were positioned side by side, one facing the source of the fire wheel and the other that of the flaming bolt. Venser saw huge, multifaceted eyes glittering just above the point of their wedge-shaped heads and heard jagged horizontal mandibles clicking together. Four sharp-tipped tails squirmed like snakes.

Someone nearby let out a terrifying war cry from directly over the second pair of gladehunters. Someone, some . . . thing dropped from the tall tree directly above them, igniting into a cloud of green and yellow flames. Impossibly, the fiery bundle accelerated as it fell, its howl growing louder and sharper.

Venser blinked. Was that a woman under all that? If so, she was doomed. The wedge-shaped gladehunters reared and coiled their tails, ready to spear the fire-woman out of the air with their sharp faces.

Two blurs of scaly green shot out at ground level before the gladehunters could strike. One swept through first monster's legs, tearing most of them off as it went. The beast screeched as gore spurted and it toppled into the mire, its attacker disappearing into the bog before Venser saw it clearly.

The second blur slammed squarely into the last gladehunter's broad midsection, driving the huge creature back and pinning it against the bole of a stunted tree. The gladehunter struggled against the odd bipedal reptile that held it, gouging the watery ground with its sharp legs and flailing its twin tails. Before it could regain its focus and its full strength, the flaming woman landed with a huge, bent dagger sticking out of her fist. The point of the knife punched through the gladehunter's armored head, penetrating all the way to the hilt. In a hideous display of strength, the woman's arms bulged and her neck strained as she sawed the blade around the gladehunter's sharp front end in a huge, crude circle, the monster flailing and keening all the while.

When her circle closed, this awful woman grabbed the handle of her knife with both hands. She pushed down, the thick blade acting as a lever, and Venser heard nauseating crack. The gladehunter shuddered, its tails twitching. Its face fell out of its head, whole and complete like an old scab dropping from a wound. The contents of the monster came pouring out as it dropped twitching into the swamp. Impatiently, the woman turned to face the lizard and shouted, "Do it."

The lizard nodded then lifted his gladehunter's faceless but still wriggling body. With no great effort he heaved the corpse on top of its crippled partner. The live insect was crushed down below the surface of the fetid water, but the lizard did not press his advantage. He dived into the marsh, and like his scaly brother, he left barely a ripple behind him.

The two remaining gladehunters roared in unison. The maimed one struggled out from under its brother's corpse and slithered through the muck away from the terrible woman. The other, the burned mantis, was still largely intact and so it leaped high into the air, hurdling its dead partner to continue the attack. It landed with a splash near the woman with the bent dagger, who was now alone between two angry, wounded gladehunters.

The fierce-eyed warrior was clearly insane, because she sheathed her weapon and goaded the gladehunters forward with both hands. She was even smiling.

The mantis gladehunter chittered angrily. "Outlanders," he said, his voice brittle and indistinct, "we will not forget your blasphemy."

"Sure you will," the woman said. "Dead bugs don't remember much."

The insects struck together, one lashing out with its long, hooked forelimb and the other with its sharp-tipped tails. The woman nimbly leaped over the first blow and kicked off of the leg that delivered it. She then caught the other gladehunter's striking tail in her hands. Her left arm twisted and the tail stretched, then snapped, spraying the monster's shell with sticky green slime. With her right hand, the woman caught the mantis's claw as it snapped for her, then she hugged herself to it.

The huge predator was strong enough to retract its limb even with a full-grown enemy clinging to it, and so it did, preparing the killing blow with its other forelimb. As it drew the woman toward him she cast her arm out, and Venser saw something sharp and shiny hurtle into the gladehunter's face.

The mantis's leg went askew as the monster shuddered and fell forward. The woman rolled off its leg and drew her dagger as she landed gracefully on her feet. She turned and showed the blade to the last remaining gladehunter. She carefully placed the weapon back in her belt and made the same beckoning gesture again, only this time with one hand and one enemy to see it.

The gladehunter roared. It thrashed his remaining legs and tail and thrust itself up, every muscle pushing and pulling its body into a vertical position. The woman was far faster than it was, toying with it as she darted behind and tackled it back down into the muck. Laughing, she forced its head and face completely below the surface of the swamp. Numb and nauseated, Venser watched as the woman cheerfully held the struggling gladehunter down until its thrashing body slowed then stopped.

She continued to hold it there for several long seconds after it ceased to move. She tossed her wild hair from her face and locked eyes with Venser. Her fierce expression did not change and she did not call out to the man she just helped rescue.

Instead, she reached out and savagely ripped the gladehunter's remaining tail from its body. She glared down at the insect, and seeing no reaction, straightened up. "He's dead," she said to Venser. Her face split into an evil sneer. "Else he'd have twitched a bit."

Turning back, she latched on to the monster's sharp anterior end, lifting it slightly out of the bog, and planted her foot in the center of its wedgelike body. With a brutal stomp, she bent the gladehunter in half until it snapped in two.

Panting, the woman hoisted dead monster's ragged tail overhead and threw the grisly item down on top of its owner. Then she turned back to Venser. "Still dead," she told him.

Venser felt cold, his skin damp and waxy. "Who . . . what?" he said, but there were too many questions jumbled together in his mind.

The rest of the strange warriors emerged from the trees and the water. In addition to the terrifying gray woman there were two reptilians and two small, dark-skinned humans dressed in red. They all seemed calm and confident, not threatening at all . . . except for the woman. But even she had protected him. Nonetheless, Venser backed away as they approached.

He yelped as he bumped into a solid figure behind him. Venser sprang toward his machine, noting two new figures half-blocking his path. One was a young girl from the same tribe as the red-clad warriors. The other was a tall, bald, dark-skinned wizard in gleaming white and blue robes.

"Easy, friend," the bald man said. It was the same voice Venser heard in his head earlier. "We're only here to help."

"Who are you? What are you doing here?" He pointed to the bodies of the gladehunters. "Do you know what you've done? They'll kill you for sure when they see this. And me."

"They'll try," the insane woman said. Venser yelped again. She was standing right beside him though he had not heard her approach.

"Radha," said the bald man. "Venser is about to go into shock. Please don't hurry him along."

"How do you know my name?"

The bald man smiled, almost guiltily. "Uhh," he said, visibly searching for an answer. "You know it?"

"Teferi, please." The young girl next to the bald man stepped forward and held her hands out, open and placating. "My name is Jhoira. We are on a mission to examine the Stronghold. Teferi is a planeswalker"—she pointed to the bald man—"Radha is from Keld"—she indicated the fury with the bent dagger—"and we're all from Shiv." Jhoira waved her hand to include the rest of the group. "Don't worry. We won't stay long."

"Actually," the bald man called Teferi said, "we didn't know it when we arrived, but we've also come to see you." He smiled broadly. "You were born near here, weren't you?"

Venser opened his mouth to answer then closed it again. He

looked from Jhoira to Teferi, then back at the gang of warriors lined up behind him. "Please," he said at last. "Just let me go."

"Oh, stuff this," Radha said. "Let's just knock him on the head and carry him with us like the luggage he is."

Venser's brain started swimming and his stomach seemed to float away inside him. He felt as if he might vomit then as if he might fall down in it.

"I don't think that'll be necessary," said Teferi. "Radha, would you catch him, please?"

Venser's vision went gray and he felt himself lurching forward. The last thing he heard was Radha's bored voice ask, "What for?"

Then Venser splashed into the marsh and everything went black.

CHAPTER 15

Jhoira sat patiently beside the unconscious Venser. She had convinced Teferi that it would be best if only she were there when the Urborg native awoke. The planeswalker agreed, but he insisted that he stay close by in order to observe.

Teferi's transport carried them all the way to the edge of the Stronghold without further incident. Now Radha and the others were setting up a perimeter in case any more Urborg natives came looking for them. Teferi had conjured a simple canvas tent to house Venser while he recovered.

Venser was lean and underfed, but he was not as wasted as the denizens of Keld. His skin was pale, almost untouched by the sun, but his hair was lush and healthy. Somehow, this lone human has taken care of himself in one of the most hostile environments in the world. Alone, unarmed, he was better off than all of the elves she had seen, in spite of Freyalise's blessing.

If Teferi was right and Venser was the Urborg equivalent of Radha, the pallid young man represented a rare opportunity. He seemed lucid and intelligent when he wasn't being attacked by monsters or defended by fire mages. If he was even slightly more cooperative than Radha (which wouldn't be saying much), he might voluntarily tell them a great deal of useful information about Urborg, the Stronghold, and himself.

Venser groaned and his eyes began to twitch. As consciousness returned, Jhoira saw that the first thing he did was reach down and check one of the larger pouches on his tool belt. She patiently waited while he verified that whatever he had was still there, and only then did he open his eyes.

"You're safe," she told him. He glanced up at her, still focusing in the dim light. "Do you remember me from the marsh?"

Venser blinked and scanned the inside of the tent. Still afraid to move, he looked back up at her and said, "Jhoira."

She nodded. "You never got the chance to introduce yourself. You are?"

The pale man sat up, propping his body on his elbow as he extended his other hand. "Venser," he said.

"Glad to know you," she said, and she was. She took Venser's hand and helped him up to a sitting position. "What were those creatures that attacked you?"

"Gladehunters. They run in packs." He shrugged. "In the wild, anyway."

"I'm quite interested in the two-tailed variety. They're called 'slivers,' and I've never seen them that big. How common are they?"

Venser shrugged. "I try to avoid them so I've only seen a few. Most of the gladehunters are people like you and me, but they will recruit anything that knows how to follow orders. You know, 'kill' and 'break that machinery' and so forth."

"You said they would come back for us and you. Will our small victory back there really bring the gladehunters' wrath down on you in the future?"

Venser's eyes shifted. "Not any more than it has in the past," he admitted. "If they had seen me there with the machine and the dead bodies, it would be a different story, but if we got away clean, they'll probably never tie the whole thing back to me. I try to keep a low profile, generally speaking, especially for the gladehunters. They come in all shapes and sizes, most of them nasty, and they really don't like people like me."

Jhoira nodded. "Humans?"

"Artificers." Venser's spine straightened and he spoke with obvious pride. "I'm a builder. I make things."

Jhoira felt a warm smile growing on her lips. "Do you, now? You have no idea how interesting that is."

"You're kidding."

"Not at all. I'm something of an artificer myself."

A flicker of fear crossed Venser's face. "You're here to study the Stronghold?"

"If we can. Our real work lies elsewhere, but some of us wanted to see Urborg for ourselves."

"Why did that bald wizard say you had come for me?"

Jhoira scowled. "Because he's a child. He likes to keep people off-balance and guessing." She regained her temper and continued, slightly less sharp. "More importantly, he thinks you might have something that will help us."

A new look came across Venser's face. For the first time since Jhoira had met him, he didn't seem frightened, baffled, or over-whelmed. His face became focused and determined. He stuck out his jaw as he spoke.

"I only have one thing of any value," he said, "and it's mine. I need it."

Jhoira noticed his hand twitching, as if it wanted to stray back to the pouch on his tool belt of its own accord.

"You can keep your powerstones," she said. "They're not what we want."

Venser was not assuaged. "But you know about them. You know I have them. You know what they're called, and you're an artificer, so you must know what they can do."

"All true, but I give you my solemn word: I would have more uses for a bag of sand in the middle of the desert than I would for your powerstones right here and now." This seemed to confuse Venser all over again, so Jhoira added, "What do you use them for?"

Still suspicious, Venser said, "I scavenge parts from the fen. I build machines. The stones drive the machines I build."

Jhoira nodded. "That is what they're meant for. I myself tend to prefer clockwork designs. There are so many ways to wind the gears, so many different kinds of energy that you can convert to mechanical—sunlight, wind, even gravity. If you factor that into the initial design, you can incorporate rewinding into the machine's initial function."

"Then you run into the perpetual motion problem," Venser said. "The clockwork eventually wears out and you spend all your time making and installing replacement parts."

"Not if you use the right metal. In Shiv, we used to make an alloy that actually grows. As the pieces wear out, they also replace themselves."

Venser was warming to her more with each new exchange. "Amazing," he said. "I don't have the facilities to make my own metals here. I'd love to get an ingot of that metal to work with."

"I can easily arrange that." Jhoira stood, offering her hand to Venser once more. "It will have to wait, though. I think if we can get a good, solid look at the Stronghold and then another at you, we'll be done here. We can take you anywhere you want to go before we leave."

Venser took Jhoira's hand and got to his feet. "Thank you," he said, "and thank you again for saving me in the swamp. It might not seem so, but I am grateful." He licked his lips nervously. "I'm not very good with people."

"I think you're doing just fine. My friends are hard to be good with, if you know what I mean."

Venser nodded. Jhoira would have bet everything she owned that he was thinking of Radha.

"This way," she said. She led him out of the tent and found Teferi waiting for them.

"Greetings, Venser of Urborg," he said. Teferi turned to Jhoira and sent, *I need to hear what you think.*

A moment, she thought back. To Venser, Jhoira said, "I am going to talk with Teferi for a moment. Please stay here or inside the tent."

Venser looked around anxiously. "Is that frightful woman about? The demon with the big knife?"

Teferi laughed. "She is."

"Does she know not to kill me?"

"I believe she does, but it's best to stay close to the tent as Jhoira says. Just in case."

Jhoira followed Teferi a few paces away from the tent. He stepped around a tree that was struggling to stay upright and spoke quietly.

"He's not the one," Teferi said. "There is no connection between him and the Stronghold rift."

Jhoira glanced back. Venser had retreated back inside the tent. "Are you sure?"

"Close to it. The rift here is different from the one in Skyshroud, but it's having the same mana-draining effect on the land. Urborg is in better shape than Keld for the time being, but eventually it'll be just as lifeless. And in the meantime, Venser has no magic about him at all."

"He's an artificer," Jhoira said. "Maybe he doesn't use spells."

Teferi brightened. "An artificer? That would explain a few things." He stared off into space, tapping his finger alongside his chin as he mused. "Maybe I should take a closer look at our new young friend."

"I think you should. He's a good man."

Teferi raised an eyebrow. "You've formed a favorable opinion of him already? Is there romance in the air?"

"Hardly. Though I expect he's also mistaken me for being as old as I look. If anything, he's probably worried about the sweet young girl forced to travel with such ogres."

Teferi laughed lightly. "How you suffer," he said. "All right, then. Let's take our new friend a bit closer to the Stronghold and see what happens. After that . . . well, I've had a chance to examine two different rifts now. Time is running out, so let's go learn what we can and see how it applies to Shiv."

"With pleasure," she said. Together they stepped out from behind the tree and headed for the tent.

Jhoira said, "What do you make of the gigantic slivers?"

Teferi exhaled. "No idea. I can't tell if they're everywhere or just everywhere we go. They don't seem to be a major danger yet, and they're not tied to the rifts . . . at least, not like Radha is." He shrugged. "We'll have to put that on the pile of questions that need answers."

"After Shiv."

Teferi nodded. "After Shiv."

Venser must have heard them coming because he stepped out and hailed them with a wave.

"Say," the artificer said. "I'm pretty close to my home here. I hate to trouble you, but if you can carry me home, could you also carry me back to the swamp where you found me? I'd like to see how much of my ambulator can be recycled."

"I'll do better than that," Teferi said. "If you'll come with me on a short flight, I'll take you and your entire machine anywhere you want to go." The planeswalker blinked. "What did you call your device?"

"An ambulator," Jhoira said. She felt the same thought growing in her head that she saw forming in Teferi's.

Venser did not notice their increased interest. "She's right," he said. "I call it the ambulator, but it's still far from functional." He laughed modestly. "Well, far from reliably functional. I have gotten it to work a few times."

Teferi floated toward Venser on a cloud of blue dust, his eyes wide and his teeth dazzling. He landed softly near Venser, who took an involuntary step backward as if Teferi were poised to slap him.

"This ambulator," Teferi said. "What does it do?"

Venser looked at Jhoira for a moment before answering, "It's a teleporter really. It's supposed to let me travel instantaneously from one place to another." He paused, continuing almost to himself. "Almost instantaneously. I can do it; I just can't do it consistently." He glanced back up. "Plus, I can't go very far, and I have very little control over where I end up. I'm just now starting to zero in on the accuracy problem. First priority was to make the trip less stressful on the machine itself." He tilted his head forward, separated his hair, and showed them an old, thin scar that ran across the top of his scalp. "And its passenger."

Teferi could hardly contain his interest. "And you've been testing this device near here? This close to the Stronghold?"

"Yes. Well, I had to. I set up my workshop here because it's close to where the parts are."

"Jhoira," Teferi called breezily. "Venser is working on a teleportation machine. Isn't that fascinating?"

"It is."

"And it's not working properly."

"What a shame."

Venser's confusion was slowly becoming irritation. "What are you two so happy about?"

Jhoira locked eyes with Teferi for a moment, then said to Venser, "Let's go collect your ambulator," she said. "I'd like to take a look at your teleportation machine. Teferi would, too. We have some experience with machines and teleportation."

She smiled at Venser's still-baffled expression and said, "I think we might be able to help."

* * * * *

"Fabulous. Brilliant. What an amazing achievement."

Teferi was laying it on a little thick, as he was prone to do. The more Jhoira saw of Venser's device, the less hyperbolic Teferi's praise seemed. Venser had cobbled together an extremely efficient teleportation matrix with very little in the way of resources. If it worked like he said it did, he had already accomplished more than most artificers did during their entire lifetimes.

He had certainly set his sights high. There were spells that could move objects and people—Teferi claimed to know at least thirty—but they were complicated and exacting things to cast. The slightest variation in the ritual could have catastrophic results for all concerned, so only experienced wizards would even dare try. A reliable teleportation machine that anyone could use on demand would be a rare prize indeed. It would also be the crowning achievement that made a journeyman artificer into a master.

"May I?" Teferi asked.

His eyes shined blue and he raised the tip of his staff. Venser nodded stiffly. Teferi reached out and touched the staff to the thronelike ambulator. Venser's machine sparkled then rose gently into the air. It began to rotate slowly.

"How does it work?" Teferi was still circling the device, walking against the direction of its rotation.

He was oddly manic, a little too interested in the machine, and it was making Venser nervous. The young artificer was also squirming under Teferi's barrage of compliments.

"Well," Venser said, "it doesn't yet."

"Of course it does," Teferi said. "Was it sitting out here in the swamp this morning? No, it was not, but it's here now. Your ambulator ambulated, my young friend, and good on you for it. Mind you, perfection is a goal, not a destination, and there's always some way to improve even . . ." Teferi's voice trailed off as Jhoira caught his eye. Almost imperceptibly, she shook her head.

Venser shifted his feet uncomfortably.

Teferi cleared his throat and said, "Excuse me. I am so excited about your work that I have forgotten how that particular cliché ends." He bowed. "Allow me to sum up: Well done, sir." From his bent position, Teferi looked up at Jhoira.

What is it? he sent. *Venser's machine is remarkable, but it's going to take decades to solve his navigation problems without the right materials.*

I can see that, Jhoira replied. *We should leave him to it.*

Teferi straightened up, still beaming at Venser. *We could save him years just by making a few simple suggestions. He'll never get anywhere at this rate, not before he's middle-aged.*

I don't think he's building it to use it. I think he's building it to prove he can.

Teferi walked under the ambulator, inspecting its undercarriage. *I want to see how it works.*

Why? I thought the point was to see if Venser was interacting with the rift.

It is, but I don't think Venser is interacting with the rift, not even through the ambulator. I think the ambulator is interacting with the rift on its own.

You think the machine is conscious? Jhoira thought of all that Phyrexian wreckage in the swamps where Venser had been scavenging.

I think the machine is connected to the rift, or at least those powerstones are. When they drive this machine, I think it travels through the rift the same way I travel through the Blind Eternities during a planeswalk. Maybe mana is the conduit to and from the rifts . . . that would explain why it's drawing so much in, but then, where does it come out?

Back to Venser . . . he's essentially built a planeswalking machine?

No. It's similar to what I do when I move within a single plane, but it wouldn't allow one to cross planar barriers. It's not a portal like the Phyrexians had. It should only be the somewhat crude but very effective teleporter Venser was trying to build, but it's not. It's more.

Teferi spoke aloud, "I think that"—he pointed to the ambulator—"interacts with that"—he gestured up at the Stronghold—"every time you use it. It would help me to know if it does and how. Venser, will you provide us with a quick demonstration of your marvelous machine?"

The artificer stole a quick look at Jhoira. She could only shrug.

"I would love to," Venser said, "but there is some structural damage I'll need—"

Teferi's eyes and the tip of his staff crackled. "Fixed it," he said. Half-turning to Jhoira, Teferi said, "I haven't changed anything about your device, Venser. I've merely replaced the parts that were clearly damaged."

"Uhh . . . thank you, but it's not safe to stay out here. The gladehunters—"

"Will not bother us." The bald man's eyes went white. "If they can still perceive us at all, they'll still have to dig for ten days to get close."

"I . . . see." Venser went to the device and stared up at it. He glanced back at Teferi.

"I beg your pardon," Teferi said. He gestured and the device slowly settled back down onto the blue platform of light.

Venser woodenly began to inspect the machine's innards. He called back, "Where would you like to go?"

"Oh, I don't want to go, dear boy. I want to watch. Take it anywhere you like, any distance, any direction. I just want to see the ambulator in action."

"Teferi," Jhoira called, "you should think this over."

The planeswalker smiled. "I disagree."

"Then at least call the others."

Venser's pale face popped around the corner. "Is that absolutely necessary?"

"Hear, hear."

Jhoira glared at them both. "The last rift we stood in front of spat out a platoon of berserkers, so yes," she said, "it is absolutely necessary."

Teferi sighed, sounding defeated, but then he perked up again. "How about if Venser goes and gets them in the ambulator? That way we can do everything at once."

"That's your solution to everything," Jhoira said, "and look how well it's worked for you so far."

Teferi's face fell. Venser said, "I'll need a few minutes to set things up. You have time to collect the others, if you like." He swallowed. "Just keep all the knives, fire, and teeth a safe distance from me. All right?"

"Done." Jhoira nodded, but she didn't look away from Teferi. He seemed chastened, but Jhoira knew that inside he was celebrating like a spoiled child who has been punished but still gotten his way.

* * * * *

Radha and the Shivans stood by, weapons ready. Teferi had dissolved the energy platform and the warriors all stood ankle-deep in the mire.

Venser was busy at his machine, still tightening and calibrating. They had placed it on one of the drier mounds that rose from the fetid water. Teferi stood off to one side, gazing contemplatively up at the Stronghold.

"We're ready," Venser said. He called out to Teferi and the others, "Anyone else want to come along?"

The Shivans only stared. Radha rolled her eyes during the silence and said, "Just get in and flip the switch, pasty. It stinks out here. I hate your whole country."

"On behalf of all us," Teferi cut in, "no, thank you."

Venser opened the door. "I'm just going from one end of this clearing to the other." He smiled hopefully at Jhoira. "We'll see if I get there."

"I'll find you if you go astray," Teferi said. "We'll get to you before the gladehunters do."

"Glad to hear that." Venser waved, sat down, then pulled a harness into place around his chest.

"Teferi," Jhoira said, "I'd like to see the rift during Venser's demonstration."

"An excellent idea." The planeswalker waved his staff. The angry red clouds shimmered and the great storm vortex faded into view over the Stronghold.

Venser unhooked the harness and stood. "One last detail," he called. He walked around to one side of the machine and reached into his tool belt. He fitted the glowing yellow powerstone into its housing and closed the panel. Then he went around and did the same on the opposite side with the second stone.

The artificer went back to his machine, sat down, and pulled the harness back on. The ambulator sat silent for almost a full minute. Then Jhoira heard a click and a metal lever being released. A series of small yellow lights came to life around the upper edge of the machine.

The Stronghold rift reacted immediately. The vortex spun faster and jags of purple lightning began to dance across its wide mouth. The lights on the ambulator glowed brighter and an increasingly loud metallic grinding sound rose over the swamp. The louder and brighter Venser's machine grew, the louder and brighter the vortex.

"Stop," Teferi said suddenly. "Venser, turn it off!" He repeated the cry in Jhoira's mind, in all their minds, his thoughts sounding close to full panic.

I can't, Venser's voice came back. *It won't power down.*

Jhoira turned to Teferi, preparing to call for Venser's rescue, but the words never came. Teferi was standing stock-still, staring fixedly at the vortex as his mouth mumbled silently. Whatever these rift phenomena were, this one had overwhelmed the planeswalker just as the one in Keld had.

A massive vertical bolt of purple energy split the Stronghold vortex down the center, followed by a clap of thunder so loud it shook branches from the trees. A gigantic, winged shape flickered into view inside the vortex, illuminated by surges of amethyst light. Sharp claws curled around the edges of the whirling cloud, then a long, loglike reptilian head hauled itself out into the skies of Urborg. The face was oddly inverted, only eyes and a beaklike face at the front end, the massive, rippled skull stretching out behind.

The dragon spread its wings and climbed high into the air. It was black, completely black, so dark that it appeared to be a solid shadow even in the bright glare from the rift below. Its eyes gleamed like purple diamonds and its small, conical teeth were pure, clean white. It was alternately real and insubstantial, shifting between solid, liquid, gas, light, and void. Jhoira could half-see the seams of its serrated scales moving against one another, but otherwise the beast's body seemed to absorb all of the light sent its way, swallowing it whole and returning nothing but rippling, gooey darkness to the viewer.

"Oh, yes," Radha shouted, her voice rising. She turned to the Shivans and said, "Let's kill *that.*"

Venser's machine continued to rev and grind. Teferi continued to stare, poleaxed by the combination of the rift and the ambulator. The shadow dragon continued to soar, circling overhead as it prepared to swoop down upon them.

Jhoira made her decision. The others could care for themselves. She and Venser were in the most danger. As the dragon banked and folded its wings, Jhoira sprinted for the ambulator.

CHAPTER 16

Teferi had been rattled, surprised, and caught off-guard far too often lately. He would have to work on that.

Venser's machine agitated the Stronghold rift, which he had expected. He was also prepared for the rift energy to push the ambulator past its limits, even ready for something nasty to emerge from the vortex. He was not expecting to be part of the problem.

For some reason, his mere presence had intensified the rift's violent reaction. Together, the Stronghold phenomenon and the ambulator were volatile, but adding Teferi to the equation made the whole thing go critical. He had been careful to keep himself clear and to consciously not influence the ambulator's peculiar connection to the rift, but everything went insane anyway.

The dragon was also completely unidentifiable, which added a lot to the confusion. The brute was not from this plane—not from any natural plane Teferi had visited or researched. It simultaneously existed here in Urborg, yet it didn't exist at all. It didn't flicker in and out of reality but was permanently trapped between the states of real and unreal.

Teferi tried to move, to cast a spell that would stop the dragon before it attacked, but his body was too distant and vague. He watched Jhoira sprint toward Venser's machine, disturbed at how detached he was from the experience. There was his best friend running into several different kinds of danger, and all Teferi could do was gape.

"Nonsense," he said.

Speaking aloud helped break through his stupor. He strenuously turned his head away from the vortex and faced the ambulator, where Jhoira and Venser were jerking at the harness, trying to get it off the captive artificer. The machine shuddered as the two pulled as hard as they could.

The ambulator was still running, still trying to process the surge of energy from the rift. Venser had designed fail-safes that would cause the device to burn out and shut down before it exploded in such a circumstance, but his machine wasn't operating according to its design. The powerstones he used were easily overloaded, especially by a massive jolt of unknown magical force. If even one of the gems ruptured, the explosive release could boil away Urborg's swamps down to the bare rock for a mile in all directions.

Worse, the rift was growing bigger as well as more violent. Here was all the proof Teferi needed that there was a connection between the ambulator and the Stronghold rift . . . for all the good it did him. He still didn't understand the connection and he certainly didn't understand how to break it.

If he didn't act quickly, something was bound to kill most of his party in the next few seconds: the dragon, the expanding rift, or the overloaded machine. All of his best spells had deserted him, and the ones he could think of wouldn't help.

Jhoira finally snapped the harness loose. Venser came tumbling out in a cloud of smoke, almost knocking Jhoira to the ground, but she caught him and kept him upright. Together they ran from the sparking, shivering machine, without the slightest chance of getting clear in time. They wouldn't make it. None of them would.

Teferi could planeswalk them all to safety easily, except for the fact it would make everything worse. At this range, in the middle of the stormy exchange between the Stronghold and Venser's machine, there was no telling where the 'walk would end, if it ever did.

"Forgive me," he said, though no one was close enough to hear.

Shiv's return was the mission, but the time rifts were the mystery. He couldn't finish the mission until he solved the mystery. Radha hadn't solved it for him; Venser and his machine couldn't. If Teferi wanted to know what the rifts really were and how they were slowly eating Dominaria alive, he would have to investigate for himself.

He had truly intended to save Shiv, but it seemed now he would have to try his final gambit here in Urborg. Though he hated having his colleagues and friends on his conscience, there was no way to take them along. Teferi reached out with his mind, locating and tagging each member of his party and then Venser. He would protect them as best he could and hope that the danger followed when he left them here.

He paused for one last moment to extend a traditional Zhalfirin farewell. *Live on, Jhoira,* he sent. *Be well and happy.*

What?

Teferi planted his staff in the wet ground, then wrapped both hands tightly around it. Jhoira's confused question echoing in his mind, he closed his eyes and planeswalked directly into the center of the Stronghold rift.

* * * * *

Teferi's voice cut through the noise, but Jhoira could hardly spare the attention. He said something that sounded very much like good-bye.

What? she sent back.

Teferi didn't answer. Jhoira stopped, allowing Venser to continue running past her, but he also stopped and looked back at her questioningly. She motioned for him to move on and turned to her oldest friend.

Teferi was standing still, resolutely staring at the Stronghold with a tight grip on his staff. What was he preparing to do?

To her surprise and annoyance, Venser ran past her, heading back to the ambulator.

"What are you doing?" she yelled, hoping to get an answer from one of them.

Only Venser replied. "The stones," he shouted. He had reached the ambulator and forcefully tore off the powerstone housing panel. "I need to recover the stones."

Overhead, the dragon roared. Venser was going to get himself killed. Jhoira wondered briefly if helping him get the stones would be faster and safer than having Radha knock him on the head and carry him to safety.

The Keldon elf was nearly salivating as the dragon descended, her dagger in one hand and a tear-shaped blade in the other. Aprem and Dassene lit up their weapons while Corus and Skive positioned themselves to fight, but none of the Shivans looked eager for this battle. It was no wonder: the Ghitu revered most dragons and hated the idea of killing one almost as much as they hated the idea of being killed by one. For their part, the viashino routinely bragged about how their tribes had driven all the dragons out of their homes in Shiv. This was Urborg, however, and Corus and Skive both knew that the odds were quite different here, only two viashino against a multi-ton dragon.

Venser retrieved the second stone and hurried back toward Jhoira. She waited until he was close then turned and ran herself, driving for the cover of the nearby trees. When she reached the edge of the copse, she threw herself behind a fallen log. She quickly and carefully peered over the log, watching Venser approach and the dragon home in.

Teferi began to fade away in the distance. Jhoira refused to believe what she was seeing, refusing to accept that Teferi would choose to leave them behind once more, but he did.

He was gone in an instant. Jhoira swallowed her rage as Venser arrived. She grabbed him by the shoulder and pulled him down behind her log.

"What's going on?" he said.

"I was hoping you could tell me. It's your machine."

Venser shook his head, horrified at the implication. "It's never done this before." The pale artificer blinked. "I feel strange."

Jhoira's view started to dissolve into a field of blue and white light. "Oh, Teferi," she said. This was all too familiar and the realization that she was being planeswalked stabbed through her belly like an icy knife. "You bastard."

"What's happening?" Venser's voice had lost all composure. "Where are we going?"

If we only knew, Jhoira thought. If only we knew enough to guess. She shot a glance over at Radha and the Shivans, barely registering that they, too, seemed to be disappearing from the marsh.

Jhoira saw no more as she felt herself go. She was drawn up and hurled headlong into the swirling vortex that glowered over the Stronghold, its eerie lightning tearing through the sea of blood red clouds.

* * * * *

As a planeswalker Teferi could go where he pleased, and he loved to travel. He had been a passenger or a pilot in just about every kind of conveyance there was: boats, airships, cycles, submersibles, and tunnellers. He had ridden on horses, camels, drakes, and winged sphinxes. He had smuggled himself in the belly of a whale. As a student he had even strapped beebles onto each of his feet and bounced along, taking giant strides in his pair of living, giggling, seven-league boots.

His first planeswalk had been a taxing and terrifying ordeal. It had felt as if he were splitting apart while falling through a bottomless pit. Adrift in the void with no sense of himself, he had been blind, deaf, and mute. When he arrived, the shock of becoming a physical being once more had given him a crippling migraine that lasted for days.

Still, nothing he had experienced prepared him for the Stronghold rift. Though he remained conscious and self-possessed, he was helpless, out of control, bullied and bounced along like an acorn through whitewater rapids. His view changed from moment to moment, sometimes fading between multiple images and sometimes flickering from one stark scene to another.

It was not the sights and sounds that pained him as he hurtled through the rift's roiling void of energy and smoke, but the jagged wounds those sights and sounds concealed. There now was Skyshroud, pale and depleted, the canyonlike rift of smoke and white haze flanking it on both sides. The rift bore into him like an auger blade and sent sharp, stabbing pains throughout his body. He saw a ghostly image of Freyalise over the trees, her sharp features stern and judgmental.

The scene before him rolled and vanished as if falling under the curl of a massive tidal wave. Teferi felt a sense of motion, of progressing forward and down. Was the massive wave that obliterated Skyshroud also drawing him to the bottom of some otherworldly abyss?

His motion slowed, and Teferi found himself high over a different forest, one with massive, healthy trees. A beautiful blonde woman dressed all in green stood balanced on the tip of a tall pine. She was weeping. Below her, two massive armies faced each other. There were huge siege engines and giant-sized warriors on each side, along with thousands of human soldiers. Each army had left a wide swathe of shattered, broken ground in its wake, and Teferi saw they had strip-mined and clear-cut huge sections of the forest elsewhere. Fire now swept through the entire region, filling the air with smoke and blackening the live trees. The war-ravaged place was clearly dying, and if the armies were fighting over its resources, they did not see the futility or the irony of their actions.

Two men, perhaps generals, met at the center of the battlefield. One was fair-haired, the other dark. They fought. The dark one fell. The blond raised his fists and screamed as if he regretted his victory. Then he drew a large, shallow bowl and held it over his head with both hands.

Teferi scolded himself. He should have recognized this scene from the start.

"That's Urza," Jhoira's voice said, "at the end of the Brothers' War." She sounded whole and healthy.

"Jhoira?"

She was nowhere in sight, and Teferi was unable to perceive her presence beyond the sound of her voice. Teferi tried to call out with thoughts and words alike, but neither seemed to work. His thoughts were low and diffuse, even in his own head.

"Teferi?" Jhoira sounded as if she were close by. "Are you here?

"I am."

Another voice answered. "Good. Now I'll get some answers. What have you done to us, clean-head?"

"Radha," he said. "This is insane. None of you are supposed to be here. I made a point of that."

"But we're all here," Jhoira said. "I can't see any of you but I can hear you."

"Well, hear this: I want out now."

"Um, hello? I don't understand any of this."

"You brought Venser too? Why?"

"Probably to keep that black dragon from eating his sorry behind. Who cares? Who cares about the Brothers' War? An ancient family dispute settled with machine soldiers. So what? Big deal."

"I didn't *bring* anybody," Teferi said. "I was trying to leave you all behind."

"Great. Thanks for that."

Below Teferi, Urza activated the sylex bowl. The battlefield, the forest, the entire continent vanished under a blinding flash of light. Before the glare began to fade, Teferi felt the same sensation of being pulled away.

"What was that?" Jhoira asked. "Are we in the past?"

"We were," Teferi said, "or at least we were somewhere else, if not somewhen." Now that the shock and disorientation were fading he began to come to grips with what was happening. At least they were all still together. "Try to stay calm."

"I really hate this."

"Try to stay calm and quiet, Radha." Teferi tumbled through the void, thinking quickly. He was still mystified by the others' presence here. He'd never taken people along on a planeswalk by accident and didn't think it was even possible. "Everyone please declare yourself. Say your names."

Voices came at him from the emptiness, familiar voices stating familiar names. It was a bit like mind-reading but easier and more direct. He could hear each individual's thoughts when they intended to share them, much like speaking to a roomful of strangers in a pitch black room. Teferi quickly isolated and identified all the members of his party.

The dead dark space around them turned an angry scarlet as the next blurred landscape grew sharp and clear before them.

"Fiers' teeth," Corus hissed.

Teferi recognized Shiv, or rather the part of Shiv he left in place. The sight of their diminished continent struck the other Shivans silent, their thoughts painful, private, and not for discussion.

Teferi tried to take in as much as he could. The current landmass represented less than a third of Shiv's original size. The southern shore was a long arc of razor-sharp cliffs that rose hundreds of feet above the water. Seen from this great distance, Teferi could mentally draw the rest of the shoreline. The perfectly round shape encompassed all of southern Shiv, several outlying island chains, and millions of gallons of sea water.

An angry red wound glowed in the sky overhead. Shiv's rift was exactly the same size as the missing portion of land. Through it, Teferi saw an endless field of smokestacks belching fire. The vast desert wastelands had become one gigantic mana refinery.

"Soon," Teferi said quietly, "we will welcome you home."

The image boiled away and left another landmass with another clean scoop missing from its shoreline. Of the party only Jhoira would recognize the northwestern coast of Jamuraa, from where the kingdom of Zhalfir once ruled the region. Now Zhalfir was gone, excised cleanly from its moorings and spirited away.

The hole in reality here was huge and billowing like a cloud. It hung over the coast of Jamuraa, clinging like a massive, semi-solid fog bank.

"Teferi?" Jhoira's voice was sharp with concern.

"We shall return here once Shiv is safely installed," Teferi said, preferring to keep his true thoughts about his homeland to himself.

Teferi suddenly slammed into what felt like a stone wall. The sensation of tumbling forward gave way to a jolt of pain as he met something immoveable. Dazed from the phantom impact, Teferi went into a wrenching, headlong plunge. As he dropped, he tried to brace himself for the next sudden stop.

After a tunnel of pure white silence, Teferi looked down from high above a flat-topped mesa. Apart from the rocky cylinder there was nothing else to see but flat, blasted desert. The wasteland had no color, but was a sepia sea of dust. It was an unnatural state, something caused by powerful magic, or perhaps by the lack of it.

There, on top of the mesa, floated a terrifying figure. She was dressed in gleaming white cloth and golden armor, her huge war helmet winged like an angel's. She stood tall, proud, and beautiful atop her mountain, and Teferi saw that while the rest of the desert was drab and washed out, the woman herself was vibrant, bright, and alive with color.

"Karona," he whispered. "We meet at last." Teferi gazed closer at the tableau and realized with a shock that he had been wrong. There was something else on the desert floor.

There was a multitude. Tens of millions of people all crawled through the dust, coated with the stuff until they were almost indistinguishable from the ground. They were abject, bent, and servile. Emaciated and weak, they were barely able to move, yet they struggled on.

Worst of all, they were hopeless, bereft of anything but the desperate need to survive. Somehow Karona had become the only way for any of them to do that, and she was making them crawl for the privilege.

The spectacle in the desert faded to gauzy white. Teferi was jolted once more, less painfully this time. He began to rise, accelerating as if gravity had reversed and he was falling up.

"What is all this?" Radha asked.

"The answer," Teferi said. "I just don't understand it yet."

A circular window formed in front of him then, purple sparks and dust churning inside its brittle pane. Teferi felt a fresh wave of disorientation when he viewed the Stronghold through the window, looking down upon the black, jagged peak from above. As he had seen Freyalise's visage over Skyshroud, Teferi saw a transparent image of a huge panther's head with its ears flattened angrily over glistening yellow eyes.

"Windgrace," Venser said. His voice had a breathless, awed quality. "We are back in Urborg."

"Keep going," Radha said.

Teferi half-expected their frenzied journey to end where it began, and he welcomed the chance to meet his fellow planeswalker

Windgrace. Instead, the circular window shattered into fragments and Teferi once more surged upward with a gorge-rattling lurch.

When he stopped he was looking down on a lush river valley. A stone shrine sat nestled between the forks of a river that ran along the western edge of a rugged mountain range. The scene rolled below him as if someone had spun the globe and Teferi shot west, traveling along the river's central fork. It led all the way to the sea, where he stopped moving and hovered over the beach.

Teferi noticed two huge spires of rock less than a mile from the shore, their points curving toward each other like a pair of pincers. Before anyone could speak he said, "Don't ask. This is totally unfamiliar to me."

Nonetheless he knew there was something very wrong here, something terrible. Whatever it was hadn't noticed them yet, but Teferi could sense its baleful face turning toward them even now.

From the sky, a flaming object fell. It was small but very bright and it angled down toward the river valley like a comet. It was heading toward the spot where Teferi had arrived, bearing down on the stone shrine.

"Oh, hells," Teferi said. He was not an expert at fire magic, but he knew serious spellwork when he saw it.

"This is going to be good," Radha said.

The burning meteor gathered speed and intensity as it fell. Teferi tried in vain to place this scene geographically or chronologically, but it was maddeningly indistinct. All he could tell was that they were somewhere on Dominaria at some point in the past. There was a rift nearby somewhere, but he couldn't pin down its location.

The meteor landed and the valley disappeared in a fiery surge of force and heat. Out to sea, silver-white light flashed at the tips of the sharp stone pillars. Before Teferi could see the aftermath, he tumbled forward again, flipping end over end through the dizzying void.

Then he was once more high above the coast of Zhalfir. The

great nation was still intact, its coastline whole and occupying its proper place on the map. His momentum brought him down closer until he was within view of a small, unobtrusive island far from any port and well clear of all shipping lanes.

Teferi recognized his former island sanctuary with a mixture of pride and regret. He had achieved great things in this facility, and he had also done great harm. In the end he had put it all to right, thankfully, so this was at least one past sin for which he had already atoned.

As if to support his opinion, Teferi's island slowly phased out of sight below. Teferi himself floated gently down as the sea around his sanctuary vanished in a curtain of frothy blue.

"Teferi," Jhoira said, "are you seeing any planeswalkers at any of these sites?"

"A few," he said, "the ones we already knew about in Skyshroud and Urborg."

"Odd," Jhoira said, and Teferi loved her for it. Only Jhoira could look at this situation, in this company, and declare one small part of it "odd."

"How do you mean?" he said.

"As far as we know, we've been seeing the past. You, Urza, and Karona, all that happened long ago. The places we've seen from this time . . . Shiv, Zhalfir, Urborg, and Keld . . . all have rifts. Only Urborg and Keld had planeswalkers watching over them."

"I'm not sure I follow."

"You seem a logical choice to be Zhalfir's protector, but Shiv has no such patron."

"I have always intended to protect Shiv as well as Zhalfir."

"But your weren't at either site."

"Ahh, but that is probably because I'm right here. Once this ride stops—"

"If it stops."

"If and when, I swear it will be my benevolent smile that

oversees the installation of your home."

Their gentle downward motion eased and Teferi broke through a grimy cloudbank to emerge over another remote island. It might have been green and lush at one point, but now it was crawling with black metal monsters. Burning oil scoured the island's surface and pooled into great lakes that filled the sky with choking black smoke. It was hard for someone without special knowledge to see why this remote location was worth flooding with troops. Teferi and Jhoira knew better.

"What's this?" Radha said. "Those look like the metal beasties we saw in pieces back at the swamp."

"They are from the same horde," Teferi said, "and the same war. They are Phyrexians. This is Tolaria at its end."

From this distance Teferi could not clearly see individuals in detail. Nonetheless, he was able to pick out the haggard, dark-haired wizard fighting his way to the island's center. Even if Teferi didn't recognize the old scholar, he would have been able to find the man by following the trail of dead Phyrexians.

"That one's a warrior," Radha said approvingly, "but he doesn't look like a fire mage."

"Barrin was a master wizard," Teferi said crisply. "He knew grand and complicated spells in all five colors.

"He's doing well for himself, but he's doomed if he doesn't get out of there."

"He knows," Jhoira said. "He's already lost his wife and child to . . . to the demons of this war. This will be his final battle. He doesn't plan to leave."

"Oh." Radha spoke solemnly, almost reverently. "Then die well, Barrin."

"He did. Teferi," Jhoira's voice had dropped to almost a whisper, "I don't want to see this, but I can't close my eyes."

"We don't have eyes to close," Teferi said. "It will be all right. The end comes quickly."

Indeed, even as he spoke Teferi saw the first licks of fire rise up from Barrin's last spell. The wizard's flames surged, burning higher until they collapsed back on themselves. The pyroclastic cloud rolled out from his position, melting the Phyrexians and dashing them to pieces against the ground and each other. The blast continued to expand until it covered the entire island. Then the angry red-orange cloud of dust and fire lingered, seething and rippling like a living thing.

The cataclysmic scene split, melted, and remerged before him. Teferi felt an unsettling internal wrench, but without the expected sense of motion. The images were changing as they had done since he entered the rift, but this time he was not leaving them behind.

The blur of color resolved itself to reveal the exact same island from the exact same perspective. It was clearly long before Barrin's final battle, as there were dozens of intact buildings and lush, green vegetation. Drawing closer, Teferi recognized Urza's time laboratory, a huge white stone building that only the most advanced students were allowed to enter.

To his mounting horror, the time lab exploded, casting its heavy stone doors off their hinges. Bolts of silver-blue light beamed out from the door, the windows, and the corners of the walls. The roof seemed to come off the building and hover a few feet above it, suspended on a cloud of brilliance. A mighty wind rushed out, knocking students to the ground and pieces of off the other buildings.

People began streaming from the open door of the lab. Some coughed and wept, others burned and bled. A thin man at the front of the group stumbled into one of the beams of silver light that had not yet faded. As Teferi watched, the man's front half aged from youth to senility to dust in less than a second. As his back half toppled grotesquely to the ground, the other Tolarians around him screamed.

Teferi was now viewing from less than fifty feet above the

ground. He could see faces and expressions now, recognizing his friends and peers and hearing the cries of the injured.

Someone shouted a warning from inside the lab. It sounded like Jhoira, but she hadn't been anywhere near the site of the accident. She only came around to save him later, much later, though the time dilation effects made it impossible for anyone to say precisely how much later. If Jhoira hadn't been there, how was Jhoira's voice shouting at him now, telling him to look away?

Teferi turned just as a small figure ran screaming into the courtyard. The boy's face and body were totally obscured behind a shroud of fire, but as he staggered forward, he looked right up at Teferi hovering invisibly overhead. The boy stopped, rooted in place as the flames continued to dance in slow, sinuous motion.

Teferi looked up at Teferi, who looked back down at Teferi.

The planeswalker had no recollection of seeing anyone in the sky the night he burned, much less an adult version of himself . . . but he had very few clear recollections from that incident. He felt a confusing rush of pity, both for the small boy he was and the man he had become. For a moment his vision flickered between that of a thousand-year-old planeswalker and a nine-year-old student. The man he had become saw himself as he was; the boy he had been saw him now.

Teferi screamed as flames engulfed him once more, burning simultaneously as both boy and planeswalker. In the depths of the Stronghold rift, Teferi's bodiless presence was ravaged by the same agony that had almost destroyed him as a child. It was far worse this time, for he had gone on to become a scholar, a wizard, an explorer, and a god, but he was still as helpless and as terrified as a nine-year-old boy on fire.

"Teferi!"

He definitely heard Jhoira's voice. No surprise there. Since the fire, she had always been there to look out for him. Whenever he asked, she would answer. There was so much he wanted to tell her, yet so much he should have never said.

Teferi struggled to regain himself. He was not a child anymore and he did not have to endure this. Time was his toy, his playground, his to direct, channel, and command. He knew a spell that would freeze the boy and the fire alike, fully stopping them in time. The effect would surround them with a thick bubble of stopped time, making it an easy matter to extract the boy and leave the flames embedded. Teferi could rescue himself now and spare them both forty years of hell and thirty years of nightmares after that.

"Teferi! Please stop!"

He did not stop; perhaps he didn't even hear Jhoira's words. The flames still danced across his face and body. The smell of his own flesh cooking was strong in his nostrils. He gestured or tried to gesture as best as he could with no physical presence. Teferi focused his mind and his power on the burning boy in front of him, the boy he had been.

Teferi cast his spell, and the world around him screamed. All disappeared, winking out like a candle dropped into a full jug of water.

Then there was silence.

CHAPTER 17

Radha was the first to awaken, so she was the first to see the strange figures that had half-surrounded them. Her instinct was to lash out, to clear the space around her and launch herself at the strangers blades-first, but her mind and body still ached from the crazy river ride they'd just been on. Bouncing from place to place with no idea where they were or where they were going seemed to be the only way these people covered ground, but Radha had already had her fill of it.

Instead of striking, Radha merely sat up and latched onto the closest stranger's tunic with an iron grip. She hauled the little man forward and glared into his eyes, less than an inch from her own. He gasped but made no other sound, his face twitching nervously.

As her catch stood trembling, Radha examined his strange features. His eye teeth had been filed to razor-sharp tips and he had animal hide markings on his face. They were not natural, but inked onto his cheeks and forehead with a tattoo needle. He looked vaguely feline, and Radha wondered if he were a priest from some sort of cat cult.

She released the little man with a shove. He retreated and gestured for his fellows to come to him. Though the group gathered in front of Radha, they made no aggressive moves and gave her plenty of space.

Radha got to her feet and looked around. If they were a cat cult they were all the same rank, because they all bore similar tattoos. All twenty of the strangers had the same tigerlike stripes on their faces and each had filed their teeth into fangs. She counted the rest of the unconscious forms dotting the cliff, accounting for everyone but Teferi.

She was confused. Radha hated being confused. The last thing she remembered was watching some nameless island blow up then blow up again. Now she seemed to be on top of a seaside cliff, overlooking two giant spears of stone about a mile out in the water.

She had been here before, during the ride through history, but it looked very different now. The only tree she had seen on the cliffs then was now a small stand of four. Where the skies had been clear of everything except the flaming, hammer-shaped meteor, now they were dotted with a half-dozen or more winged monsters.

None of the huge beasts was close enough to attack, but Radha could clearly see their luxurious fur and spectacular markings. Long muscles rippled under that fur, giving the four-footed creatures a graceful lilt as they swept through the air on leathery wings.

The little man she had grabbed stepped forward. "My name is Jiro. Please," he said, "you cannot be here."

Radha snarled. "Here I am. I'm not going away." She smiled at the man, baring her teeth. "How would you like to proceed?"

Jiro swallowed. "You don't understand. You and your friends are not safe here. No one is safe on this cliff top, not even us. This is Madara, dragon country. We are in the capitol of the whole *nekoru* nation." He gestured up at the magnificent flying beasts.

Skive and Corus began to stir nearby. Radha also heard Dassene and Aprem groaning as they awoke. The only ones still unconscious were Jhoira and Venser.

Radha looked up. "You call that a dragon?" The flying beasts were big enough, but there was nothing reptilian about them apart from their wings.

"Yes, ma'am, a very dangerous one, and there are worse ones yet. Please." Jiro gestured nervously, trying to coax Radha toward the large staircase that had been carved into the cliffs beyond the fruit trees. "You mustn't stay out in the open like this. If you're seen—"

"I said I wasn't going anywhere," Radha interrupted.

"But ma'am—"

"What's going on?" Skive slithered to his feet and stood behind Radha.

"I'm handling this," she said, without turning. "Is everyone else alive?"

Skive stretched his neck to work a cramped muscle. "Seems that way."

"Go and check, scaly. This little fellow here says we might be in danger. I want to know which of us is alive and worth carrying if it comes to that."

"I'm alive," Corus called.

"Good. I didn't feel like hauling your bulk around anyway." She waited for Corus, who had moved up alongside Skive, then she turned to the big viashino. "Wake everyone up and regroup around Jhoira."

Corus flicked his tongue. "What for?"

"Because Teferi doesn't care about the rest of us, but he'll come back for her. Keep her alive and close by and we'll take the first planeswalker out of here."

"She's right," Skive said. "We swore to protect Jhoira, and the best way to do that is to stay together."

"Sirs," Jiro said.

"Quiet," Corus hissed. He angrily eyed Skive then turned to Radha. "What about the artificer?"

"Bring him, too," Radha said. "It was his toy that sent us here.

Maybe he can tell us how to get back. If not, we can chop him up and use him as bait."

Corus turned and went back among the rest of their party. Skive stayed behind, near Radha.

She resumed glaring fiercely at the little man with the cat stripes on his face.

"Please," Jiro said again, imploring with his hands. "This is Yurei-teki's hunting ground. He is a nekoru prince. The land from here to the mountains is his, and you are on it. How can I make you understand?" He spoke slowly, emphasizing each word distinctly. "You are all fair game." He turned to Skive. "Forgive me, sir, but I have never seen the likes of you before. Neither has the prince. He will surely hunt you for the novelty alone."

Skive's tail lashed behind him. "Oh, mercy me," he said. "I'm to be hunted by a dragon, am I? This sort of thing never happened to me in Shiv." He stretched, yawning broadly.

"Sir." The little man's tone changed from polite urgency to angry admonishment. "Yurei-teki is a terrible foe. He is also my lord and master, and he deserves your respect.

Radha stepped in between Skive and Jiro. She glared down at the little man. "Prove it," she said. She flashed her hard, square teeth.

The tattooed man stepped back. "When I summon my master," Jiro said, "you will wish I had left you to the demon that haunts these cliffs."

Jiro turned and led the entire party of cat-faced people as they withdrew to center of the cliff top. When they were all assembled twenty feet from Radha and Skive, Jiro reached into his robe and pulled out a round talisman of polished jade. The rest of his tribe clasped hands and began to chant.

Far overhead, one of the winged nekoru folded his wings. The great catlike beast plummeted toward the water, but as he approached the level of the cliff he spread them once more, banking toward Radha and the others.

He was a gorgeous monster, thirty feet long from head to tail and from wingtip to wingtip. His body was covered in silky black fur that was as lush as a mink's. His coat dazzled the eye with alternating bands of orange and yellow. He bore a broad white patch across his chest and elegant white rings around the end of his long, cylindrical tail.

The nekoru's head was round and compact, and his triangular ears were in constant motion. The rest of his features were decidedly reptilian, with a small, wedge-shaped face and short, interlocking teeth. His huge yellow eyes had vertical pupils. They widened as he cleared the edge of the cliff and reared back. His wings pounded, sending a flurry of dust across the entire area, and the great nimble beast lit gently on the ground.

Jiro and the others fell to the dirt and pressed their foreheads into it. "Master," Jiro said.

Prince Yurei-teki sat comfortably and folded his wings. With his great white chest facing Radha, the cat-dragon flattened its ears and said, "Mmm. Fresh meat."

Radha smiled. She drew Astor's dagger and one of her own blades and beckoned with them. "That's right, bad kitty. Fresh meat." She struck the edges of her weapons together and sparks flew. "Come get some."

The beast's eyes flushed black as his pupils expanded. Yurei-teki struck faster than anything Radha had ever seen. The lush monster extended his body and front leg across the entire distance between himself and his target in the blink of an eye, moving more like a coiled snake than a cat.

Radha and Skive dived in opposite directions, but Radha felt the nekoru's keen claws slash through her calf. She swung her kukri blade behind her as she awkwardly spun to the ground. Radha bounced back to her feet, testing the strength of her wounded limb. The cut was not life-threatening, not even deep. Several yards away she saw that Skive had also been tagged by Yurei-teki's blow, and the viashino now carried three long, shallow cuts that sliced across both legs and his tail.

The nekoru sat on the other side of its followers, exactly opposite of where he had started. Radha could not say she had seen him move.

"Fast." He was casual, almost careless as he licked both newcomers' blood from his retractable claws. He smacked his lips and nodded toward Corus. "Cold," he said. He flicked his eyes over to Radha, ran his tongue over his claws again, and said, "Spicy."

Radha extended Astor's dagger, which had a streak of red and a crimson drop trembling at its tip. She flicked the drop into her mouth and licked her chops. "Overconfident," she said. She gestured with the blade.

Yurei-teki rotated his foreleg. His face curled into a scowl when he saw the small red stain on the gold band around his wrist. A rumbling growl started deep at the bottom of his proud white chest, rising in volume and menace as it surged up through his throat.

"*Nekozukai*," he rumbled. "Attend me. I have decided on this afternoon's entertainment."

Jiro and the others all responded with one voice. "Your servants stand ready, my prince."

"Excellent." Yurei-teki's yellow eyes glittered as his pupils contracted to vertical slits. "Now," he growled though smiling teeth. "Let's begin."

* * * * *

Jhoira awoke under Corus's watchful eye. The big viashino's shadow completely covered both her and Venser, who was sitting up nearby.

"We've got trouble," Corus said.

"For a change." She struggled to remember all she had seen,

fighting to fix the details through a haze of pain and confusion.

They had been bouncing from place to place, somehow propelled through time along a series of major planar disturbances. They had seen sites familiar and unfamiliar, with events from the past as well as the present. Her brain was still cluttered with the rush of images, and Jhoira concentrated to organize her thoughts.

Then Jhoira started. Teferi. Teferi had accidentally pulled them into the Stronghold rift and then foolishly cast a potent spell once inside.

"Teferi," she said. Corus offered a huge, scaly hand and helped her to her feet. "Where is he?"

"Not here."

"Damn it all." Her mind was warming up, loosening like a cold iron furnace with a freshly lit fire in its belly. Her vision and hearing were also returning to normal. She looked up at Corus and said, "What about everyone else? Is anyone hurt?"

"Not yet. I mean, the locals. . . ." Corus started to shake his head but then said, "Radha's handling it." The big viashino stepped aside, revealing the chaos taking place less than fifty yards away. Radha, Skive, Aprem, and Dassene were all exchanging blows with a score of strangers and a huge reptilian cat.

Jhoira watched for a full second. "What is that thing?" she asked.

"Yurei-teki, nekoru prince." Corus shrugged. "The cat-dragons seem to rule around here. That one wanted to hunt Skive and me. Radha objected."

"I see."

"She woke first," Corus added. "By the time I knew what was going on—"

"It doesn't matter," Jhoira said wearily. "Thank you for watching over us."

Her face remained impassive as the battle unfolded. Though Jhoira was furious at Teferi for putting them in this situation again, and at Radha for making it worse, at least the Keldon elf was still acting like part of the group.

Radha was everywhere at once, goading the gorgeous monster into striking at her, diving into a cluster of cat-faced strangers, dropping one of them with a sharp elbow to the top of the head, hurling her throwing blade, then charging the cat-dragon once more. She ducked and weaved between the tattooed locals, letting them take the blows she dodged. The cat-dragon prince didn't seem overly troubled about hitting his own servants.

The Shivans backed Radha at every turn, clearing space for her to move and setting up targets for her to knock down. Dassene and Aprem blasted fiery holes in the enemy formation and Skive swept in to finish off the foes Radha only wounded. The warriors had established a devastating rhythm that left the enemy perpetually off-guard and one step behind.

With a yowl of frustration, the cat-beast pounced, leaping high over the entire crush of combatants. He was aiming for Radha, counting on the confined quarters to prevent her escape.

Radha did not try to escape. Instead, she saw the monster preparing to leap and a savage smile split her face. She dropped down just as the cat-dragon sprang up, disappearing among the bodies of his servants. Skive, Dassene, and Aprem all turned to assist, but before any of them could take a step, Radha sprang out from the tangle of people with a blade in each hand.

She met the cat-dragon in midair, taking his blunt muzzle squarely in the chest. Radha's body seemed to collapse as it wrapped around the dragon's face, but she squeezed tight with her sinewy arms and legs. Positioned as she was, she was blocking the monster's eyes and safely clear of his vicious jaws, which snapped repeatedly mere inches from her belly.

The brute landed, scattering his servants. Yurei-teki roared and stood up on its hind legs, Radha still pasted to his face. He tossed his head violently and flapped his great wings, driving all of the nearby humans to their knees. Skive was too solid to be knocked down, but he did have to spike his tail into the ground to stay upright. Corus knelt down, shielding Jhoira and Venser from the wind with his broad body.

But the nekoru prince continued to contort and flail. Radha hung on tight and waited for him to tire and slow. When he did, when the beast paused for breath and to gather his strength, Radha relaxed her arms and legs but hung onto Yurei-teki's ear. From this pivot point Radha swung her long legs out and around, landing with her legs around the great beast's neck.

Radha locked her ankles under the cat-dragon's throat and squeezed. Firm as a cavalry officer in the saddle, she drew both blades and struck them together, crying, "Burn!" The dagger and the tear both burst into flame as Radha lunged forward across the monster's skull, preparing to stab down with both hands into Yurei-teki's eyes.

The nekoru prince was not yet beaten. He twisted and rolled as he rushed toward the cliff, his speed such that even Radha's long arms couldn't finish their strike in time. He rolled forward, crushing Radha and his wings painfully between his body and the rocks. When Yurei-teki regained his feet, he was balanced on the tips of his back claws, all arranged in a single line along the very edge of the precipice. All four legs, his wings, and his thick neck were extended to their maximum and his body wavered slightly as he struggled to maintain perfect balance.

The rest of the battle abruptly halted. The Shivans delivered a few more blows before they realized the nekoru's servants had broken off. The tiger-tattooed humans now stood and watched their lord's predicament with real concern on their faces.

Aprem and Dassene looked to Skive, who looked to Corus. No one knew what else to do, so everyone simply held still.

Radha's legs were still squeezing Yurei-teki's neck, but now she sat dazed. She leaned forward again, bringing her flaming daggers up and over the nekoru's eyes, but even this small shift in their weight sent the cat dragon teetering dangerously at the edge.

"Strike," Yurei-teki taunted. "Strike, little fire demon. Let's fall together. I will never touch the water, because I can fly. Even blinded I can still soar. Can you?"

"No," Radha spat, "but I can swim."

"Good," the nekoru said. "My brothers will love scooping you out of the water and dropping you back in until you swoon from exhaustion and drown."

"Too bad you'll never see it." She shrugged forward an inch, causing the cat dragon to flutter his wings. "Or anything else, ever again."

Yurei-teki rose to one foot and spun in place on the tips of four claws. He and Radha now faced inland, their backs to the sea. The graceful monster held this pose, wings extended, Radha clinging to his neck.

The big cat shuddered as if chilled by an icy wind. For a moment he seemed to forget there was a barbarian on his back and knives over his eyes as he stared out at the ocean. The prince gave a nervous little shake, and called out, "Nekozukai. Attend your master."

"Your servants stand ready, my prince."

"I grow weary of this game. The air here no longer suits me, and I wish to be engaged elsewhere. Come here and gently . . . gently, mind you . . . get this woman off me. Quickly now. No harm is to come to her or those who travel with her." The cat-dragon settled back down onto all fours then sat, displaying his snow-white chest. "Then bring me some fish. Prince Yurei-teki has spoken."

Amazingly, the nekoru closed his eyes and seemed to fall asleep. The reflection of Radha's flaming weapons vanished as his lids descended.

The tattooed servants shuffled closer, but Radha did not release her grip or withdraw her knives. Not even when all twenty were either bowing and reaching up to assist her and laying their bodies down as stepping-stones for her convenience. Radha did not even start to relax until the great silky beast below her began to purr.

Amused, Radha swung her legs around Yurei-teki's spine so that she was sitting on his shoulder with her legs hanging down. Shunning the hands of the nekozukai, Radha slid down the prince's luxurious coat and landed solidly on the ground. She growled at the servants who tried to escort her. Without looking left or right, Radha marched away from the cliff face, resolutely keeping her back to her foe.

When she was twenty yards away, Prince Yurei-teki hurled himself into the air. His great wings spread as he plummeted past the edge of the cliff, then he shot back up, rolling and twisting as he climbed higher. He let out an excited cry and swerved, homing in on a smaller nekoru in the distance. A few seconds later the chase was on, and both cat-dragons disappeared into the rain clouds that clung to the horizon.

The nekozukai seemed to forget the battle that had just happened, all but ignoring the Shivans and Radha as they tended to their own injuries. Jhoira noticed with some surprise that none of the tattooed servants was mortally wounded. There were few broken bones, a few shallow cuts, and maybe a cracked skull or two, but no one had died in the fight.

Jhoira stood, dusting herself off. "Did Radha actually restrain herself?"

Corus and Venser exchanged a look. The viashino said, "She did, actually. She said they were not worth killing and barked something about leaving the fingers alone to strike at the head." Corus shrugged. "They weren't much of a threat anyway. Skive and the others went easy on them."

"She's insane," Venser said. The tattooed nekozukai withdrew, carrying their wounded and unconscious down the sheer rock steps. Venser stood up and shook his head. "This is madness. I'm just glad you're awake now." The artificer spoke carefully, precisely, as if he'd been saving all these words up for Jhoira alone. "What happened to us? Where are we? How did we get here? Most importantly, when can I go home?"

"I'm sorry," Jhoira said. "I'm afraid I have no idea."

Well met, warriors. The bodiless voice was formal and strong, almost majestic.

"There's someone in my head," Venser said anxiously. "Is there someone in yours?"

"Yes," Jhoira said.

She was probably as jarred by the sound as Venser, but more familiar with a sudden and overwhelmingly powerful telepathic link. This was a planeswalker talking to them, or at least planeswalker-scale mind magic.

The last of the nekozukai turned and headed down the cliff stairs. Jhoira could not be sure if they heard the voice, but there was definitely fear on their tiger-striped faces. They vanished from view as quickly and quietly as a classroom of well-mannered students.

It has been a long time since I entertained so many guests. Not for centuries. Not since the nekoru came. You seem to be very special guests to me....

The voice was not familiar to Jhoira, but that meant nothing. A planeswalker could sound like anyone or anything. Something about this voice still frightened her, something deep and instinctual. Her nerves were screaming "danger" as they would if she saw the bright colors and heard the hissing of a poisonous desert snake. The laws of survival taught that when such a snake lands a lethal bite, only the envenomed is at fault.

"We are travelers," Jhoira said carefully. "We do not intend to stay."

No? The voice remained confident, regal, yet impeccably mannered. *Then we'd better get to know each other better while we have the chance. Let's start with your names.*

Venser looked at Jhoira, his eyes clear and his face full of foreboding. Corus, Skive, and even Radha hesitated, and Jhoira let herself believe for an instant that time had frozen and she'd never have to answer the voice.

Come now. It's only polite for a guest to introduce himself to his host. Young man from Urborg . . . what do you call yourself?

Venser swallowed hard.

Warrior of Keld. I greatly appreciated your handling of the nekoru, but I must know how you came to be here today.

Teferi, Jhoira thought. This could quickly spin out of her control, out of anyone's control but his. Another planeswalker was showing interest in the same two people Teferi had, and Jhoira had lived too long to believe in coincidences when demigods were involved.

Please, she tried her best to send this plea directly to Teferi's mind. *Come back to us* now.

CHAPTER 18

Now.

"Now" was the concept that introduced Teferi to the intrigues of time. As a young child, his mother had called him away from the stream's edge, "Come here now."

For once, young Teferi obeyed instantly. The strange way she stressed the final word caught his attention. Whatever treasures lay in the water, exploring his mother's tone was far more interesting.

"Why do you say that word special?" he had asked.

His mother had laughed. "It's a special word," she said. "It means 'at once' or 'without delay,' but it also means one specific moment. Each day is full of moments and they run by us like water in the stream."

Here his mother stepped over to the swift-flowing water. She raised her index finger and held it over the stream. "Moments move through the day like drops of water moving down the river. When I touch the stream and say 'now,' think of the water right under my finger." She dipped her finger in, spoke the word and then followed the river's flow with her eyes. "That spot is called 'now,' but see how even after I name it, it goes on without me, flowing away, all the way down to the sea. I will never see it or touch it again, but I can always start over." She dipped her finger in again and said, "Now."

She smiled at her son. " 'Now' is an opportunity," she said.

"When I say come here now, it's your chance to show me how clever you are. Now means right away, before the spot on the river flows out of sight."

Later he realized his mother had been adapting an old Zhalfirin homily to feed his prodigious curiosity, but by that time he had become totally absorbed in the notion of time. It seemed to be so many things: a primal force, an intellectual construct . . . and above all, a flowing series of discrete moments with direction, force, and perhaps even purpose. If one could restrict the flow with a dam, or partially solidify the water itself with extreme temperatures, one would be able to recapture the "nows" that had already flowed by—or, at least, be able to examine them in greater detail as they trickled along.

At the Tolarian Academy, Urza had seen Teferi's profound interest in the study of time and encouraged it, even exploited it. Unlike the other prodigies that the headmaster assigned to his time project, Teferi caught Urza's eye with more than natural talent and academic excellence. A planeswalker himself, Urza recognized in Teferi the potential to become as he was, to ascend to a state of infinite mind and magic. This tiny spark would remain dormant in Teferi until years later, when the catastrophic stress of being on fire in slow time ignited it and fanned it into a full-fledged flame.

In all the history of planeswalker ascension, Teferi had never heard of one that lasted forty years. Granted, planeswalkers guarded their ascension stories jealously, and when they did talk they tended to embellish. In almost every case he could find and verify, the transcendent moment was explosive, sudden, and violent. His, in contrast, happened slowly, gradually, an accelerated evolution rather than a sudden destruction and complete rebirth. Over the course of decades, every iota of his mortal being was replaced, bit by laborious bit, until his gross physical shell was replaced by the higher exalted presence of an immortal planeswalker.

Then, as one final bit of irony (and in keeping with the slow nature of his transformation), Teferi went on for another twenty years before he realized how much he had changed. After his rescue, he went back to work as an academy researcher and instructor, oblivious to his newfound status. He aged, he bled, he fell ill, he was physically and personally indistinguishable from any other young man of his class. He had no awareness of or access to his godlike abilities until decades later, when he returned home to Zhalfir and reconnected with his homeland's rich mana supply. Already an accomplished wizard, Teferi discovered he was far more formidable than he had believed—and had been for quite some time. Then, for the thousandth time, but by no means the last, he cursed Urza's time experiments and the havoc they had wrecked.

The pursuit of time had not only challenged him and defined him as a young man, it had literally made him into the being he was today. It was no wonder he was so adept at time spells and tinkering with the temporal flow—he had spent a lifetime submerged in it. A man who spent forty years floating in a bubble of water would naturally become an expert swimmer. How could Teferi fail to become an expert time wizard?

He thought of the other planeswalkers he'd known. Few had shared the story of their own ascension, but that didn't stop him from trying to find out. The transformations he had learned about were each as dramatic and unique as his own, though he often had to extrapolate backward from the beings they had become to understand the beings they had been.

Urza had ascended during the final battle of the Brother's War, which Teferi had just seen from inside the Stronghold rift. Centuries before he founded Tolaria, human Urza used an incredibly destructive artifact spell to destroy two armies at once. In the process, his spark ignited and he was reborn as a nigh-omnipotent being. Urza Planeswalker had powerstone eyes that were his greatest asset and his greatest vulnerability, for while he saw things as no one else could, he didn't necessarily see them clearly.

Freyalise had never spoken of her rise to godhood, but all the evidence pointed to an elf maiden from the Llanowar forest during the early days of elves on Dominaria. She was a worshipper of nature before she herself was worshipped, and her militant antagonism to anything other than elves combined with her love of that species to fuel her own blend of fortifying magic and aggressive combat spells.

The moment of his old friend Karn's ascension was easier to single out. At the precise moment the Phyrexian Invasion ended, Karn the silver golem merged with the Legacy, an integrated collection of powerful artifacts. Among these artifacts were several of the most potent powerstones ever created and a mechanical planar portal. Thus Karn, an artificial being without a true planeswalker spark, absorbed planeswalking machinery into his body and became indistinguishable from a flesh and blood planeswalker.

The transformation of Lord Windgrace, the panther king of Urborg, was unknown and unverifiable, but Teferi had his suspicions. Urborg was home to as many disparate human tribes as it was to nightwalking creatures, even today, but there hadn't been panther people in Urborg since the Brother's War. Somehow the pervasive corruption and predation that characterized Urborg gave rise to the noble panthers, who ruled Urborg fairly and wisely for three centuries. Windgrace's immortality kept the panthers from being a one-time aberration, and though Urborg had long been the stuff of nightmares that parents used to frighten unruly children, the symbol of Windgrace the protector still gave hope to the people who lived there.

The story that interested Teferi the most was that of Bo Levar, a planeswalking pirate and smuggler who fought alongside Urza and Freyalise during the Phyrexian Invasion. Levar lived a full mortal life as Crucias, a naval man with an entrepreneurial streak that caused him to quickly fall out of favor with his commanding officers. Discharged from a military career, Crucias became a privateer and a part-time tour guide until he and his ship were caught in the explosive aftermath of the Brother's War. Crucias ascended in that conflagration and became known as Bo Levar, an interplanar rogue who, for a price, could get you anything you wanted and deliver it to your door. This seemingly unprincipled fellow not only faithfully completed the mission Urza set for his team of planeswalkers, but Bo Levar also sacrificed himself to preserve an enlightened colony of underwater artists and thinkers. In the face of an unstoppable cloud of poisonous death, the cigar-smoking scoundrel literally gave his all to create a barrier that would protect the colony. It cost him his life, but he died one of the greatest heroes of the Phyrexian Invasion, and to Teferi's knowledge the colony still existed hundreds of fathoms beneath the waves.

Lately, Bo Levar had been something of an inspiration to Teferi. Bo Levar was a planeswalker as devoted to the sea and sailing as Teferi was to time. Levar had chosen one small corner of Dominaria to defend against the horrors of Phyrexia, just as Teferi had, and even with the supernaturally swollen ego of a planeswalker, Levar still recognized some things as larger than himself, worthy of the ultimate sacrifice.

Teferi's mind began to focus. Bo Levar had sailed the ocean and saved part of the world. Teferi himself sailed the seas of time and had also saved part of the world. There were profound similarities between them both, but insurmountable differences too. Long ago Bo Levar had done something glorious in the depths of the ocean; moments ago Teferi had done something foolish in the depths of time, something rash and witless to cap a long string of costly mistakes.

He started by conducting an impromptu experiment that had too many variables. Teferi didn't know enough about the rift, the ambulator, or his own newly unpredictable planeswalking to combine them, yet that was what he'd done. He had also become personally invested in the experiment, reacting emotionally when he saw the vision of his younger self. Last and worst of all, he had lost his nerve and tried to abort the process, abandoning the spell half-cast, which turned out to have the same effect on the rift as using lamp oil to put out a kitchen fire.

Teferi came back to himself, conscious but not fully aware. He felt solid, clothed in the body he always wore, but he was largely insensate. His eyes were open and his ears were functioning, but there was nothing to see or hear. No light, no air, not even empty space. It was as if he were enveloped by a second skin of dark emptiness.

Teferi had been to and through a great many planar voids, but this was deeper, more still, and more complete than any nothingness he knew. It was not like the endless kaleidoscopic shapes of the Blind Eternities nor the bodiless motion of the Stronghold rift. It wasn't even the ghostly nonexistence he knew from his own phasing magic. This feeling was not the absence of other feelings, but the presence of a tangible nothing. Teferi had to struggle to perceive and be perceived outside the skin-tight covering. His thoughts, actions, and deeds made no difference at all, as if he did not exist and the ebon shell was actively preventing him from existing.

It was always difficult for Teferi to admit his mistakes, but in this case he knew the cause of his current predicament and blame couldn't be placed anywhere else. Trying to staunch the flow of time during a major time disaster from a position of timelessness now seemed a rash and foolhardy act. It also had disordered the multiverse with the paradox that the multiverse had isolated him, sequestered him, removed him from the grand scheme of things entirely. He had broken too many rules and now he was forced to sit out.

Teferi felt a smile forming on his lips. Jhoira always mocked his tendency to express things in poetic terms, but it was one of the only ways he knew of to make the profound accessible. It was also a way to show off the oratorical skills he'd mastered as an apprentice to Hakim Loreweaver, the greatest storyteller in the history of Zhalfir. If poetical rhetoric was good enough for Hakim, it was good enough for Teferi.

He wondered absently why his thoughts kept turning to Jhoira. Almost as soon as he asked himself this question, Jhoira's voice cut through the interference surrounding him and stabbed deep into his mind.

Please, she said, *come back to us* now.

The curious way she stressed the last word caught his attention. When had she said it? Was it still now *now*, or had Jhoira's "now" long since flowed into the sea?

Teferi's mind drifted. He waited for Jhoira's voice to come again, so he could ask her what she meant. Also, he might be able to get a fix on her position and 'walk there. He'd like to disappear out from under the Teferi-shaped shroud that covered him. He'd like to bring it with him and display it as a unique, unnatural side-effect of his favorite type of magic.

It was not Jhoira's voice that came again. Instead, a strong, malevolent voice said, *Now. How am I to reward such useful insects?* with an eagerness that disturbed Teferi to his very core. The voice was arrogant, but it was also elusive, impossible to single out and examine.

He recognized the threat that voice represented and the recognition came with overpowering dread. Planeswalkers were the only beings with the kind of power he sensed, and only a few planeswalkers had the presence of mind to conceal it, as this one had, from all but the most scrupulous observer.

Teferi stopped trying to reach past the barrier surrounding him. Instead, he turned his thoughts and his energy inward, focusing his entire being on one simple truth. As his mother had borrowed the basics of a Zhalfirin folk tale to educate and amuse her precocious child, Teferi borrowed a mantra that his old friend Karn once told him about. It was a simple phrase that, when repeated in the face of overwhelming adversity, allowed the silver golem to persevere and prevent catastrophe.

"Jhoira is my friend," Teferi said. He pictured her face, her skin, her long hair gathered at the nape of her neck, her wide almond-shaped eyes. "Jhoira is my friend."

In his mind's eye, Teferi saw the image of Jhoira expand, pulling back to reveal the rest of her body, the ground below her, and the landscape nearby. She was standing with her back straight and her eyes wide, troubled but not despairing. He could see her mind working behind her placid expression, searching for a solution, waiting for a reply.

"Get away from her," Teferi said, his voice level and strong. The image of Jhoira blinked as if she'd heard. The look of earnest relief that crossed her face touched him. Like Jhoira herself, it was honest, immediate, and came freely, without condition.

Jhoira is my friend.

There was so much he wanted to tell her, so much he should never have said. Why was he worrying about this now? Why wasn't he rushing to help his friend, as she had asked him to?

He thought of Radha, whom he had brought along for good reasons but also in part to distract Jhoira. A Keldon, even a Keldon elf, would not have dissembled the way he had, would not have hidden his true goals. He knew for a fact that in all the recorded history of Keld, there wasn't a single berserker who had torn himself apart with self-doubt the way Teferi did every day. They were far from admirable beings, those Keldons, but they were not without their virtues.

Teferi concentrated, summoning his full force to him. Instead of vanishing out from under the dark veneer, Teferi let the magic build up inside him, holding it in check. When it began to glitter and scintillate across his body like a rain of diamond dust, Teferi let out a cry that would have done Radha proud and explosively released his built-up eldritch power.

The black sheath burst like an over-filled balloon. Oily scraps and tatters of smoke vanished in the blue-white shock wave. As the obstruction between him and the multiverse disintegrated, Teferi felt his full faculties come streaming back.

Get away from her, he sent, his tone calm and menacing. Without waiting for a reply, Teferi planeswalked straight to Jhoira's side, as full of purpose as he ever had been, more determined and clear-minded than he'd been in decades.

Jhoira is my friend. He would not leave her again.

CHAPTER 19

"Please excuse my colleagues," Jhoira said. "We are a quasi-military unit and they are accustomed to letting me answer for them." Radha harrumphed, and Jhoira was grateful she at least kept her mouth shut.

I see. And I reckon you and the young man beside you are the "quasi-" part of that equation.

Jhoira bowed demurely. "I prefer to think of us as the command element."

Excellent, but tell me, commander, why is your fellow quasi still trembling?

"This is his first mission with our unit," Jhoira said smoothly, "and as you say, he is from Urborg, therefore wary of mind to mind contact."

Ah, of course. Perfectly understandable, but you seem quite comfortable, my deceptively young friend. What is your name?

Jhoira swallowed. It didn't matter how well they guarded their thoughts, not at all. He was learning too much about them too quickly. She decided to come clean before her dissemination annoyed the unseen presence.

"I am Jhoira of the Ghitu, from Shiv. My companions are Aprem and Dassene, also of the Ghitu; Skive and Corus, of the viashino; Radha of Keld; and Venser, who as you know is from Urborg."

A definite pleasure to meet you all. Truly. A special pleasure to meet you, Venser, and you, Radha. In truth, I've never seen anyone quite like either of you. You're quite unique, even from each other.

Radha stood stiffly, her hair blown straight back by the wind. She squinted out over the edge of the cliff, sniffing the air. Her eyes were narrow and she did not speak.

How is it you all have come to my beach, Jhoira of the Ghitu?

Jhoira thoughts raced as she answered. "We were brought here. Our guide and captain lost control of his vessel. We were separated from him and wound up here."

Most unfortunate. I trust you are none the worse for wear after your . . . high-spirited interaction with the nekoru.

"It was a simple misunderstanding. We are glad no permanent damage was done."

You are too generous. They say all dragons are vain, but nekoru are particularly self-absorbed. I imagine the prince will never breathe a word of his rough treatment at your hands. He'll most likely claim to have grown bored and flown away, omitting any details that don't support his own high opinion of himself. He certainly would never admit that he sensed me coming and decided to leave.

"The prince may tell whatever tale he likes," Jhoira said. "We hope to be on our way shortly and may never return."

Oh? That would be an unhappy turn for me. I am enjoying this conversation, and we've hardly begun. For example, you haven't even told me what your purpose was before you were detoured here.

"With respect, sir," Jhoira said. "You are still a stranger to us, undeclared. We must be circumspect at least until our captain returns."

An admirable policy. I myself value circumspection quite highly. I trust that will help explain the unforgivable oversight of remaining anonymous. The voice paused, and Jhoira imagined wherever he was, he had just bowed. *Jhoira of Shiv, I am Sensei Ryu. It is not a name but a title. I lost all claim to my name and identity when I died.*

"You honor us, Sensei Ryu. I regret that you cannot be here among we living."

Indeed. Alas, I was destroyed in mind, body, and spirit by an organized campaign of betrayal. Now I am little more than a memory of a ghost, the last lingering residue of a long and noble life.

The regal voice paused. *I trust that now we are on strong enough terms for you to tell me why your unusual band has come to Madara.*

"I would if I were able," Jhoira said, "but I am not at liberty to say any more. Please excuse me."

Of course. Since you cannot answer my question, I shall answer it for you. You were all falling headlong through a network of cracks in reality. You flew through time and space, bouncing from here to there, from then to now. Your progress stopped suddenly, so I steered you here and gave you a push.

Jhoira inhaled deeply. "You did, sir?"

Oh yes, for I have developed a great interest in those cracks you navigated. As I am dead and bound to this place, I have little beyond my present surroundings to occupy my thoughts, and my present surroundings include such a crack.

"There is a time rift here?"

Jhoira forgot to be frightened, her mind digging furiously through the details of their jaunt through the rifts. There *had* been a shrine, a river, and two huge pillars of stone.

Yes. It cannot be seen easily, but I have seen it. It cuts through this realm there, between the spires of the Talon Gates.

She turned and saw the great pincers of rock that rose up from the sea. Teferi had not mentioned a rift at this site, had not even recognized the place. They all saw the Talon gates, but did he not see the rift, or was its existence just another one of his secrets?

"What is the crack?" Jhoira said. "The rift? Do you know? Do you know what caused it?"

I know it is . . . troubling. I have been dead here for a long time and lived far longer before that. This schism is older than the oldest histories of Madara, but it is not older than me. A great upheaval caused it, one of the first things to·ever happen on this world. No wonder Dominaria's history is so full of conflict—this initial defining event itself was violent in the extreme.

"Sensei," Jhoira said quietly, "what was the event?"

The particulars are complicated and abstract. I have no interest in recounting them for you now. I'm speaking of the result, of the so-called rift you mentioned. Did you know it pulls the life-force of the land to it as surely as sunlight melts the snow?

Jhoira nodded. "Did it always?"

No, little Ghitu, not until the false god Karona had her rise and fall. Indeed, as you suspected when you asked.

Fear returned, prickling at the back of Jhoira's neck once more. This entity was still flipping through her brain like the pages in a book, pulling out whatever tidbits of information struck his fancy, or even worse, he had already taken all of her thoughts and was sifting through them even as she tried to distract him.

The schism became a source of misery before Karona's War by a millennium or more. When poor, mad little Ravi rang her terrible bell and the Garden ceased to exist, the echoes of that destructive chime reached far and wide, all the way to the Talon Gates and the rift they attend. The tolling of Ravi's chime opened the rift wider and deeper, extending it all the way across the cosmos to another realm. When it reached this new place, a place where flesh and spirit existed in perfect balance, the rift disrupted that balance.

It also created a link between this world and that one, a path for any suitably powerful and opportunistic spirit to tread. Soon such a spirit found that path and used it to come to Madara, and once here she cursed it with the plague Umezawa. *The bitter seed she planted continues to bear fruit, for a member of this wretched clan arises every few generations, bent on destroying the status quo and twisting the traditions and institutions of Madara toward their own enrichment.* The voice had grown strident and bitter, but it quickly recovered its former grace and poise. *There now,* it said. *I have told you more than you knew about the Madara rift. Now you will tell me something new.*

"Sensei," Jhoira said, "you are far wiser and longer-lived than we. What could I, in my meager experience, tell you that you have not already learned for yourself?"

You are too humble, the voice said, and its tone was not complimentary, *and your experience is not so meager as your youthful features pretend. Is it?*

Jhoira swallowed again. "No, Sensei."

I would learn more of the man called Venser, he said, his voice clipped and demanding, *and more of the woman Radha. Show me your fire, warrior.*

Radha barely moved, her voice low and tight. "Nothing to show."

A canard, Keldon. You are smoldering right now as you look forward to your next battle. I think you wonder if it will be with me.

Radha did not react.

I have heard much of your tribe, of you magnificent bloodthirsty beasts. You are the first I have personally encountered. Even so, you are unique among your people, are you not, daughter of Freyalise?

Her square teeth clenched, but for once Radha seemed in no danger of losing her temper.

A pity, the voice said. *One hates to settle for the second choice, but when circumstances demand. . . .*

Young man, he said, startling Venser from a deep, almost contemplative state in which he had focused all his will on not being noticed. *You hail from Urborg?*

"I do." Venser widened his eyes at Jhoira imploringly, but she could only shrug. Anything she did to help would likely make things worse. She just wished Venser would relax. Nervous people made mistakes.

Did you come here by choice, Venser, or were you swept along as part of the group?

"I was glad to come," Venser said, a defiant tinge in his voice. The flinty tone evaporated as he continued. "But I did not intend to."

Well, the voice brightened. *I trust you do not overmuch regret the error, as it led to our meeting. I myself am already grateful for that.*

"Thank you," Venser said. From the dry, winded sound of his words, Jhoira suspected the artificer was only a few exchanges away from screaming.

"Sensei," she began, but a tight band of force seemed to close around her chest, restricting her breath.

I am not through with Venser, my dear. Now then, my boy. What is it you do in Urborg?

Venser saw Jhoira's distress, as did the rest of the party. There was an awful, gravid moment, then Venser spoke.

"I am an artificer, Sensei. I build and test machines."

Fascinating, but I gather a dedicated young man like yourself would prefer to be back among his tools rather than stranded on a lonely beach.

Jhoira wanted to shout, to warn Venser off giving the answer he was preparing to give, but she only managed to wheeze. To her horror, the sound prompted Venser to answer, rushing as if his words could restore her breath.

"Well, yes," he admitted. "That is what I'd prefer, truth be told."

I can help you, the voice said. It still came with perfect diction, perfect confidence, and perfect manners, but now it also held the soft, sinuous underpinnings of a seduction. *If you wish I can send you back instantly with but a thought. I will not miscalculate, as your bald friend did. I will not send you on an aimless journey through the void. I will simply send you home.*

Venser was no fool. He saw the looks on the others' faces; he understood he was being lured. He still had no better answer than, "You will?"

I will. I don't even require payment. I can do this for you at any time and all you have to do is want me to.

Venser blinked, confused. "Want you to? I already want you to. I just said so."

Say so again, the voice urged. *Think about the time you're missing, the spare parts you're not collecting. Think about the gladehunters turning your hard work into shrapnel and debris. You carry those stones to power machines, correct? What are they powering while you're here? What are they doing besides rattling around in your pocket?*

Can you see it, Venser? Can you see your chance for greatness vanishing because you're not there to seize it? You want to go back. You want me to come to you and take you home.

"Yes," Venser said. His eyes were cloudy and unfocused.

Ask, the voice said, reduced to a hissing whisper. *Call me to you.*

"Don't be his tool, Venser," Radha called, shouting the words Jhoira could not. "Don't do it."

Venser was already half-entranced. When he spoke his eyes were blank and his face was slack. "Sensei Ryu," he said. "Come and take me home."

All across the cloud-thick sky, gorgeous nekoru turned and fled, streaking away like startled birds. Their huge wings carried them out of sight as they hurtled out to sea, inland, up the coast, and anywhere that wasn't near the cliffs.

At last.

Venser and Radha suddenly both jerked into the air, choking on their own screams. Black light shone in their eyes, blue-gray winds whipped through their hair, and fire crackled in their silent, open mouths. The two shivered and twitched in the air as the light, wind, and fire flowed from their faces, braiding themselves into a corkscrew beam of searing energy. The twisted, tri-color beam blasted out toward the sea and then stopped dead, spreading outward as if it had struck an invisible shield.

A patch of glowing fog materialized around the beam's blocked end. The braided energy faded but the fog remained, forming an oblate shape at the edge of the cliff. The shape had a sphere of bright white light at its center that somehow cast a purple and blue sheen. A thin red line stretched up and down from the center until it had vertically bisected the oval into two perfect halves.

Radha and Venser went rigid. The swirling energy around their faces vanished and they fell forgotten to the rocky ground. Neither was visibly injured, but both were dazed and slow to move.

A dragon's head emerged from the glowing oval field, mottled green and larger than a warship's launch. Long, sharp horns curved out to the sides from the top of the head and sharp, triangular ears arced up to touch the horns. The monster's round forehead jutted up, large and bulbous over his elongated snout, giving him the air of a reptile-simian hybrid. His eyes completed the impression, blazing yellow nuggets that combined the sharp, predatory glare of a dragon with the calculating, appraising eye of a man.

The dragon paused, scanning the cliffs from left to right. A wide smile stretched across his face, displaying row upon row of saberlike teeth. He snapped his mouth shut and black lightning ripped out of the oval patch of fog, spearing out toward each member of Jhoira's party at once. All were able to dodge easily, but the blasts hadn't been intended to kill or wound, only to distract.

As she recovered her feet, Jhoira no longer saw the oval shape that framed the dragon's head like a hunter's trophy. For a moment, silence reigned as everyone waited for some sign of the monster. Then Venser turned toward Jhoira and let fly with a torrent of words.

"I'm so sorry," he said. "I couldn't stop; I couldn't think. He asked and I had to answer. I knew I shouldn't say anything but I just kept talking. What did I do—"

"Shh," Jhoira said. "It's not your fault."

"Here he comes," Radha called. She had two blades drawn but kept them at her sides, watching the dragon as it forced its way into this world.

The sunless sky swirled as a funnel formed in the clouds. The cyclone's tail lashed down and brushed the cliff's razor edge, kicking up a small burst of dust and sharp rocks. The tornado swelled grotesquely, expanding horizontally and splitting vertically in multiple places like a snake's egg at the hatching. The edges of the ever-shifting shape hardened, fixing the outline of a gigantic winged beast more than one hundred feet tall.

It roared from inside the cyclone, a heart-clenching shriek of triumph. The dragon-shape extended its wings and spread arms, legs, and tail out wide. The cyclone burst apart, casting its cruel winds out in every direction, then the monster stood revealed, rampant in ecstatic joy.

The beast's proportions were ultimately and strangely human. In every aspect he bore the subtle combination of reptile and ape and always the most formidable elements of each. His expression was wild and delighted, and his gleaming eyes radiated waves of yellow force.

The dragon's neck was short and densely muscled, his shoulders broad and solid. He had long arms and legs were separated by a barrel chest and an elongated, serpentine waist. He seemed equally natural and comfortable standing upright, stalking on all fours, or borne aloft by his huge, membranous wings.

The dread creature glided down to the edge of the cliff. He hovered there, supported more by magic than the muscles in his back or the air beneath his wings.

"I am Nicol Bolas," the dragon said, his tone calm, his words booming like thunder. "Elder dragon, planeswalker. You have earned my thanks.

"Now," he said, and the unholy light in his eyes intensified. "How am I to reward such useful insects?"

Jhoira's mind raced, driven by fear and duty. Nicol Bolas. The oldest and most dangerous planeswalker ever known. One of the original dragons, one of the great elder legends, the source from whom all other dragons flowed. Bolas had been godlike even before he ascended to become a planeswalker, and ever since he treated the entire multiverse as his personal preserve, preying upon it longer than the oldest historical texts could record. Now he was here, on Dominaria once more, and Jhoira had only seconds to find a way to survive the cruel titan's gratitude.

Get away from her.

The dragon's triumphant expression never changed, but Jhoira felt her heart leap up. Teferi had found them at last.

Then her old friend was there, tall and proud in his white robes, his staff glowing vivid blue along its spinelike curves. "Well met, Nicol Bolas," he said. "Teferi of Zhalfir hails the god-king and father of all dragons."

Bolas's sharp smile widened. He tilted his head past Teferi and addressed Jhoira. "Your missing captain, I believe." He lowered his muzzle and locked eyes with Teferi. "I know you, little wizard. You are flattery and dissembling made flesh. You seek to catch time in a jar and study it like a sample of horse urine."

Teferi was stern and forceful. "True, all true, but I have other priorities today, Great Dragon." He turned to Radha and the Shivans scattered around the area between himself and Bolas.

"Gather 'round, my friends. We're done here."

No one moved. Bolas continued to hover and smirk. "I gave no one permission to leave," he said.

"We are leaving nonetheless."

"No, time-chaser, not before I make good on the debt I owe your friends for releasing me."

Before Teferi could reply, Radha sheathed her weapons and started walking toward him. Venser quickly fell in behind her, though he could not stop glancing back at the dragon. Nicol Bolas took no action, making no move to impede them or stop their progress. Soon Skive, Dassene, and Aprem had all joined Radha and Venser near Teferi, forming ranks on his right side with Jhoira and Corus still at his left.

The clouds darkened behind the floating dragon. While his expression had not changed at all, his smile had become far more of a glower. His voice took on a sinister, echoing quality. "I find it most discourteous for guests to depart in haste," he said.

"Then I hope you'll excuse our rudeness," Teferi said, "just this once."

Bolas's wings folded and he settled to the ground. He crouched and lowered his head, his voice booming down at them from thirty feet above. "I am in a rare and expansive mood, my quasi-military friends, but I am a dragon and do not pride myself on patience." He flexed his long, taloned fingers out. They sizzled in the still air. "Your willfulness is beginning to irritate me."

"I must go, Great Lord. My work will not wait."

"If you leave now," the dragon said casually, "not all of you will make it. Those who do will not arrive whole." He crossed his arms and puffed a blast of black smoke from his nostrils. "I will, of course, follow."

Teferi's grip tightened on his staff. "Shall we duel then, O Bolas? Shall we wring what little mana we can from the rocks, the wind and the cold, lifeless tide? Let's. Let us tilt at one another and waste precious seconds of your newfound freedom and my window of opportunity. What could be wiser or more productive?

"Much has changed since you were dead, Great Dragon. Stop a moment. See what has become of your holdings, what has happened to your empire on Dominaria. The mana here was unique, among the most complex and robust on the entire plane. Madara has always offered a rich and exotic feast for the epicure to savor." Teferi smiled sadly. "Taste it now, great dragon, then tell me if you still wish to fight."

Nicol Bolas tilted his head, one eye half-closed, perhaps equally annoyed and amused by Teferi's eloquence. As he stood there, the dragon's scales glowed along their sharp edges. Moving gracefully for such a massive creature, he reached down with one clawed hand and pressed his scaled palm into the surface of the cliff. Colored light and smoke poured out from around his fingers. A bare moment passed, then Bolas straightened, breaking the vaporous connection between himself and the ground.

"Dire," he said. "You are entirely correct, little wizard. Much has changed here."

"It has, Great Dragon." Teferi seemed to relax. "What I must do may be the only way to restore this world. Will you let us pass?"

"Absolutely not," Bolas said. He spread his wings and lightning jagged behind him. "I have been a shadow of myself for far too long. You will serve as a test of this world's capacity to sustain me."

The thunder died down and the dragon contracted into himself, halving his size from one hundred feet down to fifty as purple light danced across his scales. Rather than diminishing Bolas's awesome presence, shrinking seemed only to intensify it, distilling his incalculable power into a purer, more volatile package.

"I shall add," the elder dragon said, "for someone who keeps the company of Keldons, you are remarkably careless with fighting words." Terrible fire vented from his mouth, wreathing his head in blue-black flames. "You offered a duel, Planeswalker. I accept." The dragon's eerily intelligent face twisted into a leer of unbridled hunger.

Teferi's face showed no fear. The tip of his staff flared, glowing so brightly that Jhoira had to shield her eyes. "So be it," he said.

Teferi felt a crippling chill run through him. He could do this, but his concentration and timing had to be perfect.

"Hoy, clean-head!" Radha's voice was faint and tinny to Teferi's ears.

What do you want? he sent.

She instantly shot back, *What the hells are you doing?*

I am protecting us from a power-hungry god.

You're provoking one. He said he was going to reward us.

And you believe him? You saw how he treated you when he needed to get free. Do you really want anything he'd give you?

I wouldn't hit him for offering it. Why not wait and see—

See? See what?

If he truly means us harm, and if so, then rip his guts out. If we can.

That's pretty craven talk from a Keldon.

No, it's advice from a seasoned warrior. Nobody baits a dragon carelessly, not even in Keld.

You heard him. He'll pounce if we try to leave.

So? Then he only gets some of us, and only maybe gets them. I say if you goad him into a fight now, get him all riled up, he's damned likely to take us all.

I thought Keldons always took the offensive.

That doesn't mean we walk face-first into the enemy with our hands at our sides. That's not initiative, that's stupidity.

Do what you must, Teferi thought bitterly. *Though I had hoped at least you would see the value of this. No matter. It's too late to change course now.*

Spoken like a true wizard, Radha said, *not a sailor, not a warrior, but a wizard. Good luck, you inexplicable ass. Nothing you do ever makes sense to me.*

Thank you, Radha.

The dragon's voice broke in, *May we begin, or do you plan to argue with all of your underlings in turn?*

Teferi looked up at the great elder dragon. "I'm ready," he said.

CHAPTER 20

"I'm ready."

With these words Teferi started the first planeswalker duel he'd had in more than four hundred years. The last had been against a raving mad, self-styled shark goddess in the deepest part of a maritime plane's planet-spanning ocean. He had only wanted a sample of their mana-infused coral, but she was not inclined to give it up.

That contest had not been a true test of his combat skills, as he simply harnessed the power of the gigantic sea, trapped the shark goddess in a mile-wide whirlpool, then phased her out of existence. Two minutes after the duel started Teferi had his coral and was preparing to leave. Two minutes after that the shark goddess reappeared, wondering where her foe had gone.

Madara no longer provided that kind of endless blue mana. The continent and its outlying islands were almost as threadbare and exhausted as Keld, but the magical resources here had been stronger to start. It wasn't much to work with, but it was enough for a fight that was bound to end quickly, one way or another.

Teferi now called the unstoppable urgency of the nearby tide to him, fortifying himself with the ebb and flow of the sea's endless rhythm. It would take an ocean of power to sweep Bolas aside, but Teferi hoped instead to drown the dragon in a mere bucketfull. His human shell contained the tidal force for an instant, then it expanded to more than ten times its normal size so that he was on equal footing with his gigantic opponent

Bolas did not react at all to Teferi's sudden growth beyond tilting his head to follow its progress. The dragon had risen into the air once more, reveling in the physical expression of his might, lost in the joys of his gathering strength.

Teferi shaped more of the blue mana he'd gathered, holding it in check as he arranged the ritual's complicated words and motions. The dragon beat his wings and rose higher into the air, drawing lightning to him from the clouds. Jagged energy blasted into his hands and feet and coiled around his wrists and ankles like glittering, barbed wire jewelry.

Teferi concentrated. Radha's lack of support was especially irritating, as he intended to apply modified Keldon tactics to this contest. There was no hope of matching his opponent's strength, but Teferi knew he didn't have to be faster or stronger than the dragon, just faster and stronger than the dragon expected. None of Bolas's raw might or magical skill meant much if he never employed them. If Teferi struck preemptively, before the enemy had a chance to bring all his faculties to bear, he could best even a planeswalking elder dragon.

At the very least he could contain Bolas, possibly even bind him or banish him until after Shiv was safely re-installed.

The secret, of course, was time. Stopping Bolas where he stood or removing him entirely from the time stream would end the duel as surely as overpowering him would. The dragon would almost certainly deflect or avoid Teferi's basic phasing spells, which were the simplest way he knew to stop any impending threat, even one of this magnitude. This duel called for something grander, however, something potent enough to restrain the dragon yet subtle enough to slip past his defenses.

Teferi opted for a straightforward stasis field concealed in a cone of frigid cold. Bolas was a fire dragon, but he was also connected to the blue mana that Teferi used. The dragon would recognize ice magic and might even allow it to strike him, just to show how ineffective it was. Teferi would have him then, for no matter where the cold blast hit, the underlying stasis trap would spring.

Teferi shaped his spells, weaving them together in his mind until they were indistinguishable. A surge of blue mana swelled up inside him and his feet rose off the ground. Overhead Nicol Bolas beat his wings once more, folded them, then dropped toward Teferi like a falling star.

Teferi flew upward to meet the dragon head-on. Everything hinged on his convincing Bolas that he intended to trade blows until one of them fell. He had to make this seem like a sheer contest of wills and brute power, making Bolas think Teferi was fighting on the dragon's terms.

Now. Teferi stopped short and extended his staff in both hands. He shouted in the liquid, mathematical language of time that he created for himself as blue energy ripped from his eyes and mouth. These azure beams merged with the glow from the tip of his staff, mingled for a moment, then lurched upward. The icy point of the spell's frozen cone pulsated as it streaked toward its target.

Bolas took the bait. He saw the incoming blast of ice and light, seeing how its conical point left snowflakes and specks of frost in the air as it passed. The great dragon also stopped, slowing to a hover but making no effort to dodge. Instead he confidently crossed his arms and waited.

When Teferi's spell was about to touch him, Bolas disappeared. The tip of the cone ripped through a ghostly after-image of the dragon, but Bolas himself was no longer there.

Ripping pain shot through Teferi, the same kind he'd felt on the shores of Keld. Bolas had planeswalked out of danger, apparently unaware of the nearby rift's traumatic effect. Teferi allowed himself a bit of celebration. If the 'walk was agonizing for Teferi, he could only imagine what it was like for the dragon.

Bolas reappeared in precisely the same spot. Though he still wore an overconfident grin his face was strained. Was he too proud to show the harm his dodge had done? Or was he shamming, trying to lure Teferi in? Either way, the trick Freyalise played on Teferi over Skyshroud had not harmed Bolas over Madara.

Teferi let fly another flashy spell, one designed to paralyze the dragon's body and mind without affecting the flow of time around him. Bolas exhaled a stream of fire that met Teferi's shimmering beam halfway between them, where they mingled and baffled one another, each dissolving against the other.

Now, Teferi thought again, and this time he meant *now*. He continued to pour mana into his effort against Bolas, but Teferi also reached out to the first spell he'd cast. The icy cone with the long blue trail was still rising, leaving the planeswalker duel behind, but when Teferi called it answered like a well-trained dog.

The cone curved back on its course. Nicol Bolas was focused on outlasting Teferi, his attention squarely in front of him until Teferi's concealed stasis spell slammed solidly into his back.

Teferi swallowed a triumphant yell as Bolas disappeared into a cloud of white light and sparkling blue smoke. He stared hard at the cloud, watching it harden and fall from the sky. It landed with a jarring boom. The rough chunk of opaque white ice cast off waves of white vapor that dropped heavily to the ground. Bolas was inside still, and like the block of ice he was as cold and immobile as stone.

Teferi exhaled. He had done it. Overconfidence was the only weakness every planeswalker shared, but he had exploited Bolas's first. Now the dragon was frozen in time as well as space, held fast in the grip of a spell that deflected seconds the way a seal's coat shed mild summer rain. All of the dragon's impulses were now suspended, his thoughts, deeds, and spells alike immobilized and stuck fast.

That was most effective, Nicol Bolas said, *but ultimately? Unimpressive.*

A dull boom sounded from within the iceberg. The solid white mass sublimated from ice into a cloud of steam and disappeared on the breeze.

Teferi's composure all but vanished as Bolas' face flew toward him, the titan's wild-eyed visage swelling to fill Teferi's view. The wizard tried to throw up a shield, create a decoy, even tried to planeswalk away, but he was caught fast in the jaws of the dragon.

Overconfidence is the only weakness all planeswalkers share, Bolas hissed mockingly.

Physical contact with the dragon sent Teferi into an all-out seizure. His mind became scrambled and his body jerked convulsively. His physical essence disintegrated, but Bolas's dread jaws bore down anyway, crushing Teferi's spirit as thoroughly as his bones.

Barely able to form a coherent thought, Teferi tried to delay the end with the only weapon he could muster. *How?* he sent, his thoughts ragged and weak.

Bolas replied. *There are monuments to me in every corner of the multiverse,* he said. *Visit one the next time you take the notion to turn me into a statue. Stasis?* He spat the word out as if it stung him. *You sought to imprison me in the absence of time?*

The dragon's yellow eyes appeared before Teferi, spewing madness and yellow light. Teferi thanked providence for these few unearned seconds, but he could do little else besides suffer and listen to the dragon's terrible, triumphant roar.

Time is a most formidable weapon, he said, *and perhaps the only one you use effectively, but time is only as potent as the caster and the mana he uses. Mind and will-power win duels, little wizard, not the scale of your weaponry. You commanded time to stop, to ignore me, and it would have obeyed . . . but I also spoke to it, and mine is the only voice that matters. Mind and willpower make the difference, little wizard, and yours are no match for mine.*

A cage of null time. Bolas chuckled. *As if that would hinder me. I spent centuries outside existence, separate from time or place. I was alone, adrift, bereft, and utterly forgotten.*

Because I died. I underestimated a canny little insect and I died in a created realm that could not withstand the energies released by my passing. That place ceased to exist even though I did not. Death's hand opened to claim me, but I am still a dragon. I go only where I please.

I remained in the ghostly memory of the place where I died, little more than a ghost myself. Mind, body, and spirit alike were all broken and lost, but I am still a dragon, and my indomitable will remained.

Teferi's being exploded in agony as Bolas stripped away his conscious mind one layer at a time, eroding his higher functions thought by thought.

Over the decades, my mind returned. My power followed, slowly, until I was complete in every sense but the most obvious: I was incorporeal. The body that had linked me to Madara was gone, blasted to ashes. I could not return here, nor could I escape into the Blind Eternities. I had been removed from everything real and imagined and could only haunt this wretched beach as I watched those wretched cats take half my empire.

Teferi felt his essence being torn in two, a wrenching experience that left him sundered in both body and mind. Each half of his consciousness so longed for the missing half that he was completely consumed by the ache, unable to focus on anything but his own divided self.

Now I have returned. In my exile I had occasion to study the time rift that pierces the Talon Gates. I could sense and gauge the effect it had on this world. I could imagine how it affected all the other worlds it touches. I became its keeper, familiar with every ephemeral speck and spark of its substance. That is how I found you.

Teferi's mind began to break down under Bolas' casual abuse. Sensing his victim was about to shut off, Bolas changed tactics. Physical pain assailed Teferi, though he had no physicality left. He felt his body stretching beyond its limits in all directions, his bones splintering and muscles tearing as he was flattened into a two-dimensional shape without depth or mass.

Your spark is familiar to me, Teferi Time-Chaser, but useless. If a spark could have returned me here, I would have used my own, but the Keldon and the artificer . . . did you sense their connection to the rifts when you pulled them in behind you? No matter. I was able to use their abilities even if they cannot and you will not . . . openly.

Teferi felt himself slipping away. The dragon's voice grew faint and though the constant agony did not relent, it stopped growing infinitely worse with each passing second.

This is very disappointing, Bolas said. *You have absolutely no talent for combat. Still, that is not unexpected.*

Teferi was suddenly whole again, back in the human shape and size he routinely wore. He caught a glimpse of Jhoira and Radha and the others before sharp, cutting pain ripped across both shoulders, then both elbows, then in turn across his neck, waist, knees, and hips.

The world tumbled crazily before his wide, staring eyes. He landed with one cheek pressed tight against the ground, peering up at Jhoira's horrified face. He tried to shut his eyelids, but he was as helpless and immobile as he'd tried to make the dragon.

Despite the pain, the failure, and the ruinous mistakes he continued to make, Teferi could still think. He would like to take back many of the things he had said and done over the past day. He should have skipped Urborg and gone straight to Shiv, as Jhoira had expected; he should have played to his strengths and used diplomacy or deflection to avoid a duel with the multiverse's oldest planeswalker; he should have enlisted more help at the outset of this endeavor, perhaps recruited Windgrace and even Freyalise. Together they could have gathered information simultaneously from the different sites, and when Shiv finally returned there would be multiple planeswalkers there to ensure its safe installation.

Teferi tried to blink, but even this was beyond his power at present. He found that his priorities had realigned with his current ability to achieve them, so he wished only for something that was possible, a minor boon from fortune's wheel.

He knew what was coming next, and if he could change but one thing about his current situation, it was for him to be facing away from Jhoira and the others when Nicol Bolas turned his attentions to them.

It was childish and selfish, he knew, but the truth was he'd rather not have to watch.

* * * * *

Radha stood between the dragon and the Shivans. It all seemed to happen so quickly, beginning and ending before she really even understood the stakes.

Giant Teferi had blasted the big scaly bugger and froze him solid, but it didn't seem to take. The dragon then snatched Teferi up in his jaws and they both disappeared. A few seconds later, Bolas returned with normal-sized Teferi's slack body in his outstretched hand. The dragon's claws left streaks of jagged black light in their wake, and when he opened his hand, Teferi fell from it in pieces. The bald wizard's head, arms, and legs all dropped off his trunk, which was then slashed in two across the middle.

As before, there was no blood. The pieces of Teferi's body tumbled like well-chopped firewood and the planeswalker's head landed facing Jhoira. If she hadn't warned Teferi not to pick this fight, Radha might have felt sorry for him.

"Now then," Bolas said. "We have unfinished business."

"No." Radha took another step forward, increasing the distance between her and the others. "We're done."

She was not worried about getting too close to the monster— he had proven his reach was longer than the distance between them—but Radha did hope to minimize any damage to the others if he lashed out at her.

Bolas insouciantly turned his head toward Radha. "Manners, young lady. I was speaking to the command element of your unit, to Jhoira of the Ghitu."

"I am here, Sensei." Jhoira came up alongside Radha, her expression placid. She motioned for Radha to step back.

"Young?" Radha stood fast and spoke to the dragon. "I'm eighty years old this winter. I haven't been young in a long time."

"Eighty years," Bolas said. "Adolescence for an elf. A blink for me."

Radha's grip tightened around the handle of Astor's dagger. "My grandmother was two hundred and sixty before she stopped calling herself 'middle-aged,' " Radha said. "My mother declared herself old and shriveled at one hundred and fourteen. How many years did you swallow before you no longer felt young?"

The dragon's scaly lips pulled back in a predatory smile. He huffed out a cloud of dark smoke and a throaty chuckle. "I like you, my dear. I apprehended the Keldons were a quarrelsome people, but you are downright convivial."

"We are a quarrelsome people."

"Yet you haven't bragged or bullied at all. You certainly haven't begged. You've no idea how refreshing that is."

Radha nodded. "And you haven't destroyed me, as you clearly can. Why not?"

Bolas shrugged. "You interest me. You and the artificer. Surely your captain"—he motioned to the pile of Teferi's pieces—"told you about the remarkable thing you two have in common."

"I have very little in common with that sallow, shrinking worm."

The dragon's calm ease darkened and grew sharp. "Shall I take him, then? Shall I leave you and the others be and savor his flesh between my teeth? I may find what I need from him by straining through his remains, but then again, I may not."

"Don't," Jhoira said. Radha looked at Venser, who was sweating.

"It's all one to me," she said.

"Is it, now?" Bolas's eyes sparkled. Once more they began radiating waves of force. "If I extend my hand for him now, your disinterest will hold? You will let me have him . . . and also discourage that foolish little man with the weapon made of rocks and string?" The dragon craned his huge head, looking over Radha's shoulder. She knew Aprem was standing there but did not follow the dragon's stare.

"Ghitu," she said. "Don't do it. Don't even think about it."

Aprem stepped forward. Radha's teeth clenched when she saw the bolas ready in his hand.

"Venser is under our protection," Aprem said, his pale face betraying his brave words.

"Indeed," Bolas said, "and what will you do to those who mean Venser harm? Will you strike me down? Will you ignite your awesome weapon and vanquish me with it? I believe you can do it. Do you believe?"

Aprem croaked, "I do."

"Aprem," Radha said. "Shut up."

"And stand down," Jhoira added.

The dragon's tongue flashed. "Then do it," he said.

The Ghitu man sneered at them, his face feverish and distracted. He spun his bolas vertically alongside himself so that it whistled a bare inch above the ground and an inch above his head. On the third revolution, the multiple weights burst into flame.

Now Jhoira and Dassene both moved forward, calling out to

Aprem. Instead of acknowledging their pleas, Aprem kept glancing down at Teferi's body, his face growing slacker and paler as the cold sweat ran down from his forehead.

Bolas frowned. He spoke casually, his tone jaded and bored. "Teferi used paralysis magic to counter my fire," he said, "but there are better ways to deal with an overabundance of heat." He glanced over to Radha. "Thus."

"Don't bother," Radha said, but Bolas already turned back to Aprem and lifted one eyebrow.

Something surged invisibly between them and Aprem cried out. The Ghitu staggered back and dropped his flaming bolas. His eyes widened as if perhaps he understood what was happening to him. Then the red-garbed warrior sagged inside his skin, his body sliding and contracting grotesquely as gravity pulled his now-fluid muscles and tendons away from his bones.

Aprem listed obscenely, his head half-swollen and half-collapsed into an asymmetrical horror. Dassene called her tribesman's name as the last vestiges of rigidity left him. His bones dissolved and his skin lost cohesion so that Aprem poured onto the ground. He did not splash or splatter but spread out across the surface of the cliff top. Neither his clothing nor his features blended into the larger mass as it spread, so the surface of his puddlelike corpse still displayed the distorted, liquefied remains of Aprem's lips, nose, hair, and eyes.

Dassene screamed in outrage as she drew her batons. She struck the polished sticks together and both ends ignited.

Before the Ghitu could focus her magic on the dragon, Radha tackled her high across the shoulders. They both crashed to the ground and as they landed Radha noted the Ghitu's body was hot to the touch, that smoke was pouring from under the bandages on Dassene's hand.

Fire sparked in Dassene's eyes and she struggled to shove Radha off. "Let me up," she said.

"What for?"

"To avenge. To take a piece of that smug bastard with me."

"Stupid." Radha squeezed and crushed the air from Dassene's lungs. "Wasteful. You stand down now and I'll let you go. Otherwise I'm going to knock you on the head."

Dassene redoubled her efforts. "Get off," she snarled. "Aprem and I were trained for this. We volunteered. We are *Mi'uto*, one-use warriors. We are *expendable*."

Radha looked into the Ghitu warrior's eyes, so close to her own. She tilted her head back and drove her forehead into the bridge of Dassene's nose.

"Not to me," she said.

Red blood splashed and Dassene's eyes rolled back. She went limp in Radha's arms. The Keldon elf gently lowered Dassene and rolled her onto her side so she wouldn't choke.

Radha disentangled herself and stood to face Nicol Bolas. Behind her, Jhoira and the others drew near. "Are we done here?" she shouted angrily. She turned to her party. "Does anyone else want to waste their best effort and die?" She turned back to Bolas. "Hoy, dragon," she said. "You're alive again. You're free. Why are you still here? I'd be very surprised if the thing you want most is on this rock."

Bolas's calm expression did not waver. "Perhaps, but right now, I'm enjoying myself immensely."

"All right, but we're in a hurry. Do whatever it is you're planning then pop off, will you? There's five of us standing here and none is stronger than the wizard you just shredded." She drew her kukri dagger and a tear-shaped blade, emphasizing her words with the tips. "We don't care about you." She struck the blades together and flames sprang up along their sharp edges. "Leave us be or kill us now, but Venser and I won't let you take anyone else. We all live or we all die."

Bolas laughed merrily, then he snapped his jaws together with a sharp crack. "Do you now speak for the group?"

"I do."

The dragon peered down at Radha, malevolent joy brimming in his voice. "Prove it," he said.

Radha's lip curled. She turned and looked pointedly at Venser. The Urborg native was no warrior, but he was also no fool. He drew a thin, spiked tool from his belt and stepped up alongside Radha.

Venser brandished the sharp implement and said, "Radha speaks for us all."

Radha grunted appreciatively. "Plus," she said, "I'm going to stick Venser as soon as the fight starts to make sure you never get near him."

"Hey," Venser said. Recovering, he added, "Well, I'll stick you, too. Then he gets nothing."

Bolas. Teferi's voice was thin and distant. The dragon gestured, and Teferi's severed head rose into the air on a column of empyrean light. Bolas extended his hand under the head and it dropped into his palm.

"You have something to add?"

I do. Teferi's eyes were blank white and his mouth gaped lifelessly. *The multiverse is changing. The rifts that you plucked us from are expanding. All of them. Dominaria is teetering on the tip of a needle, and Shiv's return will bring it crashing down. Not even you will be safe.*

"My, my," the dragon said. "Everyone is in such a hurry to see me go, and all with my best interests at heart." He sniffed mockingly. "I am quite moved."

Look, Planeswalker, Teferi said. *See what I have seen.*

Bolas concentrated on the head in his hand. He stood silent and still for several minutes as his face and Teferi's took on a dim blue sheen. Radha thought she saw the dragon wince slightly, but only once.

The dim glow faded. Bolas turned his palm sideways, letting Teferi's head bounce carelessly away.

"This audience is over," he said. The dragon spread his wings, and though they did not flap he still rose into the air.

Radha suspiciously watched the dragon's slow ascent. Venser still stood by her, clenching the spiked implement so tightly his knuckles popped.

"Live long, Keldon elf." Bolas opened his eyes wide and fixed Radha with a penetrating stare. She held it as he rose ever higher. "If this world does end, I will look for you and your Urborg consort in another. Survive the coming twilight," he said, as his eyes grew dark and malignant, "or I shall be sorely disappointed." Bolas extended his arms, legs, wings, and tail. Swirling masses of force and light churned behind him, a beguiling pinwheel of magical energy.

"As for me, I will travel to the place that spawned a plague on Madara. I will find the spirit that infected my empire before it was even truly mine." His eyes flashed angrily. "There will be a reckoning. I will devour the dark lady who brought Madara so much misery, then I will travel the length and breadth of the multiverse, charring to ashes every root, branch, bud, and leaf on the Umezawa family tree. Even those who have already passed from the world of the living." The dragon's face was alive with unholy joy. "Especially those. I made a vow, after all.

"Farewell, Dominaria. If the time-chaser succeeds, I shall return to you. If not, I shall always recall you as the once-brightest jewel in my hoard."

No escape, Teferi called weakly. *No safe place.*

The elder dragon had already turned and was picking up speed on his way toward the Talon Gates. His body seemed to stretch as he rocketed out to sea, lengthening into a ruler-straight streak that shifted in color and intensity from electric blue to flat black to vibrant red. The streak vanished several hundred yards from the center of the Talon Gates, but a split-second later the space inside the curved stone spires turned white. The center of the opaque oval became angry red as if heated in forge beyond its capacity, and the ground shuddered.

Radha and the others watched a massive wave surge up between the gates and the shoreline. The mountain of water gathered speed as it swept inland, seething with salt-white foam. The deluge hit and completely submerged the beach as far up the coastline as Radha could see. Though it barely reached halfway up the sheer cliff face, the wave's impact shook the whole region and knocked almost everyone off their feet.

When the tremor subsided, Radha roughly pushed Venser off her and went to check on Dassene. The Ghitu woman's eyes would be bruised and her nose painfully swollen for the next few days, but she was alive. Dassene might choose to hold that fact against her, but Radha was confident she could dissuade the firecaster from holding a grudge. If not, she could always knock her on the head again.

Jhoira stood, brushed the dust from her robes, and wordlessly went to Teferi. Radha watched her for a moment, then she rose to follow Jhoira. She caught up to the Ghitu as Jhoira was stooping to lift the larger section of Teferi's torso.

"Thank you," Jhoira said, though she did not sound grateful. If anything, the intense young woman had the air of someone who must continue, though they were no longer sure their goal existed.

"For what?"

"For taking charge. For standing off an elder dragon."

Radha shrugged, genuinely confused. "I barely amused him." She watched Jhoira collect Teferi's upper legs and put them on the ground below the torso. His bloodless body was slowly taking shape.

Radha waited for Jhoira to look up then shot her a questioning look. She gestured at Teferi with her head cocked.

"He's still our best hope," Jhoira said.

"He's in pieces."

"Earlier he was stabbed through the head, but he got back up then and he'll get back up now. You heard his voice, didn't you? He isn't dead."

Radha considered for a moment. She glanced around, spotted one of Teferi's arms, and went to pick it up so she could add it to the pile.

CHAPTER 21

Jhoira sat comfortable and cross-legged near the edge of the cliffs. Teferi's fractured body was arranged to approximate his assembled shape, the pieces separated by a bare inch at the key joints and seams. It had been hours since Nicol Bolas vanished through the Talon Gates.

Corus and Skive were currently finishing a funeral cairn for Aprem, using their claws to gouge through the rocky soil. Dassene sat numbly by, both eyes and her nose swollen and bruised.

Venser sat beside Jhoira with his eyes on Teferi but his mind clearly back in Urborg. Bolas had chosen well when he picked the artificer to beguile—Venser's work was all he had, and Urborg was all he knew. Thankfully, even Radha had grown tired of brow-beating him and now dismissed Venser's repeated apologies.

"If he had asked me if I wanted to go home," she said at last, "I would have said yes, because I did." She shrugged. "He would have gotten me instead of you."

Radha herself now stood closer to the edge of the cliffs, watching the Talon Gates for any sign of activity and the sky for nekoru. Nothing had moved since the dragon departed, nothing but the waves and an occasional sea bird. The Keldon elf was remarkably patient during their wait, almost unnervingly so. Jhoira guessed that like Venser, Radha's thoughts had returned to her homeland.

Teferi's head stirred. The planeswalker had not spoken or shared his thoughts since they gathered him together. Blue-white energy glowed in the spaces between his parts and they rose together off of the ground. Teferi's blank eyes blinked. His body slowly pulled together, knitting together at the ends and merging into one contiguous shape.

"He's back," Radha called. Corus and Skive stood and waited for Dassene, but the Ghitu shook her head. The two viashino nodded and proceeded toward the larger group.

Teferi's rich brown pupils rolled down into their sockets as the viashino arrived. He stared for a moment, focusing, then he somberly turned to them all.

"Hello," he said. "Thank you all for watching over me. I would like to pay my respects to Aprem."

Jhoira read the looks on the viashino's faces and said, "Wait until later. Are you recovered?"

"I am. Though I can't say I am none the worse for wear." He smiled, but his joy was grim and hollow. "I believe I owe you all an apology."

"What for?" Radha said. The others looked at her and she added, "Where would he even begin? There's so much."

"That is the crux of it," Teferi said. "From the start I have been relying on others to help me complete my task. I went to Freyalise because she had experience, I pursued Radha because she had mana, and I went to Venser because he had interaction with the rift. Even before I started I tried to put the onus and the impetus for my endeavors on Jhoira . . . which she politely accepted, if only to shut me up."

"Did it work?" Radha asked. "You should bottle it."

"It was partially successful." Jhoira looked to Teferi and said, "You were building to something."

Teferi nodded. "Shiv will return in two days," he said, "and I must be there to guide it safely home. I will need at least a day to prepare myself and the receiving ground, so I intend to depart momentarily. I thank you all for your help, given willingly or not. You have all been of great service to me, but that service is now concluded. I will ask no more of you, any of you, from this point forward."

"Don't be absurd," Jhoira said angrily. "Venser aside, we all agreed to help you see this through." She gestured to herself and the viashino and Dassene beside Aprem's cairn. "Shiv is our home. It's my home, and that's why you took it away in the first place. You and I agreed at the outset that this is all my fault, and I'll be thrice-damned if I'll let you make amends without me."

Teferi's face clouded. "That agreement was just a bit of face-saving irony entirely intended to be humorous."

"Bolas was right about you," Jhoira said. "You should choose your words more carefully. Things go badly for you every time you meet someone who cares more about what you say than how you say it."

"Nevertheless," Teferi said, "I won't ask of others what I wouldn't do myself, and since I'm the only one who can do what needs be done, I would prefer to proceed alone."

"That's asinine," Radha said. "If the past few days have taught you anything, clean-head, it should be that you need as much help as you can get."

Corus rose to his full height. "I came to see my home restored," he said. "Dismiss me so close to the end, Planeswalker, and you will have made an enemy for life."

"See? Your apology is accepted," Jhoira said officiously, "but your offer is not. Most of us came only to help you, and that's what we still intend to do."

Teferi watched her sharply for a few moments, then he turned to Venser. "I owe you a special apology, my friend. You never meant to leave Urborg and you never agreed to visit Shiv. You have been literally dragged into this fiasco, and I would have used you toward my own ends without ever explaining it to you."

Venser shifted uncomfortably. "I don't want to go back right away," he said quietly.

Teferi smiled, a brief bright flicker of amusement. "Don't worry," he said. "Bolas is long gone."

The artificer relaxed a little. "Oh," he said. "That's not what I meant. Corus and Skive were telling me that Shiv once had a factory that manufactured powerstones."

Teferi nodded. "That is true. Though I believe it got up and walked away during the Phyrexian Invasion."

Venser tapped the pouch on his belt. "These stones are the only thing I have that's worth keeping. There aren't two more in all of Urborg. If I had two more . . . even one more, it would cut my testing time in half." He shrugged and laughed a little. "Besides, if what you say is true, the world might end in two days anyway. I might as well be there to see it."

Jhoira almost hugged the Urborg native, not just for his casual, selfless grace, but for the effect it had on Teferi. The planeswalker smiled, a long, warm, sustained grin.

"Thank you," Teferi said. He turned slightly. "And you, Radha? Do you want to see if the world will end with a bang firsthand?"

"No," Radha said evenly, "and not just because I don't understand or care about half of what you just said."

"Oh?" Teferi's genial mood faltered. "Why else?"

"I've been thinking since we left Keld. It's been good for me to see things from a distance. I've got a few ideas I'd like to use on the Gathans. I need to get back and use them before Greht finishes building his armada and sails away."

The others stared at her, some confused, others sullen.

"What?" Radha said. "He told us we're free to go if we want. That's what I want." She turned back to Teferi and tossed her hair out of her eyes. "There's still the issue of payment, Planeswalker."

Teferi nodded. "Shall I give you all the knowledge in the *Book of Keld?* I don't have time to recite it, but I know a few spells that would implant it in your mind as if—"

"Don't bother," Radha said. "I just want a few specific things. How many corpse marker symbols do you know?"

Teferi tilted his head and stared at an imaginary point just over Radha's head. "One hundred and sixty," he said.

"How many are in High Keld?"

Teferi stared off into space for a second more. "Twenty-three."

"That's perfect." She tapped her forehead. "Give 'em here."

Teferi's eyes lit up. For the first time since his reassembly, Jhoira noticed the buoyant curiosity that normally drove him, the acute joy of new discovery.

"It's a bit intrusive," Teferi said. "I have to open up your mind to put the information in. You have to relax your guard a bit, and . . . well, doing this will bind us more closely. It will be much easier for me to reach out to you in the future."

"So?"

"So it's less like sharing your thoughts and more like letting me rummage through them."

"So? You've done that before."

"Not like this. What I'm about to do makes that seem like polite dinner conversation."

"So?" Radha shrugged. "Go ahead."

Teferi's eyes flashed blue. Radha choked and snarled as her own eyes mirrored the azure light. There was a pop and a plume of smoke, and the Keldon elf staggered back a step.

Radha rubbed her eyes. When she glanced up over her pinched fingers, she wore a wide, wolfish smile. "Oh, I can definitely use these," she said happily.

"Now," Teferi said, "if we're all agreed, I will send Radha back to Skyshroud and take the rest of us on to Shiv."

"Wait." Radha held up her hand and looked across to the cairn. There was no one by the grave site.

Dassene has silently stolen up on the group, hanging back behind Corus. Radha stepped out to see her and said, "Ghitu. I am glad you're alive. You also have information I need, but you only owe me a smack in the face. What will it take for you to teach me that fire-blasting spell you use?" She drew two blades and crossed them in front of her. "The one where you do this."

Dassene stepped around Corus, edging her way into the group. She was breathing heavily through her swollen nose.

"I will not teach you my secrets, Radha."

The Keldon elf's face soured. She sheathed her weapons.

Dassene continued. "There isn't time. In the coming weeks, certainly, but in the short term you'd better leave it to me." The Ghitu crossed in front of Corus and Skive and stood beside Radha.

"I'm going with her," Dassene said. She endured their stunned looks and went on, "I should have died battling the fiend who killed my caste-brother. Radha didn't allow it. My life is hers now, and I will give it willingly at her order."

"Dassene, wait," Jhoira said. "You aren't thinking clearly. Aprem wouldn't want this. The tribal elders—"

"Aprem is dead," Dassene said brusquely. She gestured with her head toward Teferi. "I have lost what little faith I had in this operation. I no longer wish to follow his orders, and he has released me from his service." She shrugged, her blackened eyes flat and lifeless. "I'm leaving."

"Me too," Skive said. Corus hissed angrily, but the smaller viashino stepped away and fell in beside Radha. "I'm an infantry grunt," Skive said. He lifted the mana star pendant from his chest and held it in his fist. "I don't even use magic, not really. I don't know what use I'm going to be when this large-scale mystical event happens." With a sharp jerk, Skive snapped the chain around his neck.

"I've been in a Keldon warhost before. I liked it."

Corus's tongue lashed angrily through his clenched teeth. "You're going to quit? This close to our ancestral land's return?"

Skive hissed in exasperation. "That presumes they'll ever get here. I agree with the Ghitu: following Teferi means spending half your time waiting for him to figure out which way he wants to go. I'd rather spend my last two days killing berserkers than watching him meditate, especially if we're all going to die afterwards anyway."

Corus glared over at Radha. "She bit me," he groused.

"I know. To tell you the truth, that was kind of impressive."

Both viashino fell silent but for the scrape of their tongues against their teeth. They all stood now not as one group, but two. Radha, Dassene, and Skive stood facing Jhoira, Venser, and Corus, with Teferi in the center.

Jhoira thought her friend had never looked so crestfallen yet so euphoric. He seemed a man who had gotten what he wanted but lost what he had. When he spoke, his voice was warm and patient. "Has everyone said their piece?"

No one replied.

Teferi said, "Then we are truly done here." He extended his arms wide and the curved spine-staff appeared in his hand. "Gather round, my friends and colleagues. We go back to Keld, to Skyshroud, but only for a moment." He nodded at Radha.

"And then," he continued. "At long last, we go to Shiv."

CHAPTER 22

Teferi had all but mastered the delicate art of planeswalking in close proximity to the rifts. He left Radha, Corus, and Dassene near the edge of Skyshroud, and though Freyalise did not present herself, Teferi still felt her eyes and her disapproval upon him.

There were few good-byes exchanged at the parting. There were no well-wishings, either, but quite a few angry glances.

He 'walked the remains of the group into the flushed-pink sky over Shiv, closely approximating the view they enjoyed on their trip through the rift network. The unnaturally precise arc of the coastline was exactly as they had seen it, a straight-edged scoop of land and sea. After a touch of Teferi's magic, the time rift above the sheer vertical rocks also appeared as it had before, an angry crimson window that revealed an alternate Shiv choked with mana-processors and smoke.

As he floated his team down to the searing sand, Teferi took a deep, long look into the Shivan rift. Jhoira and the others surely noticed the alternate Shiv was complete, the missing section either safely restored or never removed in the first place. With his special interest in time and the power of a planeswalker, Teferi still could not tell if the images he saw were from the future, the past, or nowhere at all. If only he knew: did a complete Shiv evidence the success of his present venture, or demonstrate a fate the nation would have suffered had Teferi left it alone?

A darker thought occurred. Was he actually seeing a Shiv from so far in the future that it negated any success he might have here today? Was Shiv destined lose all its rough natural beauty and raw strength in order to become an endless field of industrialized blight?

The permutations were overwhelming, but Teferi shook his mind clear. His plan could still work. He just had to wait for Shiv's actual return to begin before he could gauge how best to minimize the impact.

These were the lies he told himself so that he could tell them to Jhoira if she asked. Otherwise, he would never be able to see it through.

Jhoira and Corus reacted immediately upon touching the ground. First exhaling warmly as if settling into a favorite comfortable chair, their pleasure quickly turned to irritation, or at least, disappointment. It reminded Teferi of his first taste of vanilla extract, which his mother distilled from beans she grew herself. The thick, viscous liquid smelled like paradise, sweet and delicious. Touch a drop to your tongue, however, and the strong bitter taste ripped you right out of any reverie created by the scent.

Jhoira began to cough painfully and Venser stumbled. Teferi quickly cast a protection spell to preserve them from Shiv's heat and toxic fumes. Corus did not seem too adversely affected by the landscape, but Teferi included him nonetheless.

Jhoira soon recovered her breath. "This isn't Shiv," she said curtly. Before Teferi could argue, she turned to him and said anxiously, "Not anymore. We have to bring it back."

"We will."

"Excuse me?" Venser was the only one not consumed with memories of the place. He had slipped the collar of his tunic up over his nose to filter out the stale smell of volcanic gas, but the pungent stuff still brought water to his eyes. "I think I see people. Or . . . something. There."

Jhoira and Corus both focused on where Venser was pointing. Jhoira's eyes were as hindered as Venser's, but Corus closed his inner eyelids and fixed on a small spot among the waves of heat distortion and choking vapor.

"Fiers' teeth," he said softly.

Teferi looked more closely, seeing the ragged pack of strangers clearly and in detail. It was awful, to be sure, but it was not a complete surprise.

"Are they human?" Venser said hopefully.

"Not at all," Teferi said. "No human could survive here long enough to digest a meal, much less establish a tribe. No, I make it about a half-dozen viashino and twenty, maybe thirty goblins." He peered closer. "And three or four orcs."

"Goblins? Orcs?" Venser was more curious than frightened. Orcs and goblins were not a common feature in the swamps of Urborg, so perhaps Venser didn't know enough to be afraid.

"Shiv never had orcs before." Still unable to see clearly, Jhoira kept peering out into the heat. She asked, "Are the others all in one group? Goblins and viashino working together?" She turned to Corus. "Maybe the harsh climate encouraged them to cooperate."

"The harsh climate has done more than that," Corus said. "I don't know orcs, but those are no viashino I recognize. The goblins are different, too."

Teferi agreed, but he was hesitant to do so out loud. Better to wait a few more moments until the local Shivans drew close enough for Jhoira to see. Teferi did not relish the look on her face when she saw the state of her countrymen, but he relished describing them to her even less.

The goblins were not too far removed from the ugly little vermin they had been since the dawn of time. They were stunted, misshapen, squat little humanoids with muted green skin. Their pointed ears flapped as they marched and their huge noses drooped almost down to their chests. Goblins were the butt of every joke when it came to war stories and soldier's gossip, but anyone who'd met them on the battlefield knew not to take them lightly once the fighting started. They were vicious, tenacious creatures, and they were far stronger than they appeared. They did not hesitate to bite, scratch, and gouge with their crooked teeth and their ghastly long fingernails. When they carried weapons, the blades were invariably rusty, chipped, and coated with grime, and the war clubs were always improvised from random pieces of wood or discarded bones.

These goblins were slightly bigger than the norm, though they all had the same desiccated look as the elves of Skyshroud. Where the elves seemed lean and willowy, the goblins were stubby and dense, their skin pulled tight around their bones to reveal every joint, tendon, and muscle.

The larger orcs were similar in appearance to the goblins, but each stood over eight feet tall. They all had huge, hunched shoulders, sunken chests, and protruding bellies. The orcs' snarling jaws were lined with jagged, misaligned fangs. Though they were dressed in rags and appeared even more primal and savage than their goblin cousins, the orcs were actually smarter, though also more subject to uncontrollable fits of rage.

It wasn't the goblins or the orcs that startled Corus and made Teferi hold his tongue. The viashino who now approached were some of the most dangerous and feral reptilians Teferi had ever seen. Modern viashino had clearly evolved during the three hundred years since Teferi phased out Shiv. Many of these had foot-long spines along their backs and tails, others bore them on their elbows and arms. Two of the warriors near the front had wide, flat face plates with spines jutting out from their eyebrows, cheekbones, and chins. All of the viashino spines were hollow and Teferi noted drops of a cloudy liquid trembling on each razor-sharp tip. Like Corus and Skive, they were all tall and broad but moved quickly, especially through loose sand, employing an efficient half-walk, half-skate across the acrid ground.

The noise of the goblin's clumsy cadence reached them while the Shivan mob was still hundreds of feet away. The savage gang was now close enough for even Jhoira and Venser to see in detail.

"They don't look friendly," Venser said.

"I will explain who we are," Corus said, "and why we have come." The big viashino slid forward across the sand, thick muscles rippling under his scales.

"I can protect us," Teferi said. "I have a barrier that will keep them and the environment safely at bay while I make my preparations."

Corus stopped, sneering angrily over his shoulder. "These are my people," Corus said. "We don't need protection from them."

Teferi turned to Jhoira as Corus went out to meet the inheritors of Shiv. "Is he right?"

Jhoira still seemed dazed by all that new Shiv had shown her. "I don't know."

Teferi huffed, slightly annoyed. "Will he live?"

"Definitely. Corus is one of the toughest creatures I've ever known. If things go badly, he'll disappear below the sand and emerge here," she pointed alongside Teferi. "His size actually makes him faster at sand-swimming since he can shift more of it with each stroke."

The mob slowed as Corus approached. All of the modern viashino came to the front of the pack, creating a line of reptilian bodies between Corus and the goblins, with the orcs still bringing up the rear.

"What are they saying?" Jhoira asked.

"It's hard to tell," Teferi said. He was squinting hard and concentrating. "Corus has hailed them, but their tongue is rough and unfamiliar. I can work it out if I have more time and they keep talking."

"What about Corus?"

"He seems to understand them well enough."

"Do they understand him?"

Teferi jabbed the end of his staff into the hot ground. "We shall see."

One of the plate-faced viashino slid up to Corus. He was nowhere near as broad or as solid as Corus but he was as tall. They eyed each other and exchanged long hisses as their tails lashed patterns in the sand.

The conversation grew heated. The plated lizard spat and lunged forward, grasping for Corus's mana star pendant. The bigger viashino caught the errant hand and held it tight.

Tighter still, Teferi thought, as the plated lizard suddenly dropped to his knees in pain. Corus continued to crush the sharp, skeletal hand as he opened his mouth wide. His long, forked tongue squirmed among rows of sharp white teeth and Corus let out a small roar to keep the rest of the mob at bay. Then he hauled the plated lizard forward, lowered his open jaws, and bit the other viashino's arm off at the elbow.

Chaos erupted so that even Teferi lost sight of what was going on. Several spiked viashino threw themselves at Corus, the goblin horde surged forward, and the orcs roared and pounded the ground. A cloud of sand and noise rose up around the combatants, completely obscuring them from view. A goblin and a spiked lizard came hurtling out from the cloud, arcing high over the desert in opposite directions. They stayed where they landed, neither moving nor breathing.

Something moved quickly and Teferi oriented on a ripple in the sand that seemed to be rolling their way. The mob still wallowed in angry confusion back where the fight had started, but the small hump of sand quickly slid up beside Teferi.

Corus stood up from under the sand as if he'd been buried there for hours. He shook some of the grit from his scales and exhaled angrily through his nose.

"They're beasts," he said. "I told them who we were. They said, 'you've got mana.' I told them what we were here to do. They said, 'give us that necklace.' I told them that Shiv would soon be whole again, and that flat-faced skink put his hands on me." He spat a mouthful of cold greenish blood to the ground and looked at Jhoira. "I'm sorry, Lady, but right now they only see us as prey."

Jhoira nodded. "Teferi," she said. "You mentioned a barrier. I think we need it now."

"Done," Teferi said. His head and hands were surrounded by a flash of white light that slowly radiated off in every direction. The noise from the mob and the caustic breeze were both suddenly muted, though there was no visible change in the area surrounding them. The only proof that Teferi had done anything was overhead, where the wind-driven sand and the choking haze both barked up against something invisible and bubble-shaped.

"That should hold," Teferi said, "for now."

"They won't go away," Corus said. "If anything, they'll send for reinforcements and try to siege us out of here."

"Two days is all we need," Teferi said. "I'm confident we can survive a two-day siege."

Corus nodded, unconvinced. "What if they bring enough force to break through your barrier?"

"I'll strengthen it," Teferi said. His eyes flashed blue. "Or I'll send the entire population to the far side of the world. For now, however"—he turned his back to the mob—"I'd like to prepare. Venser? Jhoira? If you would assist me?"

"Of course," Jhoira said.

Venser nodded. "Just tell me how."

"Stay close by, my friend. When I'm ready, I'll show you things and ask you what you think of them. All you need to do is answer."

Teferi looked up to the great red window overhead. He closed his eyes and his ears and let his other ascended senses reach out to the time rift.

Tell me your secrets, O Shiv, he thought, and I will make you whole.

* * * * *

Freyalise appeared moments after Teferi and the others disappeared. Radha had expected the patron of Skyshroud to summon her to the center of the forest, to make her crawl and beg for an audience. She had not expected Freyalise to come to her with every able-bodied ranger in the forest.

Freyalise was ethereal and imposing as she faded into view. "You have returned, Daughter of Skyshroud."

"I have," Radha said. "Along with these others."

Freyalise turned her sharp face toward Skive and Dassene. "They may not set foot in the forest."

"Suits me," Skive said.

"And me," Radha said. She stepped between Freyalise and the Shivans. "Greht and the Gathans are out there, in Keld proper. I didn't bring these people back to battle saprolings and slivers."

"Hold your tongue," Freyalise said sternly. "I have endured your impertinence and your disobedience for almost a century, but no longer. The time has come for you to prove your worth to your brothers and sisters. The forest is beset on all sides. Seek you conflict with the Gathans? Travel to any other spot on our border and you will find them, busy with axes and saw blades. Lead my Skyshroud Rangers and drive the berserkers from our home."

Radha shook her head. "The fight isn't here; it's at the mountain."

"Your fight is in Skyshroud," Freyalise said imperiously, "and Skyshroud is here."

Radha hesitated. "So your battle plan is to drive the Gathans away from the forest. How far? We can drive them to the sea if you like and they'll be back in a week."

"Don't scoff at me, child. I have been winning wars since before the first Keldon came down from Parma."

"My plan," Radha said, "is to challenge Greht. Killing him will end the degradation of Skyshroud, and the act of fighting him will draw every Gathan within shouting distance." She stepped forward and locked eyes with the planeswalker. "If they're watching me beat him, they can't be here taking trees.

"Let me go, Freyalise," she said. "My companions and I . . . plus any of your rangers who can still fight . . . will be sure to attract Greht's attention. He will know we're coming, and he will assemble the largest 'host he can to greet us, to watch us fail. There won't be enough of them to raid Skyshroud's timber until my duel with Greht is complete."

Freyalise held Radha's eyes without wavering. Slowly, so Radha would understand that it was not a matter of her yielding, the patron of Skyshroud craned her head to inspect Skive and Dassene. Then she turned back toward the throng of rangers, over two hundred strong.

"No," she said. She turned away, casually adding, "Come with me now to the far edge of the forest. We have work to do. Your friends can stay here, or circle around to meet us, or they can swim home to Shiv for all I care. So long as they do not set foot in Skyshroud, I have no interest in them."

Radha felt pure berserker bloodlust rising in her. She slid her fingers around the handle of Astor's dagger, remembering the feel as it punched up through Teferi's skull. Freyalise would never leave herself open and vulnerable as Teferi had, but Radha still ached to see if the patron of Skyshroud bled.

"Don't insult me with that toy." Freyalise did not stop striding and did not turn her head. "Save its edge and your strength for the Gathans."

Snarling, Radha drew the kukri. With her feet once more on Keldon soil and her grandfather's weapon in her hand, hot fiery mana was hers to command once more. The dagger's blade glowed searing red.

Freyalise stopped. A crimson flush crept up her shoulders and neck as she slowly turned back to Radha.

Radha did not wait for her to finish. She inhaled sharply, concentrating on her rage, focusing it through the kukri dagger. Freyalise completed her turn just as Radha drew back the angled blade and let it fly.

The dagger tumbled as it climbed, missing Freyalise by yards. It spun on, rising until it sank deep into the bark of a Skyshroud tree thirty feet above the ground.

"What—" Freyalise began, but the explosion prevented any more. The tree Radha hit erupted into flames that billowed out and up from where the dagger stuck, all the way up to Skyshroud's threadbare canopy.

Radha drew a tear-shaped blade in each hand and shouted. "Every step of the way, Planeswalker." Her face felt hot but Radha's mind was calm. "I'll take one tree with me for every step away from the mountain."

Freyalise's skin had gone beyond blood red. Her naked eye disappeared under a film of ruby light and she stood elegant, beautiful, and deadly as fire billowed behind her.

"Or," Radha said. She left the alternative unvoiced, instead striking the edges of her blades together. The space around her filled once more with leaves of vibrant green flame that circled and danced.

There was power here and in Skyshroud, but it would never be enough. Radha's Keldon blood demanded Keldon fire, and Freyalise must be made to see that.

Radha cried out as she crossed her blades then flung her arms out straight in front of her. The flames around her rushed up to the burning tree in a swirling cloud of bright, flickering shapes. Radha's stream of green leaves punched through the column of orange and yellow flames already surrounding the tree. The firelight streaming down on Freyalise changed, shifting from flickering yellow to constant, eerie green.

Freyalise simply stared, silent and furious, as Radha sheathed her blades. The fierce warrior allowed herself to smile at last. She gestured with her eyes, indicating the area above Freyalise. Disdainfully, Freyalise tilted her head back and turned only slightly.

The tree was completely surrounded by a cloud of flaming leaves. They were yellow, green, orange, and red, and though they burned brilliant against the dusky sky they did not consume the thin, dead branches. For a moment Radha's magic had not only recaptured the full glory of Skyshroud at its peak but surpassed it.

The fire tree lit up the entire valley, even casting its intense yellow glow back into the forest itself. Below, the saproling thicket wriggled and retreated from the glow, mewling piteously. The leaf-flames quickly spread to surrounding trees, wreathing each smooth trunk and skeletal branch in the same dazzling foliage. Soon the entire outer edge of Skyshroud was crackling. When the broken trunk directly over Llanach ignited, Radha saw the captain and all of his rangers standing amazed, shock-still. Silently astounded by the spectacle, the rangers' wide eyes were filled with the reflection of Radha's fire.

"I will lead your rangers, Freyalise," Radha said, "and I will save your forest, but I will do so my way and only on the mountain."

The patron of Skyshroud remained furiously red, glowing vapor rising from her goggled eye. With a haughty flick of her wrist, she extended her hand up and Astor's dagger tore free from the center of the great blaze. Handle-first, it flew to Freyalise's hand while the planeswalker continued to stare balefully at Radha. Deliberately, Freyalise lowered the dagger to eye level.

"Come with me now, my child." Freyalise opened her hand and dropped Astor's dagger to the snow. "To the far side of the forest."

Radha planted her feet and crossed her arms. "No."

Freyalise's angry color abruptly vanished. She stood facing Radha, her proud, pale features immobile as a porcelain doll's. "You are a constant trial to me and a perpetual disappointment." She waved her hand angrily, sending the kukri dagger whirling toward its owner. Radha stood her ground, eyes narrowed, and caught the dagger by the handle with the tip a finger-length from her nose.

"You are of Skyshroud," Freyalise said, "yet you turn your back on her. She has nurtured you, nourished your roots so that you might grow tall and strong. She tolerated your Keldon blood, hoping it would make you a better elf, a war chief to protect her from her violent neighbors. Instead, that blood has ever taken you away from her, luring you with promises of ancestral fire.

"Is this your final choice? To quit the forest for the mountain, to fight not for a cause or your home, but for the sheer joy of frenzy? Now, when your home, your people, and your deity need you most . . . will you place Keld before Skyshroud?"

"Keld is Skyshroud," Radha said. She forcefully slammed Astor's dagger into her belt. "And Skyshroud is Keld. You made it so, Freyalise, and I am living proof.

"The Gathans have abused the power of this place. Under their yoke, Skyshroud lies fallow and the fires of Keld have all but gone out. I will break Gathan supremacy and redeem mountain and the forest together."

Freyalise's stoic face now twitched in frustration. "Redeemed is not restored. I tell you Skyshroud will not endure unless we all rally to defend her."

"Ahh, but I do not seek merely to endure but to conquer. Driving away the Gathans is endless, a fool's game. They will never stop coming. Greht is the key. His warhost is vast and well-organized, but that organization hinges entirely on him. Remove him and the entire Gathan army starts to disintegrate from the top down."

Freyalise shook her head sadly. "More likely the second-most fearsome will instantly step in to take command. Keldon warhosts are not so simple to disrupt and Greht's army is not as dependent on him as you suspect. Killing him . . . assuming you can . . . would weaken them all, but ultimately it will only create a temporary vacancy."

"While they are temporarily weak," Radha said, "between the time Greht falls and a new Gathan rises to replace him, while they are without a warlord, you and your rangers can be slaughtering them at will. For once the children of Skyshroud will be on equal terms with the sons of Gatha." She raised her voice, knowing that the nearby rangers were hearing every word. "Does that appeal to you, Llanach? The idea of taking the offensive? Of riding out and seizing victory with your own hands?"

The captain glanced nervously at Freyalise before answering, "All that would please me if the patron wished it so."

Radha eyes grew large and bright. "Come with me." She turned to Freyalise, a triumphant smile forming. "Will you let them follow me as you intended? Allow me to lead them into battle to save our home?"

Freyalise was fixed on Llanach, her covered eye flashing. Radha had seen many of the planeswalker's moods over eighty years, joyful, angry, stern, indulgent, but she had never seen Freyalise heartbroken until now.

The patron's voice rose, rolling out over the valley, filling the cold night air with her words. "I am going to the far side of the forest," she said, "where the Gathans make merry with our trees. Radha is going to the mountain, to confront Greht at the center of his warhost. You Rangers of Skyshroud must now choose how you will defend our home. The true sons and daughters of Skyshroud will follow me, its patron and protector. The rest . . . Radha and anyone else who follows her . . . shall never be welcome here again."

Still lit from above by Radha's flaming leaves, the assembled rangers shifted and muttered among themselves. Radha took a step toward the forest, unwilling to let Freyalise have the last word. She pulled Astor's dagger and held it high, shouting, "I mean to kill the Gathan warlord and break his army's back. I say putting Greht's head on a stick is worth ten exiles."

To her surprise, several elf voices rang out in agreement. She had expected Llanach and the others to crumble in the face of Freyalise's ire, but almost a dozen Skyshroud rangers now emerged from the ranks and were crossing the valley floor toward her. Llanach was among them, though he scrupulously avoided Freyalise's glare.

"Selfish, ungrateful children." The patron of Skyshroud whispered so softly that only Radha could hear. She turned toward Radha and Freyalise gathered her cloak around her shoulders.

"Good-bye," she said. "You will die tonight, Radha. As Greht is crushing your skull and burning the flesh from your bones, remember your home as it was, green, lush, and strong, and curse yourself for not fighting to save it when you had the chance, for I shall surely do so."

Radha bowed respectfully. "Good-bye, Freyalise. Skyshroud may wither, but it will endure if Keld does." She straightened. "And I will make Keld endure."

Sneering, Freyalise vanished from sight in a soft cloud of light. In the distance Radha heard the sound of a thousand slivers skittering and chattering Their noise receded into the deeper part of the forest, toward the far side of Skyshroud.

Slowly, the majority of the elf rangers followed their patron and the sound of the slivers, melting into the woods and leaving Radha with her small band of warriors in the valley.

She quickly counted noses as the flames in the trees dimmed. There were less than a score altogether, including Skive and Dassene.

The rangers were a mix of archers, scouts, and spearmen. The elves were each armed with a flimsy improvised sword.

"Gather round," Radha said, hunkering down on one knee. She quickly scratched a few shapes into the frozen ground with the tip of her kukri. When she was surrounded by a single-file circle of warriors, Radha tapped the crude map with the dagger.

"This is us," she said, "and this is the mountain." She slashed a series of crosses between the two locations. "There are smaller units of Greht's warhost bivouacked all through this area. If we go in more or less a straight line, we can hit five or six of them on our way to the mountain."

Llanach nodded but asked, "What for?"

"I want Greht to know we're coming. His warhost's communication is so tight they're like one huge, living thing. I want to be chopping off fingers and toes and leaving deep puncture wounds as we make our way to the head."

Skive hissed happily. Llanach nodded again and said, "What happens when we reach the head?"

Radha leaned forward and stabbed the map, skewering the symbol she had drawn for the mountain. A plume of fire shot up, startling everyone in the circle and pushing them back.

"Whatever happens," Radha said, "it'll be loud."

CHAPTER 23

Commander Hessig earned his rank by catching the previous commander's whip in his bare hand and burying an axe in the man's forehead. Greht rarely tolerated murder within the ranks, especially if it advanced the murderer, but Hessig was so effective as an overseer that the Gathan warlord allowed him to maintain the position he'd taken by force.

Lately, Hessig carried his whip coiled at his waist, rarely using it except when they went raiding. There had been precious little to raid but plenty of lumber to fell, so Hessig and his ten-warrior squad had turned their axes on Skyshroud's trees instead of the elves who guarded them. This would be his fifth trip back to the forest for wood, and he hoped it would be his last. Greht had already begun construction of his expanded armada and the ships would be ready to sail in less than a week. Hessig intended to be on the first boat out, perhaps lashing the oar-slaves for an extra bit of speed.

"Commander." The burly, scarred Gathan stood outside Hessig's tent with his head respectfully bowed.

"What is it?"

The raider looked up, careful not to meet Hessig's eye. "Both sentries on the south perimeter are missing."

Hessig emerged from the tent with his hand on his whip and a feral gleam in his eye. "Deserters?" he said hungrily.

"No," the other said. "There were signs of a struggle and blood." He sniffed. "Tasted like elf."

"Elf?" Hessig was amused but also slightly unsettled. The elves were less than a joke, paper dolls with tinfoil swords, but if they had followed Hessig out this far, they were truly desperate.

"Gather the others," Hessig said.

"Done." The other Gathan turned and began calling to his comrades.

Hessig watched impassively as the unit assembled. The elves had always been cowards, and if they had attacked the sentries then Hessig knew exactly what their strategy was. They would try to lure Hessig and his men into the thicker brush, trusting the Gathans to either come searching for their missing warriors or looking to avenge them. Every step the Gathans took in pursuit of the sentries delayed their timber raid and increased the likelihood of elf traps and ambushes.

Hessig had a surprise for them. Under Greht's leadership, even small units like this one were capable of battle magic. A commander like Hessig could strengthen and toughen the raiders under him, and they in turn would enhance him. There was no elf trick to counter a squad of Gathans in full berserker fury. Let the tree-huggers spring their trap: Hessig would make sure it broke its teeth on his flesh, then he would force the jagged pieces down the elf leader's throat.

His warriors were assembled and ready, and they were in an ugly mood that reflected Hessig's own: bored with the non-combat detail and furious that their camp had been attacked. They were ready to march out and take vengeance on any and every stranger they saw.

"There are elves about," Hessig said. He uncoiled his whip and cracked it loudly overhead. "They're waiting for us to come find them." He smiled roughly. "Instead we're going straight to the forest."

The warriors grumbled, but not so loudly that Hessig would chastise them.

"We're going to the forest for the last time," he added, and his troops rewarded him with an enthusiastic grunt. "We're going to do our job. We'll bring more wood to the beach, one more load, then we stay at that beach and wait for the ship to be ready." He cracked the whip again. "Any elf we see between now and then is fair game." He drew a short stabbing sword in his free hand. "And I plan to see a lot. The ground will be blood-sodden before my ship sets sail."

A louder, rougher cheer went up among the raiders. Hessig felt the fight inside them surge through his bones. They were strong. They were disciplined. They were hungry. This night, they would be invincible.

Something shoved Hessig from behind, driving him forward a step. His chest felt strange, burning hot but distant. His throat seemed clogged, almost closed.

Hessig looked down. A sharp, green crescent was sticking out of his chest, its smooth face smeared with blood. Hessig coughed, spattering more red on the crescent, and the strange weapon twisted and curled like a thing alive.

Before him, his assembled warriors bellowed, roared, and drew their weapons. Hessig heard the faint whistling of arrows dropping from overhead. He had no breath and his throat was full of something thick but he still tried to call out to his troops.

A thick mass of arrows rained down on his raiders before they had moved two steps. They were definitely elf arrows, their shafts elegant and polished, and the heads expertly fashioned and perfectly balanced. To Hessig their arrival seemed sudden, jarring, as one second his men were in angry motion, coming to his aid, and the next they were all knee-deep in a field of arrow shafts that covered the ground like summer wheat.

His warriors fell, their arms and legs riddled with elven bolts. Vile curses and pained moans filled the air. Their wounds were grave but not mortal. How could so many arrows miss so many vital spots?

"You're right about the sodden ground, butcher." The voice came from directly behind Hessig's ear, hissing slightly. "But it won't be elf blood."

Hessig's whip dropped from his numbing fingers. He felt a second painful shock as the strange weapon was pulled back through his chest. Commander Hessig fell, toppling forward and landing with a splash among the pink slushy mixture of warm blood and Keldon snow.

* * * * *

Radha came out of the shadows behind the command tent and sidled up next to Skive. The viashino was wiping the end of his tail clean on the Gathan overseer's leather breeches.

"Well done," she said.

Skive nodded. "A pleasure. These aren't Keldons."

"Not at all. If you're through here, go and fetch the two we left intact."

"Understood." Skive went out into the campsite, smoothly navigating the wounded Gathans being herded and dragged away by the elves.

Radha kneeled and rolled the overseer onto his back. She paused, searching her memory for the right symbol. Then she drew Astor's kukri dagger.

Skive returned when she was halfway done. "The elves are bringing the sentries," he said. He grimaced and peered down for a closer look. "Is that necessary?"

"It is." Radha finished her dire chore with both hands, a sharp grunt, and a wet, twisting crack. She stood up. "This is the third camp we've hit and I want to be consistent. Every Gathan with a whip dies and is marked. Wound the others. Leave one and only one healthy enough to run the news back to Greht." She turned and gestured with her dripping knife. "Bring them here."

The Gathan sentries were battered, bloodied, and helpless, but they were not cowed. They struggled and fought against their bonds and their elf handlers, hurling curses and snapping their teeth at any hand that came too close to their mouths.

"Shut them up, Skive."

The viashino slithered forward to the Gathan captives, opened his mouth wide and hissed menacingly. The sentries continued to struggle, but they stopped making noise.

"Greht is finished," Radha said, "and one of you gets to bring him the news."

"Your bones will bake," one Gathan said. "Your heart will crack."

"Doyen Greht will crush you," said the other.

Radha waited for them to finish. "One of you will tell Greht that the 'elf-girl' is coming for him. That Radha's Fists will destroy him and his entire 'host."

"Tell him yourself."

"If you live long enough."

"One of you will tell him what you saw here. That you saw this." Radha extended her arm so that the overseer's head hung facing the captives. Her fingers were buried in his thick, coarse hair. The sentries froze, snide defiance hardening into outrage.

The overseer's features were almost lost under a series of long, deep slashes. The dead man's face bore a rough, jagged symbol in the command language High Keld. The overseer had been a warrior, a commander, a battlefield mage who commanded a whip of fire. Now, thanks to Radha, he would forever be remembered by the mark she left on his severed head: "Goblin's Whore."

"Tell Greht," Radha said darkly, "that the mark I have for him makes this one seem like a fawning eulogy."

Angered beyond words, the sentries simply stared and seethed at Radha. She waited until she was sure they had no more insults or threats to hurl, then she called, "We're letting them go. Get ready." The elves responded by clearing a path between the captives and the north end of the camp. Archers and spearmen stood with weapons ready.

Radha carelessly tossed the severed head over her shoulder. "Llanach," she said loudly.

"Ready." The lanky elf captain stood to one side of the sentries with his spear horizontal in both hands.

Radha glared at the two captives. "Take whichever one reaches the perimeter last."

"Understood."

Radha stepped forward and shoved her face within inches of the Gathans. Green fire licked up from her eyes. "One of you has a story to tell," she said, and at last the raiders turned away, unable to hold her terrible gaze.

Radha straightened, turned, and strode over to Llanach. She nodded to the elves holding the prisoners, then she glanced back at the Gathans themselves. Slowly, deliberately, Radha opened her mouth and carefully enunciated a single word.

"Run."

The elves released their prisoners. The Gathans glanced at each other. The one on the left broke first and sprinted for the north end of the camp, but the other was only a step behind. They were fast for such big, burly men, but they were evenly matched and the one at the rear could not make up that missing step.

When they were ten paces from the perimeter, Llanach transferred his spear to his right hand. He arranged his grip, exhaled, and raised the weapon to his shoulder. Precise and unhurried, he took three long strides and let fly, heaving the spear in a high arc over the campsite. Radha watched the silver hardwood gleam as it soared.

The first Gathan hit the treeline and disappeared into the underbrush. His partner followed close behind, but just as his extended hand reached the woods, Llanach's spear came down. The sharp length of Skyshroud oak plunged through the Gathan's shoulder blades, severing his spine before bursting through his chest. The spear continued down until its tip lodged in the hard-packed dirt. The shaft snapped as the Gathan's heavy body crashed down.

Radha glanced at Llanach. "Well done," she said.

Llanach nodded. "What of the rest?"

"Leave them," Radha said. "I want them alive and frightened."

"Radha," Skive hissed. "The more of them we leave alive, the stronger Greht will be."

"True, but the more we leave traumatized, the weaker he becomes. When they hear we're using corpse markers, they'll be furious, but they'll be angry because they're afraid. Greht can't use their fear. We can."

One of Llanach's rangers ran up. "There's another Gathan camp ahead. They've got carts of wood and slaves."

"How far?"

"Ten minutes at a dead run."

"Headed for the beach? Going slow?"

The runner nodded.

She raised her voice. "New target," she called. "Bring Dassene to me. It's time for her to go back to work."

"I'm ready." The Ghitu firemage looked like she'd been through a war already, with her missing fingers and broken nose. She had been devastating in the first two Gathan camps, but Radha had to reign her in so she would have some fury left for the mountain.

"Ghitu," Radha said. "How would you like to burn some Gathan ships before they're ever assembled, along with the bastards who would have sailed in them?"

For the first time since Aprem died, Dassene smiled. Skive saw the look on her face and shuddered.

"That's the spirit," Radha said.

* * * * *

Teferi examined the Shivan rift as a botanist would a rare and poisonous flower. The very things that made it unique, the aspects most worth studying, were also its most dangerous. The fragrance from this particular bloom was intoxicating and distracting, but he did not allow it to divert his attention.

He noted with some pride that he had learned a great deal about the rifts from his detours through Keld and Urborg.

Hear that, Jhoira? It wasn't a complete waste of time.

Make sense, Jhoira sent back.

Experience is always the best teacher, and at least now I have some. All right, my limited familiarity with the rift phenomenon isn't enough to provide a direct answer to the problem of Shiv's return, but it does allow me ask the right question.

And that is?

The rift represents a rupture in the fabric of the multiverse, caused in this case by the removal of Shiv. The rupture had probably been affecting the area for decades before Karona's war turned it into an open mana drain that warps time and space. Now it's like a cracked glass bowl filled with water. The crack is the rift and Shiv's contents are leaking out, which in turn widens the crack and speeds up the whole process. Sooner or later the crack will expand enough to split the entire bowl into pieces.

To complete the metaphor, Jhoira's said, *Shiv is a rock hurled at that glass bowl. A big, sharp rock.*

Teferi frowned. *Don't complete my metaphors.*

Excuse me, Teferi Loreweaver, but I'm just trying to nudge you along. You're too fond of your own cleverness at times like this.

"Well," Teferi huffed aloud. He turned to Venser. "I can see some of us need to work on our listening skills. Jhoira is trying to help, but what she's actually doing is hindering."

Venser face stayed fixed on the circular phenomenon overhead, but he nodded. "Something is definitely happening inside the rift. It's grown much brighter and the color keeps oscillating."

Teferi's face crinkled into a smile. "I have a plan," he said, "and also, and better still, I have a few more moments to think of a better plan."

Jhoira looked pained. "Teferi, please. I—"

"Ah," he interrupted. "It's too late, my friend. Shiv has already started to come out of the special phased state that we . . . that *I* created for it."

"Excuse me," Venser said. "Do you mean to say part of the continent is simply going to drop back into place out of the sky?"

"Not exactly," Teferi said.

Jhoira jumped in before he could continue, saying, "Shiv is still here in a manner of speaking, but it's entirely out of synch in time and space. It's not going to sail into view like a tall ship into a harbor. Reintegrating it isn't a matter of physical dimensions but magical ones."

"And planar physics," Teferi said. "Remember the bowl metaphor."

"About that," Venser said. "It doesn't really work, does it? Shiv isn't a rock, it's part of the bowl. You took a section of bowl away, it sort of patched itself, and now you have this extra piece you want to force back in."

Teferi frowned. "Don't over-examine my metaphors."

"Sorry."

"Your point is well-taken, however. It will take a huge effort of will and a lot of magic to make this happen as it needs to. Fortunately, I have an ample supply of each. Would you at least agree that sustained effort and serious magic can fix a broken bowl with too many pieces?"

Venser shifted uncomfortably. "I said I was sorry."

"Teferi," Jhoira said sternly, "what is your plan?"

"My plan is still evolving," Teferi said breezily, "and I'm sorry to say, I'm just about out of time. I'll keep pondering until Shiv begins to appear, then I'll just have to go with what I have." He turned and called to Corus, who was eying the mob of feral Shivans through Teferi's hazy white barrier. "Any problems there?"

"None," Corus called. "Though I think every angry Shivan on this sad little rock is currently out there howling for our blood."

"Good," Teferi said. "One less thing to worry about." As he spoke, the Shivan rift rumbled and let loose a plume of fire and glowing red vapor.

"It begins," Teferi said. As one, they all turned to the south, toward the clean, sharp precipice that marked the outer edge of Shiv's missing section. The ocean far below bubbled and churned, lit from below by a harsh blue-green light.

A low, grating sound vibrated up through Teferi's feet, rattling his spine. At the same time a high, whining shriek sliced through his head. The air grew heavy, pressing in on him from every direction. A strong tremor slowly shook the southern edge of the island, and sea water splashed up over the cliffs, driven by the wind and the unimaginable forces building up around the entire region.

Teferi looked up at the Shivan rift, mentally preparing himself. He cleared his mind, focused his thoughts, and summoned to him all the mana he could muster.

As if emerging from a dense fog, the first hazy outlines of a massive landmass appeared. Then a familiar, throaty voice ripped through his mind, drowning out his thoughts and Jhoira's alike with its sheer manic intensity.

Hoy, clean-head! Radha bellowed. *Look at me!*

CHAPTER 24

Radha and her warhost found fewer camps to attack as they drew close to the mountain. It was safe to assume that all seven of the survivors they sent running to Greht had reached him by now, even though the Gathan warlord had not marshaled his 'host and ridden out to confront them. Radha was pleased. If Greht wasn't coming after them in force it meant he had pulled in all of his troops and assembled them here. He knew Radha was coming and he would want to make her humiliating defeat as public as possible to drive his 'host into a proper frenzy before the armada sailed.

As her choice of targets dwindled, Radha had her budding warhost close ranks and march boldly toward the mountain. It only seemed she were leaving herself wide open to attack, as Radha had sent elfish scouts ahead, behind, and to both sides. These rangers shadowed and preceded the 'host, making sure there were no special surprises lying in wait between Radha and the Gathans. The proceeded this way for over an hour until the mountain itself appeared on the misty horizon.

Radha slowed, raising an arm to keep Skive and Dassene from passing her. She pointed at the mountain and said, "It worked. We're expected."

The foothills and the base of the mountain were dotted with campfires and torches. Farther up the slope Radha saw two straight lines of fire that created a lane to a square, raised platform of stone. The stagelike structure had not been here before when she had come with Teferi, but now it also stood rimmed with torches, their flickering light giving Radha a detailed view. Scores of dense gray boulders had been carted, broken, and set in place before they were fused together by intense heat. The surface of the platform was charred black yet smooth as glass.

Radha saw those flat black rocks and steeled herself for the coming battle. It took an incredible amount of heat to even scorch Keldon stone, but Greht had half-melted tons of it in less than a week. His power was growing too strong, too quickly, and his warhost was growing right along with him.

She dismissed her misgivings, focusing instead on the opportunity they represented. Greht commanded titanic forces, especially here on the mountain surrounded by his warhost. He would justifiably expect her to make the same mistake she always made, to simply dash herself against him and see who broke first. He would also expect her to fail as she had every time before, and Radha knew she could turn that to her advantage—Teferi had shown her how even gods and titans fell when they were overconfident.

Radha slowed her pace as her 'host approached the first torchbearers. She made a soft, trilling sound to summon her elf scouts in; they responded in the same Skyshroud trail-talk. Seconds later, all eight emerged from the brush and took their places among the rangers. When the Skyshroud 'host was complete and assembled, Radha led them into the lane of torches.

Radha saw the Gathans smirk and heard them chuckling at the state of her 'host. She glanced back, half-agreeing with their assessment. Apart from Skive and perhaps herself, none of her warriors looked capable of climbing the foothills without pausing for rest.

She resisted the urge to mock the Gathans, to shout how her 'host was small, but at least none of them were serving as torch racks. Radha actually relished her warriors' shabby appearance:

the more the Gathans took them lightly, the better off she'd be against Greht. Besides, looks counted for very little in the wilds of Keld. Her 'host had already routed a hundred Gathans this night and they were marching stronger than when they started. Let the false Keldons scoff.

The smirks and jeering dwindled as Radha's 'host approached the platform. These were the upper echelons of Greht's warhost, the ones who knew for sure what Radha had been carving on their fellow commanders' faces. Radha could feel their rage and hatred for her like wind on her face. She kept her eyes wide and fixed on the platform ahead.

They were almost to the end of the lane, where the way was blocked by three formidable-looking Gathans. They were not the biggest or the most powerful, but they stood with the confidence of experience and training, stood shoulder to shoulder, one slightly ahead of the other two. Each of the sentries had a massive broadsword drawn and planted in the icy ground.

Radha stopped six feet from the trio. She felt Skive and Dassene behind her and the Skyshroud rangers behind them.

"We've come for Greht," she said.

The leader scanned her critically from head to toe. He looked as if he might yawn. "Are you the elf who thinks she's a Keldon?"

"I am Radha," she said, "and I sent runners to announce me. Didn't they make it?" She turned to Skive. "I told you we should have nailed the heads in the messenger's hands."

The three Gathans suddenly all lunged forward, each of their swords aimed at Radha. Fire bloomed from beside her and she saw Skive become a blur, so Radha concentrated on the one at the center.

She was still faster than the false Keldons, even these elite ones, and Radha smoothly brought up Astor's kukri blade up to deflect the broadsword's tip. She pushed herself forward along the blade, and with her free hand, she buried a tear-shaped blade between the Gathan's ribs. She held him up, glaring fiercely into his eyes until his body went limp.

Radha let him fall. She saw that Skive's tail had taken the other sentry's hands off at the wrist. The viashino had wrapped his sinewy body completely around the maimed Gathan's torso and appeared to be squeezing the life out of him.

A wall of greasy smoke blew over her and Radha turned. Dassene was standing with her batons crossed. There was nothing left of her target but his heavy metal boots, a pile of ash, and the melted tip of a broadsword. "You have got to teach me that," Radha said.

Now the torch-bearing Gathans began to break ranks and Radha called, "Back to back." As one, her warhost drew their weapons and faced outward.

"Oh, let them through," came Greht's gruff, echoing voice.

The Gathans immediately fell back into line. Radha waited for a moment, then climbed up the improvised steps and stood at the platform's edge until her entire 'host had joined her. Greht was there. She saw him standing at the center of the platform near the far edge, a line of five warriors flanking him on each side.

Now that she was on the platform, Radha saw how Greht had angled it so that the back was higher than the front. Her first thought was that this was to give a clear view to all of the raiders assembled below, but she also realized it made Greht and his men seem even larger.

She was amazed. There was so much more theater involved in running a warhost than she had imagined, and Greht was a cunning beast to have staged this scene so well. He could crush Radha here for his entire army to see, and doing so would serve the twin purposes of removing a considerable danger to his supply lines and strengthening his connection to his 'host.

"So, elf-girl." Greht's voice boomed out and echoed down the mountain. "This is what a forest 'host looks like." Thousands of Gathans jeered and hooted.

Radha stepped forward. "Take a good look," she said. "As Kradak himself, we came up the mountain as strangers, foreigners from another place, but we will descend it as Keldons."

More laughter, but it was more sparse and less enthusiastic. No warrior who had ever felt Keldon battle magic was eager to laugh for long at Keld's founder, especially while standing on the sacred mountain.

Greht himself seemed displeased by this turn of the conversation, but he said, "Kradak lasted through the night. You and your elves will be dead within the hour."

Radha drew Astor's dagger. It ignited. "Prove it," she said.

Greht snarled as he drew his own sword. He had switched to a smaller broadsword than he had carried, perhaps anticipating Radha's smaller, lighter weapons. Perhaps he just wanted to make a more interesting show of it for his 'host.

"Listen," Radha said to her soldiers behind her. She watched Greht stalk toward her. "You have to make noise. Cheer when I block or dodge or stick him. Rage and stomp when I miss or he sticks me."

"Why?" Llanach said.

"Because we're on the mountain." Radha turned to the elf captain, her eyes flaring. "Act like Keldons."

She turned back, let out a piercing cry, and charged. As she focused on Greht, everything outside the stone platform vanished from her perception, but she was gratified to hear roars of enthusiasm rising from her 'host.

Radha swung her dagger in a looping overhand arc. It was not so much an attack as a test, to see how fast he was with the new sword. Greht easily parried her swing and countered by shoving her roughly backward with the flat of his blade. Radha gracefully turned a back handspring and bounced back to her feet, facing Greht with her dagger ready. The Skyshroud 'host cheered again.

Radha swelled at the sound. "Too slow, false Keldon," she said.

Greht cocked his head and puffed steam from his metal mask. "Fast enough to scare you, elf-girl. I've never seen eyes so wide."

Radha side-stepped clockwise around her larger opponent. He was right—he had surprised her. Rather than slowing Greht down, his oversized muscles had more than enough power to compensate for their own bulk. His movements were short and inelegant, but they were also fast and effective.

Now Greht charged, and though Radha easily backpedaled out of range, the mere fact of his swing was enough to set his warhost howling. She ducked inside his reach and slashed at his belly, but he brought the handle of his broadsword down at her skull and forced her to jump clear.

Greht didn't even try to stop his blow, slamming the handle of his sword into the platform. The rocky stand shuddered and a thick crack raced toward Radha's feet. She hesitated, trying to gauge which way to jump, then sprang to her left.

The crack angled after her, following her flight until she landed. When her feet touched down, the forward tip of the fissure was directly below her. Greht thumped his sword again, and the cracked stone exploded, peppering Radha with sharp bits of stone and hurling her awkwardly through the air.

As gratifying as it was to hear her 'host cheer, it was doubly crushing to hear them gasp and moan. Radha came down on the platform with a loud thud. Her warhost shouted encouragement.

Rage, you idiots, she thought. *I said* rage *when he gets me.* Radha scrambled to her feet and leaped away from another of Greht's powerful swings. She had hoped to draw things out more before he started using spells on her, largely because she wouldn't last long once he did. His magic was still far more powerful than hers.

She hurled a blade at him but Greht easily batted it down with his sword. She now had only two of the tear-shaped blades left, plus Astor's dagger.

She drew a tear-shaped blade and struck it against the kukri, shouting, "Burn." The blades lit up and her warhost shouted raucously.

Greht stopped where he was and lowered his sword. He brazenly turned his back on Radha and faced his 'host below, shaking his head in exaggerated disbelief. He turned back and shouted, "Is that what they call a burn in Skyshroud?"

The mountain rang with brutal laughter.

"I see you've found a decent weapon at last. It's a remarkable blade you carry, a relic from the days of true craftsmanship. If only I had such a weapon." Greht cocked his head and paused. He reached behind him and drew Astor's other dagger, the one Radha had lost when she attacked the Gathan convoy alone.

"Oh, wait," he said mockingly. "I do." The warlord's massive fist tightened around the kukri. The fist, the knife, and half his arm ignited into blindingly hot orange flame.

"Oh," Greht said, his mock-concern rising over the roaring flame in his hand. "It seems this heirloom isn't as sturdy as it looks. Perhaps it's just not capable of handling a true warlord's full power." Greht concentrated, raising the flaming dagger and turning his metal face intently toward it. The dagger glowed like a small star, blinding every living thing on the platform.

Radha snarled as her vision returned, almost incoherent with rage. Greht now held a twisted stick of black metal in his hands. The rest of Astor's kukri dagger had melted away into slag and steam. The Gathan warlord clenched his fist, rendering the last remnants of her grandfather's weapon into a soft, falling stream of ashes and grit.

"So much for true Keldons," Greht spat. His warhost roared and stomped loudly enough to shake the mountain.

Radha forced herself to stand where she was. She remembered

the lesson of Teferi, fixing on the long-term success that she'd never win if she rushed Greht now.

Instead of attacking, Radha held her own flaming blades at arm's length. She crossed them in front of her and concentrated. As in Skyshroud, the air around her filled with multicolored leaves of flame.

Greht shook his head again. "This is too much. Attacking me with foliage?"

Radha ignored him, hearing and seeing only the flames she had conjured.

"You're embarrassing yourself, elf-girl. Here. Let me show you Gathan fire."

Greht raised his sword and plunged its tip six inches into the rocky floor. He jerked the blade free and from the wound surged a perfectly straight column of searing yellow fire. The hair spilling out from Greht's mask curled in the heat.

The geyser of flame went out. Greht turned his smoking face toward Radha.

"That's fire, elf-girl. That's heat."

"No," Radha said. "That's hot air and it won't burn, but this does." She cast her arms forward. The leaves of flame rushed at Greht, a hundred or more all headed for his chest and face.

Greht seemed to sense this was another bluff. The fire was colorful and bright but it did not burn like his. It did not generate heat that could glaze solid rock or melt steel. The Gathan warlord was an expert at fire magic and he recognized this as a flashy, hollow display.

Arrogantly, he stood unmoving with his sword down by his hip. Greht allowed the stream of flaming shapes to slam right into him, his posture stoic and unflinching as they seared minor burns into his flesh and burned black furrows across his metal mask.

Radha stood glaring as Greht weathered her flames. There were no sounds from her warhost, but she couldn't blame them because she herself didn't know whether to cheer or flee. Her fire spell had looked impressive, but the end result was so far lacking. She tossed one of her last tears at his throat, which he blocked, then she circled down to the front edge of the platform with her back to the throng of Gathans below.

Greht simply stood and watched her as smoke rose from his superficial burns. He came forward with slow, deliberate strides, his broadsword raised high.

Radha quickly began dragging Astor's dagger through the air in front of her, its tip carving a flaming trail in its wake. If she moved the blade quickly and retraced her pattern, the trail lasted long enough for her to inscribe simple shapes, even symbols.

"What now?" Greht roared. "A prayer of salvation to Freyalise? Even she fears me these days. How does that feel, elf-girl? Your patron goddess is hiding from me right now, cowering somewhere in that cesspit of a forest."

Radha turned to her host and gestured with her head, leading their attention to the flaming symbol she made. She gestured and lifted her hand, silently urging them to see what she was show- ing them.

The first tentative sounds of laughter came, but they were sporadic and they died away almost immediately. Radha felt the first twinges of despair as she realized her mistake. She should have planned for this. It was not her 'host's fault they didn't read High Keld.

Greht was too close now. Radha quickly re-scrawled the symbol in the air and then dodged as Greht's huge body barreled through the uneven line of flaming characters.

"She's writing a thrice-damned book," Greht taunted. He raised his broadsword and shouted to his men, "Is this how elves make Keldon fire?"

There was no approving roar from the Gathans, no thousand throats united in assent. Most of the raiders knew High Keld, enough to read what she was writing, and they knew it was no prayer or story. Greht stood in the sudden near-silence, his awkward, hesitant pose made nigh-ludicrous by his bulk.

Radha turned to her host, a feral snarl on her face. She growled like an angry tiger, half-roaring at them, "Laugh, you bastards." She jumped up and drew a larger flaming symbol into the air. "That," she pointed at the symbol, "means 'Piss here.' "

Greht turned toward Radha, confused but no less dangerous. As he did, her warhost saw the flaming Keldon symbol closely juxtaposed with the matching corpse-marker burned onto Greht's iron mask by Radha's flaming leaves.

Skive noticed first, but his laugh was little more than a loud, hissing rasp. The elves quickly joined in, and even Dassene cracked a smile. The Ghitu hurled abuse at Greht instead of laughter, and soon the entire Skyshroud 'host was jeering and taunting the mightiest of all Gathan warlords like a gang of children.

Greht saw the symbol burning in the air before him. His huge square hand rose to his mask and he dragged his fingers roughly across it. He probed the connected series of furrows that had eaten into his mask like acid burns. Radha reckoned he realized what she'd done to him at about the same time he realized that his 'host was no longer cheering.

Radha stepped forward, Astor's dagger ready in her fist. "You've lost them," she said, "and now we'll see who is the true Keldon."

Greht's eyes glowed red behind their metal sockets and spit sparks that continued to glow even after they hit the ground. "Yes," he said darkly, his voice painfully loud and deep. "We will see. Elf-girl? I haven't lost anything yet."

The huge berserker dropped his broadsword and raised both hands to the right side of his mask. Greht dug his fingers into the seam between the thick metal plate and his own flesh, tightened his grip, then hauled forward with all of his might.

For a moment Radha could only stare. In that moment the

rivet that connected Greht's mask to his cheek split, its wide end shooting out into the frosty air. In a hideous display of strength and determination, Greht slowly wrenched the mask off his face, inch by agonizing inch.

The rivet in his chin cracked and fell out. Greht continued to pull. Radha saw the jagged, gaping holes in his face the rivets had left behind as the metal mask began to bend, folding away from Greht's wild, bleeding, and smoking face. With a final agonizing effort, Greht ripped out the last two rivets and the corpse-markered mask flew from his hands. The twisted hunk of metal skidded noisily across the platform and disappeared.

The Gathans went wild, roaring and stamping in unison, chanting their leader's name with increasing frenzy.

Yet unmasked, Greht was somehow diminished. He was no different from any other Gathan, even with four ragged holes in his face. It was not the face of a demon or an immovable, unconquerable titan. To Radha, with his true face revealed, Greht was just another angry, ugly, bleeding berserker.

But still a dangerous one. "Now," the warlord said as he retrieved his broadsword, "we finish this."

Radha still stood amazed with Astor's dagger extended. Greht had just outdone her, actually increasing his power by recovering so quickly and completely from the humiliating thing she had done.

She nodded to her foe. "Yes," she said, "let's finish this."

She charged forward with the kukri dagger down low. Greht came to meet her with his broadsword high in both hands, blood streaming from the holes in his face. As they closed, Radha pulled back Astor's dagger and dug into her belt with her free hand. Mere paces from his foe, Greht could not stop his charge or his sweeping overhand blow. Radha saw delightful confusion in his eyes. He didn't know what she was doing and he didn't like it.

She dropped to one knee and thrust her hands up toward Greht's face. She squeezed the bottom point of Skive's mana star into the handle of Astor's dagger, her mind filled wholly with the sharp, jagged lines of the next symbol.

Greht's sword arced down at her head. She felt the power of Keld below her, felt it merge with the mana from the jewel in her hand, then Radha guided them both though the blade of Astor's kukri.

"Burn," she said, releasing a blast of pure, searing fire that slammed into Greht's face and blew him halfway across the platform. His broadsword snapped in two, the top half clattering on the rocks beside Radha.

Anger from the Gathans drowned out her warhost's cheers, but Radha heard them anyway. Still clutching the gem and the dagger together, she loped across the platform to her enemy, kicking the piece of broadsword aside as she went.

Greht was on his hands and knees, his head hung low, but he still held the bottom part of his sword. Radha stopped just outside of lunging distance and said, "Get up, false Keldon. Get up and die."

Greht's head jerked toward the sound of her voice. Radha looked at his face and savage glee shot through her. Seared deep into the leathery flesh of Greht's face was the Keldon corpsemarker "Target."

"Near here," Radha said, "in a village between the mountain and the forest, there's a blind boy. I hope he's asleep right now. I hope he's dreaming of this."

Greht gurgled and snarled. He tried to speak, but all that came out were guttural noises.

"Behold, Gathans." Radha's voice rolled out, loud and strong. "Your leader, the great Doyen Greht. Behold, and always remember how he was beaten, burned, and corpse-marked by an elf-girl with no heat." She turned and spat on the warlord. "Pathetic."

She knelt down, still clear of his sword but well within earshot. "You've lost them for real now," she said. This time it was true.

She could barely feel the once-constant and once-potent exchange of power between Greht and his warriors. "They'll never follow Warlord Target."

"No." Greht's voice was garbled and unclear. He stood and hurled his broken sword, which Radha easily avoided. "I will rule again, mana sow, and right now."

Radha rolled back to her feet, ready to fight, but Greht had not moved. He stood with his feet planted and his fists clenched, a low roar growing louder in his chest.

Below them all, the mountain responded. Greht was a Gathan, twisted by magic and Tolarian artifice, but he was also a Keldon. Even without the fury of his warhost he was still capable of devastating magic. He had survived the mountain, had completed the ritual and become a warlord, and so the fires of this harsh nation were still his to command.

At first Radha thought he would blow the entire stone platform to pieces. Greht was not shaping the mountain's mana yet, only collecting it. His scarred face smoked as the flesh upon it blackened and split. Greht's eyes disappeared, replaced by two glowing red embers. He roared for a full five seconds, then Greht's head exploded, releasing a vast gout of crimson flame from his neck and shoulders.

Radha stepped back. Greht's head continued to burn, but instead of staggering and falling, the Gathan seemed to be growing stronger. He rose and straightened to his full height. He flexed his powerful arms, raising his broken sword and a clenched fist as his prodigious roar continued. The flames around his head did not dwindle.

Radha saw him clearly in the scarlet glare. Greht's head had burned down to the bone, only vertebrae and a skull left from the shoulders up. Flames still licked around his naked skull, which was stained blackish-crimson by the infernal light. Two orange coals still glowed in his eye sockets and his square, blackened teeth clacked together in the front of his tongueless mouth.

Radha felt the surge of arcane forces around her. Greht was the dominant magic-user here, and he had summoned a great deal of the mountain's mana exclusively to himself. She still had the mana star, its power thrumming in her palm, and Astor's dagger called out to it, demanding to focus the gem's potential into true killing power. She felt the flow of mana that originated in Skyshroud but came to her through the rift above and around the forest. She felt the combined might of Greht's warhost, a rippling, churning reservoir of strength that only a true warlord could wield. If she had completed the mountain ritual, perhaps she could have claimed this resource when it deserted Greht. As it was, she could only stand and watch as the Gathan warlord's insane gambit restored his fighting form and reestablished the link between he and his 'host.

"Now, elf-girl," he said, though Radha could not determine how. "You will see how a true warlord burns."

"Yes," Radha said. "Show me, O Greht. Show me how you burn."

Then Radha struck, projecting all the mana she could muster directly into Greht. She sent hers, the pure, rich mana from the rift, along with the concentrated power of Teferi's gem. Mixed with the rush of mana Greht had already taken from the mountain, these forces gorged and taxed the warlord to his very limit. But it was the fury of a thousand bloodthirsty Gathans renewed that finally overwhelmed him.

Choking on pure power, drowning in it, Greht was unable to even cast the simplest fire spell. The blistering energies continued to pour into his body and his flaming skull glowed ever hotter and brighter. The fused platform started to fall apart, and Radha realized the great flaw in her plan: close enough to spring her trap was close enough to be caught in the blast when the forces inside Greht blew him apart.

She turned to her warhost and shouted, "Go!"

Radha then tossed Astor's dagger into the air and caught it with the blade facing downward.

"Here, you bastard," she shouted. "You can have this one, too." She cocked her arm back, got a running start, and threw herself at Greht, preparing to drive the dagger into his flaming skull with all the strength in both arms. Oddly, she thought of Teferi as her arms came down.

"Burn," she whispered, as the dagger's tip touched Greht's forehead. The Gathan warlord's body exploded, unable to contain the power it absorbed. Radha felt a flash of heat envelop her as the dagger punched through.

"Hoy clean-head!" she shouted. "Look at me!"

* * * * *

Radha came to in a cavern of complete darkness. Well, not complete . . . there was a rich red glow emanating from beneath the veneer of black, like the flashes of light she saw when she rubbed her eyes hard.

"Where am I?" Though she was aware of her jaw working and breath leaving her body, Radha did not hear her own words.

Rise, daughter of Keld.

"I'm up. Where am I?"

Home.

"Oh. Well, I need to get back to the mountain. Is Greht dead? What about my warhost?"

You are the mountain.

"I am? What are you?" When the voice didn't answer, she said, "Are you Keldon? A planeswalker?"

There are no Keldon planeswalkers. Kradak dedicated himself to the land and the land to him. Their power is shared. Keld's magic must be shared.

Radha thought for a moment. "What about me?"

You are unique. You are of Keld, but you are not yet part of me.

She spoke quietly. "Are you Keld?"

I am the covenant.

"I am not part of you."

No.

"Can I be?"

If you wish to dedicate yourself to it.

"How?"

You must give what you have and take what Keld offers. Be fire and let Keld be your fuel. Be the spark and Keld will be your tinder.

Radha heard annoyance, impatience in her own words. "I know the thrice-damned spell."

Then speak it. Speak the words. Enter the covenant.

"The words," Radha said. She knew which words, of course, but she had grown suspicious of bodiless voices. The truth was she was probably dead already, so what could it hurt?

Radha took a breath and intoned, "Coal and tinder, fire and spark, Keldons are fire, and Keld commands . . . burn."

Something hot and alive surged through her. Radha shouted involuntarily and dropped to her knees.

What is your name, child?

"Radha." She exhaled then filled her lungs to capacity. "My name is Radha."

Rise, Radha, Warlord of Keld. Go forth and burn. Shine brightly through twilight and beyond.

"Through twilight." Radha crawled painfully back to her feet. The darkness began to soften around her and she swooned, toppling back but never hitting the ground.

* * * * *

The next sound Radha heard was Dassene calling her name. She awoke below the cloud-thick night sky, the Ghitu's swollen features hovering over hers.

"She's awake," Dassene said.

"Greht," Radha muttered.

The Ghitu woman leaned closer. "Dead," she said. "Ashes and suet."

" 'Host."

"What?"

"His warhost."

"They tried to rush the platform after he blew up. We scooped you up and carried you clear."

Radha sat up, eyeing the Ghitu sharply. "You ran?"

"We strategically withdrew."

Radha grunted. She stood up, not waiting for Dassene to step back. "Where was I?"

"What?"

"Where did you find me?"

Dassene looked puzzled. "On the platform," she said. "You were lying next to the crater."

"What crater?"

"The one made by the explosion. The blast dug down almost two hundred feet."

"More," Radha said. "It went much deeper than that." She closed her eyes again. "Any danger?"

"Not presently."

"Good. Bring me Llanach and four . . . no, six Skyshroud rangers."

Dassene looked uncomfortable, and Radha said, "What?"

"You sent Llanach and eight rangers out several hours ago. I didn't think you were completely conscious, but nobody wanted to argue with you."

Radha paused. "What did I send them to do?"

"You said there was a forgotten village about halfway between here and the forest. You sent them to collect a blind boy and bring him to you."

"Good. I mean what I say even if I don't remember saying it. Now. How many are we?"

"I counted almost sixty a short while ago. More keep coming, elves and settlers." She trailed off, hesitant once more.

"And Gathans." Radha said.

Dassene nodded. "And Gathans. About ten of them asked if they could join your 'host. They claim they never followed Greht."

"It doesn't matter," Radha said, "if they were Gathans, civilians or even elves because Keld will make Keldons of us all." She grinned. "Gather two dozen who are itching for a fight. Tell Skive I want him to start tracking down the rest of Greht's timber convoys. We can use the wood, and tell him he can kill anyone he likes in the process, including his own men. Make sure the turncoat Gathans hear you tell him that."

"Understood. What about me?"

"You're going to teach me that cross-baton fire blast you use, and when Target arrives, you're going to help me make a warrior out of him.

"Target?"

"The blind boy. I intend to make him so dangerous that the mark on his face will frighten more people than it amuses."

"How?"

Radha reached out and grabbed Dassene by the shoulder. Vivid multicolored flames shot from Radha's eyes to the Ghitu's, and Dassene suddenly stood taller and straighter, her eyes clear and sharp. Her hair and skin had taken on a subtle red sheen.

"Oh," she said with a hungry grin. "Skive will love this."

Radha nodded. Her fierce dark eyes fogged over and her eyelids began to droop.

Dassene steadied her before she stumbled. "Warlord," she said, "rest here. I'll let you know when the boy arrives."

Radha started to disagree, but decided to let it go. She also let Dassene lower her back onto the woven mat, and even let herself relax, her thoughts swirling into a slow, comfortable eddy of approaching sleep.

Radha shrugged off her exhaustion and fixed Dassene with a steely glare. "Wake me when Llanach returns. Or at first light. Whichever comes first. Either way, we go back to work on the Gathans tomorrow."

Dassene nodded. "Understood."

"And then on to the slivers. And maybe the saproling thicket. . . ."

Dassene called out "Understood," from very far away. Her voice and her footsteps grew fainter until they disappeared entirely.

At last, Radha drifted off. She would sleep for eighteen hours straight and have but one, long, epic dream: she, her mother, her grandmother, and Astor all ascending the mountain together. They never spoke, and the wind kept her grandfather's long black hair in his face, preventing Radha from ever seeing it clearly.

It didn't matter. She could tell he was smiling.

CHAPTER 25

Teferi stood smiling, unashamed of the tears that flowed from his eyes. "She did it," he said. Before him, the Shivan rift roiled and stormed. "She did it, Jhoira."

"Who did what?"

"Radha. Radha won out. She's a warlord now, at one with the mountain."

"How is that good for anyone but Radha?"

"You don't understand. She didn't just beat the Gathans; she forged a link between herself and Keld. I told you there was something special about her."

"I still say how is that special? Everyone taps the land for mana."

"Radha formed her connection as an adult in one fell swoop. People are always tied to the place they grew up, but Radha was tied to the rift, not Keld. Somehow she switched from one to the other by choice, by the sheer power of her will."

"That is unusual. How is it helpful?"

"Because if she, a creature of the rift, can reconnect to the land, then I, a creature of the land, can connect to the rift."

Jhoira's face was skeptical. "I'm not sure that holds."

"I am."

" 'Connect' in what way?"

"In every way. If I do as Bo Levar did and pour every last bit of myself into healing the rift, I can seal it. A planeswalker can at least do that. Thus, no more cracks in the bowl."

"No, but the rock is still coming."

"It won't matter as much. Without the rift, Shiv phasing back into place is far less complicated, far less perilous."

"I'd feel better if you hadn't invoked Bo Levar."

"He's the benchmark." Teferi smiled warmly at her, then turned to the others. "Good-bye Venser, Corus," Teferi said. "Thank you for supporting my greatest endeavor." He turned and smiled once more at Jhoira, a thousand years of happy memories racing through his mind.

Good-bye, my friend.

Teferi winked and before Jhoira could react, he rocketed up, soaring through the barrier he had erected and on toward the Shivan rift.

Teferi. Jhoira's thoughts were right there with him. *What do you mean "good-bye?" What are you going to do?*

What Bo Levar did. What I should have three hundred years ago. He preserved one small corner of the world from Phyrexia's plagues and war machines during the invasion, same as we did. The difference was he sacrificed himself to do it. Had I done that. . . .

Had you done that you'd be dead and all of Shiv would be like the part we left behind.

Perhaps. We can't change the past . . . not even I can do that. I can do what I know is right, and I can do it right now, when it's needed most.

Teferi, no. There has to be another way.

There may be, but if neither of us can think of it in the next few seconds. . . .

What about the other rifts? What about Zhalfir? You are your homeland's protector. Who steps in if you die now?

I don't know, but I think you've already met him. Or her. Now,

Teferi said solemnly. *Watch me. Learn from what I do. If it works, seek out Freyalise, Windgrace, and Karn. I will find a way to succeed here. I will blaze the trail. You must make sure that other planeswalkers follow it.*

I can't. I won't. Teferi, I do not agree to this.

You have no choice. None of us do.

Jhoira did not reply again, and Teferi could hear her thoughts half-choked with rage and frustration. It was a good thing he didn't intend to come back because she would never forgive him for this.

Before Jhoira could call to him again, Teferi plunged into the rift.

* * * * *

Voluntarily entering the Shivan rift was entirely different from being dragged into the one at the Stronghold. Shiv's rift was only one phenomenon and one set of time distortions to contend with, for starters. The sensation of the strange un-space and un-time was even slightly familiar, as he had been here before. Most importantly, he now understood what was required of him and was fully prepared to see it through.

Watching Radha in Keld had made it inescapably clear to him. She and Venser were not planeswalkers and could not become planeswalkers, not in the sense of himself, Freyalise, and Nicol Bolas.

They had something, though, something that connected them to the multiverse's underlying structure and vast supply of magical energy. Radha could have bonded with the rift itself, merged and mingled with it to share its power. If she had, she might have been able to travel through it, as Bolas did through the Talon Gates. Instead, she had bonded with her homeland, chosen to anchor herself to Keld, to merge and mingle her force with the land's.

Teferi felt himself rise, borne up by the undeniable clarity of what he must now do. Radha and Venser had unique magical potential, and Teferi Planeswalker knew if their new spark could connect them to the phenomenon, then so could his old one.

He felt the rift affecting him, reacting to his presence. It was not alive in the sense of conscious thought, but the rift was definitely active, even aggressive. It helped Teferi to think of it as alive, as an enemy to be outfoxed.

Outside, Shiv was quickly coming back into phase with the rest of Dominaria. Teferi felt resistance from the rift and from the existing portion of Shiv as the missing landmass solidified.

Teferi reached out to the continent-sized landmass. Under normal circumstances he could probably hold Shiv in the palm of his hand and flip it in the air like a coin. Today, however, he had to treat it delicately on behalf of the millions of sentient beings who lived there as well as the feral scavengers of modern Shiv.

He could wrap himself around the returning landmass and personally shepherd it into place. Doing so would also protect Shiv from all the dangerous forces that would otherwise tear it apart, but the problem of the rift would remain. Taking Shiv away had created the fracture. Returning Shiv would only make things worse, widening and deepening the rift until it affected the entire foundation of the world, the plane, and perhaps the multiverse itself. Shiv's return alone would be difficult, even devastating, but it would be catastrophic if the rift remained.

His course was clear, as it had been since he first decided to pursue this matter outside Jhoira's workshop. He didn't need to shield Dominaria from Shiv; he needed to protect it from the rift. Shiv and Dominaria could not be removed from the equation, so the rift had to be.

Teferi prepared himself for a maximum effort, the greatest and final act of his long, storied life. Bo Levar would applaud and the entire universe would approve, even if Jhoira did not.

Teferi abandoned his physical form and became a bodiless presence, a flickering mass of mind and magical power. He extended himself into the rift, infiltrating it, blending with it, and merging with it. The rift soon felt like a part of him, a dead and callused part with no feeling or familiarity, but unmistakably part of his being. It reminded him of the clothes he picked when he incorporated in the physical world, the robes and headdresses that were not truly cloth but part of his physical shape. Now he was without shape and wore the rift as he once wore his human body.

He felt the phenomenon seize hold of him as soon as he finished merging with it. It recognized him as alien, foreign to itself, and it tried to expel him. It was strong, incalculably strong, and it was hungry.

Though it resisted him at first, the rift quickly pulled Teferi in as it recognized what he was doing, recognized the magical might he contained. He sought to become one with the rift and now it was seeking the same thing. The only difference was Teferi wanted to become the rift and disappear while the rift wanted to consume Teferi and remain.

It drew his strength from him, leeching it as it had leeched the mana from Shiv. Teferi struggled to keep his mind discrete from the rift, to maintain his own efforts for as long as he could. He didn't have the kind of mana resources that the land or the rift had, but he could access unlimited supplies of arcane energy through his planeswalker spark.

An academic to the end, Teferi could not help but wonder . . . was the Shivan rift drawing mana from him as Radha drew mana from the one in Skyshroud? If so, it would be a most interesting contest, rift against planeswalker, the insatiable trying to consume the inexhaustible.

Teferi decided to end this quickly, before regret and the memory of Jhoira's face weakened his resolve. He would pour everything he had, his very life-force itself, into the rift in an effort to choke it, to smother it and blot it out. He could shut it down, fill it in, and smooth it over so that he was the only casualty. Following his example, Jhoira would walk away knowing how to save Zhalfir and how to repair the other rifts that threatened everything everywhere.

Teferi gathered all the power he could, pulling it to him from deep within his being and from the fabric of the multiverse itself. He converted his thoughts, hopes, dreams, and emotions into pure mana. He became a magical singularity, a burst of energy so concentrated and vital that it was as dangerous as the rift.

More clear-headed and confident than he'd been since his days in the Zhalfirin court, Teferi maintained himself as the massive surge of energy he had become. Then, smiling in his mind's eye, Teferi let go, releasing that energy in a blinding, magnificent flood of liquid blue will and cloud-white fury.

* * * * *

Something is burning. Teferi's first waking thoughts were muddled but the searing, stinging sensation in his nostrils was foremost in his mind.

He sat up suddenly and suffered a rush of dizziness. His eyes rolled. When he could breathe and see clearly, he saw Jhoira, Corus, and Venser all standing around him.

"You did it," Jhoira said. "The rift is gone."

"I did?"

"That's right."

"I did it!"

"Yes, you did."

"I didn't die," he said.

"No," Jhoira said crossly. "That reminds me." She reached out and gave Teferi a ringing slap across the back of his head.

"Ow!"

"Don't try to sacrifice yourself again without telling me first." She turned, continuing to grumble to herself. "I knew you were going to do something like this, knew it right from the start when you showed me the globe in my workshop. I should have slapped you then."

Teferi slid forward onto his knees. "I really thought I would die. It felt like I was gone. There was nothing left to give." He turned to Venser. "What did it look like?"

Venser glanced at Corus. "I was distracted," he said. "There was too much to see down here, and I didn't really think to look up."

Teferi turned to Corus. "And the rest of Shiv? Have your phased-in brothers come out to greet you yet? Have you welcomed them home?"

"No one's ventured this far north yet," the big viashino said, "but I expect some of Jhoira's tribe soon. This was part of their territory, way back when."

"Splendid. Is there any other pressing news? I feel like I need to rest a while."

"The barrier's down," Corus said. "The locals have just noticed, and they're already closing the gap."

"I suppose I'd better reestablish it then." Teferi's voice was weary but jovial. "Otherwise I'll never get any peace." He stood and dusted hot Shivan sand from his robes.

Corus was right—the feral Shivans were almost within range. Teferi concentrated and extended his palms. He held the position for a moment then said, "There. That should do it."

"I don't see anything," Corus said.

"You wouldn't. It's an invisible barrier."

"It wasn't before."

"I was feeling more robust before. This barrier is different, but it will hold just as well."

There were a row of goblins at the front of the mob. One of them reached down and picked up a rock. Snarling and spitting, the wretched little monster heaved the stone high up over the strangers.

Teferi watched the rock descend, utterly unconcerned. He turned away from it and said to Jhoira, "Do you think the two Shivs will coexist peacefully? There could be problems. If I were to make peace, to somehow forestall a Shivan civil war, would that get me off the hook?"

The goblin's rock bounced off of Teferi's bald head. "Ow," he said again. To his honest surprise, his head actually hurt. He reached up and touched his smooth pate. When he brought his hand back down, his fingers were red and wet.

"Oh," Teferi said. "That's not good."

Jhoira looked up. "Are you bleeding?"

"A little."

"Planeswalkers don't bleed."

"We don't. Not usually." He smiled weakly as he crumpled to the ground, landing heavily on his rear. "I think I may be hurt."

Jhoira stood up quickly. "How many of the modern Shivans are there?"

"Fifty," Corus said flatly. "More, if you count the slivers." Streaming in from the north part of Shiv that stayed behind was an angry buzzing swarm of viciously sharp-shelled insects.

Jhoira looked down at Teferi, his head still dripping. He was totally flabbergasted and amazed at the sight of his own blood.

Venser's eyes darted from Teferi, to her, to the mob of Shivans. Corus stood quietly, his tongue flicking between his teeth.

"This could be very bad," Jhoira said. "I think we're in real trouble."

Venser sighed. "For a change."